I COULD HAVE BEEN...

Book I

D1319110

Helen Gallagher

I Could Have Been…
Copyright © 2019 by Helen Gallagher

Tellwell Talent
www.tellwell.ca

ISBN
978-0-2288-0781-0 (Paperback)
978-0-2288-0782-7 (eBook)

Bonne fête Hélène
On t'aime,
Norma & Louis
X ♡ X

For Annita
Who chose family

CONTENTS

PREFACE

Gathering its waters from lakes in the northern wilderness of Québec, the Gatineau River flows some 250 miles south emptying into the wild Ottawa River. In turn their combined waters hurl themselves into the mighty St. Lawrence just west of Montréal. As early as 1613 the great explorer, Samuel de Champlain, traveled up the Ottawa as far as the mouth of the Gatineau. Describing its location, he left it nameless and without settlers. Its inhabitants, the *Outaouais*, who had their own names for these wild rivers, were left in peace. Two hundred years would find the romanticised *Voyageurs*, fur traders, missionaries and militaries navigating these waters yet the white man's history of the *Outaouais* Region does not truly begin until the early 1800's and it is all about lumber.

The powerful lumber barons were mainly Protestant, American-Scots. Their endeavours led to the development of industries such as sawmills, electric plants, pulp and paper. Industry begets industry, none of which would have been possible without labourers and all of whom were sustained by farmers. The potato-famined Irish provided much of this labour while the French arrived from other parts of Québec to farm the land in summer and head north after the harvest up the Gatineau to Maniwaki, the springboard for the lumber fields.

By the end of the nineteenth century, the majority of the labourers were French having little hope of rising in the English controlled industries and businesses. The Irish Catholics did not fare much better. Every winter these two groups together with the Algonquin* co-mingled peaceably from Maniwaki to the wilderness of the timberland living in shanties holding as many as 100 men. They laboured as lumberjacks in the winter and *draveurs* in the spring driving the logs down river as soon as the breaking of the ice permitted.

The October migration northwards required some days travel on rough roads skirting the banks of the Gatineau. Hostels set up as rest stops every twelve miles or so on the way to Maniwaki, evolved into small villages. The work was back breaking and somewhat dangerous, giving rise to songs lamenting the hard work and the unfairness of the English boss while praising the bravery of the *draveurs*, the camaraderie of the lumberjacks and the feats of Joseph Montferrand known to the English as Big Joe Mafferaw; the *Outaouais* version of Paul Bunyan.

Two towns sprouted in the early 1800's at the confluence of the Gatineau and Ottawa River. The first was Hull on the west side of the Gatineau and then Pointe-à-Gatineau on the east side. Both towns lying on the northern banks of the Ottawa River looked across at the town that would become their country's capital. All three owed their early existence to the timber trade and had flourished into a mature tri-city area as our story unfolds in the early twentieth century.

MAPS

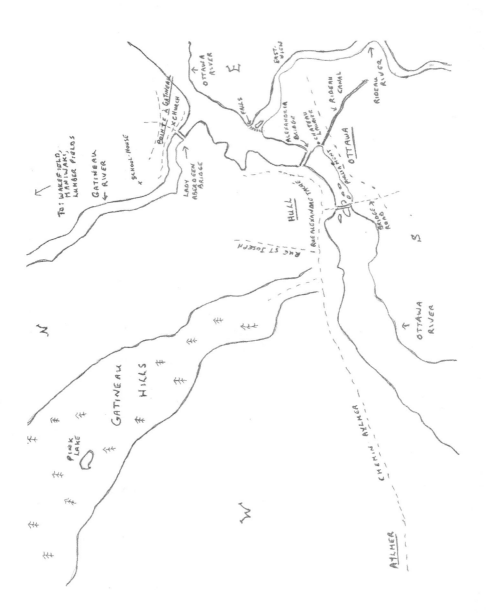

CHAPTER 1

1914-1917
War

Pain, acute searing pain, it takes over everything, blotting out the world around, leaving a person useless. In one instant Joseph Lafleur was climbing out of a musty muddy trench onto the battlefield; in the next instant the piercing pain that shot through his lower abdomen threw him back down the slope, doubled over in the foetal position. Gone were the deafening bombardments, the cries, the stench and the rats. All that was left was the pain and the horrifying fear of imminent death.

Stretcher bearers carried him as fast as they could in the dark cold night, his position remaining unchanged, clutching his stomach, each bump intensifying the pain. A brief triage at the Regimental Aid Post close behind the lines directed him to a horse drawn ambulance. The ride to the Casualty Clearing Station some 5 miles further back where the surgeries were performed was excruciating.

———◆●●◆———

At the outbreak of World War 1, Canada's army numbered a paltry 3,000 men. When the call came to defend England, men volunteered in droves; men from Halifax to Victoria; young men and middle aged men; educated men and illiterate men; rich men and poor men - English speaking men. Over 30,000 of them gathered at Camp Val

Cartier outside Québec in that summer of 1914. It was there that Canada's finest received the briefest of training before embarking at Québec's port bound for England and then on to France, to the slaughterhouse of the trenches.

French speaking men in Canada had little enthusiasm for this war. England had conquered them and France had abandoned them. This was not their war. They were busy farming their land and raising large families; they were busy working in towns for the English bosses and raising large families; the educated ones were busy, litigating, doctoring, teaching and raising large families; and the blessed ones, the priests, were busy promoting dutiful procreation.

But when the first contingent set sail for England *sans* these indifferent French Canadian men, there were those who felt left out. This *petite bourgeoisie* started campaigning for the right to be led to those bloody trenches. Men were desperately needed and so on October 20, 1914, the 22nd (French Canadian) Infantry Battalion was born; the only battalion to be formed strictly on language and culture. They would be valourous; they would die in great numbers and become known as the fighting Van Doos, the English bastardisation for *vingt-deux* (22).

Joseph Lafleur, a small town youth from the *Outaouais* region was barely 18 when he set sail from Halifax to England. Like most other young men he was excited, he would fight, he would see action, he would be brave and thus he would become a real man. The training was brutal in England, and by September of 1915 when they thought they were ready for anything, to France they went, straight to the front lines they were led. For Joseph Lafleur, the anticipated excitement and bravery quickly gave way to paralyzing fear and the taste of bile.

An interminable year had passed when the 22nd Infantry arrived in September of 1916 at the Battle of the Somme which had been raging since April. They were to capture Courcelette, a village occupied by the Germans in the Somme Valley located in the northeast of France. The fighting continued into late November and the village was freed. The allies had pushed forward a hard won 13 kilometres. The 22nd Infantry was recognized for its bravery and soldiers were decorated. Yet, it must have been a bitter victory indeed at the

I COULD HAVE BEEN...

extravagant cost of over 1.2 million dead or wounded, more or less evenly distributed between the allies and the Germans.

———●●●———

As the cold gray days coalesced one into the other, scurrying from corpse-laden fields to the equally treacherous trenches, the now inured Joseph functioned in a detached fashion. No more fear, no more bile, no more feelings, just an automaton forging ahead.

Then one dirty dreary day in November of 1916 (was it early, was it late?), the troops scampered out of their miserable hole in the ground to engage the approaching enemy on the muddy battlefield. A German Mauser rifle fired point blank deafened Joseph; all went silent and things moved eerily in slow motion. It seemed to take forever for his head to turn toward his fallen comrade, not wanting to see the angry red gap where the eyes and nose should have been. It seemed to take even longer to divert his gaze from that horror. Slowly his hand went to the blood trickling down his own face, dampening his coat; the knowledge that the blood was that of his mate finally penetrated the thick slush that seemed to surround his brain.

The automaton awoke. Only three seconds had actually elapsed; adrenalin took over. Face to face with the enemy, looking straight into his eyes, seeing right through into the depths of the stunned young German's frightened soul he speared him with his bayonet. Over and over he plunged the dripping red blade into the lifeless body with a strength the small man had never possessed. The haunting scene would replay in his mind without warning for the remainder of his life.

It was that same evening, climbing out of the trenches that his appendix burst. It was touch and go at the Clearing Station under the tents but the crude operation in the unhealthiest of conditions saved his life. During his initial recovery at the Clearing Station the horrors he witnessed left him with a feeling of uneasy guilt. He was surrounded by the maimed and the seriously injured; soldiers deserving of a medal. Where was the honour in a burst appendix when one out of every four of his fellow combatants would never return?

As its name implies the Clearing Station evacuates its patients as soon as they are either judged fit for combat or in need of further care. Three days following the operation, a feverish Joseph was put on an ambulance train bound for Étaples* to be treated at the Canadian General Hospital. Weeks of battling infection and drainage problems left Joseph weakened, wasted and depressed.

Each time he witnessed the death of a severely injured soldier his guilt needled him. Not even the cheerful ministrations of the lovely 'bluebirds', the brave Canadian nurses dressed in blue, could lift his spirits. Unfit for the front lines he was evacuated to England where a period of convalescence eventually put him back on his feet. Reassigned to the Army Ordnance Corps, he was told that the provisioning of stores, ammunition and equipment was crucial in maintaining a good fighting force and as such his work was invaluable to the cause.

These reassurances were comforting for those who felt blessed for having escaped the horrors of the front lines. For others these words fell on deaf ears feeling cheated of the perceived glories of the front lines. For Joseph, the awful truth was that he was relieved. He did not wish to return to that hell and though he had a legitimate reason for not returning, in his heart he knew that he would have done anything to stay away. He came to the conclusion that he must be a coward. The months crept by, news of the fallen in battle deepened his feelings of guilt and inadequacy until finally November of 1918 saw the end of the War to end all wars.

Joseph returned home to Pointe-à-Gatineau in early 1919, a broken old man just turned 22 years of age.

In the winter of 1918/1919, quiet reigned in the towns of Hull and Pointe-à-Gatineau. Old men, women and children hunkered down for the long snow bound winter. Conspicuously absent were the able bodied men. This was not unusual at this time of the year when the lumber fields occupied so many. But this was different, it was a disquieting quiet. Quiet, because the war fields far away had not only robbed the lumber fields of Gatineau's young men but had also laid claim to its lawyers, doctors, grocers, postmen, and other men generally not in need of winter employment in the wilderness. Disquieting, because the repatriations were taking far too long and for so many the absences would be permanent.

Under this pall, Joseph Lafleur arrived in his home town, to the family-owned general store. Robbed of his innocence and *joie de vive* his mood matched that of the town.

CHAPTER 2

1917-
The Schoolhouse

The discordant clang of the bell shook Adèle out of her reverie. All lingering thoughts of the handsome Jacques Armand dissipated as she attempted to put order to the clamour surrounding her. Twenty-four restless, hungry pupils wanted out of the classroom. Permission granted they made an untidy beeline for the cloakroom. The lunch period would be outdoors on such a glorious winter day. The cheerful blue of the sky contrasted sharply with the pristine whiteness of a fresh January snowfall sparkling with diamonds. Warmly clad with lunch pails in hand the joyful children spilled out unto the snow, their mitts, scarves and *tuques˙* dotting the landscape with bright splashes of colour; the quiet countryside now alive with the cacophony of squeals and sing-song voices.

Adèle donned her dark woollen cloak and followed out to supervise her noisy brood. Two small queues had formed by the outhouse, one on the girls' side and the other on the boys' side. Adèle would not go to the outhouse until the last of the children had left for the day. She had received strict instructions regarding the constant supervision of the boys and girls; besides, she did not deem it appropriate for her pupils to imagine their teacher sitting on that glorified hole in the ground ringed with a wooden seat. Moreover, it would be her duty as teacher of '*la petite école*˙' to clean the latrines, replenish the strips of newspaper in the small pail (or soft paper-wrappings of the Florida oranges when available) and remove the suspiciously yellow-tinged ice whilst inhaling a stench most foul.

In the rural schools of Québec during the early part of the century, edification was not the teacher's sole duty. She was more often than not a young unmarried lady of excellent repute. With her living quarters frequently located on the attic floor, the maintenance of the building became her responsibility. The school was typically a rectangular one-roomed wooden structure with a small belfry set atop the ridge of the roof. One entered the school through a cubicle annexed to the front of the building. It's most important function being that of a windbreak during the long cold winters, it also served as a cloakroom on one side and a storage area on the other where the woodpile, poker, broom and water pail could be found. Students were also assigned chores. Filling the pail with drinking water from the outside pump fell to the biggest boy, while that of cleaning the erasers fell to the oldest girl. Ringing the bell was the honoured task of the brightest pupil and it was this clanging now echoing across the valley that made Adèle jump, caught in yet another daydream.

Coats on pegs, empty lunch pails returned to the shelves above, the students trundled in followed by their teacher shaking snow off her boots; shaking the handsome Jacques out of her thoughts. Adèle enthroned herself on the straight-back wooden chair behind the large desk on the raised platform, a step higher than her pupils. She viewed her assortment of red-cheeked children with a soft heart trying to muster up the strictest of expressions to match the look of the tight raven bun crowning her head. Not yet nineteen, she did her best to hide the fact that she was no more than four years senior to her eldest pupil. Blowing warmth on frozen fingers they awaited the afternoon instructions sitting in neat rows of desks solidly affixed to the floor; girls on one side and boys on the other separated by the friendly pot-bellied stove reigning in the centre of the room providing lifesaving heat.

Adèle turned to the large blackboard behind her desk and with the perfect slanted penmanship acquired from the nuns at the convent, she wrote out four lists of problems to be solved by the four age groups under her tutorship ranging from six to fourteen. These were the children of the farmers and loggers of the Gatineau Valley. Most would not go beyond the elementary education offered at '*la petite école*'. Education was not a priority among the hard-working folk of the Gatineau Valley and Adèle would find her classroom half empty as soon as the fields thawed in late spring ready for sowing. Nevertheless, one or two of them would be gifted enough to attain the required grades and fortunate enough to get parental permission to continue higher education. The lucky few would attend the Convent for girls in the town of Pointe-à-Gatineau run by the Grey Nuns while the boys would go to the new St. Alexandre College run by the Jesuits further north along the Gatineau River.

The quiet concentration of the children, the soporific warmth of the mid-day sun spilling through the large windows along with the heat from the logs burning in the stove combined to throw Adèle into a deep lethargy. Visions of Jacques danced in her head… Uncharacteristically tall for a French Canadian, with his slim waist and broad shoulders he had looked so handsome in his uniform. Although almost two years had passed since she had seen him waving goodbye from the train, the memories were vivid. His twinkling, mocking green eyes paired with the infectious smile that created a dimple in his left cheek had eclipsed the sadness of the occasion. Once more she relived that cold grey day two years previously in March of 1915…

———◆◆◆———

It would have been unseemly for a sixteen year old convent girl to see her young man off to war. The nuns would never have allowed such a thing but Adèle had been given permission to join her family at the train station to bid adieu to her older brother, François. Louis Turcotte would miss his eldest son; the farm would be severely short-handed. He could not understand the need for this loss. This faraway war was none of their business; the young men were needed at home. With great resignation Louis and Lorraine Turcotte had donned their Sunday best, scrubbed clean the seven younger Turcotte's, and harnessed the horses to the open wagon for the long bumpy ride to the train station leaving the farm in *Grandpapa* Turcotte's safe keeping.

Adèle was chatting with her brother François and his best buddy Jacques Armand when the family group arrived on the busy platform. Knots of people, each one surrounding a soldier, filled the platform.

Lorraine caught her breath as she espied her small party; so much beauty, so much youth and energy, yet so different. The uniform could not hide the muscled upper body that gave her son of Napoleonic height an air of authority. The thick mop of romantic black curls could not soften the serious brown eyes or the resolute square jaw. Her petite daughter on the other hand was everything that is female. Underneath the long cloak, the small waist and soft curves held the promise of sensual womanhood. Above the cloak atop a slender elegant neck was a perfect oval furnished with full lips, an upturned nose and brilliant black eyes gleaming with intelligence. Cascading down the back of the cloak the shimmering raven hair was as straight as her brother's was curly. Towering over the pair, the lanky lumberjack might have been considered thin had it not been for the large square shoulders acquired in the lumber fields. The unruly sandy hair, the laughing green eyes with the ready smile imparted a sense of well-being that drew people in.

It was no secret that Jacques was sweet on Adèle. The tall lumberjack had always been welcome at the Turcotte farm. Yet, as the train drew near, the Turcotte clan was somewhat taken aback when Jacques suddenly pulled the young Adèle into his arms. Without any preamble he kissed her. It only took a few seconds for the shock to wear off before Adèle returned her first kiss with the fervour of an experienced lover. Their surroundings disappeared, eternity replaced everything.

In a strangely husky voice, he whispered, "Wait for me, Adèle, *s'il-vous-plait*, wait for me."

With the soft, warm breath of his whisper in her ear, "Oh, *oui, oui*, I will," she promised through happy tears.

The loud clearing of Louis Turcotte's throat brought them crashing back to earth. Eternity had been all too brief. A short awkward moment ensued before the shrill whistle of the train brought an anxious flurry of activity on the platform as people promised to write, shook hands, hugged, kissed, cried and said goodbye. In an instant it was over, they were gone, steaming their way to the camp at *Saint Jean-sur-Richelieu** due to depart, after too short a training, for Amherst, Nova Scotia where a brief two months of further training would see them off for England…

"*Mam'selle, Mam'selle*," cried young Gabrielle, hand waving in the air to catch the attention of her daydreaming teacher. Caught in the act, Adèle faced the snickering children. It was Friday afternoon, time to go, the restless students eager for release. The noisy exodus left Adèle thinking of her weekend plans as she tended to her tidying. There was the anticipated trip to town to visit her aunt who regularly collected the family mail from the post office. Perhaps some communication from her brother had arrived. Then there was the visit to the farm to see her family. Best of all, she would find some time after her chores to reread her brother's letters.

Lorraine Turcotte had insisted, argued and pleaded with her husband over the necessity of sending each of her children to '*la petite école*'. Though he had put up a good resistance, this was one fight he lost. In the end he was secretly glad of the outcome and proud that his children could read and write. His appreciation of his wife's foresight was unbounded when François' first letter arrived from Nova Scotia and his daughter Germaine read it to the family.

> *March 20, 1915,*
>
> *Dear Family,*
>
> *We arrive here in Amherst, on March 13. I don't think that the people in Nova Scotia are happy to see us. Me, I think that they don't beleeve that French Canadians can fite. I don't know what there problem is but they look at us in a funny way, not a frendly way. Anyway we work very hard and we are very tired at nite but don't worry about me Maman. I can take it and we are very strong and we will show them what we are made of. The food is good and there is a lot of it. I am in the*

same unit with Jacques Armand and you can bet that we will
be watching each others back. He wants you to read this to
his family. He wants you to tell them that he is well and he
is eating well and he miss everybody and he miss Adèle too.
Tomorrow we are going in the city and I will tell you next time
about it. I miss everybody too.

François

Adèle had begged to keep this letter so she could read it over and over just for that one line where Jacques had dictated a few words. Jacques missed her! And now chores completed and curled up in her big chair upstairs by the window, she chose another of these old letters. Like the others it was heavily creased from the handling and refolding.

The Armand's possessed the most rudimentary reading skills and Adèle knew that Jacques would not want her to witness his inadequate writing skills. His brother-in-arms undertook to relay his messages home. To Adèle's delight François had sent all subsequent messages dictated by Jacques intended for her eyes only under separate cover. Although the words of her lumberjack were simple, she cherished them, reread them and cried over them.

May 25, 1915

Chère Adèle,

We are on the boat since May 20. I can tell you that we got a very
good send-off at the port. We showed them those people in Nova
Scotia and in the end they all came to see us sail away. I am having
trouble writing because I really feel terible. The sea is rough and
the waves are big and it is making me really sick. Jacques is not
feeling sick and he teeses me all the time. He says it's because he is
the best draveur in Gatineau and he can roll the logs on the river
and balance on them longer than anyone else so a bit of rolling
sea is nothing. He is taking a lot of pictures to bring back for you
to see. He still has his camera and he wants to take pictures of the
whole war and sell them when he gets home. He thinks he will be

*famous. He wants me to tell you that his favourite photograph is
the one he took of you by the swing and he looks at it every nite.
When we get to England we want to ask to have a transfer to be
pilots. Me, I think this would be very exciting. Imagine, Adèle,
being able to fly! We hear that they need a lot of pilots. I did not
tell Maman about that and Jacques does not want his family to
know in case they would worry but he says that he wants you to
know everything about what he is doing and that he miss you.
He tells me to say that he thinks of you every nite.*

Ton frère,
François

The letter had not contained any of these numerous pictures
and Adèle had waited five impatient days before she could visit with
Jacques' family. Having worked up the courage she had asked if there
were any photographs of Jacques and could she borrow one. It had
been a bold move and she had blushed deeply when making her
request but to her relief, *Madame* Armand had smiled knowingly
and gone into the back room returning with the treasure.

So far François had been an admirable brother and friend so the
letters had piled up. The most recent letter was dated three months
prior. In itself that was nothing to worry about because letters sometimes arrived in a bundle after a long wait. The worrisome thing was
its content,

October 15, 1916.

Chère Adèle,

*Thank you for your letter full of news. I am happy to see
that Maman is better from that terible cold. Yesterday I also
received Maman's letter that Germaine wrote. She sent me all
the news from the Armand's and I read it to Jacques. Letters
are better than gold here so don't stop. I like the funny stories
you tell me about your students and it makes me laugh to think
of you as a strick teacher.*

It is more than a year since we got our transfer cards for the No. 8 Training Depot and we are still in Netheravon on the ground! Jacques is so good with the photography that he is still doing the developing and training others to use the cameras for reconasance. Me, I am still fixing the aeroplane engines. But I have good news. Jacques will be training to be a reconasance observer. Soon he will be in a two-seater plane with the pilot and take pictures of the enemy land. Imagine that. He is so lucky. Me, I asked to train to be a gunner because you know that I am a great shot. I think that they will let me do it and I will know soon. Maybe you better not say that to Maman. I told her I am safe in England doing mechanics and Jacques is safe doing photographs. Jacques says that he does not want you to worry because he has not gone up in the plane yet and it will not be a fiter plane, just to take pictures. Jacques says that he is thinking of you and before he used to make me read your letters to him over and over again but they teach him to read and now he reads them all by himself. So now he wants you to send him a letter just for him and soon when he is good enough he will write you one. He says that he wants to ask you something important when he gets back. Me, I think that this is good.

Ton frère,
Framçois

Every time Adèle reread this last letter, a small knot of fear formed inside her. The idea of her brother and sweetheart being in one of those flimsy aeroplanes with guns all around terrified her. But for now, with the small pile of letters in her lap, she focused on the picture of her beloved and remembered the kiss. It never failed to make her feel warm and tingly. She closed her eyes, imagined his arms around her, and dreamed of a wedding. Wishing for a new letter soon, she fell asleep.

CHAPTER 3

1915-1917
In Flight

The train was overcrowded. The body heat emanating from so many male bodies, warmed the cold March day. The noise level was high as the young men talked excitedly. Orders were to move them to Nova Scotia very soon for further training one step closer to their departure for England, one step closer to the action. There was much bravado in their voices as they spoke of crushing the enemy. Jokes making fun of the ineptitudes of the Germans evoked loud laughter, perhaps too loud, perhaps a little yellow masking the underlying fear of real combat.

The elated Jacques was still reeling from his embrace with Adèle. At first he had dreamed about it and then he had started to plan it. He had planned the where, the when and the how. Each time he had chickened out he had been left with only the dream and a new plan. But in the end it had been an unplanned spur of the moment action. Moreover, the reality had been so much more than the dream. Head back on the seat with eyes closed he was hanging on to the feelings. As he kissed her it seemed as though an electric current had coursed through his entire body feeling totally alive and as she kissed back it seemed as though he was melting, feeling totally weakened. The strength of the feelings had been unexpected, exciting and frightening.

"Hey Jacques, wake up, it's not the first girl I've seen you kiss," the laughing François said as he elbowed him in the rib.

The red-faced Jacques took on a sober look as he confided to his friend. "When we get back, I'm going to marry your sister."

"Well she's too good for the likes of you and I don't think you deserve her, but I get the impression that she won't refuse you," François replied.

"I plan on changing a lot of things when I get back. I'm not going to be a lumberjack all my life and I'm not going to drive logs down the Gatineau all my life either. Albert can take over the farm one day, he likes that but I want to live in Ottawa and I want to be a photographer."

"What?" François sounded incredulous. "You love being a *draveur*; in fact you're the best. You came first in all the competitions last year, and now you're going to tell me that one month in that photography studio on Spark Street last summer has made you soft."

"You know I love my camera, I'm always taking pictures and Mr. Jamis said that all those pictures I took at the lumber camp were really good and he says that I have great talent for developing. How you develop the picture can make a big difference and he says I've got it. I plan to take pictures of the whole war, everything about it. Mr. Jamis says that if they're good enough, I'll be able to sell them. They're going to be great photographs and I'm going to make a fortune, just wait and see."

"Sounds swell, why haven't you told me any of this before?"

"Because I knew you'd laugh at me but now that you're going to be my brother-in-law, I guess you should know," Jacques said winking at François.

"Whoa, *une minute mon ami*, she hasn't said yes yet, but if you are going to be my brother-in-law then it would be better if you were rich, *très riche*, and remember your relatives in the most generous of ways."

"Well, before I get rich we have a war to fight. Are we still going through with our plan to be pilots?" enquired Jacques.

———◆●◆———

The training in *St Jean sur Richelieu* had been short and the cold shoulder reception in Amherst, Nova Scotia had been unexpected and hurtful. However, with determined effort and active participation in the community, the battalion experienced a complete about-face. The soldiers eager for action left for England with the warmest of send offs.

The Atlantic crossing had been an ordeal for François. He had lost weight and reeled with weakness as they disembarked at Plymouth. Getting the troops, artillery and munitions from the port to the trains and then marching them to the various camps on Salisbury Plains took the better part of a week.

The march to the camp was cold, wet, and muddy. Once arrived, the damp wind wormed its way through the cracks in the floorboards of the elevated huts each holding 40 men. But to François' great relief those floorboards did not sway and the food stayed in his stomach.

"Tomorrow we put in for our transfer," François confided to his buddy. "I'd much rather take my chances in the air than get on another boat."

Jacques agreed, "We have to do whatever it takes, flying is the future and I want to start right now!"

'Right now' did not come right now as the gruelling days stretched into weeks. Summer was just not summer. Too many days were damp, cold and grey, leaving the mud to preside. The days were filled with long marches, drills, bayonet fighting, trench digging and night manoeuvres. Five hours of marching ate through the cheaply fabricated boots. They grew fitter and strong enough to find the energy for some recreation playing Lacrosse. Stiff and exhausted, sleep came quickly at night.

Although it took 12 miles of muddy roads to reach town, everyone looked forward to their leave. The pubs spilled over with the exuberance of youth; the mugs spilled over with foamy brews and the girls gushed with friendliness.

Jacques and François accompanied by fellow camp soldiers were greeted upon entering the pub with good natured shouts. "Here come the froggies!"

François pointed to a large table and nudged his friend. "Hey Jacques, look over there."

"Well, well, well, if it isn't Joseph Lafleur," Jacques bellowed as they approached the table.

"What does a man have to do to escape the riffraff of Pointe-à-Gatineau," replied a grinning Joseph. "Where have you two been vacationing in sunny *ole* England? I've been luxuriating at the Pond Farm* Spa myself!"

"We're both at Bustard Camp," laughed Jacques. "Pond Farm, eh?… Aren't you due to deploy to our mother-land soon?"

"We embark first thing Monday for the north coast. Enough of this playing in mud, it's time to get over there and give the Fritz their comeuppance."

"I hear the fighting's heavy," François chimed in. "We're expecting transfers to Netheravon shortly. I'll be servicing the fighter airplanes and Jacques will be in the reconnaissance business. Eventually we hope to train to fly the fighter planes. When you see the airplanes flying over France, give us a wave."

"The truth of the matter," said Jacques with a wink, "is that François is too frightened to face another boat ride!"

"Flying, how exciting! I'm not sure why you'd prefer that to a simple boat ride but let's drink to victory… I'm buying," offered Joseph.

To the amusement of the soldiers Jacques had his Kodak with him. Grinning from ear to ear they all wanted their picture taken. The noise level rose as usual as the night wore on but one could sense an unidentifiable something in the air on this particular night. Yes, there was excitement but also anxiety or perhaps nervousness. Many in the room would finally see action come Monday. It was what they all wanted after all… wasn't it?

The ale was having its effect. Some were tipsy, others downright drunk while Joseph became soppy and sentimental. "Eh, François, what's become of that beautiful little sister of yours? She lights up the place every time she walks into our store. She's one fine young lady and just thinking of her makes me homesick."

François caught the dark look in Jacques eye. "Adèle should have just started teaching by now but you should know that Jacques here is aiming to wed her when we get back."

"Oh, and is this a formal engagement? Does anyone else stand a chance?"

"It's formal enough in my mind, she's waiting for me and I would advise you to stay away," growled Jacques.

"Sure, sure, I get it, but a man can dream, the nights are going to be cold and lonely on the front. I hope that it won't be too long. Pointe-à-Gatineau seems so far away." Joseph moaned, his former bravado evaporating.

Although his burst appendix would shorten his stay at the front, it would still have been too long for Joseph. It would be too long for many soldiers and alas, too short for others.

Jacques and François experienced a frustrating year at Netheravon. For François it was torture to be allowed such close contact with his beloved fighter planes while doing maintenance work on the engines and then to be denied his dream of actually flying in one! Meanwhile, Jacques did enjoy putting his developing skills to work on the reconnaissance photographs, especially those that spotted the enemy or depicted live action. However, he wanted more. Photography had become everything and he wanted to fly reconnaissance, to be the aerial observer taking the photographs.

At long last, in October of 1916 the hoped-for news arrived. Jacques would fly! He was to do reconnaissance. He would be an aerial photographer. His training was extensive and François was green with envy.

"You just wouldn't believe it my friend; I thought all I had to do was photograph! But the training for observers is much more than I thought it would be. I already know all there is to know about the photography part but I've got to learn Morse code, map reading, how to use the wireless, how to shoot and everything about the plane. I'll probably be able to fly it myself in the end," complained a tired Jacques.

Feeling somewhat left out, François boasted in reply, "Well you can count yourself lucky that you've got the best mechanic ever servicing the planes."

Some short weeks later, an excited Jacques came running to his mate, "*Regarde*˙ François, my orders, I fly in the morning. I never would have believed that it would take eighteen months before I would get to see what this war looks like. Hey, what are you grinning at?"

"I've got some news myself," replied François. "I start gunner training this week. It's one step closer to being a pilot, and at least I will be flying and seeing some action."

"Maybe we'll come to regret this," said Jacques thoughtfully. "A year ago, all I wanted was to be a pilot. They're treated like heroes, champagne and women by night, but... by day they're dropping like flies out there. Everyone worships those fighter pilots and the fact that they are likely to die up there gives them an air of heroism. But you know, in the end it's the reconnaissance that makes the biggest difference to this war. Just you wait and see. I'm convinced that the information we gather about enemy operations is what will win this war.

And as far as reconnaissance is concerned we don't survive any longer than those pilots everyone worships because German Fokker planes are making mincemeat of us. All that equipment on the reconnaissance planes is making us too heavy and slow. We're nothing but sitting ducks for those lightweight Fokkers."

"Don't worry, our escort fighters are just as good now and with guys like me as gunners, they won't get a chance to touch you," replied François.

"*Euh bien... um...* suppose something did happen. My photographs... would you give them to Mr. Jamis... and... Adèle... would you tell her..."

"Are you crazy? Nothing's going to happen, we need those pictures of the enemy movements and you're the best, so just don't talk that way, it's bad luck! You can take them to Mr. Jamis yourself and become famous just like you said and you, my friend, are not going to break my sister's heart."

———◆●◆———

The glamour of it all, quickly wore off. The two friends soon discovered that it was freezing up there, it was cramped and the numerous death-defying close calls were terrifying. That these two mates were still alive by February 1917 was unusually lucky. In the face of so many fallen comrades both had lost their youthful exuberance... making them mature experienced men well before their time.

During leave, the drinking was heavy in the pubs and the willing girls were plentiful. Back in Gatineau it was Jacques who had a way with the fair sex while serious François had always been shy and reserved. Now the tables were turned. François drank, became loud, and always left with a girl on his arm while Jacques drank, became morose, and only had thoughts for Adèle.

On a cold clear day in mid-February both received orders that would take them in different directions. François would be flying the north coast of France while Jacques was on a long range mission to spot the movement of supplies, munitions and troops along the train lines of occupied Belgium. An important emphasis had been placed on German movements between occupied Belgium and France.

Jacques knew that the risk assessment for this mission was unusually high. He could feel the tension in his pilot and tried hard to shake the knot of fear wrenching his guts. Time passed uneventfully, the drone of the planes calmed his fears, and it was just too cold to think of anything else.

Four thousand feet above the western Belgium border, Jacques was busy changing plates and transmitting code. He was too preoccupied with his mission to notice the approaching menace. Out of nowhere the sound of gunfire was both electrifying and paralyzing. It was total chaos. In seconds a German fighter went down in flames followed quickly by one of their own escorts spiralling down with black billows of smoke trailing behind. Then something went very wrong, the plane lurched unnaturally flames erupting from the back as they entered a dense bank of cloud.

Losing altitude fast the pilot focused and did all in his power to keep the plane aloft. Establishing a small degree of control he searched for a spot to make a crash landing. With the clouds now above, nothing but a wilderness of trees spread before him. Short minutes went by during which Jacques had a lifetime of thoughts going through his mind. Skimming the tree tops, the plane jerked fiercely propelling Jacques out of the plane and into the tree branches. It was lights out for him before the plane crashed and burst into flames.

François returned safely that evening in time to see what was left of Jacques' mission limping in. He didn't have to be told... he knew. The survivors had witnessed Jacques' plane crashing into the Ardennes forest and the subsequent burst of flames.

The moment his fears were confirmed, all that felt nice in François died that evening to be replaced with pure hatred. It was a horrible feeling but he could think of nothing else but killing Germans.

CHAPTER 4

1917-1918
Sadness

By the time Adèle received François' letter, Jacques' disappearance was old news. The much-dreaded telegram had arrived at the Armand farm on February 26, 1917. All over the Outaouais valley these horrific telegrams were being delivered. No one wanted to open them. The task was not for the faint-hearted. Yet, it was the young Adèle who was called upon to visit the home of her beloved to read the telegram to the Armand family.

Four boys in their teens and a five year old girl huddled around their white-faced parents. The eyes spoke of unmistakable fear and anxiety. Adèle had to pry the telegram from the clutches of *Madame* Armand's hands.

The succinct telegram informed Mr. and Mrs. Armand of their son's disappearance following a plane crash near the Belgium border on February 17th. He was not expected to have survived.

With a chilling shriek piercing the room, *Madame* Armand crumpled into her husband's arms sobbing uncontrollably. The younger children started wailing, the two older boys stood in shock while silent tears rolled down Georges Armand's cheeks. For Adèle, It was as though she had received a kick to the stomach and could not breathe. She desperately wanted to get away from all this noise and misery but doubled over she just could not move.

When the crying abated and Adèle resumed breathing, too weak to stand, everyone sat. Georges Armand was the first to find his voice. *"Baptême**, that damned war... that cursed damn war! Why did we send our boys over there? Why? It wasn't our fight? Why? He was a good man, he was a good son. *Pourquoi?"*

Still clinging to her husband, Jeanne Armand murmured, "We didn't go to the train station. He said he didn't like goodbyes. Why didn't I go anyway? I could have seen him one more time. He was so handsome, *comme il était beau...* he was a good son." Fresh tears and cries started anew.

"I'm sorry, I'm so sorry. I have to go; my family will want to know. *Je suis très désolée**!" With that blurted out, Adèle escaped the distress.

And now, three weeks later, the letter had arrived. She sat in her aunt's parlour in Pointe-à-Gatineau, letter in hand. She would not open it now. Once she had completed her chores in town she would return to her schoolhouse. She would wait until tomorrow to see her family at mass and visit with them at the farm where she would give them the news from François. Apologising to her aunt, Adèle cut short the visit. Besides, she hated the sad look of concern in her aunt's eyes. Everyone was giving her that look lately and it just made her want to cry.

"Wait, Adèle!" *Tante** Hélène held her back. "It's too early, the farmers are still getting their supplies so you probably won't find any farmers heading back your way at this time. Take my buggy and pick me up for mass tomorrow. I'll ask Victor to hitch up Sugar Pie... it won't take long and you'll save time."

Adèle gave her aunt a warm hug. *"Merci, merci, ma tante,* you're always so good to me."

Tante Hélène was Lorraine's baby sister. Their family numbered thirteen children and it was Lorraine who had looked after Hélène twelve years her junior. In such large families it was always the task of the eldest girls to help out with the household chores and the younger children. Hélène had been a beautiful child both inside and out.

Although thoroughly spoiled by the whole family, she had remained sweet, caring and thoughtful. She and her brother Vincent had been the only two fortunate enough to receive an education. Both had done extremely well at the schoolhouse and found themselves furthering their studies. The Grey Nuns took in Hélène at the Convent hoping she might find her calling with their religious order. The Oblate Fathers in Hull took in Vincent for the Classical course with the same hopes. These hopes were realised when Vincent decided to do his formation for Ordination at the Seminary. It was a blessing for a family to have a child become a priest or a nun and Vincent's family was very proud of him.

Hélène, on the other hand, did not have the vocation. She had received a great deal of pressure at the convent. It was a mistake to think that the sweet, quiet Hélène was a pushover. Her resolve to do whatever she wanted was strong as were her *avant-garde* opinions. She seldom put forward these opinions and never argued with anyone which gave one the false hope that Hélène was buying what they had to say, hook, line and sinker. She would listen politely and attentively to any proposition but in the end she held her own counsel and acted in her own best interests without offending anyone.

She had worked four years as the schoolmistress at la *petite école*. For the first two years she had been hopelessly in love with a bright young man who broke her heart forevermore when he entered the priesthood. During the next two years she was assiduously courted by an older man. Adolphe Caron, a prominently successful notary in Pointe-à-Gatineau, had fallen head over heels for the beautiful, charming young lady. Raised in a poor working class neighbourhood in Pointe-à-Gatineau, Hélène's father had worked steadily at the E. B. Eddy match factory in Hull. A marriage to Adolphe would be well above her station.

Adolphe was a plain man but he was kind and Hélène felt relaxed in his company. With Adolphe the conversation flowed freely and for the first time she was comfortable enough to express her own opinions. They could discuss politics, religion, family, friends, everything and nothing. Two years after her heartbreak they were married. To her great chagrin, God had not planned for her to be a mother. Although her years with Adolphe were barren, they were pleasant, and Hélène had been content in playing mother to her numerous nieces and nephews, Adèle in particular, for whom she was godmother. Tragedy struck eight years into her marriage when Adolphe died of a head injury falling off his horse. The beautiful widow was left in favourable financial circumstances. Numerous marriage proposals were all turned down and the good-hearted Hélène devoted herself to volunteer work helping the less fortunate.

A short while later Adèle found herself in the buggy, reins in hand. It was a small two-seater with leather upholstery and an overhead covering against the rain. She thought of her aunt's good fortune but wondered if she was lonely. She loved Hélène more like a big sister than an aunt. She was so modern and open-minded. Adèle was not afraid to broach any subject and took her advice seriously. But today she had not wanted to open François' letter in her presence nor the conversation that would have inevitably ensued.

Back at the schoolhouse, she filled the pot-bellied stove with fresh wood and hurried upstairs to sit in her big chair, sunshine spilling through the window; warm air coming up through the grate.

François' November 1916 letter had been full of excitement with details of planes and flying. His last letter however, had been rife with complaints. They were freezing high up in the air and they were cramped. He had had a terrifying close call but *Maman* was not to know. Jacques was missing Adèle terribly and both of them were homesick.

With a heavy sigh, she tore open the envelope of the current missive. Two pictures fell out. It was Jacques in his uniform standing head and shoulders above an unknown man next to a small fighter plane. He was smiling broadly. In the second picture he stood by a bar next to a small man. The tears quietly coursed down her cheeks as she read her brother's words.

February 27, 1917

Chère Adèle,

I just got two letters, one from you and one from Maman. They are happy letters and it made me even more sad to read them because I know that they sent a telegram and that you would know about Jacques by now. I know that you would be hurting a lot but I hope that by the time you get this, you would be feeling a little better.

One of the pilots that flew the third plane on Jacques mission is my buddy. His name is David Baker and he said that it was a dangerous mission to begin with. Two of the planes went down and he saw it all. I don't know what they said in the telegram but I don't think that Jacques could have survived that crash and maybe it is better to face that now.

I have all of the pictures he took, there are so many of them. There are not many of them with him in the picture but there are some. I am putting the best two in this envelope. You can give one to Madame Armand. One picture is him and Joseph Lafleur at the pub. Remember I told Maman that we had met him when we were training. Joseph was leaving for the battle field that Monday. I never had any news about him. In the other picture Jacques is standing next to David Baker who is from Liverpool. That one was taken the day of his first flight. All the others I will bring home if this war ever ends. I am tired of this war and I am so homesick.

At this point Adèle studied the second photo once more. Having had eyes only for Jacques she had ignored the small man beside him. *Why yes, that is Joseph Lafleur from the store in town,* she thought. *Imagine that! I wonder if he's still alive.*

She read on:

It isn't the same around here without Jacques. I can tell you now that he wanted to marry you. I think that you know that already but he was going to ask you when he got back. Me, I wanted him to be part of the family. I am so sorry and I am so sad and I just can't shake it. Write me letters because it's all I have now. I miss you all so much, Ton frère qui t'aime, François

With heavy heart, Adèle reached into her skirt pocket for her most precious possession, the only letter from her Jacques. She had received the letter the day he died. Totally ignorant of the tragedy at the time, she had been ecstatic.

January 7 - 1917

Ma Belle Adèle,

The best thing about my last year at Netheravon is that I had to lern to read and to write if I wanted to fly. I think that I am good enuf to send you my own leter now. I got two leters from you since François told you I can read. That was the best gift I could get for Christmas. I read them all the time and they make me so happy. It is hard to send my messages to you by François because I cannot say what I realy want. What I want to say is that I love you Adèle, with all my heart. I miss you so much. When I close my eyes, I dream that I am kissing you and holding you very tite. I can still smell your hair like it had flowers in it. I was very exited to fly but now I am not so sure because it is so cold and my long legs dont fit in properly and things happen in the air that I try to shut out of my mind. I just want this war to be finished and go home and be with you. Je t'aime X X X X X X X X X X X Jacques.

The thing she had wanted most in the whole world was to have Jacques ask for her hand in marriage. With the photos and letter next to her heart she went to her bed and laid there, knees up to her chin in foetal position. It felt as though something was squeezing her heart. It was physically painful... maybe that is what it felt like to have a broken heart... or maybe she was dying of a heart attack. That would be just fine, what was the point in living anyway.

———◆●◆———

The Roman Catholic church of St. François de Sales was the envy of the Gatineau region. Today the parishioners came out in their numbers to hear the brand new organ. Caring less, Adèle sat with her family. Her red-rimmed eyes told the story of her previous night.

The sonorous organ stilled as the priest reached his pulpit. The parish became uncomfortably quiet, they knew what came next. The priest cleared his throat and began the death announcements. Social status be damned; the rich, the poor, the French, the English, the Catholics, the Protestants, none were spared. The O'Brien's lost their son Danny; *Madame* Gérald lost her husband Henri leaving her with 5 small children; Mr. Carter, the owner of the mill, lost his only son...and so the list went on.

As the faithful socialized outside after the service, Adèle espied *Monsieur* and *Madame* Lafleur. She went up to them and with a small curtsy she bid them good day and asked if they had news of their son Joseph.

"*Bonjour Mam'selle Adèle.*" *Madame* Lafleur took the proffered photo. "*Mais oui,* I remember that your brother was a friend of his," said *Madame* Lafleur. "Yes we do get regular news because he's no longer at the front. We thank God every day for this. Joseph told us that he was badly injured in battle. He went through some serious surgery and he's now serving in England in some hush hush capacity. We are so proud of him and so thankful that he's safe. *Et ton frère François,* do you hear from him often?"

"Yes we do, he's also based in England so the letters come regularly. I worry though because he's a gunner in those fighter planes and his missions are so dangerous. Anyway, I wanted to show you that picture my brother sent me of your son when he was in training."

Madame Lafleur searched through her purse and found her *pince-nez* glasses. She now looked long at the worn picture she was holding and recognising the tall soldier next to her Joseph, she gasped. "Oh *mon dieu,* I'm so sorry, I did hear the terrible news of his friend Jacques Armand. I believe someone told me that he was your beau. It is a tragedy to be sure but you are young my dear. You may not believe this now but it will pass Adèle. My prayers are with you and your brother."

She handed the picture to her husband. "*Regarde* Denis, doesn't he look happy, it's a really good picture. You must give it back to *Mam'selle* Turcotte now, it's sure to be a precious treasure."

That night she steeled herself for the next day's teaching. She didn't feel like teaching, she didn't feel like doing anything really. Lying in bed, clutching her trove of three pictures depicting her love, was all she wanted to do. Her mind wandered to her conversation with *Madame* Lafleur. *So... I'm young and it will pass... easy for her to say... what does she know? I'd love to see how she would feel if it was her precious Joseph. Why couldn't it have been him instead?*

As soon as the thought entered her mind, she felt bad. She remembered the shy polite Joseph who served behind the counter at his father's store on *Rue* St Antoine. She wouldn't wish anyone dead, what was wrong with her?

She picked out the picture *Madame* Armand had given her. This was the Jacques she knew before he left for that wretched war. This was the Jacques who had kissed her at the train station. She closed her eyes and relived the kiss for the umpteenth time.

Their mouths had parted naturally... his tongue was in her mouth and it was thrilling... now it was her turn, it was wet, warm and so soft. His arms encircled her... they pressed together. As she felt his member harden, her juices began to flow. All around her ceased to exist... the ecstasy consumed her. They were naked now and with the help of her fingers she imagined him inside her. The feeling of skin on skin... it was all too much... something was building up around her clitoris... so concentrated... almost painful... then the explosion, and the floodgates opened, the feeling of sweet release spreading through her body.

Breathing heavily, Adèle slowly came out of it. Not wanting to let go, she felt a quiet sadness. A farm girl learns about sex by watching the animals, but this… this was new and unexpected. She quickly succumbed to a deep restful sleep for the first time in weeks.

The next day came and somehow she did teach and she did get through it. Then another day and yet another went by. Days tumbled into weeks and the weeks filled the months. Those close to her worried as she hardly ever smiled and the sparkle was gone from her lovely eyes.

Just as *Madame* Lafleur had predicted, the pain did go away yet Adèle was not happy, nor was she sad. She just didn't feel much of anything except maybe on many a weekend night when she would imagine herself making love to Jacques… always with the desired effect. She ignored the fact that she had not been to confession since the first episode and pushed any niggling feelings of guilt deep into her subconscious.

For a long year Adèle bitterly mourned the loss of her Jacques but, eventually, self-awareness kicked in and she began to think of the future. Was she to become an old maid teacher? No, she had always wanted children. A life alone was not an option. There were just two things she feared about married life. Firstly, she could not bear to think of someone other than Jacques as her husband. Secondly, her dreams of motherhood did not allow for more than three or four children. She would imagine herself having time to lavish love and attention on each child before another one came along. As much as she wanted children, the thought of giving birth to a dozen of them one after the next actually terrified her.

The Church was very clear on this point… marriage is for procreation. It is the wife's duty to bear as many children as God wants her to have. If God does not want a wife to have a child then she would not be able to get pregnant. This is what had passed for sex education at the convent in the early part of the twentieth century.

As far as parental guidance was concerned, with obvious embarrassment Lorraine Turcotte had given her daughter terse instructions on how to use the rags when her bleedings would start.

Adèle had inquired, "Why am I going to bleed? Am I going to die?"

"*Mais non*," Lorraine had replied to her frightened daughter. "You're going to be a woman and all women bleed every month, it's the nature of things, that's all."

Adèle believed that the Catholic Church was <u>The</u> Church. She diligently attended Mass and recited her morning and night prayers to God with unshakable faith. That said, Adèle had many questions with no answers. Why would God want a poor couple to have so many children? Why did the upper classes who could well afford it, seem to have fewer children?

With Jacques gone, maybe she could experience something else in her life. There was no rush. She could marry some years in the future. She had loved the whole learning process at the convent. It had been over all too soon and had left her thirsting for more knowledge. As a result she read copiously; books borrowed from the convent; books borrowed from her aunt; books that told a story; geography books; history books; especially newspapers… those she devoured.

She had been following the women's movement to get enrolled into the University of Ottawa and it was only a matter of time. Most of the men she knew believed that a woman's intellect was too weak for university learning. That was patently untrue. Adèle knew that women had been attending McGill for years. There were even women doctors! She began to formulate a plan… savings… part time work! Such plans may have been grandiose for a young French Canadian farm girl but for the first time in months she was living again, planning ahead.

CHAPTER 5

1917
Belgium

"*Où* suis-je?"

From seemingly far away Jacques heard, "He speaks French!"

Then he felt the pain. Shooting pains traveling up his left leg barely masked the burning sensation on the left side of his face. It was sombre but he could make out two blurred shapes. Slowly his focus came back. A man and a woman hovered over.

"Where am I?" he repeated.

In a soft voice the woman said, "*Soyez tranquille*, you're among friends. We saw your plane crash. You were very fortunate; you fell out into a tree just before the crash. Your leg is broken but we have it in a splint and it will heal. You have a big lump on your head and the cuts on your face will probably scar. Don't worry if you show your good side you'll be as handsome as ever." She smiled encouragingly.

In a gruff manner, the man continued. "The plane exploded and I'm afraid that your pilot didn't make it. We got to you before the Germans did. It was a two seater so they'll be looking for your body. Hopefully they'll give up quickly; it's a thick forest out there. They'll never believe you survived this. It was a British plane... but... you seem to be French, where are you from? Your jacket's missing."

"I... I don't know. I don't remember a crash... I don't remember anything!"

"What's your name? Your accent's strange, from the east countryside of France maybe."

"Paul, your Swiss cousins in Valais speak with that accent," said the woman to the man.

"Do you know your name?" repeated Paul.

Jacques tried to think but his head hurt and he came up blank. He became agitated. "No, everything is blank, please, you must help me."

"Shh, shh, you need to rest. Try to drink some of this broth then get some sleep and we'll talk again," cooed the soft-voiced woman.

The broth was comforting but it was an effort and once more he lost consciousness.

"He's badly hurt. He needs to rest and eat. His memory loss is probably temporary," said the woman.

"It's nothing that won't heal," said Paul dismissively. "In the meantime he's well-hidden and safe here. He wasn't in the pilot's seat so he's probably reconnaissance. The uniform was badly torn and I'm not sure what it is but surely he speaks English since he was flying with the British. I think we can use him."

When Jacques woke up after a day's sleep, the pain had eased, his head was clearer and he was hungry. Getting his bearings he remembered the conversation with the woman and the man she had called Paul. But try as he might, he could remember nothing else. He became aware of muffled voices in the next room. His efforts to get out of bed were painful and in vain.

His movements attracted attention, and the woman appeared. With a much clearer head Jacques could see that she was young. From his horizontal position, she seemed unusually tall for a woman; slim with square shoulders – a frame that gave her a mannish look. Her chestnut coloured hair was tied up in an unruly bun promising a thick mane. Soft wispy curls escaping everywhere asserted her femininity. Her approach revealed dark blue eyes, a generous mouth and an easy smile that brightened the sombre room.

"Welcome back, I'm Angeline, how do you feel young man?"

"J'ai faim."*

Her deep throated laughter was the kind of medicine he needed. It also brought Paul into the room.

"So, the sleeping prince is awake. Is your memory any clearer... can you tell us anything about yourself... what you remember?"

"Whoa, give him a chance Paul, he's hungry and that's a good sign. I'll get food. Be gentle with him," said Angeline on her way out.

"Well?"

"First, can you tell me where I am?" asked Jacques.

"You're on a farm near Couvin, close to the Ardennes Forest in Belgium," replied Paul.

Jacques took a moment to digest this and gather his thoughts. Finally, he tried to make sense of it all. "We're at war. I know everything about the war. Belgium is occupied by the Germans. But nothing, nothing about me! How did I get here? Where am I from? Who am I? Why do I know so many things but not that? You tell me my plane crashed but I don't remember that. The first thing I remember about myself is waking up here. *Mon Dieu, mon Dieu*," said Jacques clutching his head in his hands.

"*Bon, bon*, concentrate on getting better. It's probably the shock and your memory will no doubt return. Meanwhile we need to get you some kind of identity that will not alarm the Germans. I believe you can be of help to us. Eat and rest. We'll talk again."

With the passing days Jacques regained his strength but not his memory. The young Angeline was like a mother hen around him. He learned that Angeline and Paul Roland were siblings. Although he was hobbling on a crutch, he felt much stronger and began to feel restless.

Sensing this restlessness, Paul felt that the time was right for his proposal. One night after dinner, he began, "There exists a small but well-organized network of resistance in Belgium. We act in small groups independent of one another. Some groups help our men escape to the front at Ypres. We're doing a damn good job at holding back the Huns there. Others plan and execute sabotage missions derailing supply trains and the like. Angeline and I belong to a group called *La Dame Blanche* (The White Lady). Our main job is getting information on German operations and the whereabouts of their munitions and supply depots. But it's of no use unless we get the information into the right hands and on time. This is where we think you can help."

"We need more men with a good knowledge of English, wireless transmission and the Morse code," added Angeline. "From what you've told us, you still know how to do these things".

With a great deal of eagerness in his voice, Jacques answered, "I'm feeling useless enough as it is, I'm ready to work, what can I do? Who do I work for?"

"Your orders will come from me. You'll never know who I report to, the same way I don't know who my superior reports to. That's why it works. If anyone gets caught they know precious little.

Our cousin Philippe Roland was smuggled to the front at Ypres last month. The Germans have never paid attention to this small farm so you can take up his identity. He's 25 years old and about your height and build which is close enough. I know someone who will doctor his papers with your picture. You must get used to being called Philippe. You'll also have to do your share of the farm work. Belgium is starving and the farms are crucial. No one close to us will betray you. The transmitters are moved constantly and you will travel with me or with Angeline under cover of night."

The newly christened Philippe (this was the only name Jacques knew to call himself) learned that Paul was to be away for the next three days supposedly to look at some second-hand farm equipment. During his absence, Philippe was to concentrate on getting stronger while Angeline was to fill him in on his new family's history.

He learned of their parent's relocation to the German labour camps. Thousands had met with that fate. The occupation had been brutal for many. The slightest suspicion of undercover activities or even the mere possession of a gun could mean serious repercussions for an entire family.

"The Huns rule us by fear," recounted Angeline. "In the village of Porcheresse not far from here, the villagers were rounded up, locked inside the church and set on fire. When they first arrived here, they killed our parish priest for no reason at all. They did this in many parishes just to send us Belgians a message. It worked, I can assure you. People are terrified. The Huns have burned and destroyed most of our beautiful Louvain. The worst part is that they're turning Flanders to their side, promising them independence. We can't trust anyone from there anymore. The folks around here though won't inform on us but it's difficult to recruit for the resistance. Folks are scared and want to stay out of it."

Philippe enjoyed listening to Angeline. Her soft voice was melodic and her smile medicinal. He learned that her cousin, the real Philippe, had come to Belgium from Valais in Switzerland some six years ago after his father's death which had left his older brother in charge of their dairy farm. He had wished to strike out on his own. His uncle had taken him in here to help on the farm until he could get his bearings. Philippe had become fast friends with his cousins and when the war broke out there was nowhere to go. He too had joined the resistance but his desire was to join the fight in Ypres. Paul had contacted the right people and after a six month wait Philippe got his wish.

"You're actually quite the godsend. We'll no longer need to explain his absence to the Huns should the need arise... and anyway, your French actually sounds like him when you speak with those funny A's of yours," Angeline said laughingly.

A tour of the farm designed to teach Jacques the basics, revealed that his knowledge of farming was extensive enough to assume that he must have been raised on a farm which now guaranteed his usefulness.

C H A P T E R 6

1918
Conscription

At the end of March 1918, Québecers experienced a troubled Holy Week. When parishioners should have been atoning on Good Friday, mobs of demonstrators were forming in all the major cities of the province. The French were vehemently protesting the new conscription law. Prime Minister Borden, fearful of a revolution, added fuel to the fire by calling out the troops.

On Easter Sunday, parish priests were ordered by their archbishop to read a pastoral letter from their pulpits advocating civil obedience. The more recalcitrant priests did not hesitate to add contrary opinion to this missive. More fuel to the fire!

The confrontation that took place in Québec City on the Easter Monday brought it all to a head. The troops believing that a gunshot had been fired from the crowd, fired in turn into the demonstrators with machine guns.

The newspapers throughout Québec cried blue murder against the government in that first week of April, 1918. Five deaths were reported in the aftermath of that bloody Monday. Reports of the injured varied greatly; some said as little as 20 and some as many as 70. Fearful of an arrest, many of the injured had fled to lick their wounds in hiding.

The Pointe-à-Gatineau population was enraged, something must be done. Adèle's own father, Louis Turcotte and his son Martin were among the demonstrators in Hull. But angry words and heated discussions produced nothing but frustration. In the end martial law was enforced and conscription became law for those over twenty. Whatever rift existed between French and English was now acerbated and one could hear the first real cries for an independent Québec.

Adèle's younger brother Martin, not quite eighteen, would be spared. He was a gentle young man; a great lover of nature and wildlife; but more importantly, an ardent pacifist. He would not be one to volunteer for this cursed war. This was a great relief to his parents. Louis Turcotte needed him on the farm and Lorraine worried constantly about her François. Meanwhile, Jacques' younger brother, Albert had volunteered on his 18th birthday, just weeks after Jacques death. That decision was incomprehensible for the Armands who mourned him now as though he were already dead.

On the heels of this civil unrest came a letter from François bearing bad news.

March 26th, 1918.

Chère Adèle,

Three weeks ago our plane receeved enemy fire and my brave pilot, David Baker, made a most amazing landing on the coast of France. Would you beleeve that we were rescued by Canadian soldiers from Alberta! My leg was badly injured but David was not hurt much. I was taken to Étaples to the Canadian Hospital there. I don't really remember much at the beginning because I had so much fever and I was delirios. Now I am back in England in convalesence. The problem is that I lost half of my right foot. Everyone says that it is a miracle that I am still alive after one and a half year in the planes and it is a miracle that the pilot made that great landing. It is a thriling horror story and I will tell you all in person.

I am writing to you to tell Maman and Pa because I don't know how to say it to them. So I want you to tell them in a way that they will not be worried. I am eating well and as soon as I am better I will be doing more mechanics because I can't go back in the planes with half my foot missing. The nurses are very nice here. I really like one and her name is Shirley. You can tell Maman that she is looking after me well.

I really want everyone to know that I feel good about this. Since Jacques died, I was feeling so angry all the time but it is like all that is gone now. I am learning to walk and I will have a limp but I really beleeve that I cheated death many times and God has been looking over me. Me, I am happy to be alive and all I want is for this war to end. Give my love to everyone,

Ton frère,
François

The fraternal letter was received by Adèle with mixed feelings. For the first time in over a year, François did not seem depressed. This was strange given that his injury would mark him for life. She then realised that she too did not feel overly sad. *I know why,* she thought to herself, *it's because he's grounded. This is going to lessen our worries and I'm sure I won't have trouble relating this news to Maman and Papa.*

Lorraine Turcotte lived in daily fear of receiving a telegram like the one delivered to the Armands. Contrary to her brother's wishes, Adèle read François' letter in its entirety to the family rather than using her own words.

"Oh, *mon Dieu, merci, merci,* thank you God, thank you God," whispered Lorraine, with happy tears.

Gruffly, her husband asked, "How can you be happy at a time like this? The boy has lost his foot; he'll be a cripple for the rest of his life."

Martin chimed in, "*Mais non, Papa,* can't you see… he's safe now and it sounds like he's happy. His other letters have been so angry and sad. And you know my big brother won't let a little thing like half a foot get in his way, he's the most stubborn guy I know."

Dinner had been a noisy affair that evening. The Turcotte's were all talking at once. And… well, well… who was this Shirley?

Amidst all of this Adèle followed the suffragette movement with great interest. She read in the English papers that in Manitoba the provincial vote for women had been a *fait accompli* for some time now. Finally, on May 24th, some women over the age of 21 gained the right to vote in the federal elections. It pained Adèle to realise that the Québec provincial vote would be withheld from women for what seemed would be a long time to come. The Church was dead set against it and so were most Québec males. She could not comprehend men's fear of emancipated women.

On the other hand, the enrollment of women at the University of Ottawa was imminent and Adèle spent her summer dreaming her dreams of education while helping out at the farm. When September's cold nights announced the soon arrival of autumn, Lorraine and her eldest daughter spent an amiable week making preserves, bottling tomatoes, pickles, and all manner of berries and fruit, before Adèle's return to her students.

It was the calm before the storm.

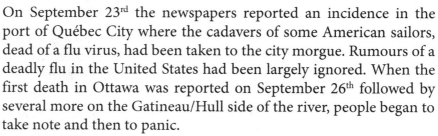

On September 23rd the newspapers reported an incidence in the port of Québec City where the cadavers of some American sailors, dead of a flu virus, had been taken to the city morgue. Rumours of a deadly flu in the United States had been largely ignored. When the first death in Ottawa was reported on September 26th followed by several more on the Gatineau/Hull side of the river, people began to take note and then to panic.

In the first week of October a calming article quoting the respected Dr. Aubry beseeched the population to practice some common sense since this flu was not as bad as people thought it was, once it was treated properly. Within a few short days the cases numbered in the thousands in the Gatineau region and the deaths were piling up. Common sense be damned, pandemonium took over.

One could wake up one morning with a fever, headache, aching limbs, coughing, nosebleeds and vomiting, and be dead by the following day. Some even cried tears of blood. Panic was well justified. Many claimed that it was cholera; some said that the black plague had returned. The religious entreated the faithful to repent as this was clearly Divine punishment.

By mid-October public buildings were closed; schools, theatres, taverns, dance halls, and even the Churches suspended Masses and services. The dead having received the briefest of blessings on the church steps were to be interred within 24 hours.

The poorer, crowded sections of the cities were most affected. In Ottawa, the working classes densely packed around the railway stations counted the most deaths. In the Gatineau region this meant the Irish Catholics and the French. That is not to say that the upper classes were spared. The virus did not discriminate; all walks of life and all manner of people succumbed. Strangely, the death toll was heaviest among young adults instead of the usual children and the aged.

In Pointe-à-Gatineau it seemed as though no family was spared. Adèle's classroom had been largely empty of students by the time the schoolhouse was closed. The isolated farms were relatively safer, so an unknowingly infected Adèle fled to the family farm, harbouring the deadly virus.

When Adèle started to experience headaches and a fever, the family tried to play it down but the terror was written all over their faces. Lorraine dedicated one whole bedroom to Adèle. Keeping all the other Turcotte's away as she nursed her eldest girl. For forty-eight hours Adèle's fate was undecided. The fever, headaches and vomiting were alarming enough but when Adèle's tearing cough brought up bloody mucous, Lorraine dropped to her knees imploring her God for a miracle. Whether it was a miracle, good nursing or simply fate, Adèle turned the corner for the better on the third day just in time to see her mother and *Grandpapa* take to their beds.

With Adèle as weak as a kitten, and both *Maman* and *Grandpapa* ailing, Germaine took up the slack. Although Germaine's ministrations could not be faulted *Grandpapa* was gone the following day. Even though seventy-four was considered to be a ripe old age, he had been strong and expected to live for some years yet. He was beloved by his family but with *Maman* sick and the two little ones showing definite signs of the flu, no one had the time to mourn him. His body was delivered for a quick blessing and burial that same day.

Seven year-old Laurent and five year-old Babette were next. Germaine ran ragged nursing the sick. The coughing was the worst. She carefully prepared the mustard poultices to put on the heaving chests. Although this old-wife remedy burned the skin, it did seem to bring some relief.

Babette protested to her big sister. "Germaine, you know that I hate mustard, why didn't you make one with sugar for me?"

This elicited a smile from the exhausted Germaine. "Just get better and I promise you a whole sugar pie, *juste pour toi.*"

Her three patients did get better and Adèle regained her strength little by little. Meanwhile, thirteen year-old Yvette ran the household while a very worried Louis and his son Martin finished their preparations for the coming winter.

When all seemed on the mend; it was Germaine's turn. It seemed only right that she suffered the least. She exhibited the symptoms of a bad cold and was on her feet within a few days.

Fully recovered, Adèle took up the slack and pitched in with household chores and the recovery of the sick. No one else got sick. It was resolved that the family would hunker down with no visits to town. Only two weeks had gone by since Adèle's first symptoms and three days since Germaine's recovery. The family mourned the loss of Grandpapa Turcotte as best they could. As prayers were lifted in his memory and rosaries were said in thanks for their own recovery, Germaine complained of feeling chilly. In a matter of hours it was obvious that the feverish Germaine was having a relapse.

The young woman's fever spiked dangerously high and her difficulty in breathing was obvious. With a fierce determination Adèle threw herself into 24 hour nursing care. Barely one and a half years apart in age, the two sisters were close confidantes. Only last month Germaine had confided her feelings for Marc Couture. She had been meeting him in town every weekend for some six months and felt that he was just as sweet on her. She had come to Adèle for advice on how to push the relationship forward with the ultra-shy Marc.

It was only last month, thought Adèle, *only last month... my God, it feels like years, not weeks. The whole world has changed in just four short weeks. No, Germaine, no, you are not allowed to die. Dear God, she's so sweet, always so thoughtful, she's too good to go, please don't take her away from me, I just couldn't bear it.*

When Germaine started to cough up blood the next day, Adèle decided that she would take her to the hospital on rue Laurier in Hull.

"*Jamais*!" avowed her father. "People go there to die. She's better with us."

"But Papa, the Providence Sisters are good nurses and the doctors will know what to do. I don't know what else to do and she's getting worse."

In the midst of this argument *tante* Hélène arrived with the post and newspapers. She had been making the trip to the farm at least three times a week to impart news of the outside world and receive news of her family.

She would speak to her family from the foot of the verandah and leave the papers on the swing chair. The distraught Adèle came running out to implore her aunt.

"*Ma tante, ma tante*, you must speak reason to Papa. Germaine has had a relapse and she's coughing blood. We must take her to the hospital. Please tell him."

"Adèle, Louis, I don't know what to advise. You'll see in the papers that the situation is catastrophic. Hundreds have died on this side of the river and it is thousands if you add those in the Capital. It may be even as high as 10,000 across the province of Québec. The doctors and nurses can't cope and it seems to me that they're dying just as fast in the hospitals. You must decide. Poor Germaine! I know that you're doing your best for her. How are the others?"

The exhausted Adèle collapsed in the big swing chair. Louis patted her back and answered Hélène. "The others have all recovered and the rest of us seem quite strong. I still believe that we're better here than in town where sickness is all around especially in the hospitals filled with infected people."

Hélène spoke softly to her niece, "Adèle, you know I believe in doctors and modern medicine but I must admit that this seems to be beyond anything. They're calling it a pandemic. People are dying of this flu all over the world and maybe your *Papa* is right. Staying away from the sickness is probably safer."

Head in hands, Adèle started to sob. Through her sobs in a pained voice, what really troubled her came out. "*Je sais*, I know. If I had stayed at the schoolhouse everyone would have been safe here. I probably caught it from one of my students and brought it here. I killed *Grandpapa* and now my precious Germaine is going to die because of me."

"Come now, none of that talk, you must be strong for Germaine, if your Papa agrees I'll take her in my buggy right now," offered Hélène.

Adèle pulled herself together. "No, you're probably right and the way she's looking now, the trip into Hull might very well kill her. I'm going back to her now and ask that you would pray harder than ever before."

The aunt took her leave with a very heavy heart, because she knew that those who relapsed very often died with their lungs hemorrhaging.

Adèle went back in. She passed her mother kneeling before the statue of the Blessed Virgin, rosary in hand. Once again she took up her post at Germaine's bed-side.

The ordeal lasted two days. Adèle nursed her sister with devotion and Germaine put up a good fight. In moments of lucidity the sisters spoke their hearts out to each other in whispers. Before going into her final coma, she spoke her last words.

"Live a good life for me, Adèle, just live every minute of it… promise me".

"*Je le promets*, we both will." No sooner had Adèle spoken these words than Germaine closed her eyes for the last time.

Sorrowfully, Louis Turcotte had forbidden his family to enter Germaine's room. Instead, they spent the last few hours of her life kneeling together in prayer.

1917-1919
White Lady

At the beginning of the war telecommunications left much to be desired. Pigeons and messengers probably did a better job. The receivers and transmitters were large enough and heavy enough to require transportation by horse-drawn carts. Necessity being the mother of invention, huge improvements developed during the war years. By 1917 reconnaissance planes were being outfitted, while on the ground, transmitters and receivers could be carried by one person. Both sides used codes; both sides received and transmitted; both sides located and intercepted enemy communications. For the White Lady, the equipment was both precious and forbidden. Discovery by the Germans meant certain death.

In a matter of weeks the new Philippe Roland was integrated into the activities of the White Lady and proved to be a good asset in their cause. Daytime would find Philippe working alongside Paul and Angeline on the farm. Nighttime took them all over the countryside. Sometimes he would travel with Angeline and sometimes with Paul. Someone always stayed behind at the farm. Transmitting equipment would be carried from one person's barn to another or perhaps in a Tavern's storeroom.

The how, when and where came from Paul who, in turn, was informed by someone else. Jacques' job was translating and sending the code he was given. Some weeks were quiet with few clandestine operations while others could mean nightly excursions.

Sometimes Paul could be absent from the farm for days at a time under cover of a legitimate reason. At such times, all of the farm work fell to Philippe and Angeline. This could be burdensome but the strong Angeline worked as hard as any man. Philippe greatly admired her strength and determination. Working side by side in the fields they fell into a quiet comfortable rhythm... words being unnecessary. It was after a hard day's work, while sipping tea, that the words flowed between the two of them. Angeline proved to be well-informed, interesting, funny and easy to talk to.

By harvest time, Philippe knew that he loved Angeline. It hadn't happened overnight. It had been a slow steady thing, from admiration, to friendship, to something more. Now he found that he wanted to be near her all the time that he would like to hold her close and let loose her hair. Yes, he judged that the word love was apt.

For Angeline, it had been immediate. The moment he was laid on the bed after the plane crash, she had loved him. His recovery had been her only concern in life. She had never been very popular with men. It was not that she was ugly, far from it. She was not beautiful either; except for her eyes... they were stunning. One could say that she had a pleasant face but when she smiled she was definitely attractive. She was not one for lipstick, nylons or frilly things.

Perhaps some might have judged her boyish appearance to be unwomanly.

So Angeline had bided her time. Never pushy, she had offered friendship to the tall handsome stranger desperately in need of an anchor. Over half a year had passed in this fashion and now sitting across from him at the kitchen table, on a night when Paul was working the cause, she saw a strange look cross Philippe's eyes. *What did I say,* she wondered.

Slowly Philippe got up, came across to her, took her hands and lifted the very willing Angeline to her feet. For a good while they just hugged. Philippe felt warm, comfortable and so happy while Angeline was in complete turmoil. He reached for her bun, took out the pins and the chestnut locks came tumbling down her back. He stepped away to take a look. The luxuriant mane transformed her while the radiance of her smile transformed him. Warmth and comfort developed into overwhelming desire. This time he held her tightly and kissed her deeply.

"*Je t'aime* Angeline. I know that I have no right. I am no one… really no one. What can I offer you; I don't even have a name."

"That is the least of it. We're first cousins and this kind of behavior is quite unacceptable," teased Angeline with a wink. "What's taken you so long, I've loved you forever."

"But you do have a point, Angeline. We are viewed by everyone as cousins. I want to court you openly. I want Paul to know."

"My, my, the slow turtle becomes the impatient hare. There's no rush. That we love one another is a good start. We're at war, everything is dangerous and upside down. We'll tell Paul. For the rest, it will be our secret until it's safe for you to be whoever you want to be."

"But what if I have a wife, what if I have a child, what if I'm a scoundrel? This is so unfair to you."

"One thing at a time, Philippe, don't spoil this moment for me. For now let's take whatever little happiness comes our way. I have a thing for scoundrels so kiss me again before I forget how it felt."

Paul was not unhappy to hear of the turn of events between his sister and his pretend cousin. A good camaraderie had developed between the two men. Each had protected the other's back on missions gone wrong and a solid bond of trust now existed.

"I agree with Angeline," Paul advised Philippe. "So far we've been more than cautious with you. We haven't even allowed you to go in town where it's crawling with Huns. There's no rush and this war can't go on forever. The Americans have joined us now and it's making a difference.

"What if my memory never comes back? Who do I become after the war? I have no citizenship, the man from nowhere with the funny accent."

"I don't want to seem unsympathetic with you Philippe because I can't imagine what you're going through. But, you worry too much. People are dying in this war, people are starving in Belgium and the future is so uncertain. We can only live for today."

"You're strong and healthy with friends protecting you and the love of a good woman," chimed in Angeline. "So you have it all, stop complaining." That said, she planted a loud kiss on his cheek and a playful slap across the back of his head.

Amidst this discussion, a car engine was heard. The two men headed for the front porch leaving Angeline in the kitchen. Heading up the beaten path was a shiny open Mercedes. A uniformed driver sat at the wheel with Couvin's *Kommandant* and his assistant comfortably ensconced in the back's leather seats. Rounding the corner not too far behind was a horse drawn wagon.

It was a terrifying sight.

"Let me do the talking," said Paul as he headed down the steps to greet the unwelcome visitors. Paul addressed the formidable German officer. "*Bonjour*, what can I do for you my *Kommandant*?"

Although deeply accented, the *Kommandant*'s French was effortless. "It has come to my attention that we have neglected to visit the farms in this region for quite some time now. An oversight to be sure as it is not our intention to neglect any of our citizens. I myself thought it a lovely day for a drive in the countryside. My *Oberleutnant* Bader will be happy to review your documents now."

"*Certainement*, they are inside. Perhaps the *Kommandant* would like some refreshment after such a long dusty drive. My sister prepares a good cup of tea."

With a nod of the head, the *Kommandant* motioned Paul to lead the way. The party headed for the kitchen where Paul presented himself, his sister and his cousin to the *Kommandant* while handing over the precious documents to the *Oberleutnant*.

"Ah, I see that you are from Switzerland, *Herr* Philippe. An unfortunate choice it was to immigrate here in such times."

"My cousins have been good to me and the farm work has been satisfying. I believe that I have been useful since my Uncle and Aunt were sent to work in Germany." Philippe used such irony in his voice that Paul had to give him a stern warning look.

"Aha, I can make out an accent… you were a country lad in Switzerland, I take it."

A more polite Philippe answered. "*Oui mon Kommandant*, I come from a long line of farmers."

The *Oberleutnant* whispered something in the *Kommandant*'s ear. "*Ah* it would seem that your paperwork is in good order, as I knew it would be of course. *Herr* Paul, would you be so kind as to accompany *Oberleutnant* Baden to your barns. He will show you how you can help replenish the much needed supplies of our government. *Fraulein* Angeline and *Herr* Philippe can keep me company in the meantime."

At the sight of the horse drawn cart, Paul had known that this was coming. Without hesitation he left with the *Oberleutnant* to assist in their plunder.

"I must say that you farmers are doing excellent work. Your farm seems to be producing well; far too much for such a small family. We commend you for your generosity today and I am quite confident that these humanitarian efforts toward your fellow citizens will continue in the future." The *Kommandant* spoke with what could only be described as a dangerous smile.

"*Naturellement mon Kommandant*," answered the soft-spoken Angeline. "We were waiting for the last of the harvest to be brought in before heading to Couvin with our supplies."

The *Kommandant* turned toward Angeline giving her a bold appraisal. Angeline had been working in the chicken coops earlier that morning. She was clad in dirty coveralls; a kerchief covered her hair; her face was grimy; her nails were black; she sat with a distinctive stoop and she kept her eyes down and half shut.

The *Kommandant* gave Angeline a disdainful look. "I see that you do your share of the work around here. I commend you and will await the rest of the supplies as soon as harvest is over. As for you, young man, you must tell me more about Switzerland. It has been a long time since I last visited your beautiful country."

Philippe's heart was beating so hard, he was sure that the *Kommandant* could hear it. He tried to hide his nervousness fearing that he was not succeeding. "My family has a dairy farm in Valais. We aren't very far from Sion. My father passed some years ago and my older brother took over the farm. I'm afraid that he and I don't always see things the same way, so, I thought it best to make my fortune elsewhere. It wasn't long after I reached here that the war began." Wistfully he added, "I must say that I do miss the mountains terribly."

"There's no need for such nervousness, *Herr* Philippe. I do not bite. You will see that this war will be over soon. Germany will restore order to Europe and there will be time enough for you to seek that fortune you speak of."

After half an hour of uncomfortable chitchat, the *Oberleutnant* came to fetch his *Kommandant*. The party left with the wagon half full headed for the neighbouring farm. The three collapsed on the porch chairs.

"*Mon dieu,*" croaked Paul. "Philippe, you must always speak to these Huns with respect. It's good that you understood my warning because for just such a lack of respect, they have been known to shoot on the spot."

"Did they buy my identity?"

"*Oui*, you would no longer be with us if they hadn't. If they decide to check out your story, it will only confirm that there is a Philippe Roland from Switzerland living here. Your accent was a big help."

Philippe turned to Angeline. "Correct me if I'm wrong, but, you had cleaned up this morning wearing a skirt and blouse, about to prepare lunch when the Huns arrived."

"That is precisely why I didn't go out to greet them with you. It gave me time to change back into an uninteresting farm hand. Young Belgian girls everywhere have been kidnapped and given to German officers as mistresses. Although I don't think that I'm exactly what they're looking for; I wasn't about to take any chances."

"I don't know about that. That grime on your face gives you that lost waifish look. Most alluring, I must say."

"Enough of that," said Paul. "I'm starving, and then there are fields to be harvested and supplies to be hidden. And you, my friend, can accompany us to Couvin on market day since you passed your identity test with flying colours today."

In the spring of 1918, The Germans threw all they had at the allies in five ferocious offensives. Some of their successes were reminiscent of their early 1914 victories. Intelligence became more important than ever.

The White Lady was working overtime with its counterpart in France. Between the daytime farming and the nighttime activities the Rolands were exhausted. One warm evening in May, they sat on the porch enjoying some rare relaxation. Paul was summing up his take on the situation.

"The attacks have been brutal and the Huns have made important inroads taking them to within firing distance of Paris. The situation may look bleak but my mole in Brussels tells me that the Germans are worried. The counter attacks are weakening them and their supply lines are failing. Their casualties in the tens of thousands are not being replaced while the U.S. army is swarming into France. I believe that they have spread themselves dangerously thin and that we're going to see an about turn."

"We're all hungry and tired. I'm also worried about this flu epidemic," said Angeline. It's spreading in all the cities and some are dying."

"*Eh bien*, if we have all of that to complain about, just think what it's doing to the battle weary soldiers," countered Philippe.

Paul tried to reassure his sister. "I wouldn't worry about the flu, it will take its course and we're quite safe on the farms."

"I'm going in to Couvin tomorrow morning to meet with a woman arriving from Brussels. Her information is top priority. You and I will leave for the French border at nightfall, Philippe. We'll be travelling through the forest to the outskirts of Fumay. We should reach there before dawn at a friend's home where my contact awaits this missive. The border is crawling with Huns but I know just the area where we can dodge them."

The next morning, after Paul's departure, Angeline and Philippe made love. Their relationship had progressed to an intimate level some months back. They were discrete and always waited for Paul's absence. If Paul knew, he made no mention of it. They were also careful. Angeline would refuse her lover if the time of the month was unsafe. The two lovers were also good friends, most comfortable with one another. Lolling about in the afterglow, Angeline whispered in his ear, "That was so, so good. If the angels could finish planting our fields we could do this all day."

"In every way you're my wife Angeline. But I want everyone to know, I want to shout it from the rooftops. I want to make beautiful babies with you. I know we must be patient but I must say these things out loud to you because I can't tell anyone else."

When Paul returned, the two men lay down in the afternoon for a good sleep. That evening as the sun set, Angeline had everything ready for her men; food, drink and warm dark clothing. The night would be moonless and the pair would have to travel with speed.

"We plan to spend tomorrow resting at my friend's farm and travel back under cover of night, so don't expect us until the day after tomorrow. Don't worry Angeline, I'll bring him back."

"I want you both back so get out of here and hurry." A quick hug and a kiss for both her men and she hastily re-entered the house to hide her tears.

———— ●●● ————

The cool night was pitch-black. Philippe marveled at Paul's ability to travel the obscure trails through thick dark forest with such speed and certainty. This was obviously not his first time. In silence they made good time.

They reached the border a little before 4 a.m. The pair slowed down as they picked their way down an escarpment to the French border. The tension emanating from Paul was palpable. It had been imperative to reach this far before sunrise as the remaining journey took place across open fields.

Traveling blind for so many hours the forest had closed in on Philippe. Having battled the panic of claustrophobia, he did not share Paul's fear of the open fields. Had he understood the dangers he may have felt differently.

Paul's fears were groundless this time as the remainder of their journey was uneventful. It was a glorious sunrise and they were received at the small stone cottage with much hugging and kissing of cheeks. First names were used for the presentations. Claude and Marie were a middle-aged couple and a thirtyish woman named Lisa was their daughter.

The frightened looking couple sat in the parlour while Lisa led the two friends into the kitchen. Paul handed over the precious envelope. Over welcome bowls of porridge, Lisa took over the meeting. Her speech was clipped, "Thank you for your bravery. Had you been caught with this, you would have been executed on the spot. I leave for Reims tonight."

The sound of a motorcar brought Claude and Marie into the kitchen. "Quick, follow us."

In seconds they were in the bedroom; the bed was pulled away to reveal a trap door; the two men along with the envelope were pushed down the hole; trap door shut; bed repositioned. Meanwhile Marie had donned her nightgown and cap, dabbed some rouge around her nose and lay under the bed covers.

All of this was accomplished in the nick of time for the wolf was knocking loudly at the front door. Claude opened the door to the unexpected *Oberleutnant*. With a surprised look Claude greeted him. "Well this is an honour! Is there something I can do for you *Oberleutnant*?"

"Yes my good man. I have been informed of your visitors. You would understand that one cannot be too careful and documents must be verified."

"Ah *oui*, my daughter is visiting us. She has come from Revin to help me with her *Mama* who is quite ill with the influenza. *Mama*'s fever has broken so we expect Lisa to return to her children tonight. Do come in, she's in the kitchen busy with the porridge. Perhaps we can spare a little more if you're hungry at this early hour."

A worried look crossed the face of the *Oberleutnant* at the sound of the word 'influenza'. "*Non merci,* that is very kind, but I don't need to come in as my aide is quite capable of doing the necessary. Were you not expecting… er… other family? I have heard that you often entertain family."

Claude gave a most puzzled look. "*Non.* Not that I am aware. We are keeping much to ourselves with *Mama* being sick."

The *Oberleutnant* instructed his aide to verify the daughter's identification and to search the house. Claude and the *Oberleutnant* discussed the weather while the German soldier went into the kitchen.

He checked the identification papers, looked around the kitchen carefully and did the same in the other small room. He hesitated at the main bedroom door. Sounds of coughing and nose blowing came through loud and clear. In the end he made the decision to open the door and have a good look while standing in the doorway.

To ensure a thorough search he checked the outhouse then reported the all clear sign to his officer. The *Oberleutnant* pursed his lips. "Well, well. Perhaps we were a little early. I have a rather long involved patrol ahead of me. I will leave my aide behind and presume on your hospitality. He will be no trouble I assure you and he eats very little. I shall pick him up on my way back tomorrow morning."

"We are happy to oblige and share our meager meals. Your aide can have the small room tonight as my daughter must rejoin her family."

The *Oberleutnant* ordered the uneasy looking aide to remain inside until his return. He clicked his heels, nodded at Claude and left with his driver.

Looking most miserable, the German soldier settled himself in the parlour with a view to the front yard. The source of his discomfort became apparent with his frequent glances at the door from whence came the coughing. Only yesterday a young woman living near their quarters had died suddenly of this influenza they said came from Spain. This house was suspected of harbouring resistance operatives. He would be vigilant but would stay far from the inhabitants of this infected cottage.

Lisa and her father went in to minister to *Mama*. Claude addressed her in a voice loud enough to carry below. "How do you feel *Mama*? You seem stronger. We have a visitor staying with us. We'll be looking after a German soldier while his *Oberleutnant* carries out his patrols."

"*Mama* you must rest now, *fais dodo*. I'll bring you food and look in often before I leave tonight. Try to sleep."

Below floor, the message was received clearly. Paul and Philippe resigned themselves to a long uncomfortable stay in this dark, damp, musty hole. A small amount of light peered through the cracks in the floorboards. They estimated their cramped quarters to measure less than six feet wide and no more than five feet in height as they could not stand up straight. Philippe lit a match which did nothing to enhance the look of the place. It seemed that they would be sharing their space with a frighteningly large rat.

The claustrophobia that Philippe experienced in the dense forest was nothing compared to the panic that was now mounting. He confessed his fears to Paul. "I'm claustrophobic and I'm finally remembering something. I see myself cramped and uncomfortable, feeling cold in my seat in the plane. There's a loud droning noise all around."

"This is a good sign. It's the first time you have a memory about yourself before you woke at our place. I know the air is stale in here but you must sit back and breathe slowly and deeply. We have to stand up as best we can and move around on a regular basis. If I understand correctly, Lisa will bring food and look in on us later."

It was, to say the least, one of Philippe's worst nightmares. He concentrated on images of Angeline in order not to think about being buried alive. Eventually the pair drifted in and out of sleep until movements from above got their attention.

Mama could be heard coughing and blowing, some scraping on the floor and then the trap door opened, the blinding light pouring in. A smiling Lisa appeared in the frame of the trap door. "It is now fifteen hundred hours; I leave in an hour. Hand me the envelope. Our resident Hun is napping in the parlour; *Papa* is standing guard. This is your meal for the day. *Papa* will let you out as soon as our guard is asleep for the night. Rest as much as possible, your journey is long. The Oberleutnant suspects too much; this rendezvous point has been compromised. You will be informed of our next venue. *Bonne chance!* God be with you."

In this terse businesslike manner, the visit was over in seconds. As the trap door shut; darkness reigned once more. Paul tore into his bread and cheese. "I'm starving. After this we exercise and rest. It will all be over soon."

"Watch your food!" Too late, the rat stole a hefty bite right out of Paul's hand.

Time passed slowly. They half stood, moved their arms and legs and then tried to nap. This procedure was repeated several times. Natural light no longer seeped through the cracks. Philippe dreamed he was in the plane. It was cold and his legs were cramped. He looked around the plane. He saw the pilot but not his face. Then he saw the equipment. Photography! It meant something.

They were fast asleep when the trap door was opened for their deliverance. Their minds were fuzzy from the stale air and their limbs were stiff from the cramped positions. Recovery time was a luxury they did not have. Before their heads could clear they were crawling across the back field with a piece of bread and cheese in their pockets.

Finally, cool fresh air and space, Philippe was almost euphoric. "It's so dark, do you know where you're going."

"I can hear the running brook. We follow that to the escarpment. The thick bushes along the banks will cover us. We also need to drink as much water as we can."

The tree line below the escarpment was reached safely. And then… voices from above… German voices. "We can't go on," whispered Paul. "A few more yards to the bottom of the escarpment and then we go left. There's a small low grotto and it's well hidden. We'll have to bide our time."

They waited in complete silence, wide awake and on edge. The voices droned on. Finally, at the break of dawn the voices changed direction accompanied by the sounds of substantial movement.

"They're coming down the path. From there they'll follow the brook. We can't move until nightfall." This was whispered through cupped hands around Philippe's ear.

Some half dozen complaining soldiers made their way down clumsily. They passed not ten yards from the intrepid pair. Once again, they had to remain in a small space for what seemed like the longest day of their life taking turns for short bits of restless sleep.

"They were waiting for us. It's obvious that there's an informant in Fumay. I don't want to think of what would have happened if we hadn't made it to the forest before dawn."

"Paul, why did you bring me on this mission? You've never brought me on one of these before and you certainly didn't need me."

"The fighting has reached a peak and this damn war is going to break one way or the other. Resistance help is more important than ever and more dangerous than ever. Some of us won't survive the missions and we need more men in the field. Consider this your training my friend."

At sunset it started to pour yet it was a relief to be underway again. The heavy rains persisted and the going was slow and rough. Soaked through, starving and exhausted, the two friends pushed doggedly forward.

"The closest farm to the forest is the Clement farm. We'll stop there to clean up. Just two farmers getting help from another farmer. I would imagine that Angeline is worried by now."

———●●●———

Was Angeline worried? She had expected their return at the same time they were hiding in the grotto still on the French side of the border. She was somewhat concerned when they had not arrived by breakfast time. However, Paul had been late before and they were due in today. Well, it was still today and there was sowing to be done. She headed for the fields where four women from the nearby village of St. Joseph awaited her. These women would put in a good day's work in return for food with which to feed their families.

By suppertime, Angeline was worried. At bedtime she was distraught. Fears always seem to loom larger at nighttime. She tried to think of all the good reasons why they would be delayed but in the end she gave way to doom and gloom. *The Huns have them. At the first hint of suspicion they shoot without question. How can I go on without my strong steady brother? My parents are probably dead somewhere in Germany. How can I bear to live without Philippe?*

After a sleepless night what had started as concern the day before was quickly building up to panic. In the light of the day Angeline forced herself to calm down and concentrate. She was not hungry but ate some porridge anyway. They were now 24 hours late. It was socked in and raining heavily. This was good for the young plants but there would be no further planting until these rains abated. She needed the work to take her mind off her fears. The house needed a good cleaning. Yes, she would clean the house.

Although washing, scrubbing and mopping kept Angeline busy, it did not occupy her mind. By noon she had seesawed from good thoughts to bad thoughts. The skies began to clear which did nothing for her mood. She felt a heavy pressure on her chest as she held back the tears. *It's the rain,* she told herself; *this weather has held them back. I won't panic until tomorrow. Oh God, please, please, have mercy. Bring them back to me. They are all I have.* And now the tears came. She sat down and let them come. Finally she lay on the floor in foetal position sobbing uncontrollably.

So loud was the sobbing that she did not hear the front door open. Philippe ran to her. "Angeline, my sweet Angeline; what's the matter?"

She cried even harder as he lifted her up. Angrily she pounded on his chest with her fists. "Don't you ever do this to me again."

Philippe removed her fists as gently as he could and held her tight. Paul moved in behind her to form a three way hug.

————◆●◆————

Paul had been right. The Germans' last big offensive in June was a failure. The tides did turn that summer of 1918 and the influenza spread with a vengeance by the end of that summer.

As was the case in the Americas, the cities were hardest hit and young adults were the most likely victims. In Belgium the piled up bodies were laid out in sheets and thrown into open lime pits for lack of wood to build caskets.

At the front, in the filthy close quarters, there was no escaping this scourge. Raving and coughing blood they could die within hours, recover in three days or ail for two weeks. There was no discrimination between the Germans and the Allies; both sides lost their men by the tens of thousands. The troops were decimated and those that survived were drained.

The most optimistic estimates put the death toll at 25 million worldwide while the more pessimistic ones go as high as 50 million. Whatever the number - the majority of the victims fell to the disease in the autumn of 1918. It cannot be a stretch to say that the influenza must have played a role in ending that atrocious war.

By the end of September the White Lady's mole at the Imperial Army Headquarters in Belgium sent word to its operatives. "The Imperial Chancellor has been told that their cause is hopeless," Paul reported to Philippe and Angeline.

While negotiations went back and forth between Germany, Austria and the Allies, things were quiet at the farm. The threesome kept as far away as possible from the towns and cities and tended to their harvest.

In November, chaos broke out in the cities of Belgium. The flu was still taking its toll, German soldiers revolted against their Kaiser and desertion was the order of the day. Lawlessness broke out and the Germans with their own problems could not cope. The long awaited November 11th armistice came under less than ideal conditions in Belgium.

The German exodus was a slow but steady flow mostly by foot, some by cart and others on horseback. In a matter of two weeks they were gone and the Belgians began the slow process of rebuilding their society.

———●●●———

The real Philippe Roland returned to the farm. Emaciated and weakened by the flu, he was happy to be home. Paul arranged for some genuine looking paperwork for a newly re-christened Philippe Roger, a friend of Philippe Roland a.k.a. Phil, both from Valais in Switzerland.

During his two years in Belgium, the only recovered memory for Philippe remained that of the uncomfortable seat in the plane and the importance of photography. He had learned to live with this strangeness and had built enough new memories to find happiness.

The churches were marrying couples in groups and among such a group in January of 1919 were Angeline Roland and Philippe Roger.

CHAPTER 8

1919
Joseph

Leaving the men folk to their socializing in the back of the Lafleur General Store where the feed was stored, Adèle ambled to the fabrics counter where her convent friend Céline Hébert was sizing up ribbons. A few months younger than Adèle, the two had been in the same class at the convent and had become fast friends.

Beauty can be a joy to describe. There exists a large palette of colourful words from which a writer can choose to paint his or her characters. The writer can delight in this variety to experiment with different forms until the desired image appears. Readers can interpret this work of art in their own fashion allowing their imaginations to bring the characters to life. It's very much the same thing with ugliness. It's a simple thing to play with the adjectives in order to horrify, repulse or evoke pity perhaps.

Homeliness is a different thing altogether. Céline was considerably taller than Adèle but beyond that she is somewhat difficult to describe. She had brown hair, brown eyes, and a straight nose with everything in its right place, in the right proportions. Céline was just simply plain. Even her welcoming smile did nothing to alter her unremarkable appearance. The enormous abdomen bursting through her coat, however, was not commonplace.

Concerned, Adèle gasped, "Céline! Shouldn't you be home? Your time must be any day now. Isn't there anyone here to help you?"

"Oh it's not for another month," chuckled the mother-to-be. "*Docteur* Fortin is sure that he hears two heartbeats. Twins run in my Mother's family you know, but my ankles are really swollen and my shoes hurt so much this could very well be my last outing. Anyway, Gérard is nearby at the blacksmith. Our mare lost a shoe but he should be here soon. Hey, why don't you come visit tomorrow after mass? I miss our chats, please say you'll come. You could ride with us. I'll make a *tourtière**."

"Oh I'd love that, but you've got to let me help with lunch. I'll bring a brown-sugar pie and I'm doing the washing up."

"*Merveilleux*, we'll chat tomorrow. Gérard's here and I've got to run."

Joseph Lafleur emerged from the storeroom in time to stop Céline from picking up her parcels. "You shouldn't be doing that *Madame* Hébert, let me take these out for you."

"*Merci* Joseph. See you tomorrow Adèle."

"*Au revoir*, be careful don't slip on the ice," replied Adèle with concern.

Within a few minutes Joseph was back inside vigorously rubbing his hands together. "Brrr... it's a cold one today. February was never this cold in England. Can I help you with anything *Mam'selle* Adèle?"

Just a year her senior, Joseph had admired Adèle since she was a little girl. He always looked forward to Saturdays; delighted when she came in and disappointed when illness or chores kept her home. This time his reaction was more intense. It was the first time he was seeing Adèle since his departure for the war, the first time he was seeing her as a young woman.

What had changed? She had not grown an inch but through her open coat he saw a shapeliness that was not there before, her face was no longer impish but more serious and so very lovely. Suddenly he felt nervous and tongue-tied. Embarrassed, he felt his face redden.

Adèle also experienced a new reaction to his presence. The Joseph that now stood before her was not the young man she had last seen. He had always been quiet with a serious look about him, but now he seemed too serious, even sad. He was thinner with a hag-gardness unfitting a twenty-two year old. A bit of life was restored to his face as he blushed and quickly looked down at his shoes.

Adèle felt his discomfiture. "*Allô* Joseph! I heard you were back. It's nice to see you again. When did you arrive?"

"I was lucky to be stationed in England so I got one of the first boats to Halifax. The problem was getting from Halifax to Pointe-à-Gatineau. The trains just couldn't handle us. It took me three weeks to get here. Anyway, I've been home for two weeks now trying to adjust."

"Your parents must be so happy to have you home safe. Our François was hurt last year and he's fallen in love with his nurse." Adèle's laugh was infectious and Joseph smiled broadly.

"So now he's gone and signed away his right to a free trip home as he plans to stay in England and marry this nurse. *Mama* is beside herself even though he promises to come home before long with his bride. We do miss him but knowing that it's all over and he's safe is going to have to be enough for now."

"You can have no idea how happy I am that it's over. I was in the trenches for a long time in conditions that I couldn't write home about. I just want to get back to normal." Once again Joseph was looking down at his feet.

Adèle felt that she had to say something to cheer up this despondent looking man. "Did you know that I have a picture of you in England in your uniform? You did look most handsome in it," she teased.

More blushing… "How can that be?"

"Oh it was way back at the beginning when you were being trained. You were standing at a bar with Jacques Armand." François sent it to me.

Joseph marveled at Adèle's ability to converse so comfortably. It put Joseph at ease. "*Mais oui*, I remember that night, your brother was there too. It was just before my deployment and I'm afraid that we all had a bit too much to drink."

Suddenly his discomfiture returned and he spoke haltingly. "Oh *mon dieu*, I'd forgotten. I am so sorry about Jacques Armand. My parents wrote to tell me."

"It's alright Joseph, I still miss him but I keep very busy. I'm still teaching and perfecting my English because I have plans…"

A loud 'AHEM' cut her short. Lost in conversation, the pair had not noticed the line of impatient customers forming behind Adèle. This time the blushing was all over Adèle's face as well.

"*Désolé,* let me pay for this writing paper quickly, *Papa* is buying feed and I must join him. See you next week, Joseph." She was gone in a flash, leaving Joseph longing for next week.

Meanwhile, outside the store, Céline grabbed a hold of her husband. "Gérard, quick, you must go into Lafleur's and invite Joseph to lunch tomorrow. He seems so lost and so sad. I've invited Adèle Turcotte so wait until she's out of earshot. It'll be such fun to have company."

"Aha, I see what you're trying to do. My wife, the matchmaker! When are you going to learn to mind your business?"

"Oh, come now Gérard, what harm can it do? Adèle is lonely and Joseph is lonely. I just want everyone to be as happy as I am."

"Alright, little miss busybody, I'll go in there when I'm done loading the wagon."

Gleefully Céline hugged herself. "Oh, what fun, they are perfect for one another. They just need a little push."

A stop at Aunt Hélène's for the post yielded a thick envelope from London. "Yippee, a letter from François," shouted Martin, Adèle's younger brother. In a more subdued voice, the thoughtful Martin added, "It's very thick but we must wait until the whole family is together before opening it."

Adèle, Martin and their Papa rode the journey to the farm in silence. With a compliant gait, the obedient nag pulled the wagon in a northerly direction along the river road; the river itself a vast field of pristine white. Two days before, Gatineau had experienced a short thaw with a light rainfall turning to snow. Before the good people of the region could be drawn into the false hope of an early spring, the cold had returned with a vengeance. The result of this weather fluctuation was breathtaking.

Every tree branch down to its smallest twig was encased in ice. In collaboration with the trees, the late afternoon sun filled the prisms with its light. Between the tiny diamonds twinkling in the snow and the light dancing in the trees, the show bedazzled the threesome.

The pine trees were not to be outdone. Winter belonged to them. Insufficient to cover the green, soft layers of snow decorated their branches. They were the only ones to retain their colour, the all-important green that kept the countryside from being called barren.

After the sunset nothing was left but the penetrating, deadly cold. The half-frozen travellers buried in covers up to their noses thought of the warm fire and the shepherd's pie awaiting them around the next bend.

By the fireplace life needled back into fingers and toes as the remaining Turcottes gathered round. The enticing aromas wafting from the kitchen would have to wait as Adèle pulled out the letter and did the honours:

January 5, 1919

Dear Family,

I am no longer in Netheravon. My documents have been accepted and I have my pay and I'm a civilian again. Shirley and I have been very fortunate. I am working at the Aerodrome in Hounslow Heath fixing the planes there. Shirley's still working as a nurse. I rented a small flat in Brentford close to my work and not far from London. I got a flat there because Shirley lives in Brentford with her mother and her brothers and sisters. The O'Brien family has suffered a lot in this cursed war because Mr O'Brien and one of his sons died at Ypres in 1917. We are going to be married next month and Shirley will move in with me. I am enclosing a picture of her because I know that you are curious. You will have guess that she has red hair when you see all her freckles. Me, I think she is beautiful!

London is crazy rite now. The soldiers are coming in from the continent by the thousands. They are very impatient to get home and many of the ones who have been fiting since the beginning have to wait. Me, I don't think it's fair. I'm not the only Canadian staying on but don't worry because I plan to keep my pay for passage home for me and Shirley. She wants to come to Canada but she has to make sure that her family is alrite first.

I wish that you could all be here with me. In London there are trains moving everywhere under the streets. They call it the Underground. You can go everywhere in London realy fast. It's a very busy place and I find it very exciting.

Shirley wants me to say hello to all my family, so hello to the Turcottes. You are always in my prayers,

François

Everyone wanted to see Shirley's picture. It was a happy freckled face with eyes that spoke of mischief. She was in her nurse's uniform, a large frilly cap covering her hair. "She must have green eyes," said Yvette. "People with freckles and red hair have green eyes, don't they?"

"It's the middle of February so they must be married by now. She looks nice," commented *Maman*. "I guess that I'm going to be a *Grandmaman* before long,"

"Just imagine *Maman*, a red-haired little boy with lots of freckles," said Adèle with a wink.

"Well somebody has to give me grandchildren. We can't go on waiting on you. You're totally blind to the young men giving you the eye at church. Mind you, I don't like most of them but young Duchamp is a nice lad. You'll end up being an old maid if you don't watch out."

"Gilles Duchamp is a nice young man, *Maman,* but I'm just not ready and I don't want to live on a farm."

"And just what is wrong with living on a farm?" asked her offended *Papa*. "This farm has provided well for you in the past. It got you that fancy education so now you're too good for us?"

"Oh, *Papa*, I love this farm. You have been the best *Papa* in the world. I had it all figured out before Jacques died and now I'm just trying to sort myself out."

Somewhat mollified, Louis gave his daughter a kiss on the forehead. "Mind you don't wait too long and find that life has passed you by, *ma chérie*."

●●●

After Mass the next day, Adèle sought out Gérard. "Where's Céline? Is she not well?"

"*Ma femme* is now in her confinement and faring well, thank you. She's looking forward to your visit, so as soon as you're ready we will be on our way."

"I'll be right back. *Maman* has my pie in a basket and I want to say goodbye to them."

In no time at all Adèle with basket on her lap, was sitting next to Gérard in his wagon. She noticed Joseph Lafleur walking toward St. Antoine Street. She chided herself for not having gone to greet him after Mass. She must make a better effort next Sunday.

It was a short ride up Greber Street and onto rue St Louis where Céline and Gérard Hébert lived in a large annex to a workshop owned by Gérard's family. Gérard's father and mother lived in a spacious apartment above the workshop with their unmarried children. The Hébert's had gained an excellent reputation for cabinet-making. Their attention to intricate detail had earned them a rich clientele in Aylmer and Ottawa while also servicing the poorer folk of Gatineau and Hull with functional furniture.

Céline waddled out at the sound of the wagon. The two women hugged as best they could under the circumstances. Freed from boots, coat, mitts, hat, and basket Adèle was led to the brand new loft that Gérard had built for his children. "If we have girls then we'll need a room for our son. I think that a loft is perfect for boys, don't you? Go on up and have a look. I'm going to have to wait until I get rid of this huge belly."

Adèle went up and came back down with the appropriate *oohs* and *aahs*. Their home was warm and inviting. The furniture lived up to the Hébert reputation and Céline's prowess with the needle had produced attractive drapes and feminine touches to the décor. "Céline is a lucky girl, Gérard. She got the pick of the crop when she married you. But, where is little Xavier?" she enquired.

"*Maman* Hébert is kind enough to keep him until my confinement is over. He'll be spoiled rotten by the time he gets back but I'm taking advantage of it and resting as much as I can."

Céline came from a fairly well-to-do family of six girls. Her five sisters were beauties taking after their mother while Céline resembled her father. Although she was the third born and lacking in good-looks, surprisingly Céline had been the first one to marry.

It hadn't been the nice dowry that had enticed Gérard, but rather the fact that as neighbours of the Héberts, she and Gérard had been close childhood friends. They were engaged upon Céline's graduation from the convent and married six months later. She produced their first son at age 19. Once the twins were born she would be mother to three children at barely 21 years old with many more years of fertility ahead. Adèle had to admire her because it was just the thing she feared the most about marriage.

The sound of an automobile pulling in brought Gérard to his feet. "Ah, that should be Joseph."

Adèle looked at Céline. "Joseph?"

"Joseph Lafleur," replied Céline in the most innocent of tones. "He seems so lonely and sad since his return, we thought he could use some company and I probably won't be receiving anyone after this week so today seemed like a good time."

Gérard opened the door before Joseph could knock. In came the young man along with a burst of cold air. "Welcome, *mon ami*. What brings you in your father's Ford? Too old to walk up St. Antoine, I see."

Joseph shed his winter garb. "I can out-walk you any day, old friend, but you did say that *Mam'selle* Adèle would be here and I thought that I could drive her back to the schoolhouse after lunch."

Joseph bowed to the two ladies. "Thank you for inviting me *Madame* Hébert and good day to you *Mam'selle* Adèle. It's nice to see you again so soon."

There was some small talk before the men sat down to a cigarette in the parlour while the ladies prepared the table for lunch.

Nothing is better than *tourtière* hot out of the oven on a cold winter day. Adèle's *tarte au sucre* received high praise and all were satisfied. Lingering, over a cup of tea, the innocuous conversation turned to politics; the women's suffragette movement to be more precise.

"I don't understand these women suffragettes. They got what they wanted. Now they want more," complained Gérard. "They're mostly English Protestants and probably all sapphists*. A great number of them preach birth control. It's most unnatural and they probably won't rest until they can be just like men."

"*C'est pas juste**, Gérard," countered Adèle. "Why would you think that my right to vote would make me manlike? And we didn't get all that we wanted in Québec. Some women will be able to vote in the federal elections but what about the provincial vote? The Prairies have had the vote since 1916 and British Columbia and Ontario followed in 1917. Why do we have to be so backwards? Do you think women inferior to men, Gérard?"

Céline rushed to defend her husband. "I can assure you that my Gérard thinks that I'm just as valuable a person as he is, Adèle, but a man is a man and a woman is a woman. God made us different and he gave us different roles. All of society is based on the family and the woman is the guardian of the family while the man is the provider. It's in the Bible, Adèle. The suffragettes are threatening our way of life. The Cardinal has shown us just how dangerous they are to all of society. If you let women live the life of a man then the family will fall apart."

"Céline! I'm so surprised to hear you speak this way. I know that the all-male Church, the all-male politicians and the all-male journalists are of that view; as are many of the rural and uneducated women of Québec. But to hear this from the top graduate of the convent is most confusing to me. You speak of your husband seeing you as a valuable person, but in actual fact you're not even a 'person' under the law in this country. You have the good fortune of being married to a most devout and loving husband but you know as well as I do how often women and young girls are being abused by their so-called Catholic fathers and brothers and husbands. Everyone looks the other way." It was a passionate outburst that surprised Adèle herself.

An awkward silence ensued.

Seeing the red-faced Adèle trying to regain her composure, Joseph came to her rescue. The usually tongue-tied Joseph now spoke calmly and deliberately.

"I must admit that the women of England played a most important role during the war. It became convenient for the country to ask them to fill in the men's shoes while they were away fighting. They stepped out of those women roles you speak about Céline. They performed all manner of male jobs, quite efficiently I might add. Now they're no longer needed and have been told to return to what people accept as women roles. Some are happy to do so but others would have liked to pursue the work they enjoyed. Now that so many young men have died, the women outnumber us. Not all of them can marry. Unmarried women will be in greater numbers. What are they to do? This war has changed the world and in this modern age, things no longer seem so clear cut for me. *Le futur est un mystère.*"

Gérard had not fought in this Great War. It was not until conscription made it compulsory that the pacifist was forced to join. He was not enlisted until June of 1918. At the completion of his training he fell victim to the flu before he could set sail. His recovery had been slow and uncertain. The newly trained Gérard regained his fitness in time for the peace talks.

Pacifist that he was, he now seized the opportunity to steer the conversation to more neutral ground. "Tell us about England, Joseph. If I remember correctly, you spent the last years of the war there."

The remainder of the afternoon went by pleasantly.

Joseph started up the Ford with his precious passenger warmly nestled under a blanket. In his mind Joseph searched for the right words to begin a conversation. His usual nervousness returned.

In the silence Adèle could almost hear the churning in Joseph's head. "I must apologize for losing control earlier this afternoon. It's a subject that disturbs me greatly and perhaps I should keep my own counsel when in company."

"Céline and Gérard did seem a little taken aback by your intensity but your views are not surprising to me nor are their's for that matter. They've lived a parochial life and I'm afraid that you'll find them in good company in Pointe-à-Gatineau.

The war, the travel and I guess also lots of reading has changed me. I make it a point to get my hands on whatever foreign newspapers come to Ottawa. I love books and I'm afraid that I read much later into the night than is good for me. This women's movement is all over Europe and the Americas. Whether the Church agrees or not, and whether it will result in a better or a worse society, this is a revolution that won't be stopped." *Well, that was easy,* thought Joseph. *I could talk to her forever.*

"I have a heroine," confided Adèle. "It's Carrie Derick from Montréal. You wouldn't believe what this woman has accomplished! She did two degrees at McGill University and then she travelled to Germany where she did all the work for a Doctorate but they wouldn't give it to her because she's a woman. Now, just where is the justice in that?"

"Isn't she the woman who became the first female university professor in Canada a few years ago?"

Surprised, that Joseph should know that, she explained further, "Yes that's right, but did you know that she's doing the work at one third the pay of the male professors at McGill even though she's doing more research than most of them?"

"Indeed, I do believe that to be unfair. If she can do the same work just as competently, then she should have the same pay. In fact I've never given that any thought before now. Most of us humans don't have the disposition to imagine ourselves walking in someone else's shoes."

"I also want to go to university. The University of Ottawa will be opening its doors to women soon. My English has improved so much that you could say that I'm bilingual now and I've been putting money aside. I plan to do some tutoring and should be able to do my courses on a part time basis… oh my, I was going to discuss this with *ma tante* Hélène and I haven't told anyone else yet. I don't know what possessed me. I would appreciate your discretion Joseph."

The fact that Joseph was the sole person privileged with this information pleased him enormously. On the other hand, the fact that these plans would probably take Adèle on a path different to his was a most unpleasant thought.

"But what about marriage... *et une famille, Mam'selle* Adèle?"

Adèle's laugh had the power to put Joseph's mind at ease. "Oh I do hope to marry someday and I do want children. I don't see that it has to be right now. I'm still young. Surely there'll be some old goat out there who will want an opinionated old maid like me... and don't you think it's time you stopped calling me *Mam'selle*. I feel like your schoolmistress. Adèle will do nicely please."

The conversation flowed comfortably between the two and the schoolhouse appeared much too quickly for their liking.

Adèle pressed his forearm with her hand. "Thank you for the ride, Joseph. I seldom get to ride in an automobile. You're an excellent driver and a good conversationalist."

Joseph went around to the passenger side to help Adèle disembark. "The pleasure was truly mine. It's been a most enjoyable day." He walked her to the door and asked her to drop by to say hello on her next excursion into town.

"I'll make sure of it." With these parting words she went inside and shut the door.

Joseph floated back to the motorcar holding his arm where Adèle had pressed her hand. In a euphoric cloud, he somehow made it back home.

———•••———

Adèle busied herself with her chores. When all was in readiness for the next day's classes, she settled into her comfortable chair, book in hand and feet tucked in under her.

Her mind wandered from her reading. *What a pleasant young man. He's usually so quiet. Who would have thought that he was so well informed and that he held such modern views! It was so refreshing to talk to someone who knows something outside of Pointe-à-Gatineau. But down deep inside I feel such sadness there. I wonder what it is.*

The afternoon's conversation brought her back to her dreams. Thoughts of university and travel to faraway lands occupied her time until a deep lethargy took her to her bed.

The following Saturday, Louis Turcotte accompanied by his son Martin picked up his daughter at the schoolhouse on the way to town. "We have a business meeting at the *taverne*. We'll probably lunch there. Shall I drop you at *tante* Hélène's, then?"

"*Oui Papa*. I have some errands to run later on at Lafleur's. I can meet up with you there between two and three o'clock. Is that good for you?"

Having settled the time and place for their rendezvous, Adèle was dropped off at *tante* Hélène's home. Her aunt had returned empty-handed from the Post Office that week. No letter had been expected from England so soon after the last.

At the lunch table Adèle found herself finally able to discuss her future plans with her favourite aunt. Hélène listened attentively to her enthusiastic niece. "There... now that it's out in the open, I feel like it's more real. Well, what do you think?"

"I'm envious, I think... yes, I'm envious. I envy your enthusiasm. But I'm also frightened for you. You see this path before you without obstacles. But there will be obstacles, great big obstacles. You would be among the first women to attend the University of Ottawa and you can expect that men will put everything and anything in your way. You speak of Carrie Derick but can you imagine the hurdles she must have faced, hurdles she still faces? Your heroine never married and she might have regretted her childlessness."

"But, *ma tante*, can you just imagine all that knowledge, her travels and her independence!"

Hélène sighed deeply. "It's enticing to be sure. You make me feel that I should be enrolling along with you. I just think that you should be aware of all the pitfalls. Your own family might feel that you're not following the will of God."

This was not what Adèle wanted to hear. "I know... I know... but I need to know also that you'll support me in this."

"*Ma chère fille*, you've always been the daughter I never had. Of course I'll support you. But what about having a family? Would you give that up?"

"I do want a family, but... well... it's just that I can't imagine loving someone like I loved Jacques. It would feel all wrong with anyone else."

"Adèle, when I left the convent you were only five years old so you would not have known, but I was desperately in love with a young man from Hull. He would come to Pointe-à-Gatineau every Saturday so we could see each other and he also attended church here for the same reason. We found ways to be alone and I can tell you that his kisses transported me to another world. To this day the mere thought of his embrace sends shivers up my spine."

Adèle was dumbfounded, a bit embarrassed, and somewhat uncomfortable to witness her aunt's candour. "But I thought you loved *oncle** Adolphe, you seemed so happy. What happened to this love of yours?"

"It was no secret. It was obvious to everyone; it seemed that we would be betrothed before long. He was furthering his studies with the Oblates* in Hull and I knew that he was a devout Catholic. Don't ask me what happened because I'll never know. On my eighteenth birthday he took me out to tea where I fully expected a proposal. Instead, without any explanation, he announced that he would be studying for the priesthood and it would no longer be possible for us to continue seeing one another. He left abruptly before he could even see my reaction."

Hélène's face betrayed the pain occasioned by this re-opened wound. Adèle stood and reached out to embrace her beloved aunt. "Oh no, how terribly awful. I didn't know. How ever did you manage after that?"

"I did manage and that is exactly the point I want to make. For months I was practically in hiding. People whispered behind my back and a broken heart is actually quite painful. I don't have to explain this to you because I know what you've been through with the disappearance of Jacques. Things are never the same after that. You never get back to normal. There probably will never be anything like Jacques again. But one does find a new normal. You've already crossed that line. I can tell when you speak of your dreams."

"But then how was it with *oncle* Adolphe?"

"Ah, *eh bien…* we were more like intimate friends. It was most comfortable and very loving. We were like-minded you see. I can only say that I was most contented. You should never underestimate comfort and friendship, Adèle. These are the things that last into old age. Our marriage is something I miss terribly."

"I'm so sorry *ma tante.*"

"Don't be sorry for me, Adèle. I want for nothing and my life is full. My work with the orphans is most satisfying. I've travelled to Montréal, Québec, Toronto and New York. What you don't know is that I plan to sail for England in June. I've recently sent a letter to your brother.

Et toi, my emancipated young lady, would understand the satisfaction I get from directing my own life; but I would advise you to think carefully about the path you wish to travel. Unfortunately, women can't have everything. There's time yet before you'll be allowed to enrol, and I do promise that I will always be there for you, whatever comes."

Adèle planted a loud kiss on Hélène's cheek. "*Je t'aime ma tante*, but I would love you more if you could find a place for me in your luggage come June."

———•●●•———

By two thirty when Adèle arrived at Lafleur's General Store, Joseph was fit to be tied. Since morning he had jumped every time the bell jingled above the door as it opened to the customers. At last, this time the jingles announced the much anticipated arrival of the lovely Adèle. Joseph asked his brother to cover for him for the next few minutes. With a knowing smile, Jean-Claude acquiesced readily.

As always he was unable to talk until Adèle broke the ice. "*Allô mon ami.* Isn't it a lovely day? Just last week we were freezing and today we almost feel like taking off our coats out there."

That was his cue. "Yes, indeed, I was out without hat or mitts and an open coat at lunchtime and it was quite comfortable."

Before he could lose his nerve, Joseph launched into his well-rehearsed speech. "My father wants me to look after some business in Ottawa next Saturday and I was wondering, *Mam'selle* Adèle, if you would care to join me. The business shouldn't take long and then I was thinking we could see how the new Parliament building is coming along. I know a place where we can buy all sorts of foreign newspapers and we could have lunch in Bytown*."

The little speech was delivered all in one breath with such speed that Adèle had to pause for it to register. The pause was too long for Joseph. "I'm sorry, I must sound terribly forward. I just thought that you might be interested in going into Ottawa and of course you must be too busy..."

"That sounds just lovely, Joseph. I haven't been to Ottawa since before the outbreak of the influenza. I believe that a change of scenery is just the thing. Could I do a little shopping in the Market maybe... or... time permitting of course, we could wander onto Rideau Street and step into Frieman's or Ogilvy's." Adèle's delight was genuine. "Why are you still calling me *Mam'selle*?"

"My father would never allow me to address a customer otherwise. I promise to address you friend to friend tomorrow after Mass."

When Louis Turcotte arrived at Lafleur's, he eyed his daughter and Joseph in their *tête-à-tête*. *Well, well,* he thought to himself, *Joseph Lafleur. Hmmm... such a quiet lad, I would never have thought him to be her type. But... he's a good lad and his father's business is doing well. Not a bad choice after all.*

"Ah... *Monsieur* Turcotte... er... can I be of service?" At the sight of Adèle's *Papa*, Joseph had visibly reddened. The nervous young man looked as though he had been caught with his hand in the cookie jar.

Joseph's discomfiture greatly amused Louis Turcotte. He remembered his own awkwardness in the presence of his future father-in-law. He could not help his knowing smile. "*Merci*, Joseph, but your brother has seen to my needs and I have just come to fetch my daughter."

Joseph was an honest man. He didn't want Louis Turcotte to think that he was going behind his back and Adèle was his daughter. With trepidation and a great deal of nervousness he addressed the man. "*Monsieur* Turcotte, I have business in Ottawa next Saturday and I was wondering if you would permit your daughter to accompany me. I would have her back at her aunt's well before dark."

"Well now, Joseph, just which of my daughters are we talking about?" There was an unmistakable twinkle in Louis Turcotte's eye.

For a moment Joseph looked confused until he saw a large grin forming below Louis Turcotte's unruly moustache. At ease, he smiled back. "I was speaking of Adèle, sir."

"I do appreciate your request for my permission son, but Adèle is of age and no longer living under my roof. I'm afraid that the decision is entirely hers."

———•●•———

It was Adèle's *Papa* who broke the silence on the way to the farm. "Soooo…, Joseph Lafleur, well, well."

Adèle mustered up as much indignation as she could. "*Papa*, please! He's just a friend. There's been nothing but sadness since Germaine passed and I thought that Ottawa and a bit of shopping would lift my spirits."

"Uh huh, whatever you say, daughter of mine."

If silence reigned in the wagon for the remainder of the journey, it was not so in Adèle's mind. Her thoughts crowded in on one another. *Papa is right of course. Who am I fooling? I do believe that Joseph has intentions towards me… it's not fair for me to encourage him this way… I have plans that don't include him right now… he's a fine person and will make someone a good husband… I'm sure that he would be a loving Papa… I'm so selfish because I do want him as a friend… he's so interesting once you draw him out… still, I must act in a way that is not misleading.*

———•●•———

Joseph was in the company of Gérard when he approached Adèle after Mass the next day.

Both gentlemen bowed. Gérard was the first to speak. "Céline sends her regards."

Joseph chimed in proudly *sans* the 'Mam'selle'. "It's good to see you again, Adèle."

"I gather that your good wife is still in one piece." Adèle handed over a basket to Gérard. "These are her favourite jam tarts. She should spoil herself while she can." Turning to Joseph, she addressed him in a moderately detached tone. "How are you, Joseph? It's nice to see you too; you're becoming such a good F R I E N D."

Gérard was anxious to leave the pair alone. "Please forgive me if I take my leave so soon, but I promised Céline that I wouldn't dally. *Gros merci pour les tartelettes.* I believe that Céline will not be the sole partaker." A short bow and he was gone.

Tongue-tied once more, Joseph looked down at his boots. Adèle was becoming accustomed to breaking the ice. "Well, Joseph, are we still planning on going to Ottawa next week."

"Oh, most definitely, provided we don't get a blizzard. Father is lending me the Ford for the day. I can pick you up at the schoolhouse around nine in the morning if that's not too early. It's a long road to the bridge at Chaudière and my business takes me to LeBreton Flats at the E. B. Eddy offices. I should be done in less than an hour leaving us plenty of time to do a little sightseeing before lunch with good time to visit the big stores on Rideau Street."

"Well, I see that I'm in good hands, my F R I E N D. Please, come over and say hello to my family."

With Joseph in tow, Adèle headed for her family who were gathering together in preparation for the journey home. "*Maman, Papa*, you know my F R I E N D Joseph Lafleur."

Everyone was oblivious to Adèle's enunciation except for *Papa* who did his best to hide his smile. Pleasantries were exchanged and before long the family was homeward bound.

Joseph decided to take a walk to calm his nerves. He ambled along the riverside on Jacques Cartier towards the meeting of the two rivers that made up his world. His mood matched the splendour of the day. Adèle's references to their F R I E N D S H I P had not registered.

Joseph was falling head over heels in love. Visions of Adèle danced in his head. Totally giddy, he opened his arms to the skies and laughed out loud unaware of passers-by. *I think she likes me. Please God let her like me. Please God send us a beautiful day next week. Oh this feels so weird. Am I going mad?* He reached the family home above the General Store just as dizzy as he had been at the outset of his walk.

CHAPTER 9

1919
The Courtship

The interminable six days' wait did come to an end after all. Joseph rose early that Saturday, completed a number of chores at the store and discussed with his father the business at hand in Ottawa.

Denis Lafleur noticed his son fidgeting. "I guess you'll want to be getting ready. The schoolhouse is a good way up the river and you'll want to be on time for your meeting.

Sooo… *Mam'selle* Adèle… she's a fine young lady that one. It would be a good match for her as well, I dare say."

Joseph reddened. "*Pa*, I'm just getting to know her. You are way ahead of things."

"Uh huh… go on get out of here, don't keep the young lady waiting."

Joseph exercised great care in his appearance on this promising day. The only suit he owned was comparatively new. The three piece dark-brown mixed tweed was acquired in London, the capital of men's fashion at the time. He attached a starched collar with rounded ends and starched cuffs to his white shirt and embellished the ensemble with a brown tie speckled with tiny gold dots. His tan leather boots laced up to the top of the ankle. In deference to the little vanity that Joseph possessed, the heels were elevated to heighten his stature.

With a generous dab of Brilliantine he plastered his hair down and carefully put a straight part just left of centre. The mirror reflected the face of a serious-looking young man. Under a high brow, the features were well proportioned. The ears were small, perfectly shaped and close to the head. The eyebrows were generous without being bushy. The chestnut eyes were warm and intelligent. It was probably the thin mouth that was responsible for the serious look. Altogether it was the face of a nice-looking young man without qualifying as handsome. *Hmmm... it might be time for me to grow a moustache. People might take me more seriously as a businessman.*

It did not turn out to be the perfect day requested in prayer but one could not be too greedy because the overcast day was quite mild. As such Joseph donned a brown woollen flat cap that matched his outfit but his short well-used navy coat had a jarring effect. It couldn't be helped... it was that or his big black coat and it was not cold enough for the long heavy garment.

When Joseph arrived at the schoolhouse punctually at nine, Adèle was in the anteroom fetching her cloak. Purely by chance she too had donned her newest attire of browns and taupes. The smoky brown skirt of soft wool was looser than her everyday ones. Belted above the waist it reached well above her ankle, just below the calf; shorter than her usual just-above-the-ankle ones. A shorter overskirt reached a third of the way down the underskirt giving the opulent look described in the Sears Roebuck Catalogue. The material had been a birthday present from her aunt while Céline had provided the superb handiwork. Her taupe blouse had loose sleeves gathered in a cuff at the wrist. The V neck trimmed with lace was fashionable and alluring. A feminine boot with pretty buttons and a slim heel would have complemented the young modern look perfectly. Alas, having splurged on the blouse, Adèle could not permit herself new boots. The lovely outfit showed up the old unsophisticated boots with the thick heels and Adèle now regretted her frugality.

Seeing the motorcar drawing up, she put on her cloak, hat and gloves; with handbag on her arm, she left quickly to meet Joseph before he could reach the schoolhouse. Three homes below the hill along the river enjoyed a full view of the schoolhouse above. It would be unseemly for Joseph to be seen going inside the schoolhouse with Adèle on her own.

Joseph gave Adèle a thick woollen blanket to cover her lower body and they took off in good spirits.

With the 'hellos' and 'how-are-yous' out of the way, Joseph uncharacteristically initiated the conversation. "My brother Jean-Claude will be leaving Pointe-à-Gatineau by the end of May. He intends to live in California."

"Goodness, what takes him so far away?"

"Well, he's fascinated by the motion picture industry. His buddy James O'Malley went there to escape conscription and he's been writing to lure him there. He writes about the warm climate year-round and the mighty Pacific Ocean."

Adèle interrupted, "I must admit that a year-round warm climate seems enticing enough for me. But what about the store, he has a future here."

"Well, he's never truly liked working at the store. Jean-Claude spends his money at the cinema, on cameras and anything to do with photography. He does what's necessary at the store but he always longs for his free time. He says that Mary Pickford is making hundreds of thousands of dollars and the production studios are making even more. Can you even begin to imagine such outlandish amounts of money?"

"Good grief, what are we waiting for, let's get on the next train, *toute suite*," laughed Adèle. "You know, my Jacques wanted to be a professional photographer."

Joseph was the first to recover from an awkward pause.

"Now that you mention it… that night at the pub… you know… you have a picture of us… well… the fellows were all begging him to take their photo to send to their family or their sweetheart. He didn't mind at all, in fact, he seemed to be enjoying himself. He took time to position each soldier correctly and he took away the empty bottles and glasses off the bar in the background."

Adèle was silent; a faraway look in her eye. Joseph steered the conversation back on track.

"In some ways, I sort of envy Jean-Claude. I too would like to travel but I'm about to get much more involved in the merchant world."

Adèle returned to earth. "Oh, how do you mean?"

"There's a grocery called Laflamme's on rue St Joseph in Hull. Henri Laflamme wants to retire and his only son died at the Somme. The unfortunate man's wife died giving birth to their second child, a daughter, and he never remarried. Well, the daughter is married and has lived in Montréal for ages. Sooo... Monsieur Laflamme wants to sell us a share of his business. E. B. Eddy is offering us the loan we need for this venture."

"This sounds exciting but if *Monsieur* Laflamme wants to retire, who's going to run the grocery?" asked the perceptive Adèle.

"Well, that's just it. I've always worked in the food section of our general store and Jean Claude in the dry goods. Robert is seventeen now and my father plans for him to take my place and I would head *Marché Laflamme*. Since there's no son to continue his business, *Monsieur* Laflamme wants it to remain as *Marché* Laflamme, sort of like a legacy. *Pa* will back the loan and *Monsieur* Laflamme would be with me for a year before he retires. The contract says that the business would be mine upon his demise." This last bit was said with a self-satisfied-smile spanning from ear to ear.

Adèle could see that Joseph was feeling proud. "How wonderful for you Joseph! It would seem that congratulations are in order. *Monsieur* Laflamme seems a generous man."

"I'd have to say yes and no to that. He's an old friend of my grandfather so it was super that he chose us to buy in... but... I'll be paying my way. It does mean, however, that all those fanciful thoughts of freedom and travel aren't for me," he sighed.

"When does all this take place?"

"We're training Robert and we should have a new hand by the time Jean-Claude leaves... so, I would say before the summer starts. I'll have to move to Hull. The flat above the store is quite large and *Monsieur* Laflamme is moving in nearby with his younger sister, *Madame* Gauthier, who has recently been widowed. It's a lot of responsibility but I'm ready for it and I might add that I have some new ideas I'd like to try out."

They passed over the newly renovated Lady Aberdeen Bridge over the Gatineau River leading to Hull. "Goodness, but I must be boring you."

"Contrary to what they say, women do have the capacity to understand business," replied Adèle with some irony in her voice.

"Small businesses run by women are sprouting up everywhere and very successfully I might add, despite the difficulties they face from certain men."

Flustered at having touched such a raw nerve, Joseph started to backtrack, "Oh, I didn't mean anything of the sort, Adèle. What I meant was that I have been talking about myself for way too long."

"Joseph, the thing I like most about our F RI E N D S H I P is that we can talk about ourselves and anything at all for that matter without feeling constrained."

Adèle was very sincere about this. Most days were spent teaching children. The topics of conversation at the farm were usually restricted to family matters. Her good friend Céline and her husband were exceedingly devout and ultra conservative. So many subjects were taboo that it was best to tread lightly. This left her *tante* Hélène with whom she could converse freely on any matter. It was gratifying to be able to do the same with a seemingly liberal young man who was her contemporary.

"*Moi aussi,* I feel the same way. I'm usually not much of a talker but I feel comfortable talking to you. I probably shouldn't have been talking so openly about our business, *Pa* might not approve but I felt safe in confiding these matters to you."

"You can rest assured that your confidence is well-placed. You can count on my discretion as I believe I can count on yours."

As they crossed the Ottawa River on the bridge at Chaudière they marvelled at the harnessing of the cauldron-shaped falls in preparation for the new electric plant. On the Ottawa side of the river the E.B. Eddy offices awaited their arrival on Bridge Street just a short distance further.

The couple was kept waiting some ten minutes in the reception area before one of the higher-ups at the match factory offices came to greet them. Joseph presented his friend Adèle to the manager and after handshakes and a few banalities the two men retired to an inside office while Adèle occupied herself with last year's copies of McCall Magazine.

Many of the women depicted on the covers and fashion pages sported short hair, most with soft curls. Adèle's beautiful mane was assembled into a loose bun at her nape. It was not as severe as her schoolmistress look with the tightly wound bun atop her head, nevertheless, it wasn't very modern. The short hair seemed liberating and the soft curls were so feminine; one might even go as far as to say seductive. Perhaps she should give serious thought to having her hair cut and styled.

What a foolish thought. It would be an expensive undertaking and my hair is so straight, I would constantly have to style it into curls. I could wear it like the lady on page 4, a short straight bob... no... that looks too masculine.

Adèle's thoughts were interrupted when Joseph emerged from the office. He thanked the secretary and motioned to Adèle that they could leave. His satisfied look told Adèle that the business had gone well.

Joseph waited for them to be settled in the Ford before saying anything. "I'm pleased to say that we can now put things in motion. *Pa* and I will meet with *Monsieur* Laflamme, one more visit to E.B. Eddy to sign the loan papers and then it will all be in the hands of the notary. My dear *Mam'selle* Adèle you have the grrrreat privilege of sitting next to *Monsieur* Joseph Lafleur, the future proprietor of Marché Laflamme, rue St. Joseph, Hull." Joseph was laughing in good humour.

"*Regarde*, Adèle, even the skies are clearing."

Bubbling with happy chit chat, Joseph steered the car unto Wellington Street. The mixed traffic was heavy and slow. Buggies, wagons, motorcars and pedestrians jostled for position. "It's been at least six months since I set foot in the city and I swear I can see twice as many motorcars as before. I know that there are over 150,000 people on this side of the river but the hustle and bustle always takes my breath away," Adèle admitted.

As they slowly passed the Parliament buildings, Adèle remarked, "Well, I really can't see much progress since last I saw it. It's been three years since the big fire but then I suppose that much of the work is going on inside away from our eyes."

"Parliament has been in session at the Victoria Museum since the fire which is unfortunate for me because I was a regular visitor to the museum before the War. Anyway, they expect to be out of there soon I hear. Have you been Adèle?"

"The museum? *Mais oui*, just before the war broke out in the summer of 1914 *Papa* took us all to see the dinosaur. It was quite the outing. Babette was too young to come but Laurent was there and when he saw the beast, he started to cry and wouldn't stop until Maman took him out. The rest of us were completely awed."

A few minutes further on, Joseph was looking for room to park the Ford on George Street. That accomplished, there was time to amble through ByWard Market and to purchase copies of the New York Times, the Toronto Star and *La Presse* from Montréal. They soon settled into a cosy tea house on York Street for a much anticipated lunch.

"If you're wondering what that loud noise is," laughed Adèle, "it's my stomach asking me if I've abandoned it."

"I'm just as famished, let's order before we both faint."

Adèle was thoroughly enjoying her outing. The food was well prepared and the best part is that she didn't have to cook it nor do the washing up.

The museum continued to be the main topic of conversation.

"Do you remember *Père* Jacob's sermon not long after the dinosaur was put on display?" asked Joseph.

"*Non*, I can't say that I do. To be truthful, I must admit that I tend to drift off during his sermons. He dwells on hell, fire and brimstone most of the time and it would seem that the very act of breathing is sinful. Perhaps I'm being harsh but I see God in a different light."

"I quite agree with you and I assure you that this particular sermon was no different. He went into a complete rant about Darwinism. He pronounced it to be a mortal sin to view that dinosaur. The museum could not have asked for better advertisement. The good people of Pointe-à-Gatineau went in large numbers and filled the confessionals afterwards."

Adèle was giggling. "Yes, I can just hear him now. But, seriously though, don't you think that evolution is quite farfetched?"

"You may very well think less of me for this, Adèle, but I do believe that there is much truth in Darwin's findings. It was easy to get books on the subject in London. Most of the modern scientists are in agreement on the subject. I hope that I haven't shocked you and I assure you that I'm a devout Catholic despite this."

"I'm not shocked, Joseph, but I'm greatly surprised. You are actually the first person I've known who believes this. Mind you, I've never had this kind of conversation with anyone else and I doubt that anyone I know has ever read a book of science."

"I'd be happy to lend you some of my books. I have two that are written with the lay person in mind. You would find them easy to follow. However, it might be better for you not to mention this field of study. Most good Catholics feel very strongly about Darwin."

"Yes, I would so like to read them! It probably won't change my mind but then I'll be better equipped to argue with you on the subject. Oh my, what would Céline think? You're right this is better kept between us."

Joseph was delighted with the conspiracy, it felt intimate.

"Now you can understand my desire to enrol at the University of Ottawa. There's just so much to learn."

It was time to leave the tea house and Joseph directed Adèle and this unwanted turn in the conversation to another avenue. An hour was spent in the big department stores on Rideau Street before it was time to head home in order to arrive before the sun set.

The drive home seemed shorter and the two young people spent their time amiably discussing family.

Upon crossing the Lady Aberdeen Bridge, Joseph enquired, "Am I still dropping you at your *tante* Hélène's home?"

"Oh, no… I'm so sorry… I forgot to mention that I'm returning to the schoolhouse. *Papa* will be picking me up tomorrow morning on their way to Mass. This is quite a detour for you. I should have said something this morning when we set off."

Joseph was happy for the extra time with Adèle. "*Aucun problème*, we've made good time and I really love driving. I'm going to miss this car when I'm in Hull."

At the schoolhouse Joseph walked Adèle to the front steps. Both parties were sorry to see the day end. A small slip on a patch of ice unbalanced Adèle. Joseph reached out and held her upright close to him. Too close. Joseph held her for longer than was necessary. The moment was long and tense. Both wanted more; both knew that it could end things.

Joseph let go gently. His voice croaked; he cleared his throat. "Well… er… I want to thank you for your company…"

Adèle interrupted. "It is I who must thank you. I enjoyed everything about today and I feel that we are going to be the best of F R I E N D S. I'll want to read those books you offered but for goodness sake don't bring them to church tomorrow. I'll pick them up at the store next Saturday. Goodbye for now." She disappeared into the anteroom.

And so it went for the next few months. The two became fast friends. Joseph's move to Hull in May didn't change a thing. Joseph had unlimited use of *Monsieur* Laflamme's buggy. There were more outings to Ottawa; a couple of movies at the cinema that elicited opinionated talk; a couple of theatre pieces in Hull (one they disliked and one they could not agree on); a Sunday lunch at the farm; then one at the Lafleur's; and one at Aunt Hélène's.

Above all, it was the discussions that drew them so close; politics, religion, science, suffragettes, drama, you name it.

Consequently, on weekends, Adèle was spending less time at the farm and more time overnighting at her aunt's on many a Saturday after a date with Joseph… no… not a date… she would never call it a date… an outing.

Everyone awaited the announcement of a proposal. The pair already behaved like an old married couple.

Joseph was prepared to continue in this happy fashion for a while yet, but his mind was totally preoccupied with trying to figure out the best way to carry this friendship to the next level.

Marché Laflamme was faring well and the easy-going Henri Laflamme gave Joseph the leeway he needed to test new marketing methods. He purchased a used Ford pick-up which served the business well for transporting goods and doubled as his personal method of transport.

But, the apartment above the store was too big for him. It needed to house a family and Joseph was ready; he was ready financially; he was ready emotionally; he was so ready sexually; he was ready for Adèle. Her beauty bewitched him, her intellect captivated him; her humour charmed him; she truly had him mesmerised and he wanted none other.

Most of his horrifying nightmares in the trenches were replaced with dreams of Adèle that often resulted in sticky sheets. *Père* Jacob would have branded them as impure, lascivious, obscene, certainly worthy of mortal sin in need of confession. Joseph routinely confessed having impure thoughts but his dreams could not be helped, they were not of his willful making... hence those went unconfessed. Had Joseph been honest with himself, however, he would have had to admit that he would have readily willed these dreams had it been the only way to experience them. Thank God for beautiful dreams!

Adèle was mostly happy with the way things stood. She and Joseph had joined the Ottawa Public Library. There were no bounds to Adèle's curiosity. Jules Verne had long been a favourite and she now added H.G. Wells to this list.

The history and geography books were pleasurable but the science was exciting. She learned that the solar system was one of many forming a galaxy called the Milky Way; there was even a theory that other galaxies might exist beyond this; she studied evolution (accepted the evolution of the planet and the animals but not that of man who was undoubtedly created as is, and by God himself; but most significantly, she learned about her own body and its reproductive functions. University awaited and Adèle sent in her application for the autumn term.

She derived much satisfaction from her friendship with Joseph but something was missing. Her sensual reveries of Jacques were now quite rare. Recently she had had some downright erotic dreams involving Joseph. During the Friday night after school closed for the summer season she awakened in the midst of an orgasm.

It was now Saturday morning. The schoolhouse was in need of a thorough cleaning and as such she would not go into town today. She dawdled in bed a while longer.

Why would I have such a dream? Joseph and I are not that way. We are F R I E N D S, nothing more. I wonder what it would be like to kiss him... hmmm. There was a niggling in her groin. *Why do I get these feelings all the time? It's the same when Joseph is too near me... it's all so strange.*

Père Jacob says that the women should be pure creatures and that it is the men who have sexual desires that are sinful unless they are within marriage. It's the conjugal duty of the wife to assuage these desires. Well, I have news for Père Jacob; women get sexual desires too. I don't think that they can be helped or only happen when you're married. Sometimes I'd like to be held tight and be kissed just like it was with Jacques... actually... it's much more than just sometimes.

I think it would be nice with Joseph. I enjoy being with him so much. He would be a loving husband, I know it. I'm just not ready. I really want to go to university. Why couldn't we kiss anyway and still be friends. In her mind the word 'friend' was no longer heavily emphasized, it now possessed a much softer tone. It was... well... friendlier.

There's so much to do today, I must get these lazy bones out of bed. Tomorrow we'll all be at the church picnic and... well... we'll see.

———◆●◆———

Père Jacob was under the weather so to speak, so it was up to his aide, the young *Père* Tremblay, to deliver the Sunday sermon. Adèle was delighted. It was obvious that everyone felt the same way as all remained awake throughout the entire delivery. His homily spoke of the great love of God toward mankind; His longsuffering patience; and His great joy in embracing a forgiven soul returned to the fold. It was the perfect sermon to set a joyful mood for the church picnic on this glorious early summer day.

Procession-like, the parishioners laden with baskets made their way to a large field on the banks of the Ottawa River. Blankets of every colour were laid on the ground giving the field the appearance of a great big granny quilt.

Off came jackets and ties. The men rolled up their sleeves to their elbows and a good number of women followed their example. Straw boater hats were the order of the day making it difficult to differentiate anyone from afar. Many of the younger ladies sported skirts in a variety of pastels. The various intonations of male and female voices intermingled with the squeals of happy children. Altogether it was a most cheerful scene.

The fare was not to be outdone as lunch baskets of all shapes and sizes contained everyone's best recipes. The custom was to share one's goodies with everyone else. And so one brought the best potato salad, the best fried chicken, the best *tourtière,* the best bread, the best cake, the best pie and all manner of pickled vegetables.

Babette totally adored '*oncle*' Joseph and she monopolized his company. An unusually quiet Adèle was sitting slightly apart deep in thought. She was hatching a plan. Friday night's dream had left her on edge. She wanted to see what it would be like to kiss Joseph. It was a purely selfish desire but she wanted it more than anything right now.

Now that school was over, Adèle would be house-sitting for her Aunt who was still in England and not due back until August. After the picnic she would throw caution to the wind and lure Joseph inside. The trick was to get Joseph to do the deed without her seeming forward.

"Adèle, Adèle, are you off to the moon somewhere? Come, have some potato salad."

Maman's voice interrupted Adèle who was blushing deeply, feeling guilty of her sinful thoughts. "*Merci Maman*, I'm feeling ravenous and without a doubt you make the best potato salad but I'm afraid that I'll be sauntering over to the Fortin's for strawberry pie," Adèle teased her *Maman.*

As the afternoon wore on, full bellies and the warm sun had a tranquilising effect. The noise level died down, many of the parishioners drowsed. The children had run themselves ragged and were now into some quieter sit-down play. Adèle wanted to go home as soon as it was appropriate before she lost her nerve.

It was Louis Turcotte who made the first move. "Come on everyone, it's a long way home and we're all tired. Let's pack up and head for the wagon."

"I left the pick-up in the church yard so I'll walk you to your aunt's house if you wish," offered Joseph.

Adèle was grateful. "That's so kind Joseph."

Families were beginning to pack up. It was the proper time to leave. Joseph was no more talkative than Adèle. They walked in silence until Joseph remarked, "You seemed very quiet today, is everything all right?"

"I'm very tired; I think that I might have overworked myself yesterday. Everything is such a mess at the end of the school year and I wanted to get it all out of the way since I would be closing up to stay at my aunt's for the next few weeks."

It was back to silence. If Adèle thought that she was being improper in her sinful scheming, it was nothing compared to the heavy planning going on in Joseph's head. He had a head start on Adèle since he had been plotting for weeks and he could now see an opportunity presenting itself which he fully intended to seize.

The aunt's house had indoor plumbing and he would ask to use the facilities as soon as they reached the house; a perfectly reasonable request.

Having reached the front porch, Joseph could not get the words out of his mouth before Adèle spoke up in a funny squeaky voice, "Would you like a cup of tea before heading for Hull, Joseph?"

Joseph who had been rehearsing his lines was taken aback. "Um… er… yes, yes, that would be just the thing. *Merci.*"

Not a thought was given to nosy neighbours; the pair entered the house. Joseph placed his hat and jacket on the rack and was led into the parlour. The fire burning within Joseph was too much to bear; crazed out of his mind without further ado he grabbed Adèle by the arm and drew her roughly to him. Close up, the passion in his eyes was unmistakable. He barely managed to get a whisper out, "I love you Adèle."

Mouth pressed to hers he embraced her tightly.

It took a moment for Adèle to recover from the shock of this sudden unexpected turn of events. But her fires were burning too and this is exactly what she had wanted. She opened her mouth and let him explore. The familiar knot of painful pleasure started to spread below her abdomen. This was just so delicious. To Joseph's surprise she returned the kiss with ardour. The shock that coursed through Joseph's body caused his erection to harden.

With bodies pressed tightly together, the erection incited Adèle further. Moaning she began to rub her pudendum against his penis.

Joseph joined in the rhythm. Neither had expected the kiss to last so long and to go so far. Their movements became frantic. Joseph cried out as he ejaculated which caused the sweet release of an orgasm for Adèle.

Trembling and exhausted they dropped down on the sofa. Trying to recover their wits, they remained silent in their embarrassment. A peek at the wet circle in the crotch of Joseph's pants confirmed what Adèle thought had happened. It was no wonder; she had behaved like a complete tart.

With difficulty it was Joseph who spoke first. "Adèle, I am so, so, so sorry. I never meant for things to go so far. I've wanted to kiss you since forever." He tried to hide his wet spot with his hands. He was so obviously embarrassed.

Adèle tried to comfort him. "Joseph, the fault is equally mine. I too wanted to kiss you. I've been taught that only women of ill repute behave as I did just now... you see, I'm just as much to blame."

"You too, wanted to kiss me?"

"Well, silly man, couldn't you tell?"

"Adèle, I want to marry you. I want to be with you all the time. I will do everything in my power to make you happy... *s'il-vous-plait*... say you'll have me." There... it was out.

Adèle did not look away. She held Joseph's gaze and thought carefully before choosing her words.

"Joseph, I take what you have just asked me very seriously but we have just experienced something... um... surprising... to say the least... and you know that I have plans of my own. So please give me some time to digest it all. We both have much to think about so let's agree to talk about this again next week."

Joseph let out a long heavy sigh. With a smile, he tried to bring some levity to the situation. "I had planned to inveigle my way into your aunt's house by asking to use your facilities. As you can plainly see, this is no longer a deception but a necessity."

"You are the sweetest man I know, Joseph."

1919
The Best Laid Plans

That week, Adèle had planned to luxuriate in her aunt's comfortable home reading some forbidden highbrow French literature she had found in Hélène's bedroom. Flaubert, Balzac and Zola could not hold Adèle's agitated mind.

Try as she might, Adèle was unable to put order to her thoughts. Confusion reigned.

What was I thinking? It was a dangerous experiment from the start. Down deep, I knew that it would change everything. Why did I have to know what it was like to kiss Joseph? Everything was going so well. Why did I invite him in? Why? Why?

But then again, could I have stopped it? Joseph had planned to come in. He would have done the same thing. I shouldn't have allowed him to kiss me. But then again, could I have stopped it? I really couldn't have stopped it, could I? I had no will of my own at that point.

It wasn't what I had expected. I thought it would be sweet and nice. It was so much more than that. It wasn't the same as Jacques though. With Jacques it was like electricity was going through my body. It was more like I was... enraptured... like rising above anything earthly. It was as though Jacques and I became one ecstatic person. With Joseph it was more like I was hypnotised. The feelings were just delicious and I couldn't stop myself. There is no point in comparing the two because Jacques is gone.

Every time I've let myself dream of the kiss with Jacques I've had a sinful outcome; and now I can't get Joseph's embrace out of my mind and these thoughts generate the same sensual feelings. From what I've been reading it seems that it's natural for women to be sensual. We don't ejaculate but I know that I've been experiencing what they call orgasms. I'd always thought that married women let their husbands do it to them because they love their husbands and because it's their conjugal duty. When our hog gets behind our sow, he squeals and grunts while she just continues to chew on her slop. Ma tante Hélène tells me that this is exactly what grandmamma had told her to expect but ma tante says that it was nothing of the sort. She said that it was intimate and pleasant and that it brought the couple closer together.

My feelings are more than pleasant though. Do other women go through what I'm going through? I think I would love that part of marriage. I don't think that I would've made a good nun... maybe I would be better suited for a 'lady of the night'. Oh God... help me... am I sinning... should I go to confession. I can't bear the thought of saying any of this to Père Jacob. I just couldn't.

Joseph wants an answer. Do I love Joseph? If I loved Joseph would I have to ask that question? I know that I loved Jacques. Why did I love Jacques? Every time he came to the farm Maman made sure that Yvette was sitting by us reading or playing with her doll. I can't remember ever having a real conversation with him. I just remember that he made me feel giddy.

I didn't really know Jacques, did I? What did he like, what were his dreams? It was François who told me Jacques liked photography. Jacques didn't read books. Did he know anything outside the lumber field and the farm? That's a horrible disloyal thought... he would have evolved during his time in England and if he had come back we would have gotten to know one another and become friends as well as lovers.

Joseph wants an answer. I know everything about Joseph and he knows me inside out. We talk like bosom friends... we can talk about anything at all. We don't even have to agree... in fact sometimes it's great fun when we disagree. What would it be like without Joseph... hmmm.

It was a lonely thought.

I got over Jacques. Surely I would get over Joseph especially when there'd be so much going on at university. I'll make new friends with intelligent women who are like-minded. There's another world out there. Our discussions will be most entertaining. And my sexual life... that will have to be put on hold... will I find another Joseph later on?

Why isn't ma tante here at a time like this? Things can never go back to how they were. Joseph wants a wife and a family. I know that he would cherish me and care for me but I would be happy to simply continue as friends... it wouldn't be fair to Joseph though. Who am I fooling... the next time we were alone, I would want more than friendship. Joseph wants an answer.

Whatever I decide I lose something important in my life.

And so Adèle's mind continued in this disarray for the entire week.

———◀●●▶———

Across the Gatineau River, in Hull, Joseph's week could only be described as tortuously turbulent. He was truly suffering. In some ways, he too regretted having carried things further, simply because it would either end in marriage or nothing at all and his gut told him that it would probably be the end of everything.

He slept badly. His wakefulness was either caused by an ejaculation induced by erotic dreams of Adèle... or... he woke up in sweats from nightmares in the trenches. Whatever the cause, these wakeful periods in the black of the night were filled with pessimism regarding Adèle's answer. It was during the daytime that he allowed himself to hope.

He would imagine Adèle side by side with him sharing in the running of the store. His Adèle was the type who would want to be in the midst of things. He would imagine nights of passionate lovemaking. The depth of Adèle's ardour had been totally unexpected. He too had been taught that this kind of intensity was experienced by the male. During their embrace he had felt just how much each was under the control of the other. That he, Joseph, could give Adèle so much pleasure was an exhilarating thought.

Joseph wasn't a virgin. In England the soldiers had been given talks on sex and birth control. The talks had meant to terrify the soldiers by describing the debilitating effects of sexually transmitted diseases. Nevertheless, they were given prophylactics just in case.

On two separate occasions a somewhat inebriated Joseph with a couple of his comrades had ended up paying for a prostitute. The expensive two minute experience had left him depressed. He had, of course, visited the confessional following each of these sinful acts.

He knew now that sex with love would be an entirely different matter. He longed to possess Adèle, to make her writhe on the bed, to hear her moan. What if she said no?

Where would he find another woman such as her? It had been his experience that in mixed gatherings the men held together as did the women. The overheard snippets of the female conversations had always been about children and the household, an unfamiliar territory for him. He knew no other woman who combined beauty, intelligence and passion into one.

By and large the folk of Pointe-à-Gatineau were of the poor working class. Between the church and the laws of the land, women were nothing but baby machines. Apart from rudimentary reading and math skills, the school system taught the girls how to sew, cook and clean. Most importantly they learned their catechism and their role in a Catholic society according to the Bible. The luckier ones had a bit of geography and history thrown in.

Most of these girls were married between the ages of sixteen and twenty, ill-prepared and uninformed in sexual matters. The babies then started coming year after year. These exhausted women (if they survived childbirth) had time for nothing other than child rearing and drudging housework. They learned how they were expected to conduct their lives from the misogynist pulpit.

In fairness to these women, it was not that Adèle was unique. It was that she had a better education, the time and curiosity to read and people like *tante* Hélène and Joseph with whom to explore thoughts outside this narrow, close-knit society.

Adèle was quite correct. There was another world out there. There was a world of science, exploration, invention and big business. A world populated by brilliant people who would move the world forward. Bit by bit women were moving into that world. The twentieth century so far was an exciting time of innovation and discovery and promised to be a century like no other.

But for Joseph, she was one of a kind and life without Adèle was unimaginable.

———————●●●————————

The following Saturday, Adèle received word of an invitation for herself and Joseph to lunch the next day after mass with *Monsieur* Laflamme. His sister was away, visiting her niece in Montréal. Neither slept that night.

Mass was a blur and the drive to Hull was mostly silent. Whatever platitudes were spoken did not lodge in the memory banks of either party.

This was the first time that Adèle was being received by the kindly old gentleman and she really did try her best to be sociable but it was an obvious struggle. Her discomfiture did not bode well for Joseph and in turn his attempts at civilities were not his best effort.

Henri Laflamme had not lived to this ripe old age without being able to recognize something of human nature. The aura was unmistakably heavy and these two young lovers needed some privacy.

"Well, I'm afraid that I must beg your leave, *Mam'selle*. My life has gone full circle and I'm afraid that after Sunday lunch I'm in need of an afternoon nap, as would a new born babe. The tea is steeping and you'll find the chairs on the veranda to be quite comfortable. Joseph knows his way around." He bowed, "Joseph, *Mam'selle* Adèle, *c'était un plaisir.*"

The coupled mumbled their thanks and repaired to the veranda, cups of tea in hand. The small house was set back from the road affording them some modicum of privacy and the large chairs were indeed comfortable.

More silence.

Joseph could take it no longer. "Adèle, please, you must put me out of my misery."

Adèle started to cry softly. Joseph waited. With great effort Adèle composed herself, dabbed at her eyes and nose with her hankie.

"Joseph, I care for you more deeply than I have for anyone else. Although I've no doubt that you will make an excellent, loving spouse and a good father, you know that marriage at this time would not be in keeping with the life I envisaged. I'm sorry but I've sent in my application to the University of Ottawa for the coming term.

You've been an outstanding companion for me. Indeed, no one understands me or knows me better than you do. I cannot bear the thought of losing your friendship and do wish with my whole heart that we could continue the way we were."

Joseph was completely still trying his utmost to remain in control of his emotions. Failing utterly, he spoke louder than he would have wished.

"ADÈLE, I NEED A WIFE - NOT A FRIEND! Can you not see how much I love you? I do want your friendship but I want much more. I want you, body, mind and soul. I want a family. I want... this is too distressing..." Joseph's voice cracked. He remained speechless for a long moment while Adèle resumed her weeping.

Joseph rose and drew himself as straight as his 5'6" would permit him. His voice was strained, "I'll drive you home, Adèle. I wish you every success at the university and will look forward to hearing good things about your progress. I'm afraid that it would be too arduous for me to continue seeing you." He held out his hand to help her up.

The miserable drive home was too long yet the time to drop off Adèle came too quickly.

"Joseph, I am so sorry."

"Adieu, Adèle."

CHAPTER 11

1919
Confession

Adèle stood on her aunt's porch looking forlornly at the back of the departing pick-up truck. She was in shock.

If the previous week had been difficult, it was nothing compared to the coming weeks. At first Adèle was reliving the agonies following the death of Jacques. These acute emotions, however, didn't last long. A few days later Adèle emerged from her cocoon of pain. This latest state of mind could hardly be called an improvement. She found herself in a state of utter solitude and desolation. It was hot and oppressive… and… there was no one to talk to.

It was mid-July and her aunt was not due to return until late August. She was alone with her thoughts. She wallowed in self-pity.

Eventually when rationale returned she came out of her selfish misery and began to think more coherently. *Joseph is right. We've enjoyed a rapport beyond that of most couples. And then there was the kiss and… well… what else could he think after that. Everything seemed perfect for marriage and he is so ready. He really loves me and to offer him friendship when he has so much more to give is truly an insult. I've hurt him badly. I wonder how he is. I hope that he doesn't hate me now. There I go, being selfish again. If he has to hate me to get over me then so be it. He must find someone else. He deserves the good family life he wants.*

This magnanimity did not alter the fact that Adèle was desperately lonely. Half the pleasure in reading a good book or a controversial newspaper article was in sharing and debating it with someone whose opinions you valued. She would never have thought that a university education would end up costing her so much.

Oblivious to the debacle, Louis Turcotte picked up his daughter after the Saturday shopping that she may have a good home cooked dinner at the family farm. The wagon was full. Martin, Luc, Yvette and Annette sat atop the provisions singing happily.

Papa was barely heard above the ruckus. "So we finally get you to ourselves. It's so kind of you to remember that you have a family," he teased.

If Adèle was unusually quiet, it went unnoticed with the clamour that continued all the way home.

By dinnertime, however, it was obvious that something was amiss. Adèle did not join in the boisterous bantering that was the usual fare at the Turcotte family dinners. Louis Turcotte had never subscribed to the notion that children must be seen and not heard. He loved children. Adèle had told him once that her friend Céline had grown up in a household where the children were required to keep silent at the dinner table. Louis had surmised with some degree of amusement that the poor man had probably felt vulnerable in the presence of seven women talking at once.

After dinner, Adèle offered to do the washing up with her mother. "*Maman*, let's give Yvette and Annette some time off and I'll do the dishes with you tonight." The girls did not wait to be told twice; they ran off with a loud whoopee...

Lorraine gave her husband a meaningful look and the two women moved to the kitchen.

"What's wrong, Adèle; have you had a disagreement with Joseph?"

The tears rose to Adèle's eyes and she threw herself around her mother's neck. "Oh, *Maman, je suis misérable.*"

Lorraine let her daughter cry for a bit and then she sat her down at the kitchen table. "*Là, là,* tell me what happened."

In the recounting of the events, Adèle realised that it was the first time that she was informing her family of her application to the University of Ottawa. Yes, it was true that she had not seen much of her family but… had it been a deliberate omission? She was well aware of her parents' beliefs that Adèle had flights of fantasy when it came to her talk of higher education. She had known that they would disapprove.

"Adèle, Adèle, Adèle; *non*, I'm not hearing right! You turned down Joseph Lafleur to go to university! Have you lost your senses? *T'es complètement folle*!*"

Tears began afresh. "*Maman*, you don't understand…"

"No, I don't. Help me to understand. I've seen the two of you together. The two of you are in a little bubble when you're together. No one else exists. Any fool can see that you're in love with each other. Do you not love Joseph… because if you don't… you certainly have put on a good show."

"No *Maman*, it's not a show. I care enormously for Joseph and we do get along like two peas in a pod. Joseph himself understands my desire for learning. I just want more out of life."

"You want more than a loving husband and a family? Will your books replace that? Have you any idea how lonely your life will be?"

The past week had taught Adèle exactly what that would feel like and suddenly she was not so sure of herself. "*Ma tante* Hélène is quite content on her own."

Lorraine became angry. "What kind of idiotic notions has my sister put into your head? I'm going to have a serious talk with her."

"No, *Maman*, she has nothing to do with this… she isn't even here… and yes, I do know how much I'm giving up. That's why I'm so miserable and the last thing I want is to lose my family as well."

Lorraine softened. "*Ma pauvre* fille*, I believe that this is a monumental blunder on your part, but, you will never lose your family come what may. You should see yourself… it's obvious that you haven't been sleeping. Get yourself to bed. Your *Papa* will help me with the washing up… leave it to me… I'll tell him."

At daybreak, Louis found his daughter in the big swing on the porch. "Come Adèle, let's go for a little walk."

They walked in silence as Louis was trying to put order to his thoughts. "Adèle, the world is changing in ways that I can't understand. I'm well aware of your sympathy for the women's movement and I know that once these things get going there's no stopping it. Change will come... change has already come, women vote, some women even wear men's pants, women go to university... I don't know where it will all end but I do think that that there will be a big price for society to pay in the end. *C'est pas naturel* and you, Adèle, are going to pay a very big price for going against your nature. I've been criticized for being too lenient with my children and now I see that I'm partly to blame."

"*Papa,* how can you say that? Did you want to bring up automatons or did you want to bring up thinking people? My mind is made up. I have every intention of marrying someday and having a family. It's just a few years' difference, that's all. Please support me in this."

"No, Adèle, you don't have my approval. You'll always have my love and your family will always welcome you but I never could approve of this unfortunate decision of yours. I believe that you've missed your chance for true happiness."

For all of *Père* Jacob's sermonizing against the innumerable breeds of sin, the good people of Pointe-à-Gatineau never made the attempt at conquering the sin of gossiping. News of the break-up spread as quickly as had Jacques' disappearance two years before. At that time Adèle was awash in sympathy and condolences. This was indeed a different kettle of fish.

Though many versions were bandied about, the common thread that held the story together was that Adèle had shamelessly encouraged poor Joseph and then unceremoniously dumped him.

Any outing undertaken by Adèle was an ordeal. Previously she had enjoyed the approbation of the community and was counted among the favoured young people. Now it would seem that there would be no Christian forgiveness for this fallen angel.

Adèle went out only for the essentials and always at the quietest time of day. She sat eyes front at Mass and hurried back to her aunt's house without any of the fellowship. She was spared Joseph's sad demeanour who now attended Mass in Hull. She was not spared the dirty looks, whispers and innuendoes as she ran the gauntlet from the church to her street. Adèle became a lonesome recluse.

It was customary for *Père* Jacob and *Père* Tremblay to stand on either side of the church entrance after Mass in order to greet the parishioners on their way out. For weeks Adèle had escaped this greeting by pressing through the middle when the crowd was heaviest. On a particular Sunday nearing the end of August, *Père* Jacob stepped forward and grasped Adèle by the arm.

"ADÈLE TURCOTTE!" Everyone stopped and waited for what promised to be grist for the gossip mill.

In his best preacher's voice for all to hear, the priest continued, "I have not seen you in the confessional nor at the communion table for many months young lady. What have you to say?"

In abject mortification Adèle wrested herself free and ran all the way home. She flung herself on the sofa and remained there sobbing without eating lunch or changing her Sunday dress. Exhausted she eventually fell into a troubled sleep until repeated knocks at the front door roused her.

It was a dishevelled, swollen-eyed Adèle who opened the door to *Père* Tremblay. "Please my child, may I come in?"

Showing no surprise, Adèle despondently let the young priest in and offered him a seat in the parlour. Her manners intact, Adèle addressed him in a tiny voice, "May I offer you a cup of tea *mon* Père?"

The cleric's heart went out to the dejected young woman. "I am so sorry about what happened at the church today, *Mam'selle* Adèle. *Père* Jacob meant well. I've heard the unkindly whispers and I know that you're going through a difficult period. I came to pray for you and to tell you that you are not alone."

Adèle's sigh came from somewhere deep; she let his soft voice minister to her bereft soul.

"The Bible tells us in Revelations 3:20 that Jesus is standing at the door of your soul knocking. He's asking you to let him in because he wants to fellowship with you. He loves you Adèle, He died for you and he's not about to give you up. Won't you hear Him knocking *mon enfant* and let Him in. He is the Friend that you need at this time. Let me pray with you now."

The loving words of the prayer washed over Adèle and she was overwhelmed. Through tears of relief she whispered, "I'm ready for my confession *mon Père*."

From his deep pocket the priest pulled out his stole, kissed it and put it round his neck. Adèle began, "Bless me Father, for I have sinned, it has been... um... maybe as much as two years since my last confession.

Formalities over, the floodgates opened and she told all... the pain of Jacques death... her sinful thoughts... her masturbations... the kiss that had gone too far with Joseph... her desires to go to university and hence her break-up with Joseph.

With forgiveness granted and penance proscribed, Adèle felt extremely light. Smiling she repeated her offer of tea; she was famished.

A steaming teapot with a plate of biscuits was placed on the small table before the sofa. "*Mam'selle* Adèle, you should know that there is nothing wrong in your desire to further your education. Christian women can have many vocations. Indeed, there are more women than men alive so it stands to reason that not all women can marry."

This was music to Adèle's ears, although she couldn't see why the education meant that she would not marry.

"However, I do have an important question for you to ponder. Have you sought out the Lord in these plans that you have for your future. Is this what the Lord has planned for you? It's only in following His will that you can find true happiness."

"To be truthful, *mon père*, for the longest time my nightly prayers have consisted in reciting the rosary. I promise that I'm going to take all of this to the Lord."

The visit ended shortly thereafter and Father Tremblay left the house with his stole still around his neck. Realizing his absentmindedness, he removed it while going down the front steps. This was not lost on the prying neighbours who would report that Adèle had made her confession. Furthermore her sins were grievous enough for the confession to have lasted over an hour.

True to her word, Adèle did bring her troubles to the Lord in prayer. It's difficult to attempt to describe the feelings of the newly converted to the unconverted. Balm had been applied to Adèle's soul and she was walking on a cloud feeling as light as a butterfly. In this refreshed state she was able to pray earnestly. She poured out her heart to her Saviour. She prayed for Joseph and wondered how he was doing. She would have to see him soon and ask for his forgiveness. Finally, she asked the Lord for a sign that she may walk the right path.

The signs came, one good, one bad.

The following Sunday Adèle braved the malicious parishioners and walked head high to her pew where her family sat. To everyone's delight it was *Père* Tremblay who climbed to the pulpit. His eloquent sermon on forgiveness pulled at his flock's heart strings.

After Mass Céline made a beeline for Adèle before she could escape. She spoke in a contrite attitude, "Adèle, I beg your forgiveness for having abandoned you, during your difficult time, my dearest friend."

For Adèle, this was the first sign from God that all would be well. She embraced her old friend and whispered in her ear. "I missed you so much."

"Come, have lunch with us. You have been alone far too long and we have so much catching up to do."

"*Merci*, Céline, but I'm following *Papa* in the buggy today as I plan to lunch at the farm. How about tomorrow, for tea, when Gérard is working and we can have a *tête à tête* just us girls."

With a time agreed upon, Adèle headed towards her family. She was agreeably surprised by the nods she received from many of the parishioners. *Thank you Père Tremblay; you are truly a man of God.*

The family was delighted to see Adèle in good spirits for the first time this summer. The chatter was spontaneous and lively. Adèle slept over as the hour was getting too late for her to ride home alone.

Adèle hummed her favourite ballads on the ride home the next day. She eagerly looked forward to tea with Céline. She thirsted for companionship as much as a woman lost in the desert thirsted for water.

That afternoon, the old friends rekindled their fellowship. With the pleasantries out of the way, it was time to bite into the real meat of the matter pressing on their minds.

Céline began, "The rumours were awful and you ran away after Mass every Sunday and Gérard thought it best that I stay away for a while. I told myself that the twins and Xavier were keeping me too busy to see you anyway. That was so wrong and now, I really want to hear your side of the story."

Céline let her friend speak without interruption. Adèle told all, without elaborating on the kiss of course. She ended with *Père* Tremblay's visit that resulted in her salvation.

Céline was slightly infatuated with the young cleric as were half the women of the congregation for that matter. "Oh my, but *Père* Tremblay is truly an angel sent from God. I hope that he remains with us after *Père* Jacob retires. His sermons are so uplifting, don't you think?" Adèle nodded that she concurred.

"But I don't understand why you always seem to complicate life, Adèle. Why you would give up a nice man like Joseph Lafleur and the chance of a family for some more learning is totally beyond me. You could have married Joseph and read books to your heart's content for the rest of your life."

"Sometimes I do wish that I could see life as simply as you do. You do seem so fulfilled but we're different and I can't explain it any other way except to say that as different as we are, I do value our friendship so very much."

It was Céline's turn to confide in her friend. "I'm expecting again and we're hoping for another little boy. Gigi and Lou-Lou have been such good babies and a real blessing."

"But, the twins are only five months old; are you up to it?"

"Well, I didn't think that I would be in a family way again as long as I was nursing, but two boys and two girls would be just perfect and we're happy."

"Yes, I can see that. I too would love such a family but then what comes after... eight more... you're still young."

"We will take whatever God has in store for us, Adèle!"

Adèle thought it best to change the subject so she turned to village matters for she had much catching up to do with the news and gossip of the summer including the upcoming nuptials of Katie O'Malley the Saturday after next to which both Céline and Adèle had been invited.

Adèle was certain that Joseph would be there as the O'Malley's and the Lafleur's were close. She hoped that there would be an opportunity to speak with him privately.

God had forgiven Adèle, the friendship with Céline was rekindled, family matters were good and *tante* Hélène was due in on Friday. It is odd that only just so many things are allowed to go right before the inevitable bad turn occurs.

Thursday's post yielded a letter from the University of Ottawa. Adèle could feel her heartbeat pulsing in her ears as she stared at the envelope. Eventually she tore it open with little decorum.

The university was sorry but their quota was full. They were promising her a much better outcome if she were to re-apply for next year as her name would be among the first.

Adèle was stunned. She had never allowed for the possibility of this outcome. She sat seemingly unaffected, her mind blank. When the letter's message finally sank in, the first thought that came to mind was, *this is another sign.*

Adèle was confused more than she was disappointed. *I can certainly wait another year. It would permit me to be in a better position financially. They practically guarantee an acceptance for next year. But what is God telling me? It would be easier to understand if they had refused me outright. Does he want me to wait... or... was I supposed to have accepted Joseph's proposal?*

Adèle found herself becoming agitated. She remembered *Père* Tremblay's admonition. She knelt in prayer and asked the Virgin Mary to intercede for her and gave up the problem for the Lord to solve. She rose from her knees in a calmer state of mind. She would wait to discuss matters with her aunt. Things would no doubt become clear, she was in good hands.

Tante Hélène was travelling on the overnight train from Halifax to Montréal and she was met at the station in Ottawa by her excited niece at noon on Friday.

Hélène was exhausted from her travels. The sea voyage had been rough and she had not slept on the train. Once the two women had lunched and related the essentials about family, Hélène took to her bed leaving all that had to be said for the next day.

Hélène had corresponded with family and friends during her three month excursion. As a result she had not expected to find Adèle in such a calm contented state. "Your last letter was heart rending, Adèle. You seemed so forlorn and confused. Are you starting university shortly then?"

"The university will not take me until next year, but I'm not despairing, far from it. I'm expected to return to the schoolhouse this week to prepare for the new school-year. If I was so alone, it was that I had forsaken the Lord, *ma tante*. I'm close to Jesus now and have left my life in His hands and those of the Blessed Virgin who would be the best person to understand a young woman."

"Ah... I see! That union with the Spirit is a powerful thing. When did this occur?"

"Last Sunday, *Père* Tremblay came to visit when I was at my very lowest. You have no idea just how wretched I felt this past summer. He spoke kindly to me, he pointed me to Jesus and he heard my confession. The Lord truly is a refuge *ma tante*."

Adèle related all of the summer's events in a way that she had not been able to write. Hélène listened attentively, her eyes opening wide in horror at some of the more painful details with a 'my, my' or 'how awful' thrown in.

"And what of Joseph, how is he faring?"

"I've not seen nor heard from him since the day we parted. I'll probably get my chance next week at the O'Malley wedding. I've every intention of apologising but I won't make myself a nuisance as he must have the chance to rebuild his life."

"I must say that I'm happy to see that you've achieved peace of mind but I must caution you that the euphoria of the newly converted abates in time. The Lord and the Virgin Mary will continue to strengthen you if you let them, but problems don't disappear and you'll be expected to make decisions."

"I've also realised that I'm prone to being selfish and we've talked enough about me. Now, I want to know all about François and Shirley... and... *ton voyage à Paris naturellement.* I swear that someday it will be me."

Adèle was regaled with the highlights of her aunt's sojourn in London and Paris. She had also enjoyed the company of the unassuming, down-to-earth Shirley. "She's also very funny and easily makes people laugh. You wouldn't recognise François. He's fat, talkative and happy. He plans to return home with his bride in the New Year."

That night Adèle repaired to the guest room feeling overjoyed. Notions of travels to faraway places danced in her head. She looked forward to church tomorrow and the big family lunch planned at the farm where *tante* Hélène would be distributing souvenirs as well as gifts from François.

CHAPTER   1 2

1919
O'Malley Wedding

Early September and already the leaves were showing tinges of yellow and orange; soon the trees would be clothed in their finest attire. Adèle's finest lay before her on the bed in the attic of the school-house. She reminisced as she inspected the outfit she had worn on her first winter outing to Ottawa with Joseph. She remembered his appreciative look and his compliments when she had removed her cloak at the tea house. It all seemed so far away. *Well, it will have to do, I've not bought anything new and it's cool enough for it today. At least my new shoes will help give it a fresh look. In any case, this day belongs to the bride and all eyes will be on her.*

Papa arrived early to pick up his daughter on his way to town. "What's in the valise?" enquired her father.

"It's my outfit for the wedding; I intend to make full use of *ma tante's* indoor plumbing. I'm going to pamper myself to a hot bath and Auntie promises to give me a lovely hairdo and let me have some of her perfume from Paris. I've got modern shoes with slender heels so you see *Papa*, I'm sure to be the next best thing to the bride and will most assuredly find myself a husband, who... I promise... I will bring straight to you for your approval," laughed Adèle.

Louis Turcotte laughed along with his daughter but he did hope that a husband would be forthcoming before a year went by and she started afresh with her university nonsense.

Hélène hovered around her niece's toilette. First she had cut some thin strands of hair bordering her face and gave them a curl. She was now braiding ribbons in an intricate bun at the nape of the neck. The adorned bun looked classical and the soft wispy curls framing her face looked alluring. "I do like the new short hairstyles but I think that in your case it would be absolutely sinful to cut off this God-given gift. I, on the other hand, have decided to go to Ottawa and get the latest of hairdos... AND... I'm buying an automobile!"

"WHAT?... Wow!... When?"

"*La semaine prochaine*. How would you like to learn how to drive?"

"Oh *ma tante*, I would really love that. How exciting!" Yes, this is the kind of life she would like for herself. She could earn a good living with an education, she could travel... she could... well... time will tell.

———◆●◆———

The Irish population of the Gatineau area, being Catholic, often intermarried with the French Canadians. The O'Malley's themselves were a union between an O'Malley and a Lamarche. Today Katie O'Malley would be marrying Bertrand Poulain.

The church was full as the good people of Pointe-à-Gatineau never missed a wedding. It was imperative that one could describe everyone else's appearance. The congregation was abuzz when the organ finally struck its first chords. All eyes turned to the back of the church. Everyone prepared to *ooh* and *aah* appreciatively as the bride made her appearance on the arm of the proud father.

She did look lovely. The smooth satin dress gathered below her bosom flowed fairly straight down to her ankles revealing a white high heel shoe with a muslin flower attached to the strap across the top of her foot. The bouffant sleeves tied at the wrists gave the dress its panache while the simple tulle veil flowed some ways behind the bride. Contrasting all this white was a small bouquet of peach coloured dahlias held at her waist. Her beaming smile was easily discernible through the thin veil.

Next in the procession came the maid of honour, Lizzy O'Malley. Adèle did a double-take as did many others. *When had she gotten so grown up... and... so beautiful. She must be... let's see... maybe eighteen years old. When did her red hair turn such a lovely auburn? Her short curls seem so soft and that pale green dress matches her eyes perfectly; even if it is a bit too short. She looks like she just stepped out of a McCall's magazine. It's most practical to have her dressed in something that she can wear again.*

Once the ceremony began, Adèle started looking around the church as discretely as she could, hoping to locate the pew where Joseph was sitting. When she finally detected him she caught him looking straight at her. Both reddened and immediately lowered their eyes. Adèle lost some of her hard won composure.

Joseph had known that he would see Adèle at Katie's wedding. He knew that it would be difficult for him but he had to get used to it. The Gatineau area was too small and they were bound to meet from time to time.

Broken-hearted, he too had suffered during the summer. The store had kept him too busy for the kind of loneliness that Adèle had endured but through it all he had felt utterly miserable. Although he had steeled himself for his first look at Adèle since his *adieu*, he was overwhelmed by his feelings of love.

She's more beautiful than ever. When will it all end? I've got to get a hold of myself. We'll no doubt have to greet one another and she mustn't think that I'm pining away. I wonder what she's up too. Soon, she'll be attending university surrounded by men she'll find interesting. Her Papa has nothing to worry about. It won't be long before one of these learned men will marry her. Why didn't I tell her that I could wait. What was I thinking... if I could manage four years of the war, surely four years of courting would be heaven on earth compared to that. Then again it seems that all she ever wanted was friendship. She did tell me often enough and I just wouldn't listen.

The newlyweds had the good fortune of a cool but sunny day. The well-wishers greeted them on the front steps of the church and once the wedding party was well photographed, the invited guests headed for the reception.

The O'Malley home was plainly structured but quite large. The furniture in the sizable dining room had been either removed or pushed to the wall to make way for dancing and the sprawling kitchen had a good variety of dishes arranged on the large table. Many had brought food, each item being the dish they were best known for. Guests were milling about inside and out.

Adèle was rehearsing her apologies to Joseph. She asked Céline and Gérard to excuse her as she went in search of Joseph. *I'd better get this over and done with.*

She espied him on the far side of the veranda. He wasn't alone. There was Lizzy hanging on his every word, showing a set of perfect white teeth as she giggled in a way that indicated Joseph to be the wittiest man at the gathering. As she giggled, her curls swayed and her bosom shook. Her V neck was decidedly too enticing.

Joseph seemed captivated.

It was lights out for Adèle's soul right then and there as she now proceeded to commit one of the seven deadly sins.

Jealously is an extremely powerful reaction and most unbecoming. *She's a bit too curvy if you ask me. The men might be ogling her now but give it a few years and a couple of children and she'll be fat.* She made a quick about turn and sought some privacy. Impossible... people everywhere wanting to say hello.

Inside the fiddler began tuning his instrument; an accordion and harmonica added to the racket. Everyone's attention turned to the dining room. People crowded the doorways and windows to watch the two quadrilles waiting for the cues from their caller, 'Little' Joe Lamarche.

Although 'Little' Joe was short, he was anything but little. Satisfied with their harmony, the music struck up and the caller began prompting whilst playing the spoons; the dancers followed, stomping the floor in harmony.

"Round your partner do-si-do,
Round your partner here we go,

All your hands in a great big ring,
Circle round with the dear little thing,

Allemande left with the corner maid,
Meet your own and promenade."

The music quickened; laughing, the dizzy dancers whirled. Adèle watched as Joseph twirled Lizzy round and round her skirt rising showing entirely too much leg. She was sorry now that she had declined Gilles Duchamp's invitation to dance.

The loud music, the stomping feet, the boisterous crowd all became too intense for Adèle. She escaped to the far end of the veranda. Lost in her thoughts she didn't notice the change of pace to a quiet two step nor did she hear the soft footfall behind her.

"Adèle."

She froze momentarily at the sound of the familiar voice. Recovering quickly, she turned to face him.

"Joseph, how nice to see you." *Darn it, why couldn't I have said something a little more intelligent.*

Joseph's smile was genuine and it was infectious. *I'd forgotten how lovely her smile can be.* "It's nice to see you too. Someone told me that your aunt has returned. I can imagine that this must be a happy time for you."

"Yes she's been back a week. We never stopped talking for three days straight," Adèle laughed. "François sent us all presents and we heard all about his bride and his life in London. Oh, and *tante* Hélène also went to Paris. She visited the museums, walked the Champs-Élysées, went to the little cafés in Montmartre with artists all about... and... I'm babbling... sorry."

Joseph laughed. "I missed your babble. I'm glad to see you in good spirits."

"I too have missed our chats. Now tell me about the store. Have you heard from Jean-Claude? I have so many questions; I don't know where to begin."

"Come let's sit." They conversed at length, in low voices, heads close.

Jean-Claude had written describing his life in California and the film industry. Joseph had made some changes at the store and Henri Laflamme wanted to retire in the spring. The pair fell into their comfortable little world as though they had parted only yesterday, oblivious to prying eyes and wagging tongues.

"Have you moved to Ottawa yet?" enquired Joseph. "The university term must be starting soon."

"Oh my, I guess that you wouldn't have heard. I wasn't accepted for this year because they had too many applications but they practically guaranteed me a place next year... so... I'm back at the schoolhouse and ready for Monday to face the little monsters!"

"*Je suis désolé* Adèle; I know how much this meant to you..."

"Oh, don't be. It was difficult to accept at first but you'd be surprised to see how I've changed in some ways. I'm much more patient and this way, I'll probably be in a better financial position when it's time to move to Ottawa."

"Adèle Turcotte... patient... will wonders never cease," teased Joseph.

"What about you Joseph? I was really hoping to see you here today to apologise for having misrepresented our friendship and for any pain I may have caused you. I'm glad to see that you're moving on."

"I don't want to argue with you at present but we both know that there was no misrepresentation because it was never just a friendship. A choice had to be made and you made it."

Adèle reddened. *Well, he's not going to let me get away with that, but, he's right.*

"What do you mean... you're glad to see that I'm moving on?"

Adèle blushed deeper still. "Well... um... Lizzy O'Malley."

Joseph threw his head back in a loud guffaw. "Oh ho ho... do I detect a note of jealousy?"

Adèle gave him her most indignant look. "*Vraiment*, Joseph, get over yourself. You must have noticed how Lizzy was looking at you. I'm sure that everyone else also thought that something was going on between you two."

Joseph seemed greatly amused now and he chuckled. "To be sure, Lizzy O'Malley has turned into a fine young lady but beyond that I would have trouble knowing the first thing about her unless she stopped her infernal giggling. Did you know... even my 'hello' is the funniest thing!"

This news was very pleasing to Adèle. "Now you've got me giggling."

A commotion brought the couple back to earth. The bride was ready to throw her bouquet. One of the young maidens pulled at Adèle dragging her to the assemblage of unmarried women standing at the bottom of the front steps. Above them on the veranda, backing the group, Katie hurled the bouquet over her head into a multitude of hopeful hands.

Adèle's hands lay by her side while Lizzy standing beside her had hers outstretched. The bouquet hit Adèle in the chest and bounced off landing squarely into Lizzy's waiting hands. The triumphant look that Lizzy gave her was not difficult to interpret.

Everyone cheered for Lizzy and then cheered some more as the newly-weds prepared to leave for their honeymoon; two days of sheer luxury at the prestigious Château Laurier in Ottawa.

"How are you getting to the schoolhouse tonight," enquired Joseph.

"I'm sleeping at *ma tante's* tonight and *Papa* will drop me off tomorrow after church on the way to the farm. I've promised *ma tante* to disclose every little detail of the wedding."

"It's a short walk to your aunt's but it might be best if you had some company on the way."

"*Merci*, I'd love that."

Joseph left Adèle at her aunt's door with a polite tip of his hat and wished her a good night.

Hélène had been looking out for her niece. "Was that Joseph Lafleur?"

Adèle took off her hat and gloves. "Yes it was, and don't you look at me that way. It was all very friendly and much easier than I had imagined. I apologised for any hurt I may have caused him and we ended up talking about anything and everything. That is as much as I will say about Joseph Lafleur... now... do you want to hear about the wedding or not?"

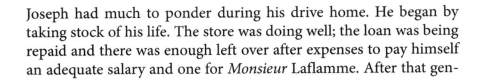

Joseph had much to ponder during his drive home. He began by taking stock of his life. The store was doing well; the loan was being repaid and there was enough left over after expenses to pay himself an adequate salary and one for *Monsieur* Laflamme. After that gentleman's retirement in the spring, everything would be his, leaving only the loan to contend with. In a few years' time, once he was solidly on his feet, it was his intention to open a branch in Aylmer a few miles to the west of Hull. Just two days ago, Henri Laflamme had called him a shrewd businessman.

He wasn't a bad looking fellow and he was no dolt. He was also aware that a few young ladies, some from Pointe-à-Gatineau and others from Hull, had found ways to make their availability known to him; not all of them as forthright as Lizzy O`Malley... but... the ladies did have their ways of letting a man know.

What would I do with a girl like Lizzy O'Malley? Her well-endowed bosom immediately popped into his mind. He started to undo all those little buttons that went down from the V in her alluring blouse. A soft girdle pushed her firm breasts up into the overflowing bodice; he pulled down the bodice and imagined the nipples erect. His loins stirred. *Well... yes... there is that... she's definitely enticing.*

What would we talk about? Hmm.... I could keep company with some of my more interesting clients. I've supped at Maître Labelle's table and the conversation was provocative and quite lively. Lizzy could stay home with the children as she would only giggle embarrassingly throughout the whole affair. In the end we would be living separate lives except for the bedroom of course. And when old age takes over and the children are settled, what would we have then?

I still love Adèle. He sighed. *I think she has feelings for me too... I know she has feelings for me.* He remembered the kiss. *I've missed her so much... no... I'm not going through any more of that. She wants a friend... I'll be her friend but I'll not be found in an embarrassing position like last time. Only friendship until she wants more. If I have to wait until she's ready, then so be it. Suppressing my desires will not be an easy matter but it's better than being without her.*

———◄●●►———

Adèle managed to keep the conversation on neutral ground with her aunt. But alone in her bed it was a different matter. Prayers did nothing to calm her. *I guess ma tante was right. Life is not always so clear-cut.* The day's events had proved just how much she had missed Joseph's company. The prospect of a long, lonely winter was terrifying.

Lonesomeness aside, it was altogether another matter that preoccupied her the most. Her intense reaction to Lizzy O'Malley frightened her. *I was so jealous. I don't remember ever feeling that way before. I wanted to scratch out those beautiful green eyes of hers. I'm not a violent person. Joseph is mine and no one else can have him... only... Joseph is not mine. I gave him up. Holy Mary, Mother of God, what am I to do?*

———●●●———

A wonderful thing happened the next morning at Mass. For all to see Joseph Lafleur entered the St François de Sales Church and walked down the aisle with the erect posture of a confident man. Reaching the fifth pew he squeezed himself in between Adèle Turcotte and her little sister, Babette. Alas, it would seem that Babette was doomed to be as bad a giggler as Lizzy O'Malley!

The courtship was both the same and different. It was the same in that familiar activities resumed such as the cinema, the theatre, shopping in Ottawa, reading and discussing international newspapers and so on.

Added to this were invitations to dine at *Maître* Labelle's table. Maurice Labelle, a relatively young man in his mid-thirties, aspired to enter federal politics in the next election and as such he entertained often. The young lawyer's first wife had died giving birth to their second child. He had recently remarried an Irish/French-Canadian young lady twelve years his junior. A graduate of McGill University, Mary Kelly was an ardent feminist.

Crowning Maurice's head was an ample amount of wavy, sandy-coloured hair meticulously parted in the centre. His generous mouth was surrounded by an impressive full beard and moustache combination that took nothing away from his penetrating dark brown eyes. The hair both atop and below was neatly trimmed. In fact, his entire appearance, both in apparel and stature spoke of neatness. Maurice Labelle looked every bit the part of a future Member of Parliament.

His conjugal choice for a partner would no doubt enhance his chances at the polls. Mary Labelle was as tall and as trim as was her husband. Although modestly dressed, she wore the latest fashions in good quality clothing. Her straight black hair was perfect for the modern bob hair-cut. If one were asked to describe Mary Labelle, one would mention her intense violet eyes for they were the most remarkable feature in an otherwise ordinary face. It was her unseen qualities that put her in a class apart from the norm by virtue of her exceptionally keen intellect and her graceful social disposition. Devoted to one another, the well-respected couple was going places.

Evenings at the Labelles were a source of sheer delight for Adèle. The varied guests were generally from Ottawa and Hull. It would be incorrect to describe them as like-minded for the debates that regularly ensued from a diversity of topics were compelling and at times heated.

Three years older than Adèle, Mary enjoyed the young teacher's company. Their views held much in common. Mary had advice for Adèle regarding her desire to attend the University of Ottawa.

"You may well be surprised to know that I wouldn't recommend the University of Ottawa for you. Did you know that the few women that enrolled this term were nuns whose curriculum is greatly curtailed to theology and literature? I suppose that they can't trust anyone but nuns to share classes with men... *humph...* Your chances would be much better in Montréal. All universities will discriminate against you but at McGill you would be in good company with many more women studying various disciplines. You would have a choice between the sciences and the arts... and... last year they finally admitted women into medicine."

"I'm afraid that McGill is not in my budget. But where did the lady doctors in Toronto and Montréal obtain their degrees before?"

"Some went to the United States. I've a friend who went to the university in St Paul, Minnesota. That's not next door so we were all certain that she would remain in the United States but she has returned and is practicing in Montréal. Harriet Brooks has left for Cambridge in England to pursue a further degree in physics and we expect great things of her. I promise you Adèle that we are on the cusp of a new age for women worldwide."

"I believe you and it's so exciting. I just want to be a small part of it all. What about Laval University in Montréal?" Adèle enquired.

"Most people now call it the *Université de Montréal*. Yes, you could try there... although... their prejudice runs deep. Marie Lajoie was their first female graduate eight years ago and would you believe that she was refused the Prince of Wales Scholarship which she rightly won? Worse still, at Laval University in Québec, Marie Sirois was not even allowed to attend her graduation ceremony to receive her diploma. It was mailed to her! The Catholic universities make it much more difficult for women... but... I do know that you'll get through whatever you decide, nevertheless, you must also realise that it won't be a bed of roses."

Among other highlights of the courtship was learning to drive *tante* Hélène's new automobile. The Model T Ford was a shining, dark blue four-seater with brilliant yellow spokes in the tires and polished wooden framed windows. Joseph undertook to be driving instructor for both the ladies. Adèle, being the younger of the two became proficient in considerably less time than her aunt.

In November Joseph accompanied the two ladies to Montréal. Adèle saw this as the first step towards world travel and as such she was terribly excited. The party boarded the evening train on a Friday. Hélène had organised a two night stay at a good friend's place on rue St André close to *Parc La Fontaine* for herself and her niece while Joseph stayed at his paternal uncle's home just seven blocks further south.

They visited the big department stores on rue Ste Catharine; Morgan's, Ogilvy's and Goodwin's. They attended Mass at the magnificent Notre Dame Cathedral and visited the imposing art museum on Sherbrooke Street. The hubbub of a city more than twice the size of Ottawa animated Adèle. She marvelled at the imposing façades of the financial buildings on rue St Jacques. "I've never seen so many motor vehicles as I've counted no more than two horse drawn carts and two buggies on this whole street," commented Adèle. They rode the street cars and walked miles taking in the sights that Montréal had to offer. The exhausted trio did not reach home until late Sunday night.

The courtship was also different mainly because Joseph's comportment was different. His behaviour was that of a true close friend and never anything more. He was interesting, sympathetic and caring. He never pushed for more nor intimated that he expected more. Above all else, he avoided physical contact with Adèle. Joseph was playing his cards differently this time around.

It was everything that Adèle had hoped for. She could outline her future plans in detail to Joseph and he would listen attentively with helpful suggestions and comments. There was an activity planned for every weekend filled with thought-provoking conversation.

So why did she feel that something was missing?

It must be obvious to the reader by now that our heroine possessed a healthy libido. Through prayer and self-restraint Adèle had had some degree of success in controlling her desires when she was alone. It was a different matter when she was in the company of Joseph. It was a torment at times for her to be in close proximity to the young man who had once awakened her senses and made her lose all control. Adèle yearned to be touched. It would be so lovely just to be held close to Joseph. But then... she knew that she would want more... she knew that he would too. She began her nocturnal fantasies once again.

In the confessional *Père* Tremblay was very understanding, (the young priest had his own demons to contend with); he admonished her to continue praying and he absolved her. Adèle should have guessed that Joseph was having much the same experience at the confessional in Hull.

On one particular evening, for whatever reason the conversation had turned to Adèle's visit from *Père* Tremblay during her aunt's absence. Joseph started to laugh heartily.

"What is so funny, Joseph Lafleur," asked Adèle in a huff.

With a smirk on his face, Joseph answered, "I was told by some busybody, I don't remember who now, that *Père* Jacob had let everyone know at church that you were a scarlet woman." He paused to laugh some more. Before Adèle could speak, he continued, "Wait, there's more. You were such a sinner that it took Father Tremblay half a day to hear all of your sins."

"And you think that's funny?" She watched as Joseph was trying his best to put on a straight face... and then... she too broke into peals of laughter.

"Seriously though, it's not a laughing matter when you consider that I'm convinced that *Père* Jacob called you out because he had heard my confession and put two and two together," Joseph disclosed. "As far as I'm concerned that was a breach which I've yet to forgive him for. I'm now confessing at the St Joseph Cathedral in Hull."

"Really! So that's why he called me out. What an awful man. You have no idea just how mortified I was that day."

"The moment I heard... *ah oui*... now I remember... it was Jeanne Fournier who told me... anyway, I came very close to phoning you at your aunt's."

"I wish you had, I was at a low point. But *Père* Tremblay was wonderful. He was with me for an hour; that much is true. He was sympathetic and very helpful with his advice. I wish they were all like him."

——————●●●——————

By the time December rolled around, Adèle's thoughts were conflicted. She was not enamoured with the curriculum at the University of Ottawa; she could not afford McGill, she was hesitant to leave Joseph for Montréal. Christmas was a time for family but she would be with hers and Joseph with his. *It would be so nice to celebrate Christmas together... even better with children of our own.*

One weekday afternoon when her students were on Christmas holidays, Adèle was having an intimate tea at Mary Labelle's home in Hull.

The two liberal women were having a frank discussion. Adèle decided to venture into Mary's personal life. "I have some questions that may be of a personal nature but I can assure you that I don't wish to be nosy... but rather... it's in the hope that it may help me in my own decisions."

"Goodness, you sound so serious, do go on."

"You've studied economics as well as literature. Did you not wish to continue or find employment in these fields? What made you decide to marry Maurice?"

"Ah... I see. It's young Joseph, is it?"

Adèle blushed.

"I'm not at all offended by your questions. I believe in speaking plainly. I don't fear the words, menstruation, pregnancy, or even vagina for that matter. It's ridiculous how we tiptoe around what is totally natural in the female and use polite phrases like 'in the family way.'"

"But, I digress and to get back to your question... at barely sixteen years of age I was a victim of a serious motorcar accident. There was much internal bleeding and it was thought that I would die. My womb was damaged beyond repair and as a result I can't carry a child."

"I'm so sorry to hear that."

"No, no, don't be. I came to term with it years ago. But I believed that no one would ever marry me so I embarked on studies and threw myself into women's rights. I met Maurice during the Easter demonstrations against conscription. The attraction was immediate. We were compatible in all aspects. Maurice was looking for a wife and mother for his two boys. The fact that he already has children made it less compulsory for us to have our own. Adam and Charles are bright, inquisitive and I just love being their mother."

"Maurice and I are partners in his political ambitions. I believe that I can be of great help to him and it's something we can share. As for my own ambitions... well... I too have political aspirations for which I'm prepared to fight and for which I will have my husband's support. To be honest with you... I'm not the kind of woman who would have been happy as a maiden for a lifetime... if you know what I mean." She winked at Adèle.

This was an eye-opener for Adèle. It provided a different kind of lifestyle for her to consider. Later that day she reviewed her situation: her family wanted her married; Céline thought she was crazy to have passed on Joseph; her Godmother wouldn't commit herself but she obviously liked Joseph immensely; Mary Labelle seemed to think that marriage was a good thing;... what did Adèle want?

It was time for her to make up her mind. She had been sending mixed messages to Joseph for almost a year. Either she married him or she went to university and broke it off that he may find someone else. Whatever she chose, it would cost.

She looked long and deep within. Adèle wanted Joseph for her husband and she wanted to have a family with him. The University of

Ottawa no longer interested her. She would like to study in Montréal but she found it daunting; not that it would stop her from doing it… but… she really didn't want to leave Joseph.

Adèle started to tremble; she took some deep breaths to calm herself. *I have just made a huge decision. I want to marry Joseph and I want to do it soon. I have wasted enough of our time.*

The trick was how to get Joseph back on track. He was a devoted friend but he was keeping his distance. A girl just can't go around asking a guy to marry her.

CHAPTER 1 3

1919-1920
A Game Of Hockey

On the Saturday, two days after Adèle's monumental decision, the plan was for the menfolk to attend an Ottawa Senator's hockey game at Lansdowne Park. Louis Turcotte and his son Martin were to accompany Joseph and his father, Denis Lafleur. However, Adèle was determined to be with Joseph that day and somehow inveigled the men to take her, her sister Yvette and *tante* Hélène with them. Since all three of the ladies loved the sport and understood all of its intricacies, it was judged that the women would be worthy companions.

Yvette was beside herself with excitement and Adèle was in the same predicament but for different reasons. As far as propriety allowed her, Adèle was determined that Joseph would perceive her change of heart.

It was a cold clear day and our festive party was dressed appropriately. The men thought that the weather was perfect for good ice and were buoyed by the fact that the Senators were poised to make the playoffs for the Stanley Cup. The rendezvous was at *tante* Hélène's. The men rode with Joseph in the Ford and the ladies followed with Adèle at the wheel of Aunt Hélène`s new automobile.

They took the closer Alexandra Bridge and once in Ottawa they went all the way up Bank to the park entrance. Inside the Aberdeen Pavilion, Adèle nearly knocked her aunt over in order to secure a seat next to Joseph.

To the great delight of the audience, the Ottawa Senators were getting the better of the Québec Bulldogs. The crowd stood to their feet and roared for each of the Senators' goals. Adèle also stood, tightly squeezing Joseph's arm in her excitement (though it was a ploy, the excitement was real). The excuses for pressing Joseph's arm were many. Each time Adèle made eye contact with Joseph she gave him her best smile. Harry 'Punch' Broadbent skating fast and furious scored the winning goal with seconds to go. What a game! Our small party was ebullient as they left the pavilion.

Denis Lafleur dropped off the three men at *tante* Hélène's. Everyone was invited in for a hot cup of cocoa. The men relived the salient points of the game while the women busied themselves in the kitchen. An hour later, the Turcotte's were on their way home except for Adèle who had made sure to ask her aunt for a night's hospitality. In the kitchen Adèle had whispered in Hélène's ear her request for a little time alone with Joseph. Her aunt had replied with a nod and a long inquisitive look, but Adèle gave nothing away.

Feigning a headache, Hélène excused herself. "The afternoon's excitement has left me hoarse and headachy. Would you mind very much if I took my leave? Don't stay up too late Adèle and please lock up for me. Goodnight Joseph, drive safely."

Adèle rose from the armchair to give her aunt a kiss.

"*Eh bien*, I suppose that I ought to be on my way also," said Joseph making an effort to rise from the sofa.

"Do stay a while Joseph," said the spider to the fly. "It's early yet and we haven't had a chance to chat with all the madness at the pavilion."

Adèle sat herself down next to Joseph on the sofa with a warm open smile.

"You have to admit though; it was a terrific game." For no reason that he could discern, Joseph suddenly felt wary.

"Quite thrilling actually," agreed Adèle. "Would you like some more biscuits?"

"*Non merci*, I made a bit of a pig of myself just now."

This is going nowhere. I've got to change the subject, thought Adèle. She took the plunge. "You know Joseph, I've been thinking. I've decided that I don't want to go to the University of Ottawa anymore."

"So I guess that you'll be going to Montréal then." There was disappointment in Joseph's voice.

"I'm not sure. I really can't afford McGill. Montréal is far away and I would be far from my family."

There was a long pause. Joseph was trying to process this new tack on Adèle's part. *What is she trying to say? All she has ever wanted was to go to university.*

"I'm not following you Adèle. Don't you want to go to university anymore?"

"Well… you know how much I would love to go to university… but… it might not be right for me."

Adèle was looking straight at Joseph, her mind furiously sending him every kind of telepathic message possible.

Is she saying what I think she's saying? Does Adèle want to get married? Whoa, I'm jumping the gun. I've no intention of going through this again.

"Adèle, you're confusing me, *j'comprends pas.* Just exactly what do you think would be right for you?"

Adèle wasn't prepared for a forthright question. *Wow. Where do I go from here short of proposing myself? Why isn't he picking up on this?*

"Well… I've been examining my life in detail during the past few weeks… and… I don't believe that I'm meant to be single. Well, of course you know I always said that I would marry someday… but… well… um…" Adèle looked down; suddenly dejected; no more bravado.

Now that Adèle had stopped talking, Joseph could heard her loud and clear. His heart thumped so loud that he thought even *tante* Hélène could hear it from upstairs. As thrilled as he was there existed in him (as in all of us) a bit of the devil. He knew that it was small-minded of him and malicious but he wanted a little revenge.

"Are you saying that you want to get married instead of going to university? Have you met someone?"

Adèle looked up, "Joseph! How could you say something like that?"

All it took was one little tear escaping the corner of her lovely right eye and Joseph was undone.

"Forgive me Adèle, but surely, you must see how confusing this is for me. You're hitting me with an unexpected about turn."

Propriety went out the window, "*Je t'aime* Joseph." Now the tears flowed freely.

Joseph put his arm around her and cupped her face with his free hand gently kissing away every tear till he found her mouth. It was a loving kiss and before it could ignite the way it had on the last occasion Joseph broke it off. He held Adèle close to him and whispered. "I think that I've loved you since you first started coming in the store with your hair in braids."

Holding Adèle at arms' length, Joseph got down on one knee and for a second time he asked the question. Adèle was laughing and saying yes, yes, all at the same time. Joseph joined into the happy laughter.

Upstairs Aunt Hélène looked up from her book when she heard the laughter. It gladdened her to know that her niece was happy and wondered what could have been so funny. *They really would be so good together. I wish that Adèle could see what everyone else sees.*

———◆●◆———

At church the next day Adèle approached her mother. "*Maman*, this may be very last minute and an imposition but would it be possible for you to invite Joseph and *ma tante* for lunch? It's very important to me."

"*Certainement* Adèle, I can always throw in a few more potatoes. What's this in aid of anyway?"

"Oh, I'll tell you later *Maman*… shh… the sermon's starting."

After Mass, Lorraine made the invitations as requested. When *tante* Hélène began making excuses due to her meal waiting at home, Adèle gave her an imploring look. Her godmother saw everything in that look and somehow she guessed. "Well on the other hand it can in no way match your cooking Lorraine and I can have it as leftovers, so, yes, I'd love to come."

Joseph addressed Adèle's father. "*Monsieur* Turcotte, would you like to try a ride in my pick-up? I'd be honoured if you rode with me as I'd enjoy going over the finer points of yesterday's game with you."

Louis Turcotte found this a bit strange but, why not? "Martin, take the reins, I, shall be motoring home." he addressed his son in a la-de-dah tone.

"Lorraine, why don't you and Yvette ride with me and Adèle. That way we can reach home before the wagon and get the food prepared," offered Hélène.

Once on the way, Joseph wasted no time. "Monsieur Turcotte, you may be quite surprised to hear me asking this... but... I'm requesting your daughter's hand in marriage... and... to be clear sir... I am talking about Adèle."

Louis stared at Joseph dumbfounded. "Well, I'll be... wait a minute... you <u>have</u> asked Adèle?"

Joseph burst out laughing. "She did say yes more than once, sir."

"*Sacré Cœur*! I love that girl dearly but I've never understood her. You'll be having your hands full, my son... and... you have my blessing."

When the wagon reached the farm with the famished brood, they found *Papa* by the fire enjoying a pipe with Joseph and the women in the kitchen getting the meal ready.

Once all were seated round the long table, it took a few seconds before the noisy family realised that Joseph had stood and was tapping his glass with a fork to get everyone's attention.

Joseph cleared his throat. Adèle glowed as he took her hand in his. "It is my great pleasure to announce that Adèle has accepted to become my wife."

A few seconds of shocked silence and then loud congrats, laughter and much thumping on Joseph's back ensued. Louis for his part fetched a bottle of gin that they may toast the good news.

"So, when is this happy event to take place," enquired *tante* Hélène.

"Well, we haven't actually set a date but we want it to be very soon and we thought we could discuss that with *Maman* and *Papa*."

"Just how soon does this have to be?" Lorraine asked warily.

The family went quiet. Adèle's laugh rang out, "Oh no *Maman*, not that soon. It's just that I feel that I've wasted enough time and would like it to be soon. Joseph feels that way too."

Lorraine was visibly relieved. "It's not customary to have a winter wedding but I don't see why not. It can be done provided it's not too big."

"Next week is Christmas and it seems like a good time to be publishing the bans at Church and then we could set a date for the first week in February maybe. How does that sound to everyone?" Adèle asked.

The rest of the day was spent in working out the details of the first Turcotte wedding. Joseph planned to meet with Adèle and then left early in order to stop by his parent's home to inform them of the happy news.

The wedding date was set for Saturday, February 7th and the bans were read out at church the following Sunday on December 28th. Not many were surprised at the news of the upcoming nuptials of this much talked-about couple; the few days before the official announcement had given ample time for word to have spread. The actual wedding date, however, did elicit some raised eyebrows. Some furious mental calculations were occupying the minds of many. Most concluded that all seemed in order but they would be looking out for the date of the first-born just to be sure.

Meanwhile, a letter from François arrived in late January. It contained some good tidings and had obviously crossed the one from Adèle announcing her good news. The important part of the letter was as follows:

> *The good news is that Maman is finally going to be a Grandmamma sometime in early July. We are over the moon. Before we settle down to all this responsibility I have decided to take my bride on the honeymoon we never had. We will probably never get the chance to travel again so we are going all out. We have foolishly put all of our savings to this end. Me, I think its alrite because I start working on the planes at the Rockcliffe Air Station in March, so we will be just across the river from you. I have been writing to get this job for the last six months and with my good references, it all went my way in the end.*
>
> *We leave for Le Havre on January 28th. We plan to go to Ypres in Belgium. Shirley wants to say goodbye to her father*

and her brother who fell there at the battle of Passendale. We will be in Paris for a few days and then set sail for New York. After a few days there we will take the train home....

Lorraine was ecstatic. "*Quelle joie!* Adèle is getting married, François is coming home and we are going to have a grandchild. Louis, I couldn't be happier."

Adèle added, "Oh dear, they're on their way to France now and my letter will reach London too late. He'll be very surprised when he gets here and finds out that his little sister is also married."

Louis' eyes were moist. "Our son has become quite the mechanic it would seem. It means that we're going to have to buy a truck at some point so we can get around easily to visit with our grandchildren in Ottawa and... in Hull of course," he winked at Adèle. The children cheered and whooped at the mention of a truck.

———●●►———

Clickety clack, clickety clack... the sound of the wheels on the train tracks had a hypnotic effect on the twosome heading for a three day honeymoon in Québec City; at the Château Frontenac no less. Joseph nodded off and Adèle was reliving memories through a somnolent haze.

The wedding had been as small as was possible with two large families to consider. Louis Turcotte could not afford a grand wedding. Family members had brought copious amounts of food to the intimate reception at the farm. The gifts were modest except for the beautifully crafted rocking chair from Céline and Gérard. "For rocking the babes to sleep," the couple had declared in unison smiling broadly.

I'm going to be a mother someday, Adèle thought dreamily... clickety clack, clickety clack... She was suddenly roused by the thought that followed. *We're going to be making love... tonight...*

The weeks leading up to the wedding had been so busy that she had not given her honeymoon much thought. Furthermore, she had not seen Joseph as often as before and when they did meet he had been adamant that they were saving it all for the appropriate time. "I'm through with all of these confessions," Joseph had laughed. "The nice thing about this short engagement is that we won't have to wait long before we can righteously love each other to our hearts content in the sight of the Lord."

The week before the knot was tied, uneasily, Lorraine had approached her eldest daughter. When Adèle realised that she was about to get the mother-daughter talk, she tried to help her mother out.

It's alright *Maman*; I've read a whole book on female anatomy and reproduction. I know what to expect."

"Well, I really don't know just what young people are reading nowadays but reading about it and doing it, are not the same thing. I know that Joseph is kind and gentle so he won't mistreat you. It only really hurts the first time and it's never for very long. You'll grow accustomed to it and your husband will love you for it. You'll do just fine."

It was the memory of this little talk that was now troubling Adèle. Adèle had been counting on the feelings evoked from dreams of lovemaking with Jacques and more recently with Joseph. Her *Maman*'s little talk didn't make it sound all that appealing.

Clickety clack, clickety clack... the book had mentioned the hymen but as it resembled more of a textbook, there was no description of lovemaking. *Tante* Hélène had once described the whole procedure as 'pleasant'. As they approached their destination, Adèle's confidence in her knowledge dwindled.

Clickety clack, clickety clack... would it be surprising to know that Joseph was thinking along similar lines? He had thought of nothing else but his honeymoon over the past weeks. The recollection of their memorable kiss was the jumping off point for his plans. It all had to be perfect. He was aware that his love for Adèle was probably more intense than hers was. He believed that she did love him in her fashion but he loved her enough to last them both a lifetime. Encouraged by her reaction to their most sinful kiss; their lovemaking promised to be marvellous. As they approached Québec, Joseph's confidence grew.

Adèle had seen pictures of the famous Château Frontenac perched above a steep escarpment overlooking the mighty St.

Lawrence River. But the photos as well as her vivid imagination had not prepared her for this grand a scale of opulence.

"Oh, Joseph, *mon amour*, how can we possibly afford this?"

"I've been planning a long time for this very day, mon amour, and anyway, their rates at this quiet time of the year were very attractive to a poor fellow like me."

The small room was richly furnished with original paintings adorning the walls and their own private bathroom. Joseph was the first to use the facilities. Smelling of scented soap he emerged in a wool blend robe opened to reveal a blue-striped pyjama. He told Adèle to take all the time she needed as he sat himself down in the lone armchair newspaper in hand.

Luxuriating in a hot scented bath, Adèle did take her time. Her preparations included a dab here and there of *tante* Hélène's French perfume. She then examined her naked body. Her petite frame was perfectly proportioned. She would have liked larger breasts but at least they were rounded and firm. Looking down at her thick black thatch, she wondered what other women looked like down there. She would wear nothing under her nightgown but hopefully she wouldn't have to remove it and hopefully the lights would be turned off.

The nightgown was a gift from her godmother. For the most part it was plain silvery silk that lingered on her curves when she walked. It was the bodice that drew the eye. The chest covering was made of sheer material with a lacy motif that did little to hide her bosom. Thin spaghetti straps left her shoulders and arms bare except for her lustrous black hair cascading front and back. She wore no robe over the negligee.

Bowled over, Joseph failed to notice his bride's nervousness. Dropping the paper and tearing off his robe, he rushed to Adèle, took her in his arms, and kissing her they fell to the bed.

Joseph lost all control. He tugged at his pants with one hand freeing his already erect penis and pulled up Adèle's lovely gown. He pushed her legs open, fumbled around until he found the honey pot and forcefully thrust his member in. He ejaculated to the piercing sound of Adèle's cry the moment her hymen gave way.

Complete silence. He rolled off a stunned Adèle. Joseph sat up, his back to his love, eyes shut, head in hands. "I'm so sorry, I'm so sorry."

With tears slowly running down her cheeks and a mixture of blood and semen running down her inner thighs, Adèle went to the bathroom. *Who was this man? Where had her friend disappeared to? Is this what it was all about? How was it going to be for the rest of her life?* She washed it all away. Confused she sat on the toilet seat working up the courage to re-enter the room.

When she finally came out she found Joseph in bed staring at the ceiling. She quietly got into bed pulled the blankets to her neck and presented her back to Joseph hoping that somehow she would fall asleep.

Joseph was in a most wretched state. The tension that lay between the two bodies was palpable. Nothing, absolutely nothing had gone according to plan. What had possessed him? He had ruined everything. He had lost her. *No, I can't let this happen. I have to make this right. I can do much better.*

Joseph turned on the light and tentatively reached out to Adèle. She froze. He gently turned her on her back. In her eyes he saw both sadness and anger.

"Adèle, you are so very beautiful, I lost control and I'm sorry. It wasn't supposed to be like this." Adèle relaxed slightly; fresh tears appeared at the corner of her eyes. Softly, Joseph removed each tear with the tiniest of kisses. He kissed her forehead, her nose, eyelids and cheeks in the same manner.

He felt her body relax a little. He kissed her neck. Light kisses. He kissed her shoulders. He felt her body begin to give way to his caresses. He kissed below her throat. Through the sheerness of her bodice, he saw that her nipples had puckered in anticipation. Joseph removed all the blankets and gently began to remove Adèle's nightgown.

She stiffened.

"Shh… shh… *je t'aime*, nothing bad will happen." She let him remove the gown. Joseph took off his pyjamas.

In the soft glow of the light they lay bare to one another.

Joseph looked…

Adèle looked…

Across his chest she saw a mass of soft brown curls that narrowed into a strip reaching all the way down to a mound around his manhood. This was her first live view of an adult penis and it was beginning to stir. Before she could get frightened again she quickly looked away up to his eyes… it was the sheer excitement in Joseph's eyes that began her own stirrings.

The more he stared at her breasts, the more the nipples puckered begging to be touched. His gaze went south. As she watched his bold examination of her pubic area, she felt a warm glow. Gently he pushed her legs wide open. He beheld the pink bud of her clitoris peeking out between her labia. He now looked into Adèle's eyes and she saw it all there: wonderment, amazement and yes, unbridled lust. This look was as powerful as any touch and Adèle's body began to move, her eyes imploring him to stop looking and start doing.

He accepted the invitation. He cupped one breast in his hand, kissed it all around, licked the brown areola that defined her nipple area and then suckled her. He gave the same loving attention to her other breast. Adèle moaned and began to move. Alternating from one breast to the other he explored between her labia and stroked her clitoris with his fingers. He found her opening. She was so wet. With her juices he rubbed gently in and out and around her clitoris and back again.

His most passionate dreams now became reality. Adèle was moaning and writhing, her body glistening with a light sweat. It was she who pulled up her knees and drew him to her. Determined not to repeat the previous fiasco, he was slow and gentle. Adèle responded with the thrust of her pelvis in perfect synchrony. Joseph let her take the lead as she quickened the pace. When Adèle felt the familiar knot of painful ecstasy tighten all around her clitoris her movements became frantic searching for the releasing explosion. The shudder of her orgasm triggered Joseph's own eruption.

They lay side by side breathing heavily basking in the afterglow. Joseph turned to his wife… she was crying silently. The tears were streaming. Horrified, Joseph asked, "Adèle, *ma belle* Adèle what's wrong?"

Adèle smiled through her tears. "I'm just so happy, I love you so much, Joseph."

The next morning, the famished newlyweds had a sumptuous breakfast and went for a walk on the Dufferin Terrace. The large wooden walkway by the Château skirted the edge of the cliff offering a magnificent view of the St. Lawrence. As Adèle walked arm in arm with her husband she felt a little sore between her legs; not enough to hurt, just enough to deliciously jog the memory.

They walked the terrace and later they made love; they went ice skating and later they made love; they thrilled their way down the monster ice slide further along Dufferin Terrace and later they made love. It was everything a young couple could wish for their honeymoon.

Life was perfect.

CHAPTER   14

1919-1920
Belgium –
The Aftermath

The Belgium left behind in the wake of the Germans' decampment was not a pretty sight.

The initial resistance to the invasion had been met with over-kill on the part of the Germans. If one discounted the British propaganda stories of Germans eating boiled Belgian babies and the German propaganda of their benevolent protection of the Belgium populace, the truth somewhere in between remained grim.

Thousands of acres of farmland were laid to waste. The flourishing pre-war industrial sector of Belgium gave way to the sole industry of fuelling the German war effort; its machinery dismantled and appropriated to this end. The once efficient railway system was in shambles. Many public buildings such as universities, churches and the like lay in ruins while thousands upon thousands of homes were destroyed.

The small Northwest corner that had remained in Belgium hands from Ypres to Nieuport suffered the brunt of this war, its towns ravaged right down to rubble. As a result Belgium's small army lost 40,000 of its soldiers. Meanwhile in occupied Belgium some 60,000 civilians perished, at least 6,000 of them summarily executed. Over

1.5 million were displaced; some fleeing successfully to other countries, others forcefully sent to labour camps. These are the losses that can be quantified.

But how does one measure the state of mind of the wounded, the widowed, the orphaned, the hungry and the countless unemployed? The German occupation was appropriately dubbed by the allies, 'the rape of Belgium'.

Despite these horrific setbacks, Belgians were a determined lot and they set about the reconstruction of their country. The government fully expected to be reimbursed by Germany for the war atrocities. With these expectations Belgium borrowed extensively and miraculously found itself back on its feet inside a decade.

Due to the scarcity of food, the farms that survived fared well in 1919. As the Roland's prepared for planting in April of that year, their expectations were justifiably optimistic. Two fields that had lain fallow were ploughed anew with the labour of the Roland family, who now numbered six strong, further aided by women from the St Joseph village.

Mr. Roland senior had returned to the farm in late January without his wife. At the onset of the war they had been dispatched to different labour camps. It had taken him eight anxious weeks of searching much of Germany before learning of his beloved's demise two years earlier. Physically, the camps had weakened and emaciated him, a condition that was remedied with Angeline's good ministrations. Mentally, the camps had robbed him of his *bonhomie*, a condition that seemed incurable.

In early March Paul Roland had married the fearless Caroline Boucher who had been his handler during the resistance. Her bravery during the war years had captivated him and her recent announcement regarding her pregnancy had thrilled everyone. Meanwhile, Philippe and Angeline were expecting their firstborn in early October.

The real Philippe Roland, better known as Phil to the family, was assiduously courting one of the pretty girls from St Joseph village working their fields. Wedding bells seemed inevitable. The farmhouse was happily bursting at the seams but two women (soon to be three) in the same kitchen is an unworkable situation over a long period of time.

A month earlier, Philippe and Angeline had begun the construction of their rudimentary home to the east of the main house. If all went well with everyone pitching in they expected to move in early June.

On a beautiful evening in early May, the family was enjoying a warm sunset on the porch and celebrating the news of Belgium's adoption of universal suffrage.

"This is going to change everything, mark my word," asserted Paul.

"*Humph*, I can't understand why they didn't go all the way while they were at it", queried Caroline? "I understand that the widow of a dead soldier suffered a great loss but how does that make her more eligible to vote than I would be? Did I not do my part during this infernal war? What about the bravery of Gabrielle Petit and Edith Cavell? They gave their lives for the resistance, for Belgium. *C'est complètement fou*¨!"

Paul and Philippe knew only too well how necessary the women had been in the resistance, working bravely side by side with the men and if Phil had survived the war it was due to the unstinting devotion of the nurses who were themselves in constant danger. They nodded their agreement except for Monsieur Roland who believed that allowing women to vote was the end of civilization as he knew it.

"That is bound to change soon. *Bientôt, tu verras*. The fact that they have included some categories of women is a sure sign. A few more years at the most and we'll all be at the polls." Angeline comforted Caroline in that soft soothing voice of hers.

"*Mais c'est contre la nature*. If we go against nature that way, our society will change for the worse," warned Monsieur Roland.

"Oh, *Papa*, society is already in shambles." Paul was passionate when it came to politics. "Look around you. Belgium is in ruins. We're going to need everyone on board to recover. Universal suffrage is going to put people in power who will come up with the labour laws necessary for the ordinary folk of Belgium to go forward and rebuild our nation."

"*C'est vrai*," Phil said in Paul's defense. "Nothing will ever be the same again... and that goes for the whole world. The war has changed us all and the rebuilding belongs to this new generation of both the men and women who have survived this tragic war."

Philippe listened attentively, still unsure of his status in this Godforsaken country. He served the resistance for Belgium, he farmed for Belgium, he married a Belgian woman and he would vote in the election. He had no other history so he clung to this family and this country and he was thankful. Yet, he did not possess the great pride of nationhood that a lifetime of memories engenders in one's heart.

In less time than one would expect, law and order was restored in Belgium and the people went about rebuilding their country, rebuilding their lives.

Philippe and Angeline moved into their cozy love nest, vacating the little room at the Roland main house, making way for Phil and his new bride Ginette, leaving Monsieur Roland the only occupant of the front room which had gone from parlour to bedroom to accommodate the crowd.

The able-bodied worked hard that summer, leaving the lighter chores to the expecting mothers. Life fell into a comfortable routine.

Philippe had acquired a camera and resumed his love of photography, his only memory. His pictures reflected his mood. His pastoral scenery depicting all aspects of farm life was serene, peaceful, and almost sleepy. His favourite subject matter, however, was the picturesque town of Couvin.

During the German invasion the fortified towns of Namur and Dinant, just north of the farm, had suffered destruction and massacre. The out-of-the-way town of Couvin, nearest to the farm, on the quiet Eau Noire River had not met with the same fate. Philippe loved to stroll along *rue de la Falaise*, up *rue de la Ville* and into the narrow lanes of the old town dominated by the beautiful Église St. Germain de Paris.

The site had originally been occupied by prehistoric tribes; digs also attested to Roman occupation; the church, various European duchies, the Netherlands, France and Germany had had their turns; the town had been burned and ransacked on numerous occasions. And yet on these age-old lanes among the timeworn buildings, oblivious to centuries of upheavals... time stood still.

Philippe's photos of Couvin portrayed the quaintness of the houses, the majesty of the church and above all else the beauty and magnificence of the surrounding scenery. Philippe was in a good place with himself.

One early September morning while tidying after breakfast, Caroline heard a blood-curdling cry emanating from the chicken coops where Angeline was gathering eggs. The cry had produced the necessary adrenaline for Caroline, heavy with child, to sprint like a gazelle the distance to the coops in record time.

She found her sister-in-law doubled over in obvious pain. "*Mais Angeline, qu'est-ce qu'il y a?* What's wrong, here, let me help you."

The three young men followed by Ginette were bounding across the fields in response to the piercing cry. "It's a few weeks early but I believe she's in labour," Caroline guessed.

Feeling too faint to walk, Philippe carried his beloved to their cabin and laid her on the marital bed. Once more she contorted and screamed. Philippe was gripped by fear and clutched his stomach as he too felt a pang sharing Angeline's pain.

Ginette ran into the room breathless from her run across the fields. She quickly assessed the situation and took command. "I've delivered the last two of my sisters; I know what to do. Caroline go boil lots of water; Phil fetch the midwife from the village, Géraldine Marois; the rest of you, out you go."

Philippe kissed his wife on the forehead. "*J'suis là, mon amour.* We're going to have a beautiful baby. I'm just in the next room; I'll see you both soon." Phil left for the village and Paul was sent back to the fields.

Philippe paced the front room as the women came and went with pots of boiling water, towels and sheets. Meanwhile the screaming continued at regular intervals. He had no memory of any childbirth. Was he one of many children; had he been there for the birth of his siblings; did he already have a child? Was anyone missing him? Each of Angeline's scream was matched by an intense pang in his own innards.

Two excruciatingly slow hours ticked by on the mantel clock before the midwife arrived. Ginette came out to greet the midwife. *"Bonjour Géraldine, je crois qu'il y a une petite complication."*

"Complication…complication! *Mon Dieu,* Ginette what do you mean?" Phillippe asked frantically.

"Là, là, calmez-vous. I'm here now and all will go well but I must tend to her immediately. Stay calm, it will be over soon." Géraldine hurried Ginette into the room before inquiring about the 'complication'.

"The baby is feet first", Ginette informed the midwife.

"What does that mean?" Angeline was already exhausted, gleaming with sweat.

"Pas de problème, ma chérie," cooed Géraldine. "I can pull the baby out but it will take more time and I'm going to ask you to be very brave and not to push too hard."

Hours went by; the screams intensified at shorter intervals; the men came in from the fields a little earlier than usual to stand by Phillippe. Meanwhile, the women continued their to and fro with pots of boiling water, a worried look on their faces which did nothing to assuage the men's mounting fear.

Monsieur Roland led the men in prayer. His rosary came out and they recited the familiar words. Philippe had not habitually been devout. He accompanied the family to church on Sundays and enjoyed the hymns. Beyond that, he had not given religion any thought. But now he found himself repeating the words with great fervour.

The screaming stopped.

Where were the baby's cries?

Philippe could take it no more. He burst through his bedroom door. So much blood… blood everywhere. Caroline and Ginette were crying softly, Géraldine was bundling a small package and Angeline seemed to be asleep.

Géraldine spoke to the tall man standing in shock. *"Je suis très désolé Monsieur Roger.* It was a difficult breech birth and your daughter was strangled by the umbilical cord. It was too early and she had not yet turned. Had she come out the right way I could have slipped the cord off. Your wife is hemorrhaging. I'm doing everything to stop it but she's exhausted. She needs your strength and your love. Talk to her and encourage her."

Midwifery could be extremely rewarding. There was no greater joy for Géraldine than to hold a new life and hear the first cry. But in the early part of the 20th century women literally risked their lives to bring a new one into the world. Each time something went terribly wrong, Géraldine lost a little piece of herself and wondered how much longer she could do this work.

Philippe somehow managed to put his fears and pain aside and brushed his lips on his wife's cheeks. Angeline slowly opened her eyes. Philippe held her hand.

"*Mon amour,* I love you so much."

"*Le bébé?*"

"We have a beautiful daughter just like her mother. She's asleep now, you can see her later." Philippe had no difficulty in lying as he imagined with all of his heart that it was true.

"*Je t'aime Philippe.*" As she drifted off to sleep, these would be the last words Philippe Roger was to hear from his beloved wife.

The blood kept flowing… so much blood. Philippe held her hand until her last breath.

The small sad group in the front room had been informed by Ginette of the tragedy that was unfolding in the next room. When they heard the primordial howl that came from Philippe's entrails, Monsieur Roland answered with his own while the rest sobbed uncontrollably.

Philippe was angry.

He was immersed in rage; he wallowed in it; he reeled from it; he indulged in it. He was angry with the midwife; he was angry with the baby that killed his wife; he was angry that Caroline was about to give birth; he was angry that Ginette had just announced her pregnancy; most of all he was angry with God.

What kind of a being would take away everything from a man, not once but twice? Even Job had been allowed to keep his second family. This was supposed to be an all- powerful, kind, loving God! People could be cruel but God ought to know better. Either He was uncaring and unconcerned when it came to the human race (there was plenty of evidence to support that theory), or, there was no God.

Once again Philippe found himself without roots. His Belgian family tried to reason with him but the truth was that Philippe was like a shroud of darkness snuffing the very life out of everyone around him. Angeline's death hurt the Roland's deeply and would affect them for the rest of their lives; but with the imminent birth of Caroline's baby and another on the way, they were prepared to move on.

The fecundity and marital bliss surrounding Philippe was too much to bear. He needed to ache some more and vent some more and hope to get it out of his system. It was necessary for him; it was unfair to the Roland's.

Philippe's decision to tour the country in order to photograph the restoration of Belgium was met with mixed feelings. He would be missed, he was loved and his pain worried them, but the pall would be lifted and that would bring some relief to everyone's suffering.

They said their goodbyes, hugged and kissed on both cheeks with the entreaty to be well and return soon.

Philippe planned a circuitous route going northeast starting with nearby Dinant and Namur; then continuing on the same track to Liège and turning northwest to Louvain and Brussels; the pilgrimage ending in the 5% of Belgium that had not fallen to the Germans between the northern port of Nieuport and Ypres in the west.

Other than Couvin and its surrounding areas, whatever territory Philippe had covered in Belgium had always been in the dark, preferably on moonless nights, and never as a tourist.

He would be gone for months.

Ringed by forts, Liège, Namur and Dinant on the River Meuse are towns permeating in old world charm. All three towns had fallen to Germany's 'Big Bertha' canons in less than three weeks. Dinant had witnessed the summary execution of over 600 of its men, women and children as a warning to those who dared resist.

Philippe was not there to photograph the charm. Massacre and destruction best suited his frame of mind. Any beauty that had been left intact or even the hustle and bustle of the reconstruction efforts, were ignored.

If it was devastation he sought, he was well rewarded in Louvain, the once beautiful university town where a library of precious ancient manuscripts had been cherished were now gone.

The Germans had hoped to walk into Belgium unimpeded. Due to what they called 'unlawful' resistance, their march through Belgium to get to France had been severely delayed, giving the enemy dangerous preparation time. Louvain was to pay the price. For five days straight it was gunned, burned and pillaged; its citizens killed helter-skelter in their hundreds.

With each photograph Philippe's rage grew.

The travel was difficult with the rail system still under heavy repairs in many areas. Philippe was willing to work for a lift in a wagon or a truck; for a meal and a room. With so little to offer, people were generally kind to the taciturn young man with the funny accent.

Thus he made his way along his itinerary as the days shortened and grew cold; the heat of his anger keeping him warm. It would seem that there existed no other man as miserable as Philippe felt; yet, the worst lay ahead.

In the month of January Philippe had reached Nieuport. From Nieuport to Ypres he trekked through the muddy region in complete disarray. He no longer knew what to feel so complete was the devastation.

It was here in Passendale, in Flanders and Ypres that the allies and Belgians had faced the Germans for four long years destroying until all was flattened, killing until millions had fallen.

All of Philippe's rage had not prepared him for the ravages he now witnessed. Most days were cold and gray, the terrain muddy and barren strewn with bits of barbed wire and pieces of metal; a lone dead tree upright among burnt out trunks lying around; a wall standing on its own, the remainder of that building in ruins. The pictures told a story of utter desolation and for a while this mood replaced the fury that had burned in Philippe these past months.

By the time he reached Ypres his mood had turned to great sorrow and sadness. The former inhabitants exiled at the beginning of the conflict had now returned. The reconstruction consisted in building simple wooden structures that they may have shelter before any real restoration could begin.

On January 29th Philippe's heart broke. He was photographing some trenches left behind; in his mind he could smell the stench, hear the cries, and he felt the fear. When he came upon a dead branch stuck into the ground holding up a soldier's helmet. He took the forlorn picture.

Did this soldier die? Was he young? Was he lonely? Was he afraid? Was someone waiting for his return home? And what about me... is someone, somewhere, waiting for me? Why did so many have to die? Why did Angeline die? Why did my baby die... Who am I? Philippe fell to his knees sobbing. The ghostly screams of the dying suffused his mind. He joined them, crying out in anguish, pounding on his chest to make the hurt go away. He ached with grief. He cried until he was dried out and exhausted.

Eventually he pulled himself up and made his way back to the town. The catharsis had drained him of all emotion and he now sought somewhere or someone who would take him in for the night. He tapped on the shoulder of a man walking ahead of him arm in arm with his lady.

The short stocky man turned to him. They stared at each other long seconds.

"Jacques? JACQUES!" The man's face registered shock.

"FRANÇOIS!" Jacques was wild with happiness.

Just a flick of a switch in his brain and it was all back, every bit of it; playing marbles in the snow with François as a boy (he felt the frost in his fingertips so vivid was the memory); his family; driving logs down the river; Adèle on the swing; the planes; everything.

With great roars of laughter the two men hugged, clapping each other on the back, a confused Shirley looking on.

"C'est toi mon ami, c'est vraiment toi!"

Suddenly François broke away, violently shaking Jacques by the shoulders, laughter giving way to anger. "*Sacré-Cœur,* what are you doing here? Where have you been? We were told you were dead, how could you do that to us?"

Caroline looked out the window when she heard a motorcar approaching on the clear Friday evening of January 30th. "*Venez voir, venez voir!* Everyone, come quick!"

The Rolands trooped out of the house. There was Philippe, a young couple at his side. It was bedlam; everyone wanted a piece of Philippe; kissing, hugging, babbling.

When good upbringing reasserted itself, with a certain degree of curiosity the clan turned to the couple. They stood agape as Philippe introduce his best friend François Turcotte from Québec, Canada and his wife Shirley from London. He then took a deep bow, "*Et moi,* Jacques Armand, at your service."

They sat around the kitchen table listening to Jacques, imbibing a celebratory bottle of Geneva gin; Shirley doing her best to follow with her rudimentary French. Jacques was all talked out. For hours, François and Shirley had listened to his Belgian story and now it was the Rolands' turn to hear the Canadian story.

"So, that's where the funny accent comes from, I knew it wasn't from my neck of the woods in Switzerland," asserted Phil.

The latest addition to the family, little Geneviève, was bounced around on everyone's knee. Jacques also congratulated Ginette proudly pushing forward her small rounded belly and heard all that had transpired since his departure at the end of September.

It was late at night when they finally turned in, bushed from all the emotion. Jacques was surprised to see that Phil and Ginette had not moved into his cabin. "We were waiting for your return to discuss how best to proceed."

"*Je suis tellement fatigué.* I can't keep my eyes open. There are decisions to be made but it can wait until tomorrow." Jacques, François and Shirley headed for the cabin. "You two take the bedroom and I'll stay in the front room. I barely have strength to light the fire. *Bonne nuit.*"

By the time Jacques saw them settled in the bedroom, had the fire lit and spread the blankets on the couch, he was wide awake. It was the first moment he really had to himself since the fateful tap on François' shoulder.

Like a deflating balloon he was spiralling down to earth. He looked around the small cabin they had built with their own hands. There was Angeline, smudges on her face; dishevelled in her farmer's overalls stretched tight over her rounded belly. She was caulking the cracks between the floorboards. He could hear the sweet sound of her soft voice; melodic, sexy and now haunting. It was so real; what was she saying? He reached out to touch her and the delicate vision vanished, wisps of sadness and longing trailing in its wake.

Here in this cabin he was Philippe, husband of Angeline; his family were the Rolands. His sweat had mixed with the very earth of this farm and he had put his life on the line for Belgium. But Angeline was gone and there was no doubt in his mind that he was also Jacques Armand from Pointe-à-Gatineau.

Except for the actual plane crash, his memory was intact. Strangely, it was as though he had flown the reconnaissance mission yesterday; the three year gap non-existent. He had left home a youth on the threshold of manhood; he was no longer the same young man. The war had made experienced mature men of these youths well before their time. Jacques was in the uncommon position of having matured into two men.

Adèle scratched at the periphery of his mind but he dared not bring her to the forefront; here in Angeline's home, it seemed disloyal. He thought of his family and visions of home danced in his head as he drifted off to the land of Nod.

The next morning at breakfast in the Roland's kitchen, it was time for planning. "We want to be in Paris by tomorrow for a short stay. It's our honeymoon, you know. *Un peu tard*[*] but, better late than never. *Après,* we sail from Le Havre on February 4th for New York. After a brief visit in the big city we'll board the overnight for Montréal and on to Pointe-à-Gatineau."

All heads turned to Jacques. "*Et toi, mon ami,* will you be joining us?"

"It will be difficult to leave my home in Belgium, *très difficile*. But I truly wish to see my family and it's been too long. So as soon as I can earn enough to buy my passage I'll follow you, François."

"Ahem." Paul cleared his throat so as not to give away his emotional state. "With you and our Angeline gone, there'll be a void that can never be filled." His voice cracked. "Ahem... but you belong with your family Phili... er... Jacques and our family, our farm, our country even, owes you a debt of gratitude. You weren't around long enough to enjoy the fruits of your labour last autumn. The farm did very well and your portion will more than pay for your passage to America."

This little speech made Jacques' eyes water. "*Merci mon ami, mon frère,* you gave me a life when I had none. I now have two families. So be it, after I tie up loose ends François, I'll join you at Le Havre on the 4th. We sail together then, but only because you travel with a nurse and I won't have to look after you when you're seasick."

———◀●●▶———

The S.S. France dominated the port at Le Havre with its four massive red stacks. All areas of the ship were open for touring before departure, after which the various classes were to be relegated to their proper position in life. Our threesome wandered in the first class lounges and dining rooms.

"*Mon dieu, quelle opulence!*" gasped Jacques.

"It's no wonder they call it the 'Versailles' of the Atlantic." Shirley was just as breathless.

Their tiny interior cabins grounded them to reality.

True to form, poor François suffered badly the entire week of the crossing. First class travel would have been wasted on him. Shirley remained loyally by his side and Jacques was left much to himself.

At the point of no return, Jacques began to experience a certain amount of apprehension. Seven years had elapsed since he left home. Everyone would have changed; he had changed. How would he be received? His memories of Adèle were fresh however, his letter declaring his love uppermost in his mind.

His present feelings were confused and complicated to say the least. The young Jacques yearned for her and reeled at the thought of their embrace giving the older Jacques feelings of betrayal as Angeline crowded his mind. He also reasoned that the barely seventeen year-old Adèle he had known, no longer existed. According to François she was quite the feminist with grand plans of attending university. Where would he fit in?

These thoughts were too complex and worrisome and so he turned to the practical. François, bless his soul, had preserved all of his war-time photographs including his precious negatives. Together with his substantial collection of post-war Belgium, he planned to look up Mr. Jamis in Ottawa to see if his work had potential. Whatever the outcome, he would reside in Ottawa and make his career in photography.

Warmly dressed, François dragged himself to the deck joining his travelling companions and the rest of the passengers for their first view of the Statue of Liberty. Immigrants fleeing a war torn Europe jostled to get a good view of the Promised Land; full of hope and optimism, they cheered.

Back on *terra firma* François was ebullient. "*C'est fini pour moi*, I won't be returning to Europe until aeroplanes begin regular crossings."

After London and Paris, our travelling companions were not newcomers to big cities, yet New York was something altogether different. The skyscrapers towered as much as 21 stories above them, the streets were jammed with motorcars, Negroes were in large numbers and the atmosphere buzzed with noisy excitement.

Among the highlights for the three tourists' New York visit were the American Museum of Natural history where they marveled at the hall of African Mammals and stood agape before the mighty Tyrannosaurus Rex; attendance at the Broadway musical 'Irene' at the Vanderbilt theatre; and skating in Central Park.

As much as François and Shirley were thrilled with their visits to Belgium, Paris and New York, the time had come to complete their journey homeward. François was happy with anticipation while Shirley wondered, somewhat uneasily, how she would fit into her husband's large French family; a little homesickness creeping in. Jacques for his part was experiencing a growing nervousness.

The overnight train to Montréal's imposing Windsor Station arrived early in the morning. Our trio stretched their legs before their connection to Ottawa. They walked the streets of Montréal nearby, Jacques and François delighting in the familiar French-Canadian chatter all around; Shirley a little apprehensive.

Before long it was time to re-enter the massive wide-open arches of the château-like Windsor Station and board the overnight coming from Halifax snaking its way west through Québec City and on to Montréal and beyond. Directed to the back of the car with Jacques in the lead, the passengers followed in single file behind him.

Jacques came to an abrupt stop causing a chain reaction collision behind him. On the aisle seat right before his unbelieving eyes sat the most beautiful woman. "Adèle!!" Without thought or hesitation he took her by the hands and lifted the petite beauty up into his arms.

1920-1921
Home Again

It was over before it began. For one thing Adèle was not participating in the embrace and for another there was a blasphemous outcry from the irate passengers bumping into one another behind him: "*Merde*·... *Tabernacle*·... Ouch... *Maudit*·..."

Meanwhile, the small man sitting next to Adèle was rising from his seat, "*C'est ma femme!*"

Jacques unhanded Adèle and for a short awkward moment our five stunned characters starred at each other. Almost immediately they all spoke together and much like the passengers behind, their words collided.

"Jacques, c'est toi," exclaimed Adèle... "*Ta femme?*" Queried Jacques... "SIT DOWN!" yelled a passenger... "Adèle!" said an excited François... "François, c'est bien toi, mon frère!" Adèle squealed... "What's happening?" Shirley was so confused... "MOVE, *TABERNACLE!*" shouted another.

With that, François took charge. "Shirley, Jacques, quick go sit in the seats two rows further on. I'll sit in this empty seat across from Adèle. We have a lot of explaining to do."

The grumbling passengers settled and when the hubbub died down François addressed the young married couple. "Joseph, you must forgive us. We weren't expecting to see you here and we had no idea you two were married. It was somewhat of a shock because the last we heard, Adèle was contemplating a university education." The whistle blew; the train wheels slowly grinding along the tracks. "Somewhat of a shock you say," Adèle interrupted. "You bring a dead man on our train and you talk about shock."

"*Du calme, Adèle,* tell us how this came to be," Joseph wanted to understand.

"Well that's a long story," answered François in a weary tone.

"We would appreciate the short version then," Joseph persisted.

François launched into a short discourse; he had the curious newlyweds' full attention. "Jacques was flung from his plane just before it crashed. Belgian farmers rescued him. He was badly hurt; broken bones, black and blue everywhere, some deep cuts and a concussion that left him bereft of all memory."

"*C'est incroyable,*" gasped Adèle.

François continued. "The Belgian family took him in and nursed him back to health. In time he recovered physically but his memory did not. He took on the identity of a cousin from Switzerland to avoid German imprisonment or worse. He served the war effort bravely in the resistance. I can assure you that the invaluable information his cell provided contributed much to the defeat of the Germans in their last big offensive."

"*Quel courage!*" Joseph's own perceived cowardice reared its ugly head.

"How did you find him," asked Adèle. "This covert work must have been dangerous."

"Wait 'til you hear the tales. We found him at Ypres wandering around taking photographs of the devastation. The moment he laid eyes on me, his memory returned, intact." Amazement in their eyes, the pair sucked in their breath.

"He has suffered much recently and he isn't the same Jacques you knew, Adèle. You see, he too married but tragically he lost both his wife and his infant daughter in childbirth a few months ago. Shirley and I have found him taciturn and prone to dark mood swings. He has changed."

"*Pardon,*" Abruptly Joseph straddled Adèle to get out of his window seat. He made his way further back to where Jacques was explaining things to Shirley.

Joseph addressed Jacques in a formal manner. *"J'suis désolé* Jacques, please, accept our apologies. We had believed you dead. François has informed us of your misfortunes over the past three years. Adèle and I are so sorry for your loss."

"I'm sorry too, and I'd no idea that Adèle had married."

"You could not have known. We're all in a bit of a shock. Anyway, I'm extremely pleased to see that you didn't perish in that accursed war. We'll have lots to talk about." Joseph gave a short bow of the head and went back to his Adèle.

Overhearing, Adèle thought; *what a nice man I married. Yes, nice... very nice. Why is it that we so often use that word when trying to make ordinary people sound a bit more interesting? Nice... it's really an underrated word.*

Jacques' return home spread rapidly throughout the small communities of the *Outaouais* Region. When Maître Labelle heard of Jacques exploits, during one of his *soirées,* he contacted the 'Ottawa Citizen' to give them the story. Desperate to escape the limelight and preserve his privacy, Jacques declined the 'Citizen's' request for an interview.

Once the happy reunion had taken place with his family, he was duty-bound to travel to the headquarters of the 22nd Regiment for a sort of de-briefing and his honourable discharge. Not only did Jacques receive this honourable discharge along with his back pay but to his immense surprise, he was publicly awarded the 'Distinguished Flying Medal"

There was no escaping the newspapers after that. His story appeared in 'La Presse', the 'Montréal Gazette', the 'Globe' from Toronto and the 'Ottawa Citizen', among others.

When our local hero approached Mr. Jamis, Ottawa's foremost photographer, he was received with a great deal of interest. "Your photographs have a lot of merit. Some of your aerial photography gives a unique perspective and your daily life in the training camps come to life. However, I do believe that we have enough here to publish a pictorial account of the 'rape of Belgium'. Words could never do justice to the story you tell in these poignant photos. I'd be pleased to collaborate with you on such an endeavour."

"It would be an honour." Jacques was excited. "Is there any way that you could use my services in your studio? I'm in search of gainful employment."

Mr. Jamis smiled broadly. "I do remember the summer you apprenticed before the war. I was right in thinking that you showed promise. We have great new techniques for developing film which you'll appreciate. The pay is small but you can easily augment this with journal photography."

"Is that a job offer?"

"You start Monday." The two men shook hands.

During his down time Jacques' thoughts turned to Adèle. *They thought I was dead so I should have expected Adèle to marry. After all, I too married. I should have also expected Joseph to make a move; he was always mooning over her at the store... still, I can't imagine him to be her type. It would have been less of a surprise if she had gone to university... somehow I can see her doing that. Mon dieu she's more beautiful than ever.* A frisson went up his spine. *I loved Angeline with all my heart but I still love Adèle. How can that be? Get a hold of yourself, man. She's a married woman.*

Joseph for his part had uneasy thoughts about the hero's return. With a certain amount of envy and jealousy he recognized that Jacques was the picture of manliness. To make matters worse he was decorated for his bravery. *What is Adèle thinking about all this? She loved him once, does she still love him? How can I measure up to such a man? I've never done anything brave and I certainly don't cut the same figure.*

His trench warfare dreams returned as they always did when he was troubled. In his dreams he saw Jacques flying like an angel overhead, dripping in medals while he was on the ground running away from the battle, severely wounded soldiers all around him shouting coward, coward! Awake, trembling and sweating, he kept reminding himself that he had done no such thing. It was not his fault that he had to be carried away on a stretcher.

And what of Adèle's thoughts? Joseph would not have wanted to know. On the train in Jacques' arms, she had been within a hair's breadth of melting into his powerful chest before Joseph's outburst announcing their marital status had frozen her.

He's more handsome than ever. That scar on his forehead and down his temple makes him look so manly. I'd forgotten how tall he is. I wanted him to continue holding me... I know how wrong that is... but it's what I wanted... I so badly wanted to give in. Lord, please forgive me.

She tried to imagine his life in Belgium. The newspaper accounts were hair-raising. Granted, they had to sell newspapers, but still, he was so brave. Unfortunately, her thoughts wandered to his family life where he had lived as Philippe. Try as she might, she could not block out thoughts of Jacques and his wife making love. It was unstoppable. Each time the same terrible jealousy she had experienced when thinking of Joseph and Lizzy O'Malley, possessed her.

Fortunately, these alarming thoughts experienced from time to time by our three troubled souls, did not consume their lives. Life does go on. The normal day to day humdrum is usually the norm for most people... and so it was for these three.

Jacques found enjoyment in his work, making a name for himself in journal photography and becoming quite artistic in the darkroom.

Joseph immersed himself in his grocery store and resumed his interest in business and the sciences.

Adèle found the large apartment above the store to be quite a change from her attic room at the schoolhouse. A staircase led from the street up to a generous veranda along the length of the building. Double doors on the veranda led into a large parlour and dining room. The roomy kitchen had enough space for a kitchen table and a back stairs leading down to the grocery's storeroom below. A door led out of the storeroom to an enclosed back yard. There was space to park the truck, a sizable lawn and an apple tree in the middle. Apart from the master bedroom there were three other bedrooms, all three empty of furniture.

This was quite a luxury for a young childless couple and Adèle felt a little lost in this grandeur. *It seems so big and empty but it has everything we need to raise a family. It's obvious that this apartment hasn't had a woman's touch in ages. I'll soon remedy that…*

She threw herself into re-decorating and making the old furniture left behind by Monsieur Laflamme look refreshed with the use of colourful cushions. A bit of lace here and there, new draperies and pictures on the walls made it homey. She had brought a few of her own personal possessions, among them the shoe box holding François' letters, Jacques' one precious letter as well as family pictures, the three of Jacques betwixt the collection. The personal knick-knacks were displayed on end tables while the box was put away in a cupboard corner, unvisited and forgotten. The Héberts' rocking chair in the corner of the master bedroom awaited.

Although Adèle's duties upstairs took up a good part of her day, she also found time to work side by side with her Joseph downstairs.

She continued her daily prayers to the Virgin Mary and as for her sinful thoughts, she regularly confessed those to *Père* Tremblay and left it at that.

Together, Joseph and Adèle resumed their conversations and debates, their visits to the library and the theatre as well as their encounters with their many friends.

Life was comfortable. If there was any fly in the ointment, it was the fact that the Jacques issue was a secret the couple could not discuss. In June such a small fly was easily buried deeper into the ointment when Adèle happily announced to her husband that they should expect their first child in late February.

There were many kinds of Catholics in Québec. There were those of great faith who bought the teachings of the Church and the admonitions of the priests, without question. Adèle's parents (and indeed the majority of the poor folk) fell into that category. There were the hypocrites with little belief who attended mass regularly just for show believing it to be necessary for their own advancement in whatever endeavours they pursued. You could put Maurice Labelle and Mary Kelly with their political aspirations in that category. Then there were those who gave a great deal of thought to their beliefs, accepting what seemed right to them and discarding what seemed to be something made up by men of the cloth to suit some earthly church agenda. Adèle and Joseph fell into that category.

Joseph was an oddity for a man of his upbringing, education and class. He was a devout Catholic in almost every way except for the Old Testament writings which he took as allegories meant to teach the people of those times about God, His creation and His relationship with His creatures. The six day creation was simply unsupported by scientific evidence. If it wasn't a sin, there was no need for confession.

If Adèle had managed to be without child until June, it was not due to a deficiency in her conjugal duties. Adèle as a believing Catholic viewed childbearing as a sacred duty of matrimony. Birth control efforts that killed sperm or ova were probably wrong. Potions that resulted in the death of the embryo were definitely murder. But, having read copiously on the subject and given it much reflection, she could find no sin in the rhythm method of birth control. If it wasn't a sin there was no need for confession.

Adèle assiduously watched her calendar, inscribing little marks on certain days whose meaning was known only to her. She had wanted some time alone with Joseph that they might settle into married life together before embarking on parenthood. At the very least, it certainly put to rest the suspicions held by the parishioners at the sudden announcement of their wedding.

Nonetheless, she knew that you couldn't stop rumours in this nosy community. If they waited too long then the good people of Pointe-à-Gatineau might speculate that she was using birth control; or maybe she was barren; worse still, maybe Joseph was not getting any loving! Joseph and Adèle made their happy announcement to the satisfaction of the righteous and the great delight of family and friends.

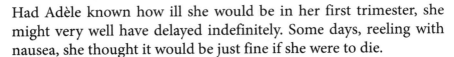

Had Adèle known how ill she would be in her first trimester, she might very well have delayed indefinitely. Some days, reeling with nausea, she thought it would be just fine if she were to die.

She had her morning rising down to a workable routine. Before lifting her head from the pillow she reached out for the soda cracker placed on her bedside table the previous night. She ate it. She then waited for the nausea to subside. The next step was sitting up in bed. If all went well and the cracker stayed down, she tried a little water. At this point she usually experienced more nausea. She would wait for it to subside. The final step was standing up making sure that she was holding on to something or someone because this action invariably caused waves of nausea and at times, fainting.

The rest of her day did not go much better. Their social life was severely curtailed not to mention their sex life. Joseph was patience itself taking up the slack in household chores and supporting his wife in every way possible.

"I wish that I could carry our little one for a part of each week to give you a break," he would often say.

"*Mon Dieu, t'es un grand bébé, Adèle Lafleur.* Motherhood is not for the weak. Buck up, you can do it," chided her friend Céline.

"*Ma pauvre p'tit fille, là, là,* it will pass and you will forget all about it. Just think of your beautiful baby," her *Maman* commiserated and comforted.

Maman was right. Three months into her gestation, although emaciated, the nausea did disappear. Adèle was so relieved and happy. Her *Papa* had always said, "You have to experience a hammering headache to appreciate not having one." Overflowing with hormones, Adèle bloomed.

The couple resumed their busy life.

They visited François and Shirley who had settled in a small two-story wooden house on Park Street in the Eastview* area of Ottawa. The Ottawa Air Station in Rockcliffe was easily accessible from there. François was full of talk about the planes and the future of aviation. "Just you wait and see, we'll be flying large numbers of people across the Atlantic and even the Pacific in a fraction of the time it takes to go by boat," he predicted.

At first, François had been terribly disappointed that Adèle had married Joseph Lafleur. He would have loved to have Jacques as his brother-in-law. He knew that they had loved one another once and he worried that Adèle had made a terrible mistake. But as he got to know Joseph better and saw them interact as a couple, his fears were calmed.

"Whoa, the next thing you know you'll have us flying to the moon," laughed Joseph. François seemed happy with his work and Joseph was pleased for him.

Shirley had been well during her entire pregnancy which had permitted her to work some night shifts at the hospital before she began showing too much. The extra money had helped them furnish their home and prepare for the baby's arrival. Now, she devoted all of her time to her husband and especially to the first of the Turcotte grandchildren, little David named after her father.

The fascinating maternal bond that was obvious between Shirley and her newborn delighted Adèle. She put her two hands over her own stomach and whispered, "Soon, *mon amour,* soon, we'll be together."

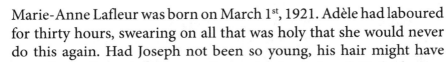

Marie-Anne Lafleur was born on March 1st, 1921. Adèle had laboured for thirty hours, swearing on all that was holy that she would never do this again. Had Joseph not been so young, his hair might have turned gray from the amount of worrying he endured. He had never prayed so hard in his life, promising novenas, pilgrimages, whatever it took for the Lord to spare his wife.

As miraculous as childbirth is, the real miracle is the total dismissal of the pain and suffering when the tiny wrinkled being with the scrunched up face is placed in the mother's arms. Joseph's eyes watered as he approached the bed. There, in that bed was his whole world. There was no one more beautiful than this woman who had given him the most precious gift that life had to offer. He was overwhelmed, the tears flowed joyfully.

1921
A Shopping Spree

For Adèle the spring of 1921 passed gently in maternal bliss having suffered no more than a week of mild baby blues. Marie-Anne was a good baby and within a month the infant was sleeping her nights giving her mother the rest she needed to regain her strength.

Her younger sister Annette, now fourteen years of age, stayed with them the first month to help out. It was exciting to be in town on a busy street in Hull. Being an aunt twice over now made her feel so grown up. She tended to most of the household chores and had to beg Adèle to be allowed to change diapers and hold the little niece she absolutely adored.

Joseph installed a small bassinette behind the counter downstairs so that Adèle and Marie-Anne could spend part of each day at the store with him. Customers *oohed, aahed* and cooed at the baby. For Joseph and Adèle, it could not have been possible to be happier.

Although they rarely ventured out during those first few months, they did have company. The proud grandparents, Louis and Lorraine Turcotte came to see the latest addition to their family as well as Denis and Rose Lafleur for whom it was the first grandchild. Yvette had married the young farmer, Gilles Duchamp, who had once hankered after Adèle. They also came to visit; Yvette visibly in the family way was blooming.

Céline and Gérard arrived one Sunday with their brood; Xavier now three years old; Gigi and Lou-Lou beginning to toddle around and baby Alexandre in Céline's arms. "*Ma chère,* you have lots of catching up to do." She patted her belly. "We're hoping for a boy by the end of the year."

"*Félicitations,*" Joseph clapped Gérard on the back and went for the bottle of gin. "*Une petite célébration!*"

Adèle got up to hug her friend. "Will you be alright?"

"*Pourquoi pas?* What kind of question is that? Of course I'm going to be just fine.

She's probably right, thought Adèle. *She hardly gets nauseous and she pops them out with little effort. She's nice and plump and seems to have them well in hand. Still...*

Monsieur Laflamme came for a visit with his sister, the widow Gauthier, who promised she would babysit from time to time to give the young couple a break. Maurice and Mary Labelle came to pay their respects with invitation in hand for a *soirée* the following week. "It promises to be interesting," winked Mary.

This was to be Adèle's first real outing since the birth of Marie-Anne. Unlike Céline who seemed to get a little fatter with each child, Adèle had lost weight due to the severe morning sickness of the first trimester.

"Oh Joseph, *regarde-moi.* I look like a lost orphan in this outfit. It's too loose, too long and way out of date."

Her last new outfit consisted of her honeymoon suit, too warm for June but she could wear the skirt with her one lovely V-neck blouse. Her closet was full of clothes suitable for a classroom mistress and a few skirts that were let out to accommodate her bulk during pregnancy.

"You look like the most beautiful little lost orphan I have ever seen in that outfit, but I agree with you. It's high time you treated yourself to a new wardrobe especially now that you're regaining your figure. A shopping spree is definitely in order. I'm sure Mary would love to help you with that."

"Have I told you lately that I love you, Joseph Lafleur! Marie-Anne has been fed; Madame Gauthier is on her way to babysit so hurry up, comb your hair and let's go or we'll be late."

It was a balmy June night so they walked the distance to Labelle's large brick residence on *rue* Alexandre-Taché. Mary greeted them at the door. Her violet eyes gleamed against her shining silver dress. Sleeveless with a low waist, it left her calf exposed. She looked stunning. During the ritual kissing of cheeks, they could hear familiar voices coming from the parlour.

Their faces registered some surprise when they saw Maurice serving drinks to François, Shirley, Jacques and a gentleman who was a stranger to Joseph and Adèle.

"I knew you would be surprised," laughed Mary.

"We're having a veteran's night with a purpose in mind. And… we have an announcement to make," said Maurice with some hoopla.

"But first, please meet my friend, Daniel Peterson. Daniel, this is the upcoming young business man I was telling you about, Joseph Lafleur, and his vivacious wife, Adèle."

Daniel rose and shook hands with Joseph, bowed and kissed Adèle's hand lightly, "Vivacious, I have yet to find out, but beautiful I can see already. It's a pleasure *madame*."

Conversations at the Labelles usually alternated between French and English but it would seem that English would be prevalent this evening in deference to Shirley and Mr. Peterson.

When everyone had been served, Mr. Peterson rose to his feet, raised his glass and saluted his friend, "A toast to *Maître* Maurice Labelle, Hull's new Liberal candidate for the federal elections later this year."

Amidst cheers and congratulations, Maurice spoke up. "Thank you, I'm counting on your support."

"You have my vote," interrupted Joseph.

"Thank you Joseph and since this is the first election in which all women can vote, I'm also counting on your vote Adèle."

"You have it," countered Adèle.

"Actually, this will be the first election for Jacques, Shirley and myself as well," said François. "I'm sorry that you're not running in our county but I can tell you that we all have strong Liberal leanings."

"Here, here," Maurice raised his glass. "Daniel Peterson will be managing my campaign and you can be certain that he intends to rope you in Joseph with your business connections in Hull… and you Adèle, we'll need women encouraging other women to vote."

"Would you believe that some women will not vote because their husbands have told them not to?" Mary was quite indignant.

"We're going to be up against much prejudice, I'm afraid. I myself expect to get resistance when I try to persuade my own mother but I intend to prevail," said Adèle, her right fist in the air.

Just when the political discussion had run its course, the two young lads, Adam and Charles were led into the parlour by the nanny to say their goodnights. They were presented to the newcomers, François, Shirley and Jacques. Adèle admired the boys who had proper manners and were not at a loss for conversation. Then after the kissing of cheeks and goodnights, they were led upstairs to their room.

At the dinner table, Mary broached the subject for which she had brought this little group together. "I'm writing a book on the role of women in the war. Jacques, I understand that you have first-hand knowledge of women in the Belgian resistance."

"Women who gave their lives for the cause," Jacques volunteered.

"Great, that is exactly what I want to hear. And you Shirley, you were a nurse during the war. Your perspective would be invaluable to me."

Shirley looked pleased to be part of something. "Oh, I do have quite the stories for you."

"Excellent. Joseph, François, I heard that you were both wounded and I want to hear your accounts of our brave 'Bluebirds.'"

Joseph winced at the word 'wounded'. "I'd be happy to help although I've done everything to forget that time, the 'Bluebirds' were indeed brave and tireless."

Maurice chimed in, "I know what you mean, Joseph; I have friends who still have nightmares about their time in the trenches. I, myself, saw no action. Something's wrong with my vision and I'd never have been able to shoot straight. I served as an officer, at the training camps in Nova Scotia.

I must confess to being something of a coward so I can't see how I could have survived the trenches let alone flying in those tiny planes facing enemy fire with nowhere to go but down. I have great admiration for the three of you. I salute you."

A lull in the conversation ensued, each man lost in his own thoughts, unwanted memories pushing their way forward.

"Well, enough of this maudlin talk, Mary has something special in store for dessert."

The evening progressed pleasantly. Accounts relating the bravery of women in the war were offered. Then the three 'world travelers' were pressed for descriptions of London, Paris, Belgium and New York. The Labelles had been to New York but Mary dreamed of going to Europe as did Adèle for that matter.

Joseph and Adèle were the last to leave. "Mary, I was wondering if you plan to go shopping anytime soon. As you can see, I'm in need of a new wardrobe."

"Actually you're in luck. Jacques was with us all afternoon. We posed for our family portraits as well as a good portrait of Maurice for his campaign. I'm due to pick up the photographs at the end of the week. We can go into Ottawa together."

"That would be great; I'm looking forward to it."

"I'll be in touch with the particulars."

They said their goodnights; the kisses and hugs were heartfelt.

When the couple arrived home, Marie-Anne was wide awake and hungry. Adèle nursed her in their bed with Joseph looking on admiringly. The infant drank her fill with gusto and once satisfied the couple spent time enjoying their precious daughter. The normally coherent couple were reduced to cooing, baby talk and clucking noises; a language Marie-Anne seemed to understand perfectly as she rewarded them with smiles and newly acquired sounds of her own.

After she was tucked in her bassinette for the night, the feelings of tenderness and love engendered by Marie-Anne still permeated the room. Joseph and Adèle made love... slowly... gently... lovingly. Sleep came easily.

I COULD HAVE BEEN...

The next morning, Adèle awoke before sunrise. Fully awake, it being Sunday, she chose to dawdle in bed and let her mind wander before the cries of her daughter demanded breakfast.

Jacques has changed so much. He barely spoke last night. He used to laugh all the time; always joking and teasing. The funny thing is that François has also changed. He used to be so shy and quiet. It's almost as though they've switched personalities. Well... not quite. It's not that Jacques seems shy... more like sad... someone with a lot on his mind.

He's so handsome though. I'd love to see the sparkle return to those beautiful green eyes of his. If he had returned after the war, I would have married him. I wonder what my life would have been like... hmmm.

She began to undress him in her mind. Before she could get aroused beyond no return, she stopped herself. Guiltily she thought; *this is wrong* and she replaced that thought with that of the warmth and caring of the previous night.

Then she started to worry. *Oops... was I safe last night? Let me see...* She started counting. *It should be good... well barely... two more days and it would have been dangerous. In any case I'm nursing and they say it's safe until you finish... then again that doesn't seem to work with Céline... I want Marie-Anne out of diapers and walking before the next one.*

Unknown to Adèle, her spouse was also awake, his back to hers and his own thoughts running rampant.

I wish I could be more like Maurice. I mean... really... he actually admitted to being cowardly. He was actually relieved to have missed any action at all and he said so. He didn't seem the slightest bit ashamed of that and he was full of praise for those of us who were in the thick of things.

I can't help feeling that I cheated when my appendix burst. Why in the name of heaven did I have to tell my parents that I'd been wounded? Now, they've gone and told everyone and I'm stuck with this lie. I'm nothing but a fraud. What would Adèle think if she knew that François and Jacques are true heroes and I'm just a liar? I guess I have to live with this now but I can make it up to her… I can be the best husband possible and the best father.

———◆●●◆———

The ladies had agreed to leave for Ottawa just after lunch on the Thursday following the *soirée*.

Settled in Mary's dark blue Buick, the pair set off for Sparks street where Mary knew just the shop and where Mr. Jamis had his studio. "How much time do you have available," Mary inquired of Adèle.

"Marie-Anne has been fed and is in her bassinette downstairs with Joseph. Madame Gauthier has promised to help out and she won't need nursing for another five hours. In any case I left some extra milk just to be sure."

"Excellent! We haven't had a good *tête-à-tête* since the birth of Marie-Anne. What's motherhood like… do you regret leaving out university?"

"*C'est merveilleux.* I never expected it to be so wonderful and Joseph is so good with her. I know what a cliché this sounds like but it truly is a miracle; a little piece of me and a little piece of Joseph all wrapped in a beautiful little package, all ours.

And, no, I don't regret missing university. My life is full right now and I feel nothing but contentment and happiness. But you are the one with so much happening; writing a book and campaigning with Maurice… it must be exciting."

"Yes it is. After I pick up my portraits, I'm meeting at three with Maurice at Daniel's office just around the corner from Mr. Jamis' studio on Wellington Street. I'll be an hour at the most so you can shop some more or spend some time going through Jacques photos of the war which I highly recommend. We should be home by 4:30 at the latest."

This hadn't been in Adèle's plans. "We'll see. What decided you to become a writer? I can't begin to imagine writing a whole book. Although I'm passionate about books, numbers were really my forte."

Deep in conversation they were surprised to see that they had arrived at their destination so soon.

Adèle knew that the Labelles were well-off and she had worried that Mary would take her to shop somewhere unaffordable. She was relieved to see that Mary's selections had taken the Lafleur's pocket-book into consideration.

Two hours later, Adèle was carrying parcels containing two dresses, a couple of skirts and blouses, a cloche hat and shoes with two inch heels, a strap around the ankle.

"So, what about your hair; when are you going to take the plunge. A short raven bob; it would be so alluring."

Adèle laughed, "I need more time. I'm just not ready to let go. If I wear my bun in an intricate weave at the nape like today, the cloche hat will go on down to my eyes as is the style. I'll be able to look down my nose at everyone... la de dah."

They arrived at the Jamis studio just before three as scheduled. The bell above the door jingled and Jacques came out of the dark-room in the back.

Jacques blushed deeply. "Adèle, what are you doing here?"

"Tsk, tsk, manners *Monsieur* Armand. Adèle is my shopping companion today."

Jacques recovered quickly. "Of course, I was a bit surprised. It's Adèle first visit to our studio. You look well, Adèle, motherhood suits you."

Adèle had also needed a moment to recover when she saw the handsome Jacques emerge from one of the two doors leading to the back. "Why, thank you, Jacques."

"You're right, my manners are bad. Please, do sit down ladies. *Madame* Labelle, I have your portraits right here." He opened a drawer behind the counter and came up with some large brown envelopes.

"*S'il vous plaît*, I've told you to call me Mary." She took out the contents and exclaimed, "Lovely... just lovely. *Regarde* Adèle!"

"I believe that Maurice has arranged the payment. Now, you must both excuse me as I'm due at Daniel Peterson's office." She turned towards Adèle, I'll be back at four and I would strongly rec-ommend that you prevail on Jacques to show you his war-time pho-tographs. They are exceptional."

She was out in a flash at the sound of the tinkling bell. They were alone. It surprised Adèle to think that this was the first time that she had ever been alone with Jacques.

"Um… where is Mr. Jamis?"

"Oh, he's doing portraits, very important actually. He's photographing the Governor General and his family."

"*C'est remarquable.* How are you enjoying your work? Those portraits of the Labelles were indeed better than the usual family photos."

Jacques lit up. He talked about all the new techniques for developing. He could as well have been speaking in a foreign language. Adèle knew nothing of photography; all she knew was that his green eyes were sparkling.

"Do you really want to see the photographs from the war; I have lots with François in them. I've also got some good ones of New York."

"I'd be delighted but I really don't want to keep you from your work."

"Don't worry about that, I can finish later tonight. Upstairs is the studio and the other half is a small flat where I live so I can work whenever I want. Sometimes I'm down here in the dark room until late at night. Come follow me."

She followed him through the other door leading to the back. They left the door open that he might hear the tinkling of the bell. Inside was a long, wide table covered with photographs in what seemed to be some kind of order. The walls were covered in photographs with many overlapping due to the lack of bare wall. There were four straight back chairs and a heavy piece of furniture about five feet tall that housed many drawers. Two windows opened to a back lane and a small staircase along the side wall led up to what she presumed would be the studio and his flat.

"These here on the table are being arranged for a book that has been accepted for publication about the 'rape of Belgium'. Mr. Jamis will also be submitting some of them to National Geographic." Jacques could not hide the pride in his voice.

He went to a drawer and pulled out a pack of photos. "Now, these will interest you, *tu verras.*"

Adèle walked over to him. She was delighted to see photos of Jacques and François, thinner and younger, innocent of war matters at that point. There were pictures taken in Nova Scotia... one of François on the deck of the warship looking miserable... their barracks... muddy faces... the flimsy looking planes.

Jacques towered over Adèle, bending he pointed out and explained the whereabouts of each picture. Adèle was genuinely delighted. Before her eyes she could see François' letters come to life. And then... and then... a picture François had taken of Jacques. Adèle sucked in her breath.

There was Jacques; sitting at a tiny table; totally concentrated; writing a letter. There had only been one letter; the simple letter where he had declared his love for Adèle.

Jacques went silent. There was no need to explain the photograph. Adèle looked up. It was his eyes that did it. She was lost. They were both lost. Too many years of dreaming, wondering and denying.

For a short moment the embrace was slow, hesitant; they were exploring. Then the dam broke and the flood could not be stopped. In mere seconds Jacques had carried Adèle up the stairs. As he put her down she pulled him down to her mouth. It was brutal; almost savage. They practically tore the clothes off each other until they lay on his bed naked like in their dreams, only better than in their dreams... so much better.

There was no talking... rasping breathing... hungry kisses all over the other's body... she grabbed his rock-hard penis... he was a big man in every sense... she pulled him in. He filled her completely... her body... her soul... her mind... her every sense. The world outside this very bed did not exist. Adèle was ecstatic.

There was nothing gentle about Jacques' thrusts. Adèle arched her body to meet with his every lunge just as roughly. She scratched his back and bit his shoulder as her orgasm shook her body. Still, he went on... it was too sensitive... she wanted him to stop... she wanted him to go on forever. An animal's growl came from deep within as he climaxed.

No more than fifteen minutes had elapsed since the embrace downstairs. They lay next to one another, recovering their sanity, exhausted from the intense fervour.

In seconds, reality asserted itself. Adèle visibly paled, "*Mon Dieu,* what have we done?"

The store was open for business downstairs. Anyone could have walked in… anyone could still walk in. "I'm sorry Adèle, I'm so, so sorry. I never meant for this to happen."

"Stop Jacques, we both meant for this to happen, we have been meaning for this to happen for years. We're equally to blame. But, you must try to understand that I shall be doing everything in my power to stay away from you in the future. We must never refer to this again. It must remain a secret for the rest of our lives. Please Jacques, for my sake, it must be so."

"I do understand and I promise. I'll lock this memory away in a tight little box in a far corner of my mind. But you should know that from time to time I'll be going to that box to open it a crack for a peek inside. I still love you Adèle."

And now, fear getting the better of them, Jacques hurried into his clothes leaving Adèle in the bathroom to do her best with her dishevelled appearance. He rushed downstairs in case a customer should arrive.

No sooner had Adèle returned looking proper than Mary breezed into the studio to the sound of the tinkling bell. Adèle grabbed her parcels and made for the door. "*Merci* Jacques, your photographs were truly interesting but we really must go now, Marie-Anne will be crying for her milk. Let's go Mary."

"Wait up, where's the fire Adèle. *Au revoir,* Jacques."

"You're very quiet. What is it?" Mary inquired of her friend during the ride home.

"It's the war photos, I guess. Some of them can be quite upsetting." *And now the lies begin,* thought Adèle.

Adèle hurried through the grocery store and took a peek at the empty bassinette. "*Bonjour* Joseph, can't stop; Marie-Anne will be starving. I'll see you upstairs after you close. Byeeee…"

She sent Madame Gauthier on her way with hurried thanks, nursed Marie-Anne and poured herself a hot bath to cleanse any signs of wrong-doing.

For the most part women are usually big on guilt. Some say that it's even worse with Catholic and Jewish women; the Catholic women having the advantage of confession.

Adèle's mother as an example, always made certain her family ate the best parts of the chicken leaving a wing, a back or perhaps the neck for herself. The one day she chose a juicy leg, her enjoyment lasted until the last bite after which the guilt set in.

No confession would erase the kind of guilt Adèle was feeling. *Fifteen minutes, just fifteen minutes of my entire life and the rest of it is ruined forever. Nothing will ever be the same again. Who was that person? It just isn't me; I behaved no better than an animal.* She began to feel the pleasure knot starting to form below her stomach. *Stop it... stop it. Yes... yes, I know, I've never felt anything like that in my life and I never will again and I must never ever think about it again... never. How I wish I could take it all back.*

How can I face Joseph? He's sure to know just looking at me. How could I betray him like that? There can be no better husband. I'm nothing but a harlot... me... Adèle... an adulteress. Marie-Anne has an adulteress for a mother. Mon Seigneur Jésus, you may have forgiven 'La Magdalene' but I just can't pray right now. I may never be able to forgive myself.

The adulteress part is bad enough but I'm going to have to add 'liar' to the list. Joseph must never find out. It would hurt him deeply and it would ruin our family. I'm going to have to find a way to live with this. Unlike Hester Prynne I can't go around town displaying my scarlet letter for all to see. I'll wear it inwardly but like her I'll live the best life I can for my family. Perhaps one day there'll be forgiveness but not now... not yet.

Joseph stuck his head around the bathroom door. "*Ma Belle,* so early in the bath? I see many parcels; I must see you in your new finery; *une parade de mode.*"

"Sure, before bedtime. "I'm coming out now and we can have some supper before Marie-Anne wakens."

At the supper table, Joseph asked Adèle to describe her day. She winced inwardly and put on a brave face. She spoke of the shops, Marie's book synopsis, and... "We picked up her family portraits at Mr. Jamis's studio. They really were quite lovely. Jacques showed me some of his war photos. François was in many of them and it was interesting to see life in the training camp in England. You were in the same area, right?"

"Yes, we were all at Salisbury Plains but I was in a different camp nearby. All I can remember is the eternal mud everywhere," he laughed.

"That was certainly evident in the photos… but… the photographs taken in Belgium were very upsetting. I saw what the trenches looked like, Joseph. You must have suffered."

"Well, it was a long time ago." Joseph cleared his throat. "How is Jacques enjoying working with Mr. Jamis?"

"I think he's found his calling. I'm happy for him."

Joseph was looking intently at his wife as she spoke of Jacques. She seemed calm. "Well, we don't have a camera and just about everyone has one. We need to take photos of Marie-Anne."

"You're right…." And so this normal every-day conversation continued between man and wife. Adèle was relieved that she could describe her day without any lies except for those of omission naturally. She had not said that Mary and Mr. Jamis were absent but she had not said that they were there either. Joseph had not asked but he probably would have assumed that they were there.

That night Adèle modeled her new outfits for Joseph. It was so easy being with him, she actually found herself laughing. When she took off her last outfit, Joseph gave her that special look. "*Désolé*, Joseph, but it really is not the right time and I'm afraid we'll have to wait a few more days."

"But you're still nursing."

"Look how well that's turned out for Céline, and she's a perpetual nursing machine."

"*Bon, bon*… but you're so hard to resist."

Adèle was bending to pick up some of her clothes that had fallen to the floor when suddenly she felt a sharp pain in her gut as she was suddenly hit with a thought… *Oh my God, oh my God, oh my God… no… no… no!*

She rushed to the bathroom so that Joseph could not see her panic. Her stomach was in knots and her mouth dry. It was hard to breathe. *It's the wrong time of the month. I hadn't thought of that.*

Now she was praying. *Dear sweet Jesus, Mary Mother of God... I beg of you... pleeeease... I mustn't be pregnant. I can't do this to Joseph, he's done nothing wrong... punish me any other way. Please.*

———●●●———

The week following the evil deed was a busy one. Adèle buried herself in housework, cooking, caring for Marie-Anne and learning the business bookkeeping. Joseph found her to be an easy pupil with a facility for numbers. She delved into these accounting lessons every night until sleep overtook her.

However, walking around with a black soul is arduous work so by the end of the week she found time to slip into St. Joseph Church for confession. Although St. Joseph was steps away from the store, the couple regularly attended St. François-de-Sales in Pointe-à-Gatineau in order to be with family. But there wasn't a chance that Adèle would confess this sin to *Père* Tremblay. At St. Joseph she had the anonymity she desired for what was to be the most difficult confession of her life.

She could hear the shock and disapproval in the priest's voice. Not that adultery was unheard of as it was a common enough occurrence among the men of his parish; but it wasn't every day that the good women of the Gatineau area confessed such a sin. Most probably the majority of adulteresses did not go to church in the first place.

The priest took time to counsel Adèle. He wanted her to understand the enormity of her sin and he wished to assess the depth of her repentance. Finally, when the priest realised that Adèle was crying, he relented and granted the blessed forgiveness she craved, setting some solemn prayers for a novena as penance.

At the sound of Joseph's soft snores, Adèle let her tears flow freely that night. She prayed to the Virgin Mary with heartfelt fervor. She asked that Joseph be spared and never have to suffer because of her sin. She thought of the way her life would unfold from now on.

That thing with Jacques, it was an intense infatuation I had never resolved. I can see that now, yes... infatuation... and ... a longing... lustful, if I have to be honest, from way back before Joseph. Well, it's resolved now. I do have feelings for Jacques and I may very well have them all of my life but I really don't know Jacques like I know Joseph.

He's gentle, patient, loving, interesting… we can talk about anything for hours. He's a good father, such a good husband… he loves me… he's a beautiful person. I'm so lucky. The thought of living without him terrifies me. I truly love Joseph.

What if I'm pregnant with Jacques' baby? My monthlies have been so erratic since the birth of Marie-Ann. She placed her hands on her stomach… one bridge at a time.

She put her arm around Joseph and pressed herself against his back. For the first time she understood her feelings for Joseph. Somewhere in the back of her mind there had always been the notion that her one true love had been Jacques and that she had settled for Joseph. If any good could come out of her folly with Jacques, it was that she no longer had any doubts about the nature of her love for Joseph.

"*Je t'aime mon amour*," she whispered to Joseph's back.

Joseph stirred. He was pleasantly surprised. One doesn't remember each coupling in the lifetime of a marriage but this would be one that would rank high in Joseph's memory along with his first honeymoon night. The first he would remember for its passion and discoveries, this one brought them to a higher plane, it was an uplifting experience; one could actually say it was spiritual.

In the afterglow Joseph was overwhelmed with emotion. "*Cherie…*"

"*Oui, Joseph?*"

"I'm remembering the Old Testament verse, 'And Adam knew Eve, his wife…' It always struck me as odd that they used a word like 'knew' to say they made love."

"*Mmmhhh…*," purred Adèle.

"Well, just now… what we did… well, it all makes sense. It was more than sex, more than loving; I was 'knowing' you and it was the same for you."

Adèle came to. "What an absolutely perfect thing for you to say. But how do you know that I felt the same way?"

"I know because we were one."

CHAPTER 17

1921-1922
Green Eyes

When the first wave of nausea overpowered her, a week late with her monthlies, Adèle despaired. She should have worried more about paternity issues but she was too ill to care. Who cared whose child it was, she didn't want this child, any child, not now, not so soon. She returned to her survival routines and *tante* Hélène moved in to look after her niece and grandniece.

Joseph suffered as well during this time... to be clear... we are not talking about the same kind of suffering; it is certain that Adèle would have gladly exchanged her predicament for his in the blink of an eye. But he did worry about Adèle and he missed her. He missed her by his side at the store; he missed her lovemaking, he missed their lively conversations, he missed her laughter; for Adèle's only focus was finding a position that would minimize the nausea and vomiting which was usually prone in her bed in total despondency.

Three months droned on and as was the case when carrying Marie-Anne, the sun rose bright one morning in September and the ordeal was over as suddenly as it had begun.

Hormones coursing through her body, Adèle became her old self once more. She convinced herself that the child could just as well be Joseph's and refused to ruin everything by worrying until there was something to worry about. This feat was easier said than done but the determined Adèle devoted herself to domestic life.

She lavished attention on Marie-Anne who would have to share her mother with a sibling before she could take her first steps. The couple's companionship resumed; working side by side; the dinner conversations; the intimacy.

Adèle was chomping at the bit to be out and about. Her first outing was a tea organized by Céline. "Bring Marie-Anne. Katie O'Malley... I mean Katie Poulain... but she'll always be O'Malley to me I guess... anyway... she'll be here with her Johnnie."

It was the picture of perfect domesticity. *Père* Jacob would most assuredly have beamed at the sight. Céline's three eldest were helping little Johnnie to walk, squealing with laughter each time he fell; Alexandre was crawling at a good pace; Marie-Anne was babbling baby-talk; and the three pregnant women looked on with pride. Céline had put on so much weight it was hard to tell what was fat from what was gestation. Katie was visibly showing a small rounded belly while Adèle was too early on to really show.

Céline teased her good friend. "I thought you were going to have them far apart. Thought you could fool God, did you? Well, it seems that whenever we mere mortals make plans, God seems to play a joke on us for being so arrogant."

"*Tu as raison, Céline.* It certainly wasn't the plan," replied Adèle.

The women talked of their children's mischiefs and virtues; proven cleaning methods; tried and true recipes; and their husbands. It was certainly a change from an evening at the Labelles'.

Though the children could not possibly have understood, they lowered their voices as the talk turned to bedroom matters.

"I find it odd that *Père* Jacob preaches diligently about relations being only for procreation but he won't give us a rest when we're pregnant," wondered Katie, not for the first time.

"Well it's my understanding that the wife's conjugal duties continue through pregnancy in order to keep the sanctity of the union. Men are naturally beasts and they must be kept from straying, *tu comprends?*" Céline was all-knowing when it came to church matters.

"I know what you mean; Bertrand was waiting to pounce on me the moment the six weeks were up after Johnnie's birth." Katie giggled.

"Well, it isn't all that bad. It's always over in a few minutes." Both Céline and Katie laughed.

Adèle was very quiet. It wasn't the first time she had heard this kind of talk. *I guess I must be as much of a beast as the men are. I can't be the only one. Ma tante Hélène enjoyed her lovemaking with mon oncle Adolphe and Mary always has a naughty look on her face when the subject comes up. I feel sorry for Céline and Katie; they're missing out on an important part of their relationship.*

"You're very quiet; I see the way Joseph looks at you. I bet you don't escape often either." Céline's curiosity was piqued.

Adèle laughed it off. It was none of their business. "Well as you can see..." She pointed to her belly.

———●●———

The next outing was to be a memorable one. Madame Gauthier was happy to see Adèle in good spirits and only too willing to look after Marie-Anne. Film night was once more reinstated.

The acclaimed French film, '*J'Accuse*' directed by Abel Gance had finally reached Ottawa. "I'm not sure I'm up to seeing a film about the war," Joseph admitted.

"Everyone's talking about it. It's supposed to be a movie with substance for a change... but... we could see something else... film night is supposed to be a pleasant experience after all." Adèle acquiesced with a tinge of disappointment in her voice.

The ever sensitive Joseph did not miss that hint of disappointment and although he had his misgivings about the film, he was also curious to see what everyone was talking about. "*Non, non, ça va...* let's go see what's so special about this film."

To say that the film was substantial was an understatement. To bring reality to his film, the director had used actual film clips from the war front. The plot was a complicated twist of friendship (two war comrades); adultery (Edith, the wife of one comrade sleeps with the other); rape (Germans capture and rape our heroine); an illegitimate child; an avenging father; the hero gone mad; and the rising of the dead soldiers from their graves to add an even more gruesome touch. Excellent lighting effects and the chosen music brought home the drama. At the end the audience filed out of the cinema in complete silence.

The beauty of the full moon on this crisp autumn night in September was lost on our couple. On the drive home, each sat silent, deep in thought. Adèle studied the heroine, Edith, who slept with her husband's friend; while Joseph replayed the war scenes and the dead wounded soldiers rising from their graves.

"Well, how was it?" enquired Madame Gauthier.

"*C'était terrible*. It was just too gruesome, I don't think you would enjoy it Madame Gauthier," Joseph warned.

"It's very sad and it has a bad ending," added Adèle.

"*Pas pour moi alors, bonne nuit.*" Madame Gauthier took Joseph's arm as he walked her to her door a short way up the street.

As they settled in bed, Adèle knew that they would be discussing the film; they always did. *I don't want to talk about this one. What did he think of Edith's betrayal? He probably thought she deserved to be raped by those vile German soldiers.*

To Adèle's great surprise, Joseph turned off his light and with his back to Adèle, he mumbled, "*Bonne nuit.*"

Adèle tossed and turned as she thought of betrayal. The film hit too close to home and she saw herself in Edith, the heroine. Two hours ticked by and just as she drifted into a troubled sleep, she was aroused by a frightening scream.

Joseph sat bolt upright, bathed in sweat. "*Mon Dieu*, Joseph, are you alright? What's the matter?"

Joseph was trembling. Adèle put her arms around him. He put his head on her shoulder and for the first time since she had known Joseph, Adèle heard him cry. It was soft at first; Adèle tightened her embrace and he gave up control, sobbing.

When he had let it all out, Adèle reached for his handkerchief and handed it to him. "Was it those nightmares of yours? It was the film, wasn't it? I'm so sorry, we should never have gone. Those horrible war scenes; maybe if you tell me about it, the dreams would stop."

"I'm nothing but a coward, Adèle, you married a coward. I was never wounded; it was my appendix that burst." There it was finally out.

"I don't understand, your mother said you were wounded."

"I was too ashamed to be away from the front just because of my appendix while soldiers were maimed and dying around me. My operation went very badly and when the infection set in they moved me to England. The day I wrote to my parents about my predicament I was in turmoil. The soldier in the bed next to mine had lost both legs. He died in agony that day leaving a wife and two children behind. So, in my letter, I lied."

"*Mon pauvre Joseph!* How does this make you a coward? You fought bravely for over a year in those infernal trenches."

"It never occurred to me that my mother would make me out to be brave. I was never going to tell that lie to anyone else. I was shocked the first time it came up in conversation and I just sat there without correcting anyone."

"Tell me about the trenches, Joseph; tell me about your nightmares."

"Above everything else, it's the stench, Adèle. It never goes away. If I smell a dead rat or any dead animal on the road, the trenches flash before my mind wherever I am. It just reeked of rotting flesh, urine, moldy damp, rank sweat and fear. You could actually smell fear."

Adèle held his hands in hers. "Go on."

"There was the noise of gunfire, bombardments and the cries of the dying. The silence was even worse. Sometimes everything went silent and you could hear your bones shaking. The worst usually happened after the silence."

"We screamed blood-curdling war cries as we climbed out of the trenches to fight the enemy. It was supposed to scare the enemy but I think we screamed to steady our nerves and stop ourselves from thinking. You just forged blindly ahead because if you thought for one moment that you were running to your death; chances are, you froze and you were sure to catch a bullet."

"I dream of those muddy, freezing hell-holes, Adèle. I see the walking dead soldiers sightless, missing limbs; just like in the film; but some nights... some awful nights... I have my worst nightmare. That's what I was dreaming about just now... and... I'm not sure I should be burdening you with that one, Adèle."

"You need to tell me Joseph, it must come out and I do want to know."

"I fired my gun into the approaching enemy and when I saw Germans fall, I never really knew if it was my gun or that of a comrade that made its mark. This was a normal occurrence... but... I actually killed a man, Adèle.

"It was war, Joseph. You were there to kill the enemy. It was a Hun you killed, right?"

"You don't understand. My trench mate, Jean Laroche, was running beside me; it was so misty; we were shooting blind. A bullet caught him right in the face and he went down." Joseph paused and Adèle waited patiently.

"The German soldier was practically on top of us. He came to a standstill when he saw what he had done; then he looked at me; he was visibly confused... and I... *Mon Dieu...* he was so scared, he was so young. Joseph's voice cracked. He let go Adèle's hand and started to pummel the pillow with his fist. "I killed him; over and over again I stabbed him with my bayonet. I was out of control, it was like someone else was doing this and I couldn't stop. I was covered in blood, warm blood... some of it was Jean's and some of it belonged to the young soldier... none of it was mine. He never tried to fight back, Adèle... he just looked at me, like if he was surprised. I can't forget the hole in Jean's face... I can't forget the look in the German boy's eyes... I can't forget the blood. I just want to forget." Joseph sagged, his energy spent.

"Joseph, you weren't much older than a boy yourself. Friend or foe, none of you young men should have ever been in such an impossible situation. You should never have lived in those inhumane conditions or seen any of those frightful war horrors. None of you were who you really are because you were all living an actual nightmare.

But you're right. I can't begin to understand. I wasn't there. It must have been agony and you very nearly died, who cares if it was a burst appendix or a bullet, every one of you who survived the trenches is a hero in my book. I'm terribly sorry that you continue to suffer with these nightmares and I can only hope that they will occur infrequently and perhaps one day, it will be over.

Dieu Merci, you're alive. You're a good man Joseph, a wonderful family man. Remember always that you have great purpose in life, we need you and you'll always be our hero."

A burden lifted from Joseph's shoulders that night and though the nightmares never disappeared completely, they did occur far less frequently.

————◖◗◗————

Four women ran for the 14th Canadian Parliament on December 6th of 1921. William Lyon Mackenzie King would head the government with his Liberal Party. The more significant result for women's rights groups was that Agnes McPhail became the first woman Member of Parliament for the Progressive Conservative party. It was a small beginning and a beginning that would not bear much fruit until the 1960's.

The Liberals won most of the Québec seats and as such Maurice Labelle became Joseph and Adèle's new representative. The month of November had been most hectic as our couple threw themselves into campaigning for Maurice.

As was the case when Adèle carried Marie-Anne, she enjoyed four months of well-being before her small frame became too heavy for comfort during her final two months. After the excitement of the elections it was the happy Christmas commotion. It was Rose Lafleur's turn to receive her son's little family for the *réveillon*`. Marie-Anne was crawling over everything, squealing with laughter as she tore paper wrappings off the presents to her hearts content. She was the centre of attention despite the fact that Joseph's sister Marie and her beau Charles Cournoyer announced their engagement. Rose Lafleur was delighted at the thought of more grandchildren.

Adèle was full of energy that winter. The couple received visitors for dinner; went out to dinners; and enjoyed their Saturday date nights. Adèle liked working at the store, interacting with the clients and keeping immaculate books for Joseph. She availed herself of family and friends' offer to babysit that she might go into Ottawa with Mary from time to time for a luncheon or a visit to the library. The deed already done, she found that her intimacy with Joseph was uninhibited and frequent.

By the time February rolled around, the backaches set in and her ankles swelled. She was relegated to the sofa with her feet up and found the wait tiresome especially since the baby did not seem to be in any hurry.

Docteur Fortin was watching Adèle carefully because of the swelling ankles. "*Docteur* Fortin says that this baby is lazy," complained Adèle. "He thinks that the baby is fully ready and I should have delivered by now."

Joseph cringed when he saw his petite Adèle completely engulfed by her enormous belly, waddling to the kitchen as best she could on short legs that she herself could not see. "Sit, sit, I'll do the dishes. It can't be much longer now, you just rest."

Expected just after mid-March, Monique did not make her appearance until March 26th, 1922, fully ten days late and almost four weeks after Marie-Ann's first birthday.

The delivery was excruciating. Marie-Anne had been a small 5 pound baby but Monique was a big at 8 pounds and Adèle was small with a narrow pelvis. The bleeding was difficult to stop and the mid-wife called the Doctor when she feared a hemorrhage. After the birth Joseph refused to remain in the family room. He sat by Adèle holding her hand throughout encouraging her. The midwife looked after the baby and the Doctor busied himself with staunching the bleeding.

It was only after the all-clear sign that the couple in exhausted relief could gaze upon their new daughter. "*Regarde* Adèle she looks just like you. She's so beautiful and she already has a full cap of black hair. But see how long she is. This little beauty won't be a pipsqueak like her mother... oh no... she's going to be tall just like the Savard's. All my mother's brothers are tall; that's where my brother Jean-Claude gets his height from; and you have to admit that my mother is tall for a woman. Can't tell what colour her eyes are going to be yet. Marie-Anne's were so obviously black right from the beginning. Maybe she'll have my mother's hazel eyes, wouldn't that be lovely, Adèle. *Elle est parfaite...* Adèle? You're very quiet, are you alright?"

Joseph had been babbling away and Adèle was watching him enthusiastically examining his new daughter from head to toe. She didn't see the likeness to herself, one never does actually. She didn't see Joseph in her but... then again... she didn't see Jacques in her either. All she could think about was that she was tall... tall like Jacques? She would have liked to have been sure right from the beginning.

"I'm just so sleepy, Joseph."

"*Fais dodo ma brave Adèle.* I'll take care of Monique, look, she's fast asleep. Get your rest." He kissed his beloved.

The next day, infection had set in, fever was raging and the Doctor was back. It took two full months of bedrest before Adèle fully recovered. Marie-Anne had been farmed out to *tante* Hélène's. Annette was back looking after the household chores and helping with Monique when she wasn't in her bassinette downstairs with her *Papa*.

Although back on her feet, Adèle was not quite her usual animated self. She was delighted to have Marie-Anne back with her but it upset her that she had missed her first steps. She cared in every way for Monique but... perhaps because she was mostly absent during the initial weeks, she had not bonded with her as she had with Marie-Anne.

More than that, she worried that Monique was Jacques' child. She would be tall and her eyes were not quite green yet but almost. She had convinced herself that Monique was not Joseph's daughter and this caused her a great deal of anxiety and guilt. She had been too complacent about her tryst with Jacques and she believed that Monique had been sent to remind her of her sin. In her mind Monique was a punishment rather than a joy.

The frightening thing was that in Adèle's stead, the bonding had taken place between Joseph and Monique. He was obviously besotted with her and at three months old she reserved the best smiles for her *Papa*. It was probably a good thing that everyone said that Monique looked exactly like Adèle because if Joseph found out, it would kill him. *Maybe she does look like me,* thought Adèle, *but those are Jacques' eyes... those are his eyes.*

In addition to carrying around this heavy guilt, Adèle spent more time upstairs with Marie-Anne who was walking and getting into too much mischief to be in the store for long periods of time. However, the most disquieting thing about Adèle's lack of oomph was the fact that she was terrified of pregnancy. She was persuaded that another pregnancy would kill her. She kept a strict calendar that left very few days for her Joseph.

Joseph had nearly gone mad when he thought he might lose Adèle. He gave her all the time necessary for her recovery. The only bright spark in his life had been Monique. At first Marie-Anne was away at *tante* Hélène's and his only distraction was Monique. Now that Adèle was judged fit he knew that something was not right but he couldn't put his finger on it. The fact was that he missed Adèle.

One evening in August at the dinner table, Joseph decided to say what had been on his mind. "I miss you Adèle."

"Mais, t'es drôle toi. What a funny thing to say, I haven't gone anywhere."

"You're up here all the time now. We haven't been out much and you come to bed after I've fallen asleep. We hardly see each other and we only talk about the children."

"Well, Joseph Lafleur, someone has to clean, do laundry... not to mention all those diapers... get the meals, do dishes, take care of the girls... and Monique started sleeping her nights for the first time this week... she hasn't been easy." It came out as a bit of a tirade.

"Whoa, *ma Chérie,* it wasn't a criticism. I understand all that you're saying but the fact still remains that, I miss you." He held her hand in his and gave her his best smile.

"I miss you too."

They talked... and talked. There was the upcoming wedding of his sister the following week. They planned to see 'Oliver Twist'. They discussed Dickens. It was time they invited François and Shirley for dinner. Joseph helped with the dishes and when the children were tucked away for the night, they got into bed together.

The calendar was not as strict as she would have liked but things were within the safety net. Adèle surrendered herself. *Why can't it always be like this? Joseph is really special and I did miss this... I missed him. We've got to be so careful not to lose what we have.*

Two weeks later Adèle was vomiting.

1921-1922
A Job Offer

Contrary to his promise to Adèle, Jacques was a frequent visitor to the little locked box in the corner of his mind. He was drawn to the treasure inside as forcefully as a pirate to buried Spanish gold.

After a few long peeks he no longer bothered to lock it. He had imagined her naked before but now he was seeing the reality of the roundness of her small breasts and the fullness of her shining curly thatch so thick and black against her ivory skin. He wished he had taken the time to bury his face in it and many a night before sleep took him, he imagined himself doing just that, deeply inhaling the scent of her; his stiff shaft in hand.

Jacques never felt guilty about these nocturnal events. He had given up on God the day his family had been snatched from him. To make matters worse, his return home revealed that his second chance at happiness had also been snatched away.

Guilt did manifest itself, however, when he was thrown together with Adèle and Joseph at unavoidable social gatherings. Jacques was jealous of Joseph and the fact that Joseph was a really decent chap did nothing to lessen the jealousy but it did make him feel guilty. He would never have believed that he was capable of taking another man's wife, let alone the wife of a person he had been friendly with.

With Mr. and Mrs. Jamis he had been to the theatre to view
'*J'Accuse*'. The photographer in him delighted in the excellent cine-
matography but the story could not fail to depress him as it did most
viewers. Almost every scene in the film left the viewer with food for
thought, most of it unpleasant.

Like Adèle the story of betrayal affected Jacques the most. *I'm
not that kind of guy... Adèle's not that kind of person either. I've turned
her into a scarlet woman... she must be having a terrible time dealing
with that. Joseph seems to be good with her. What kind of man does
what I did? I guess it's true what people say... given the right circumstances, people... ordinary folks... can have a moment of insanity and
are capable of anything... even murder they say.* That thought did little to assuage his feelings of remorse.

He was a frequent guest at François' and their friendship was
solid. He found Shirley to be a salt of the earth kind of woman with
a wicked sense of humor. Little David thought the world of this tall
'uncle'. Jacques felt at home with these people as he did with his family on the farm and as he had with the Roland's in Belgium. He was
a logger, a farmer and an artist. He liked to work with his hands. He
enjoyed conversations about his father's farm, François' mechanics,
sports of all kinds, and the plight of the labourer. He joined a parochial ice-hockey team with François who participated as an assistant
coach. He played with passion.

Evenings at the Labelles were a different thing altogether. Not
always *au fait* with the latest in literature, world events and politics,
Jacques felt uncomfortable and out of place. When he declined a
number of their invitations it was not only to avoid running into
Joseph and Adèle but also because it just wasn't his cup of tea.

But he was no hermit, and so he did run into Joseph and Adèle
from time to time at family gatherings and at François' home. At
each encounter, a flash of the other's nakedness never failed to
pop into their minds. Try as she might Adèle could not stop the
momentary memory of his long muscular body with the many little scars on his chest, a souvenir of his plane crash. She was sorry
that she had not taken the time to kiss each one. With great will-
power she would shelve the thought hoping that her blush was not
too obvious.

At one such gathering at the Turcottes' farm sometime after Christmas he overheard Adèle telling Yvette that she was due around mid-March. He did the math. He sat in shock. *Sacrifice*, c'est pas possible. There's a good chance... no... that would be too cruel. Pauvre Adèle, she must be going through hell. Should I talk to her? No... the best thing for me to do is to leave her alone. I need to get away from here... for a while anyway. I still love her and that's no good for me either...*

"Hey, you... you look like you just saw a ghost." Martin waved his hand across Jacques' face.

"I think you may be right," said Jacques with a hollow laugh.

The next day Jacques carefully checked the date of Mr. Jamis' appointment with the family of the Governor General back in June. He had good reason to 'beware of the ides of March'. Each day that passed after that without hearing of the new arrival was met with a sigh of relief.

When François telephoned him with the news that Adèle had delivered a big baby girl, Jacques was clearly delighted. He convinced himself that the delivery was too late to have been his child. He rejoiced for Adèle yet he was aware that he was experiencing a certain amount of mixed feelings. He still felt the loss of his wife and child. He would love to have a family especially with Adèle. A small part of him would have liked the child to be his.

He was lonely.

Meanwhile back on Park Street François turned to Shirley after the telephone call, "*C'est curieux*. It seems to me that Jacques was as pleased as though it were his own child being born. I believe that he's still carrying a torch for Adèle. I do wish he would meet someone."

"He's a handsome fellow to be sure, but he hasn't much in the way of *joie de vivre*. If I were single, I would find him difficult to approach. Methinks your friend is hurting." Shirley patted her husband on the shoulder.

A few days later Jacques was worried sick when François gave him the news of Adèle's life-threatening predicament. He paced the small area of his apartment. *This can't be happening again. I know she's not mine and she'll never be mine but she mustn't die. I just can't take any more of this. I've got to get away.*

The life-changing letter from National Geographic arrived at the Jamis Studio on the first Monday in April, a week after the birth of Monique and the day after hearing that Adèle would pull through pending a long recuperation.

The previous summer, Mr. Jamis had submitted a number of Jacques' best photos along with newspaper clippings relating to Jacques wartime story. He had given up hearing from them; it had been a long shot at best. Jacques was now staring at the fat envelope sitting on the counter from the National Geographic Society.

Mr. Jamis was excited and getting impatient. "Go on, open it. Fat envelopes always bring good news."

"Well, here goes." Jacques tore open the envelope and handed it to Mr. Jamis. "Here you read it out loud, I'm too nervous."

The National Geographic Society was impressed with the photographs depicting the devastation in the aftermath of the war. They were mounting an expedition to the areas most affected by the war for a sort of before and after story. They wished to use a number of his bleak photos and wanted to contrast them with the ongoing reconstruction efforts across Europe.

One of their experienced reporters, Frank Gresham, would be researching the story. Would Mr. Armand be interested in joining Mr. Gresham as his photographer for the story? It was felt that his talent as a photographer and his experience of the war would be an asset.

The proposed date for their departure was set for the end of May. Should Jacques accept the contract he was expected to be in Washington no later than mid-May in order to familiarize himself with National Geographic; their photography department; and the mission in particular. There were pages detailing the contract and the travel to and from Europe.

Mr. Jamis laid the missive back on the counter, took off his glasses and smiled broadly at Jacques who was whooping whilst doing some sort of Indian dance. Had Shirley witnessed this spectacle, she would have retracted her comment about Jacques' lack of *joie de vivre*.

———●●●———

The six weeks prior to Jacques departure were extremely busy. He was intent on completing all of his work with Mr. Jamis and spent his personal time practicing his colour photography. There were the usual preparations for a long voyage and the family visits to say his goodbyes. He also sent a letter to Paul Roland informing him of his upcoming trip to Europe, hoping that they might get together.

One evening at François' place, Jacques made a request. "I haven't seen Adèle since well before she gave birth and I know that she's still recuperating but I would like to see her before I go. Is she receiving any visitors?"

"As it turns out, I haven't seen her either. I spoke to Joseph two days ago and he told me that Adèle was bored to tears and would love to have visitors. Shirley and I promised that we would stop in on Sunday after Mass. Why don't you accompany us?"

"*C'est parfait.* Sunday it is then. Pick me up on your way there. I was so worried we were going to lose her but I understand that she's making steady progress."

"We were all worried. When Joseph called, I was happy to nurse her. It was a full week before the fever broke and we could begin to hope for the best. She may be a wee little thing but there was plenty of fight in her. Her *tante* Hélène has Marie-Anne, Annette has moved in to help, and Joseph keeps Monique by his side most of the day. A couple more weeks and she should be back to normal again," recounted Shirley.

When the threesome arrived after Mass, Adèle was installed in the upholstered armchair with her feet up on a stool, a blanket covering her lower body. Pleased to have company, Joseph offered drinks all around.

Jacques hoped that his shock at seeing Adèle so thin and pale did not register on his face as he bent down to kiss her cheeks.

"*Mon Dieu,* Jacques you look as though you've seen a ghost. I don't look as bad as all that; I'm the picture of health compared to last month." Adèle's laugh and her radiant smile were all that was needed to restore her beauty.

Jacques returned the laugh. "You're as lovely as ever, but," he turned to Joseph, "my friend you've got to start feeding her or she will disappear altogether."

"Like the little lady said, she's positively fat compared to last month." Joseph's loving eyes were on Adèle.

"So, tell us all about your big news… Washington… then Europe… I'm green with envy. We were so thrilled to hear that one of ours will be working with the National Geographic. Will we see your name along with your photographs?" Adèle was excited for Jacques.

With his gaze firmly on Adèle, Joseph thought; *she's so beautiful when she's animated like this. The company will do her a world of good.* He turned to Jacques.

"We love the magazine; we never miss an issue. It's the next best thing to travelling when you don't have the means or the time to go to these faraway corners of the world. What I enjoy most is the beautiful color photographs. Will you be doing any of those?"

"I've been experimenting with autochrome color for a while now. It's expensive and far from perfect but I find the result worthwhile."

"Why do you say it's far from perfect?" Joseph's scientific nature was piqued.

"Well, for one thing, you need a longer exposure so nothing must move and you have to use a tripod in all circumstances. It's best for still images. The result is somewhat grainy and not sharp like the black and whites."

"Oh, but that's what makes them so beautiful," chimed in Adèle. "It gives them a kind of haze… makes them a bit unreal… like an impressionist painting."

"You seem well informed. I'm afraid I wouldn't know one painting from the next," said the practical Shirley.

"She reads voraciously especially since she was ordered to two months bed rest. Poor me, I almost have to carry a cart to the library each week." Joseph stumbled around the room with arms out as though he was carrying a heavy load. "Her latest craze is the arts."

"And now, I shall make it a point to read about photography, in honour of our famous Gatineau photographer," Adèle's tone was mocking. You don't suppose there are famous women photographers? Now there's an area I hadn't thought of."

"*Mais oui*, there are a number of excellent women photographers. Imogene Cunningham comes to mind. She's mainly into flowers and such. Then there is Eliza Scidmore. I believe that she's a woman after your own heart, Adèle."

"Tell me more."

"Well she's a member of the board at National Geographic and has traveled the Far East extensively. Her Japanese photography is remarkable. She hand tinted the cherry blossoms and you should see the colours in the kimonos. I really hope to meet her."

"Yes but you haven't explained how the colour gets in the photograph," Joseph persisted.

While Jacques spoke with Joseph and François about glass plates, dyed starch grains and light, the two women chatted.

"I must confess, Shirley, that I sometimes envy women like Eliza Scidmore and that Imogene person… I forget her name… "

"Oh, you'll feel differently when you're back on your feet; you have a good life here, Adèle." Shirley was not one for self-pity and had little use for complaining. "Well, well, just look who just arrived; if it isn't the little princess herself."

Annette had entered the room with a wakeful Monique in her arms. Shirley got up and rushed over to gawk.

"Oh look François, look at those eyes! How splendid! You brilliant little thing you… we're going to be fast friends you and me… dazzling green eyes in a sea of French Canadian brown." Shirley cooed at the infant. "It's a sign of good luck you know… where in heaven's name did you get those peepers from?"

Adèle and Jacques exchanged a quick furtive look that spoke volumes. Joseph took his daughter from Annette. "It seems that we have skeletons in our closets in the Lafleur family. I understand that my great-grandmother was the love child of a Scottish lumber baron."

Jacques clung to this life-raft of news. *It has to be Joseph's daughter then.*

"I never knew that," interrupted Adèle.

"Aha, *mon amour*, I can still surprise you." He turned to Shirley. "My mother has hazel eyes and my uncle Jean-Marie has eyes as green as yours Shirley."

"Well then, Jacques, what's your story." Shirley winked at Jacques. "Perhaps your beautiful *Mama* had a secret liaison with a wealthy Scotsman and your *Papa* came to her rescue and married her to save her honour."

Everyone laughed. "You should be writing romance novels, Shirley… next, you should have me hunting down this wealthy Scotsman who left my mother dishonoured and penniless, demanding my rightful share of his fortune."

"*Oooh…* how exciting!" Annette's young imagination was running wild. "Families around here are so ordinary, this is much better… and we could have an old fashioned duel in the story, Shirley, what do you think?"

"Now see what you've started, Shirley," admonished her husband. "I believed it's time we let Adèle have her rest."

There was kissing of cheeks all around; wishes of good luck; promises from Jacques that he would write; and a long last look at Adèle when no one was watching.

CHAPTER 19

1922
Washington

The train journey to Washington took the better part of two days. In Montréal he took the overnight train to New York. In New York Jacques had to transfer from the gargantuan Grand Central Station to the equally impressive Pennsylvania Station to catch the train bound for Washington. As he stood in the cavernous waiting room, his excitement mounted. *What an enormous room… this city is amazing. I'm glad this is the last leg… I'll be in Washington tonight.*

Disembarking from the train, Jacques picked out a heavily bearded man from the crowd who was possibly in his forties, holding a piece of cardboard with JACQUES ARMAND written in bold black capital letters.

He made a beeline for this man and introduced himself. The man shook his hand. "I'm Frank Gresham and very pleased to make your acquaintance, Jack."

"It's Jacques."

"Yes, that's what I said, Jack. Let me help you with these bags, my car is nearby."

Once the bags were safely stowed in the trunk, the party of two took off. "You're to be my guest during your stay in Washington. I live alone with my only child and there's way too much space for the two of us."

"That's very kind of you; I had expected to stay in a lodging house."

"We have a full two weeks before we embark for France. You'll have time to familiarize yourself with our mission and find your way around our photography department which I believe will be much to your liking. You'll also find that Washington is lovely in the spring."

They made their way to the attractively tree-lined Q Street NW. The Chrysler came to a stop in front of a solid three-story red brick townhouse with large bay windows sporting neat white trimmings.

In the foyer, Jacques admired the ornate crown molding, the elaborate chandelier, intricate floor tiles and the curved staircase with highly polished natural wood balustrades. "Are you hungry?" enquired his host.

"No, thank you, I had a full meal on the train."

"Well then, it's late and I would imagine that you must be tired. I'll show you to your room on the third floor. Tomorrow being Sunday you can sleep in and come down for breakfast in your own good time. You'll find the kitchen at the end of this corridor and the bathroom facilities on the second floor facing the staircase."

The bags were placed in the small guest room and the two men said their goodnights. The faint breeze coming through the window was pleasant. Jacques walked over to the window which looked out onto the quiet street and took a deep breath. Turning around he studied the room that was to be his home for the next two weeks.

The small rectangular room had a masculine feel to it. It held a single bed, a night-table, a wardrobe and a comfortable looking arm-chair; all of which were of a highly polished natural wood with complex carvings. The wallpaper had a cream background with a motif of sailing ships. The drapes, bedspread and linens were plain. All in all, the room spoke of comfort and it was not long before Jacques had emptied his bags and settled into the deep sleep of a weary traveler.

◆●◆

A bright sunny day welcomed Jacques to his new life. Hoping that a plain white shirt and pants was the suitable attire for breakfast, Jacques made his way down to the kitchen with bacon aromas growing stronger to guide his way.

Jacques had nothing to fear about his casual appearance as his host was in pyjamas and robe. "Come have a seat, you'll find that we are quite casual on Sundays. The staff is off, we're not church goers, we keep our own hours, we eat in the kitchen and we fend for ourselves. How do you like your eggs?"

"It's not necessary for you to go to any trouble Mr. Gresham; I can also fend for myself."

"And so you shall, but not today. I'll play host for one day, show you where everything is and then you're on your own... and please... call me Frank.

"In that case, I'll have them scrambled, Frank."

The kitchen had obviously been modernised with the latest appliances and it was large enough to house a large table with six chairs. A bank of windows over the sink looked out onto a cheerful garden.

Footsteps were approaching. "Ah, time for you to meet the prodigy."

The lad of about sixteen was quite the sight to behold. His dirty coveralls and shirt were splashed with paint of every colour. A disheveled mop of short blonde curls sat atop his head and his face wore more than a few smudges of yellow paint. The messy appearance disappeared as soon as Jacques looked into his eyes. Seemingly bottomless pools of blue beckoned... *plunge in at your own risk.*

"So this is Jack. He looks much more like the lumberjack he once was than a photographer."

Irritation vied with shock as Jacques suddenly realised that he was in the presence of a petite young woman. This was no lad.

"I'm afraid you must forgive my daughter. You will find her irreverent at best. She was raised to be a free thinker and sometimes I believe that her mother and I made a colossal mistake. Jack, meet Jodie."

Without as much as a 'pleased to meet you', Jacques left his manners on the table as well. "How did you know I was a lumberjack?"

"What a curious accent... it's not at all the same as the French from France. I haven't quite decided if I like it yet. We read the newspaper clippings about the lumberjack from the wilds of Canada turned war hero."

So this was the drawback. Nice house, nice room, nice host, great job... but he would have to put up with this annoying young woman for the next two weeks.

"I see you've been up early in your studio and yellow seems to be the order of the day." Frank looked warmly at his daughter.

"The light was just perfect, Daddy... just couldn't let it go to waste." She gave her father a peck on the cheek and turned to Jacques. "Apparently, I'm quite the budding artist and if you're a good boy, I'll invite you to see my etchings." She winked provocatively.

Jacques' dislike deepened. *She's scandalous... rude... a brat, how can her father allow her to behave in this manner?*

"Etchings, hah, probably more like children's scribbles," Jacques retorted, hating himself for sinking to her level.

"Jodie, behave! Why must you always seek to provoke? Now you have poor Jack playing your game. But then again, if you two want to act like squabbling siblings, I suppose we will function as a normal family for the next two to three months."

Months! She can't be coming with us. "Will you be accompanying us, Miss?" Jacques voice sounded a little frightened.

"No... it is you who will be accompanying us; my father and I are a team... and... it's not Miss... it's Jodie." She picked up a slice of toasted bread, kissed her father once more and left with a wave. "Ta ta, must go, the creative juices are flowing."

Whoosh, electricity and energy followed Jodie and the kitchen was suddenly empty and quiet.

Frank looked at the visibly stunned Jacques. Breaking the silence with his laughter he put his hand on Jacques, shoulder. "You'll get used to her. She obviously took a liking to you and she's testing your mettle."

"She took a liking to me! I wouldn't want to see her when she doesn't like someone."

Frank looked sad for a moment. "No, indeed, you wouldn't want to see that."

"I'm sorry, Frank. I really didn't mean to criticise... it's just that I've never met anyone quite like Jodie."

"She was right, you know. We are a team. We were in India in 1903 when she was born. My wife and I were dedicated to travel and discovery and hadn't planned for a family. Jodie was a surprise but it didn't change our lifestyle. Our twosome just became a threesome."

"So, she went everywhere with you? What about schools and friends?"

"We home-schooled her and I daresay, she received a superior education to that of organized schooling. Our assignments were often lengthy and Jodie played with the local children wherever we happened to be. She learned to speak Spanish fluently during our stay at the Machu Picchu site. More than all of that, she learned her geography and her sociology firsthand.

Being the only child on these expeditions, she was spoiled by everyone. Thrown in with scientists, anthropologists, philosophers, writers, artists and free-thinkers from around the world she became wise beyond her years. You'll find her most interesting when she decides you're worthy of her affections."

Who in their right mind would want to be worthy of her affections, she should worry more that I won't find her worthy of my attention. Jacques was indignant.

"What happened to her mother, if you don't mind my asking?"

When he saw the pain in Frank's eyes, he was sorry he asked.

"We lost Miriam four years ago in New Zealand. It was a drowning accident." It was all he would say.

Frank took a deep breath and found his smile. "Now, eat up, no time to waste, I want to show you around our fair capital. I'm afraid that you've missed the cherry blossoms."

Frank was a good tour guide. He knew the history behind the scenes and he had an entertaining way of describing Washington. "I'm going to drive you by the White House but I'm leaving our National gardens for next week because we will all be attending the dedication of our Lincoln Memorial which is at the opposite end of our Washington Monument, that tall obelisk we keep getting glimpses of as we drive around; so the best for the last then."

"Actually, I've been meaning to talk to you about that. Seeing as I'm already here, the Ottawa Citizen has asked me to cover this event. I understand that President Harding will be speaking at this dedication. Anyway, it shouldn't interfere with any of my duties at

National Geographic as I'm just there to take the photographs and send them by courier."

"I don't foresee any problems. Every bit of work helps the pocket." Frank winked.

"Tomorrow morning I'll introduce you to the head of our photography department and you will be pretty much in their hands this week. Friday we'll be attending an evening at our chief editor's home, Gilbert Grosvenor. I hope you brought your best suit. Monday is the dedication of the Memorial and for the rest of the week we'll be meeting as a team to plan our little expedition. We sail on the 28th. Any questions?"

"I was hoping to see the originals of some of National Geographic's most famous photographs."

"Don't worry about that. The lads at the photo lab will be sure to show off. Who knows, you may very well be in that hall of fame yourself someday. Play your cards right, Jack, and you might be asked to join our permanent staff."

Jacques enjoyed his daytime activity at the photo lab. He was fascinated by the comprehensiveness of the dark rooms and he mooned over the large collection of famous photos; some autochrome photos by Arnold Genthe; American Indians by Edward Curtis and the exotic Japanese ladies in their kimonos by Eliza Scidmore among the scores of photographers that had their work on display.

Lost in photography, his days whizzed by happily. Evening time on Q Street however, was something else altogether. Unaccustomed to having servants, he quickly decided that this was the way to live. Through the sterling efforts of Coco the maid, his clothes were laundered and pressed; his room was swept, dusted and polished. Meanwhile, Bessie, the largest black woman he had ever seen, was serving up cordon bleu meals and Joey the gardener come handyman kept everything shipshape.

Despite the delicious food, Jodie found a way to spoil evening meals for Jacques. Always in her dirty coveralls she continued her barbs and Jacques gave back as good as he got. Frank, for his part, looked down on the pair, bemused, as a father might look at his two quarrelsome children. She seemed to be thoroughly enjoying the repartee, Jacques was not.

"Tell me Jack…" Jacques winced and stopped her mid-sentence.

"It's not Jack, its J a c q u e s. I know that you speak fluent Spanish and I know that you have a working knowledge of French and I know that you could say my name properly if you wanted to." You could almost see the smoke coming out of his ears. She got under his skin; an irritation he just couldn't shake. Thankfully the perpetually messy Jodie spent most of her time behind the closed doors of her studio.

"Sure thing Jack, now don't go getting yourself all in a snit."

Jacques gave up. It would seem that he had now undergone another name change in his life. He ate silently refusing to look at Jodie or answer any more of her questions.

Knowing that his unfashionable three piece suit was not up to inspection, Jacques was determined to carry himself proudly and put his best foot forward at the Grosvenor's party. He looked forward to meeting the who's who of National Geographic in particular Eliza Scidmore.

In the foyer at Q Street, Frank and Jacques' patient waiting was about to turn impatient when they heard Jodie's footsteps coming down the staircase.

"You look ravishing my darling daughter, but we must hurry as we're already quite late."

Mesmerised, Jacques had yet to budge. For some reason, Jodie's laughter reminded him of cascading water heading down a lively brook.

"I do clean up on rare occasions you know." *He's quite a piece of manliness, our lumberjack. Paul Bunyan has nothing on him. I could easily get lost in those green eyes,* thought Jodie as she took a long hard look at Jacques.

Jacques took in Jodie's garb. He could discern delicate shoulders under her gauzy stole. With a deep V her silky blouse was held up by thin shoulder straps. Gathered below her small bosom, it flowed down loosely just above the knee to reveal matching loose-fitting trousers, the pant legs opening wide at the ankle. The entire outfit's colour matched her eyes.

Her generous lips were painted red and whatever she had done to her eyes had an astonishing result. If anything, it was her hair that had undergone the greatest transformation. No longer dishevelled, her cap of soft curls had a silky shine. For a moment Jacques imagined running his fingers through them. The only discordant note in his opinion was the funny little bunch of feathers atop her head that purported to be a hat.

Except for working coveralls he had never seen a woman in trousers before. If anyone could carry it off, it was Jodie.

"Come on you two. Stop gawking at each other."

More wonders lay ahead for our country mouse. The Grosvenor residence was the closest thing to a mansion Jacques had ever been invited to. The glittering reception hall was packed with people in finery. Most men sported tuxedos and the women sparkled; he espied two who were also in trousers with silver glitz on the hems by the ankles.

Jacques promptly forgot the names of all the people he shook hands with. Everyone seemed to be engaged in some kind of witty conversation. This was much worse than a soirée at the Labelles.

"Oh, oh, here comes George. You're on your own you two." Frank disappeared into the crowd.

A slick looking young man made a bee line for Jodie. "Well if it isn't the devil's daughter herself. What mischief have you been up to?"

"Much less than I would expect a crook like you to get into," laughed Jodie. This time it didn't sound anything like a running brook.

The slick young man enfolded Jodie in his arms. "Oh how I do love you dearest Jodie. I can always count on you for a good laugh."

She presented Jacques to George. He looked down his nose at Jacques' suit and some banalities were exchanged. "We must press on, George. Jack needs help navigating through these shark infested waters. Take my arm Jack. Ta ta George."

"Jodie, stop, please. Can we sit for a moment?"

Jodie looked at Jacques curiously trying to assess his mood. "Come, follow me."

They entered a sitting room where a number of the older folk were quietly chatting in small groups. Jodie chose two armchairs in a corner of the room by an expensively draped window.

"Is something the matter, Jack?"

"I can't do this Jodie. It's all a game and I don't know the rules nor do I want to learn the rules." *Why am I telling her this? She's going to tear me apart and laugh at me for days to come.*

"You're quite right. It is a game. I'm good at games and I always play to win. It's how I survive in Washington. Luckily, most of my life is spent on expeditions, in some of the remotest parts of the world among peoples who have little to no material goods. Life is real there. The people are genuine. Sometimes without a common language we find total communication just using signs. It can be so simple, so straightforward... I'm hungry... I hurt... I'm sleepy... I'm sad... I'm happy... I love you... so simple. It's in places like that where I'm most at home."

"Well, you could have fooled me. This is the first real conversation I've had with you. Could we not bury the hatchet and do more of this?"

"We'll see." Jodie gave him a smile that warmed his entire body. "Come with me, I've someone real I'd like you to meet."

Jacques groaned. "Oh, alright."

Jodie led Jacques across the room. An older lady was sitting across from another mature lady with an empty chair next to them. The two were deep in conversation. The elder of the two was dressed in complete opposition to Jodie. In muted beige tones her outfit reached up to her chin almost with sleeves to her wrists and fell modestly above her ankle. A little lace at the neck and wrists was the only concession to frivolity.

Jodie spoke softly to this woman. "Auntie Eliza..."

Eliza Scidmore looked up. "My darling Jodie, you're a breath of fresh air, as ever. What have you brought me? Is this the young photographer from Canada your Dad was telling me about?"

"Yes Auntie, his one desire in life is to meet with you. Jack Armand, I'm pleased to present Eliza Scidmore and her friend Mrs. Colleen Johnson."

Jacques shook each of the ladies' hand. "*Je suis enchanté.*"

"What a nice young man. I hope that after this you can aspire to loftier desires in life. We must arrange for more seating."

"Oh no Auntie, I know that I'll be out of my depth when the two of you go into your photography language. I'm off to greener pastures."

"No photo talk for me either," said Mrs. Johnson. "It's high time I found out what mischief my husband is up to."

Left alone, Jacques became a little tongue tied. The lady came to his rescue. "Frank showed me some of your photographs. There was one that particularly stood out for me...."

And so the conversation began. Eliza Scidmore was an introvert by nature and not one to make small talk or speak of herself. They found a common language in photography and Jacques enjoyed the rest of his evening.

◆●●◆

Saturday mornings, Bessie went all out with breakfast. It was more like a feast than breakfast. The various dishes were laid out on the buffet in the dining room; eggs Benedict, bacon, sausages, meat pies, refried beans, kippers, pancakes, corn bread, porridge, jams, jellies and a large fruit plate.

"This may be a silly question, but how are three people supposed to eat all of this?" Jacques' stomach felt full just looking at the amount of food.

"Don't you worry, nothing will be wasted. Some of these leftovers are for tomorrow when the staff is off and the rest will go to help feed their families. Now dig in," ordered Frank.

Jodie breezed in, late as usual. She took one look at the buffet. "I can't stomach anything this morning, too much champagne last night. Bessie, can you bring me some dry toast and orange juice, pleeeease."

"How was your *tête-à-tête* with your heroine, you seemed engrossed? She doesn't usually speak to anyone that long." Frank was reading the papers and Jodie kissed him on the head as she made for her seat.

"I found Miss Scidmore to be intelligent and extremely well-informed."

"Now, how could someone like you possible know that?"

Here we go again. I'm going to ignore her. "Is she really your aunt?"

Jodie looked thoughtfully at Jacques. *Hmmm... he didn't bite.* "No, but she's been in my life since I was born and I've called her auntie as far back as my memory goes. She was my anchor when Mommy died; Dad was in too much of a mess to deal with anything."

As was the case with her father, Jodie's eyes betrayed her pain when the subject of her mother came up. Jacques changed the subject. "Well, I truly enjoyed that part of the evening but please tell me that I won't need to buy a tuxedo."

Jodie laughed. "These parties are part of Washington life I'm afraid, but you can always decline. Auntie Eliza usually does; you were lucky to see her there. You might want to reconsider the tux though. I believe you would cut a handsome figure in one of those."

"A compliment... wow... I don't believe it... was that really a compliment or is there something awful to follow?" Jacques was contorting his face into exaggerated looks of surprise.

Frank peered over his paper. "I told you she liked you."

"Let's not get ahead of ourselves, now. Like is a strong word, why don't we graduate to tolerate which makes you eligible to enter my studio." Though Jodie's words were mocking, the look in her eyes said something else. *That was stupid. I don't really know this guy. What's the rush... what if he laughs at my work?*

Jodie's bravado was all gone and she looked down but Jacques hadn't missed the vulnerable look in her eyes. *All of a sudden she looks like a scared little girl. This is no time for teasing.* "I'd be honoured, Jodie, but you should know that I really don't know much about art so you'll have to be patient with me."

Frank had put down his paper when he heard his daughter's invitation. *Oh, oh... what is she doing? Her art is everything to her... only those she trusts completely get to see it... and I wouldn't blame him if he made fun of her art after the way she's treated him this past week. He couldn't possibly know how fragile she really is.*

"Well then, if Jacques knows little about art perhaps he would prefer to do something else." Frank was giving them the way out.

"On the contrary, I really would love to see your work."

"I'm suddenly hungry." Jodie went to the buffet. "Finish up Jack; you'll need fortification before entering my inner sanctum." Jodie's laugh rang false.

Jodie led Jacques slowly up one flight of stairs. She hesitated at the closed door of her studio. "Here goes, then."

They entered.

Dumbfounded, Jacques was overwhelmed by colour. Canvasses covered the walls and they were also on the floor leaning on the few bits of furniture; a large chest, a chaise, a small table and her easel. He was unaccustomed to the modern way of painting. He stood silently trying to make sense of the bold colours.

Little by little he discerned that they were landscapes. Large splotches of different greens with coloured stems were trees. The undulating valleys with their patchwork of varying hues gave the effect of a quilt. He walked around, carefully examining the paintings. He stopped and stared for a long time at a large canvas of brilliant greens, reds, oranges and yellows. *How does she do that? The sun almost looks as though it was drawn by a child; a yellow circle with lines of rays. But a child could never make it feel so bright and so hot.* The painting was bathed in light.

"This is beautiful." Jacques meant it.

Jodie had been standing in a corner holding her breath. Now she was beaming. "Half the painting was on me the day we met, especially the yellow." She giggled like a little girl.

"I remember it well. You have a cloth covering your easel; is it a work in progress?"

"It's almost finished." Jodie's voice was hesitant. "You can see it if you want but I really would understand if you thought it was strange and didn't know what it was about. Surrealism is not for everyone."

"Let's have a look then."

Jodie removed the cloth.

It was strange; not at all what Jacques would call art... more like a drawing. Jacques made out three huge pairs of eyes. You could tell they were eyes. Two plain arcs met to form the corners of the eyes and large lashes were drawn on the upper arc with smaller ones on the lower arc. A child would have drawn an eye in this fashion. In the first pair of eyes there was an open window where the iris should have been. Through the window in the first eye, there were pretty blue flowers and small blue doves. In the window of the second eye there were black snakes on a blue background, and what looked like a small devil.

Below was the second set of eyes. Jacques looked up at the first set to compare and he could see by the shape of the arcs and lashes that these were a man's eyes while the eyes above were female. Once again the windows were there but in each case they had bars like a prison window, this time inside the window was a green background completely blank.

Below that, the third set of eyes was remarkable. The first was a male eye with the most luminescent green oval pool in the middle, a diving board on one side. Sitting on the diving board was the form of a naked woman, her only feature being a small yellow thatch on her head. You could tell by her posture that she was contemplating diving in.

The next eye was female with the same pool and diving board in place of the iris. This time the pool was a silky blue. The human form was male with a light brown thatch on his head; also seemingly contemplating a dive.

Jacques was sitting on her stool examining the painting in great detail. After a long time, Jodie asked in a whisper, "Well, does it mean anything to you?"

Jacques hesitated, trying to find the right words to answer her. "Yes it does. Perhaps the man is afraid to take the plunge in those inviting blue waters because he fears what he sees through the second window of the woman's eyes above… and perhaps the woman needs to find the key to allow her in behind the bars of the man's eyes to see inside before she takes the plunge. As inviting as it seems, perhaps they're not ready yet."

"And perhaps they're just funny eyes; just me trying to dabble into the bizarre world of surrealist painting." Jodie spoke lightly with a laugh, bringing the tour of her studio to an end.

The week before their departure was indeed a whirlwind of activity. On the Monday, Jacques was bowled over by the size of the Lincoln memorial and awed at the height of the Washington Monument. During the dedication he was able to take a great number of pictures with President Harding on the podium.

There were the planning sessions at National Geographic and the endless packing at Q Street which included a newly acquired tuxedo for Jacques following Frank's recommendation. "Haven't you seen my photos of Ypres? Do you really believe that a tuxedo would be the appropriate garb?" Jacques had asked sarcastically.

"Perhaps not but we will not be travelling third class for the crossing and then there is Paris…" Frank had insisted.

Jodie for her part, see-sawed between insults and proper behaviour. Jacques ignored the insults and enjoyed the good moments with her.

The day before they left, Jacques went into Jodie's bedroom to help carry out her luggage. On the dresser was a large autochrome colour photograph of a nude. He picked it up to examine it. The slim body was arched backwards provocatively in such a way that her head was thrown back and her face not visible. The nipples on her small breasts were erect. The colour was done in such a way that you wanted to run your hand over the silky skin. It was such a strong feeling that Jacques did just that. As he ran his fingers over the nude, he exclaimed, "This is extraordinary. It's alive."

"It's an Arnold Genthe. Do you recognize the model?" Jodie had an odd look on her face.

"No, I know most of his work but I've not seen this one before."

Jodie, spread out her arms and took a deep bow. "Tadaaa… you are looking at her in the flesh."

Jacques immediately took his hand off the photograph. "I don't believe you. Your father would never have allowed it."

"You really are old-fashioned. There's nothing shameful about our bodies. Genthe is a good friend. He did one of my own mother; at my Dad's request. Surely the photographer in you can see that this is a work of art."

"I'm not made that way, Jodie. I'm just not of your world. I would want my wife's nudity to be seen by me alone. So if that's old-fashioned, then go right ahead, call me old-fashioned."

Needless to say, the Genthe work of art was firmly imprinted on Jacques mind and he did nothing to shake it.

CHAPTER 20

1922
The Expedition

Whale watching turned out to be the highlight of an otherwise uneventful but pleasant crossing. A young boy first spotted them. Passengers reached for their binoculars and rushed to starboard.

The naked eye could make out two spouts in the distance. Patiently the passengers waited until they were rewarded when one of the whales broke water. The other followed shortly to the *oohs* and *aahs* of the onlookers.

Jacques had camera in hand trying to capture what was too far off when suddenly, not a hundred yards off, the monster leaped out of the water to the surprised cries of the passengers. Although the captain did his best to follow the whales, within a half hour the show was over.

"Tell me you got it all." Jodie was flush with excitement. "In all my travels, this is my first sighting. It was magnificent."

"I'm certain I got some great shots. Twice we sighted whales on the crossing to England in 1915. I took pictures but the results were disappointing. One photo shows a spout and the other a sort of undefined lump."

"They're awesome creatures; quite majestic. Look how happy they've made everyone." Jodie pointed at the groups of passengers smiling; excitedly recounting the experience.

"Yes, they are imposing creatures. I remember thinking how lucky they were back then in 1915. They were peacefully going about their business totally undisturbed by the fact that most of us were rushing to our deaths."

"Oh, no… we're not allowed to be sad on this ship. There will be enough sadness ahead on our journey. Come, let's change for dinner. There's a great jazz combo on the programme for tonight."

Before arriving at Le Havre, the trio poured over maps and their plans for the coming months. Paris would be their base camp. Starting at Amiens they would circle around going next to Arras, and then to nearby Vimy in France, entering Belgium to visit Ypres, Louvain, Namur and Dinant. There was a planned visit to the Roland Farm before re-entering France to cover Rheims their last stop before returning to Paris.

———◀●●▶———

They were received with open arms at the elaborate home of *Monsieur* and *Madame* Raymond Marquis in Paris. Jodie had explained that they were good friends with her Mom's family. "Auntie Isabelle… another auntie who's not a real aunt… well she and my Mom went to school together. And their families were close."

Auntie Isabelle took Jodie by the hands. They exchanged cheek kisses. "Look at you! The young girl is now a woman… *une belle femme.*"

Grunting under the weight of the baggage Frank added his views, "You mustn't be fooled by appearances, dear Isabelle, she may look all grown up, but she's the same silly girl you so kindly took in two years ago."

"Frank, *s'il te plait*, put those bags down. The servants will see that they're delivered to your rooms. In the meantime I'm sure you can use some refreshments and then you may want to settle in and rest before dinner, later…"

Madame Marquis was interrupted as a young man came barreling down the majestic staircase, laughing. "Jodie, Jodie, Jodie, *ma chère amie!*"

"Olivier!" Jodie ran to his arms to be lifted up and twirled around like a little girl squealing with pleasure.

Frank turned to Jacques, smiling, "I rest my case."

Jacques was introduced to Isabelle Marquis and her son Olivier as Jack Armand. *"S'il vous plait madame, appelez-moi J a c q u e s."*

"Ah, Jacques, certainement, vous êtes français, but I don't place your accent."

"Jack hails from Canada... Québec, to be more precise and he's the very talented photographer attached to our mission," Frank explained.

The party repaired to the drawing room for refreshments; echoes of the happy chatter of old friends reuniting left behind in the cavernous foyer.

The weary travelers were relieved when they were finally escorted to their respective rooms on the third floor for a much needed rest. Jacques felt somewhat out of his depth. *It's a good thing I took Frank's advice and bought a tux.* Jodie had whispered that dinner was formal just before she entered her room. *I guess Jodie's Mom must have been rich if her family was friendly with this family and if she did some of her schooling in Paris. I wish I could come down with something and have a legitimate excuse for skipping dinner. Madame Marquis says that her husband Raymond will be there and she intends on sitting me next to him. He's not a photographer let alone a lumberjack or farmer... what in heaven's name are we going to talk about.*

At dinner, Raymond Marquis monopolised Jacques. He was contemplating expanding his business to Canada and was interested in knowing everything about Québec. Jodie was listening intently as Jacques had not shared much of himself with Jodie.

Isabelle was in deep conversation with Frank while Olivier was trying his best to get Jodie's attention away from his father's dialogue with Jacques. "Jodie, what say you, we do the cabarets in *quartier Pigalle et Montmartre* tomorrow night?"

As always Jodie was taken in by the charming French accent in Olivier's English. She found it sexy, so different from Jacques' accent which was more... well... different. "I thought you'd never ask. I'm looking forward to Jack's reaction... he's quite the country bumpkin you know."

Olivier had not meant for Jacques to accompany them but he would find him a girl and he could have Jodie to himself.

As they left the table, *Madame* Marquis addressed Jacques. "I know that your time in Paris is very limited but I would strongly advise you to visit Notre Dame Cathedral before you take off. It is the most magnificent in France and you will be seeing nothing but ruined cathedrals from hereon in, *c'est tragique*."

Jacques took her advice. In the company of Jodie, he set off for a day of sightseeing and photography. He was bowled over by Notre Dame and delighted with the charm of the bridges over the Seine. The warm sunny day was conducive to a friendly stroll arm in arm along the Champs-Élysées. They sat outdoors at a small café. Jacques marveled at the Eiffel Tower. "It's not as tall as the Washington monument but it has a lot more style. The gardens everywhere are lovely."

"When we get back, I'll take you to the *Bois de Boulogne,* now there's a park. So far Paris is my favourite city but there's so much of the world that I've yet to see so who knows what city will steal my heart next." Jodie looked up at Jacques. "I was listening in on your conversation with Raymond last night and it gave me the desire to visit Canada. I believe I'd especially love the rivers, lakes, and the wild forest. I think I'd like to go when there were mountains of snow."

Jacques took advantage of the moments when Jodie was being civil with him. "Funny, I took you more for a city girl."

"You've only seen me in the city and you're right. When I'm in the city I love everything about it; the lights, the museums, the shopping, the hustle and bustle and the nightlife. It's in the cities that I love to play." Jodie's blue eyes twinkled with mischief, her voice on the verge of laughter.

"Well then, why would you especially want to see the wilds of Canada? What about *Montréal* or historic *Québec*?"

Jodie looked down and in an uncharacteristic tone, she spoke softly. "Because it's in nature that I find my soul…"

They sat quietly for a few moments, Jacques not knowing this side of Jodie, not knowing just what to say.

Jacques broke the awkward silence. "You want to travel for the rest of your life then? Will you never settle down with a family?"

Jodie laughed out loud. "Come on Jack, try to imagine me a wife and a mother. My Dad has a lot more years of travel left in him and I plan to accompany him."

"He's lucky to have you. It would be lonely without family."

"I guess so; they hadn't planned on having a family you know. Now he says that it was the best thing they ever did. He tells me that I was the only reason for going on after Mom died."

"He's probably right... and when he's gone... what will you do then... no husband... no children?"

"Why must you always be so annoying, Jack Armand!" She let go his arm.

"Me... annoying... look who's talking..." and so the familiar bickering resumed.

After dinner that night the two young men of the household were chatting in the foyer waiting for Jodie to come down. A study in contrasts, they made a handsome pair in their tuxedos.

Of medium height, Olivier's build was slight, his features finely chiseled. His coal-brown hair was slicked back shining with brilliantine, his black eyes also shining. Between the nose and the heart shaped mouth was a fine line moustache that looked as though it had been drawn with a black pencil. His tuxedo was cut from expensive cloth; the white dress shirt was immaculate and the gloss in his shoes a virtual mirror. Though the overall effect was that of a good-looking young man, it was artificial and slightly effeminate.

Whereas, Olivier's expensive get-up made him look good, Jacques made his modest garb look good. The sandy-coloured waves in Jacques hair were properly combed, but free from confining gels. The full moustache he had been sporting for the last year was well-groomed giving him the desired look of strength and maturity. His daily morning regimen of sit-ups and push-ups provided him with the physique to fill out his tuxedo. In an unpretentious way, Jacques looked the embodiment of manliness.

When Jodie finally made her appearance, she took Olivier's breath away and left Jacques with mixed feelings. Her arms and shoulders were bare, the blouse barely above her breasts. She was all glitter and shine with rows of long beads dangling around her neck. A cloche hat covered her hair pulled down to her eyebrows. Her ruby red lips and eyes heavily made up certainly made her look womanly.

Jacques hated cloche hats. *Jodie has lovely hair, why hide it? Her bodice is too revealing, just look at Olivier ogling her. What has she done with her eyes… they're amazing. She does look beautiful… but… well… she looks a bit like a hussy.* As disapproving as Jacques might be, the truth was that he was as turned on as Olivier was.

"What have I done to deserve the two most handsome escorts in all of Paris?" Jodie gave an arm to each man conferring upon each one a most lascivious look; Olivier giving back as good as he got; Jacques turning beet red, looked away.

On the ride to Montmartre Jodie was blabbing away about the famous painters who had eked out an artist's life there: Renoir, Van Gogh, Picasso, Pissarro, Dali… On and on she went, explaining that most of the artists had moved to Montparnasse since Montmartre had become too expensive after the war. The now commercialised district was the venue for cabarets, cafés and famous clubs like the Moulin Rouge, the birthplace of French cancan.

After touring Montmartre up on the hill, they settled for jazz at *Le Grand Duc* in Pigalle. Cutting through the smoke filled air, they found an empty table and ordered drinks. A tall gangly girl was making a beeline for their table. "Ah, Martine, *tu es là.* I've arranged a companion for you Jacques, you lucky man."

Jacques was furious while Martine couldn't believe her good fortune. Jacques was able to recover his good manners as presentations were made. "*Enchanté Mam'selle.*" He kissed the blushing Martine's bony hand.

Jacques and Martine made small talk about his origins but half his attention was on Jodie who was shamelessly flirting with Olivier. He was relieved when the band struck up making conversation impossible.

It had taken Jacques a long time to get used to jazz. At first it was nothing but discordant noise. It was too loud and at times the trumpets sounded like screaming people. But somewhere along the way it got under his skin, like an irritation making him want to move to get rid of the itch; gyrate might be a better word. Jodie had taught him the dance moves on board the ship. Jacques eventually discovered that he had no choice but to let the jazz take over, abandoning himself to the mesmerising sounds.

When jazz slowed down its beat to the woozy sound of the saxophone, Jacques would become spellbound, the music coursing through his body. But on this night at *Le Grand Duc* the beat was fast and Jodie was pulling Olivier to the dance floor giving Martine the courage to do the same with Jacques. Feeling the music taking over his limbs, Jacques was easy to persuade.

As he followed the angular girl to the dance floor in her loose outfit, it occurred to Jacques that she looked something like a walking clothes hanger. Abashed at his unkind thoughts he abandoned himself to the music, all else around him faded leaving only the hypnotising sounds.

The foursome, out of breath, sheens of perspiration on their skin, returned to their table when the band took a break. Olivier ordered a bottle of champagne.

"Jazz seems even more popular here than in America," noted Jodie.

Olivier loved jazz and was well versed on the subject. "You can thank your famous Jim Europe and his Harlem Hellfighters band. They entertained the troops all over France during the war. Your own army refused to live with them because they were Negro, so they fought with us and acquitted themselves bravely. Look around you, many of the Negroes you see here remained after the war, living in Montmartre because they felt more comfortable here. Their music is appreciated and I believe that this is only the beginning for them. There's a move afoot to bring over your most famous jazz musicians and singers."

Jacques noted that Blacks were socializing with Whites, a number of couples being mixed.

"You wouldn't see that in Washington," Jodie had read his thoughts.

The exhausted foursome left for home in the wee hours of the morning. After dropping Martine off at her home, Jacques had to put up with listening to Jodie's flirtatious dalliance with Olivier. *Her behaviour is outrageous; she'll soon have him in her bed.*

Early the next morning the travelers repacked. Feeling headachy and sleep deprived Jacques took charge of his photographic equipment. Jodie looking as fresh as a daisy managed her art supplies and Frank carried their clothing which was greatly reduced to the bare necessities. All their finery would remain with the Marquis until their return.

At breakfast Olivier and Jodie appeared as cool as cucumbers, behaving like siblings. Jacques was sorry he had fallen asleep as his head hit the pillow for he had hoped to monitor any noises coming from Jodie's adjoining room. He studied them closely trying to discern any telltale signs. When Jodie caught him staring she gave him a wink. "What's the matter Jack, the old man can't take the pace while we younger folk can stay up all night."

Jacques quickly looked the other way. She had gotten to him again. It suddenly dawned on him that his relationship with Jodie was much like the one he had with jazz. She had gotten under his skin, a truly annoying irritation. Unlike jazz he had no intention of abandoning himself to the sensation.

The distance to Amiens would be covered by rail. Once in Amiens Frank intended to purchase an old farm truck with a good tarpaulin that would cover their belongings. They expected that many a side trip would necessitate horse-drawn wagons and often times long walks across fields. Hotels would be few and far between. Their best hopes were farm houses where their money would be welcome. The worst scenarios had them sleeping under the tarpaulin.

All three were dressed the same; loose fitting pants tucked into comfortable hiking boots, plain long-sleeved shirts rolled up above the elbow and floppy wide cloth hats. Each had a similar change of clothes and a jacket for cool weather. They also brought along a pair of dressier pants for the men and a plain skirt for Jodie.

As they gathered in the foyer after lunch to say their goodbyes, Jacques was astonished at the change in Jodie. Devoid of all makeup in her hiking clothes, she looked more like the young man he had first thought her to be. *This can't be the same person.*

1922
Reconstruction

Amiens, Arras, Vimy and Ypres were towns that had been closest to the front and each had seen their share of actual battle. Their lovely cathedrals and architectural treasures lay in ruins and a large portion of their populations were rendered homeless.

Frank interviewed the town officials while Jodie spoke with the women and children. Although both had a working knowledge of French they were grateful for Jacques' fluency.

Seen from afar, Jacques did not see much change since he had left Belgium yet a closer look revealed that much had been accomplished. The victory that had been celebrated with much fanfare under the *Arc de triomphe* in Paris was not as ebullient near the front. Their victory had not exactly delivered the land of milk and honey.

It is difficult to rebuild a town without first rebuilding its population. Some sort of spiritual and mental rebuilding had to take place. Families were torn apart waiting for their loved ones to return. For the fortunate, they were found in hospitals and prison camps. For the less fortunate there was some closure in having a body to bury. However, many would wait in vain, not knowing. Volunteers worked untiringly in the lost and found departments set up everywhere. It was necessary for people to mourn their loss.

While thousands waited to reconnect or simply make their way home, the second order of business was the clean-up. Trenches had to be filled in. The towns had to be cleared of rubble while the fields had to be cleared of dead bodies and bits of bodies as well as the detritus of army materials and the more dangerous unexploded munitions. As the promised help of British de-mining experts delayed, the impatient populace undertook much of this themselves, often with deadly consequences.

Even more critical was the reestablishment of transport; railways, roads and canals. There was a need for carts, wagons, horses and motor vehicles. The decimated farms were in need of fowls, other livestock and grains.

Throughout these phases of reconstruction the allies were a team. Help came from all quarters especially the Americas. Labour was imported from Poland, Italy and even China.

Though a visitor's eye would travel naturally to the lofty ruined spires of the Cathedrals and then down to empty streets where homes once stood, by the time the small National Geographic expedition arrived in June of 1922 much of the work outlined above was completed. Neat rows of small pre-fabricated wooden structures housed those who had lost their homes and the actual reconstruction of the towns was underway.

As is often the case, it was the people with the least that proved to be kindest. Ruined farmers struggling to get back on their feet were the first to offer a share of their meagre food supply. They offered a bed where they could and a barn loft when they couldn't. By the time they reached Ypres at the end of June they had had to spend only one night under the stars at the back of the truck. It being a cool night they had huddled under the tarpaulin for warmth.

The work was intense; the conditions were harsh, and most stories were sad. The trio never complained, knowing very well just how fortunate they were to be living across the ocean far from this wreckage. Amid the sadness and sorrow, the discouragement and despondency, Frank and Jodie also found optimism, confidence and a great deal of bullishness to forge ahead toward a brighter future. Jacques found much to photograph that spoke to these two sides of the coin.

As the days stretched into weeks, Jacques and the two Greshams grew quieter as though under a pall. Their conversations were often limited to the revision of the day's work. Try as they might, they found it difficult to embrace the optimism they so desperately wanted to capture for the magazine feature.

It was in Ypres that the Greshams were most appalled. It was in Ypres that Jacques was the most hopeful. They had not seen it two years before. Jacques had.

He knew that he would have to make the trek to the trenches where he had done his best work, where he had broken down, where he had felt his insides being torn out. Jodie wanted to accompany him and Jacques wanted to go alone. He couldn't find the words to explain it to her so they went together.

It was a dreary misty day much like the one he had experienced two years before. Where there had been only mud, there were now some weeds and wild grasses although, if truth be told, the mud had the better of them. However, things looked different enough for Jacques to have a certain difficulty in finding the right spot. Then he saw it. There was no mistaking the dead tree that had not been removed and the tell-tale hump in the earth where the trenches had been filled.

"What's so special about this place?" asked Jodie trudging through the mud.

"It's here that I took the shot that National Geographic liked so much and I need to do an after-shot. It's not going to be easy to find anything to photograph that shows much promise in the future. Everything is as dreary as before."

But, his keen eye did find something. The branch in the ground with the soldiers helmet hanging on it was gone as was the trench. However, the dead tree was recognizable; it was obvious that the mound covered the same trench; and right where the branch with the helmet had been was a patch of weeds with some pink wildflowers.

He positioned the shot exactly as before. He hoped that the clump of flowers done in colour right where the soldier's helmet on the branch had been would speak volumes.

Suddenly, behind the hump of the former trenches, a young boy emerged holding a long piece of wood. He fell to the ground and started crawling on his belly holding the stick like a gun. He aimed, "Bang, bang, bang," he yelled.

Jacques clutched at his heart, fell to his knees... paused... let out a cry... and feigned an exaggerated death rolling unto his back.

The boy got up, his gun now a crutch, he hobbled to the side of his enemy. *"Vous êtes mort monsieur?"*

"Oui, je suis mort," answered Jacques.

The boy giggled. *"Vous parlez drôle, monsieur,* and dead men don't talk."

"What did he just say, I didn't catch his accent?" Jodie enquired.

"He says I talk funny."

"Well, he should hear you in English if he wants to hear funny."

"Bonjour, my little man, what's your name." Jodie crouched down to the boy's eye level.

The boy giggled once more. "You talk funny too. *Je m'appelle Reynald, et vous?"*

Jodie smiled warmly, *"Je m'appelle Jodie.* How old are you?"

The boy pulled back his shoulders and stood at his straightest. *"J'ai neuf ans, et vous?"*

Jodie laughed, "Nine years old... my, my... you are quite grown up." Judging by his small stature she had expected to hear him say that he was six.

"I'm nineteen." Jodie pointed to the stump below his left knee. "What happened to your leg?"

The smile on Reynald's face was replaced by a frown. I was helping to find the mines and... BOOOM!"

Jodie took his small dirty hand in hers. "Where are your mother and father?"

"Papa died in the war. *Mémère* says he's a hero." Reynald managed to look proud.

"Mémère, is that your mother?"

"Non, I live with *Mémère."*

"That's your Grandmother, right?" Jacques had interpreted *Mémère* correctly.

The boy nodded.

"Do you have brothers and sisters?" Jodie persisted.

The boy's lower lip quivered and Jodie regretted the question. "Francine was helping with the mines too and... BOOOM." Tears spilled over making inroads onto the muddy cheeks.

Jodie gently took him into her arms and when the crying stopped, she looked through her pockets and gave the boy some coins. "Take these coins to your *Mémère* and tell her I said that she should buy you something sweet to eat. You're a good boy Reynald."

Reynald wiped his nose with the sleeve of his rag of a shirt, gave Jodie a big smile and hobbled away through the mist toward the ghostly looking ruins of Ypres.

Jodie stood and watched the boy disappear. She hung her head down and when her shoulders started to shake, Jacques went to her.

He took her into his arms, her head barely reaching his heart. Then the sobbing began... loud wails... her whole body shaking with sobs.

Jacques remembered his breakdown in this very place. *What is it with this place?* He tightened his embrace.

The sobbing gradually subsided into crying, then low moans and finally seemed to stop. Jacques held her by the shoulders and pushed her away gently to look into her eyes. The big blue pools were overflowing, lingering tears quietly running down her cheeks.

Jacques was drawn involuntarily, aching to take the plunge. She looked so vulnerable, so sweet, her lips begging to be kissed. Then he remembered the painting, the eye with the open window where the snakes and the little devil lived; he stopped himself. *Oh no, I can't do this. I know I'd regret it. She'll tear me apart.*

Jacques took Jodie by the arm. "Come, we'll find that place where we're to meet with your Dad and have something to drink before he arrives. I'll tell you about my time here two years ago."

Back into town they found the place, not much more than a hole in the wall; they ordered drinks and food.

Once they were served, Jacques opened the conversation. "From the time we reached Amiens you've not been yourself. Then in Arras and Vimy it's gotten worse. You hardly ever talk anymore and you haven't been painting."

"How do you know that I haven't been myself? You really don't know me Jack."

"Well if that's how you want to be then we'll just wait here for your Dad in silence." Jacques sounded exasperated.

"I'm sorry Jack. It's just that… well… I've seen poverty before you know, and shacks and hovels. Much of our travels took place in remote areas lacking in what we call civilization. The funny thing is that the people were generally happy. I grew up playing with village children who often lived in huts. The children usually helped with chores and farming for part of the day and in some places everyone sang as they worked. But then we also had time for play. We played with sticks and stones and makeshift toys of all kinds. We ran about the place screaming with laughter. We genuinely had fun."

"This is so different. The devastation, the ruined homes, the broken families and the endless stories of loss; it's getting to me. It would be one thing if it was all caused by some natural disaster but man did this. It was man against man. The signs are everywhere that man is nothing but a cruel beast."

"I know exactly how you feel Jodie. Those pictures my boss sent to National Geographic were taken two years ago when I took a trip through Belgium after my wife and child died. Things looked even worse then and I hadn't come to grips with the death of Angeline. The weird thing is that I had a complete break down when I reached Ypres in the exact same place where you broke down today and where the young boy cried. I sobbed even louder than you did. It was moments after that I met my friend François and recovered my memory."

"My goodness, the place is haunted." Jodie looked awed.

"I believe so. It's a place where death hangs like a shroud. It just seems to encompass you at first; then it enfolds and imprisons and squeezes your heart until it breaks." Jacques made a wringing motion with his hands.

"Yes, you have it exactly right. I feel much better now though." Jodie did look recovered.

"You needed to let it all out, but I think that you have to try to see the positive from hereon in. It's what the mission is all about. I assure you that things are moving in the right direction."

"I'm glad you were there Jack. I wouldn't have wanted to be all alone. When Mom died, I felt so alone. We were extremely close-knit the three of us. But when I lost her, I also lost Daddy to his grief. He wouldn't even look at me. I learned later that it was because I look so much like my Mom and he couldn't bear it. I was fifteen and my Mom was very open with me, teaching me to be a woman."

"For two years I was so lost. Then something happened three years ago. Auntie Eliza had a conversation with my Dad that went on for hours behind closed doors. I heard my Dad cry. Anyway, whatever was said changed everything. My Dad was back in my life. He tried to explain what he had gone through and asked for my forgiveness."

"I'm glad for you. I have a big family and we're all close and then I have François. We need people." Jacques consoled.

"Whoa, just a minute, I have Daddy and it's all I need. I can't help loving him but I don't want anyone else in my life. It hurts too much when something goes wrong so the best thing is to keep it simple," Jodie affirmed.

"You'll never know what you're missing and I feel sorry for you Jodie."

Jacques could see some tart insulting remark about to make its way out of her mouth when Frank arrived in the nick of time.

"Why so glum... I hear the food's great here." Frank looked like a man who had had a fruitful day so far. "Don't eat too much; we're invited to have dinner with *Monsieur* Brabant and his family, a most interesting councilman who has given me interesting insights and statistics."

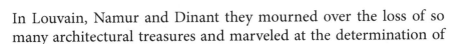

In Louvain, Namur and Dinant they mourned over the loss of so many architectural treasures and marveled at the determination of the people to rebuild their cities and towns to their former glory.

Jacques was enjoying his photography; Frank was gathering copious information; and Jodie had resumed painting.

She managed to capture the sadness of the ruined structures while painting what looked like flowers clinging to the grey walls to convey hope. In the foreground stooped old men walked amidst colourful blobs of children playing.

Jacques peeked over the shoulder of the artist hard at work. "Ah, the sins of the past and the hope for the future; am I right?"

"Well something like that, I suppose." With palette in one hand and paintbrush between her teeth, Jodie used her finger to smudge some of the bright blobs on the canvass.

Jacques was pleased to see her painting again. She was back to her old self and he much preferred the teasing and barbs to the morose silence of her previous weeks.

The Rolands did not enjoy the modern convenience of the telephone but Jacques' letter had told them to expect him in late July to early August. As such, they had been on the lookout for the last couple of weeks when the old pick-up truck rolled down the farm's driveway on an early August evening.

Caroline sounded the alarm and the entire family rushed out. Jodie had been driving and before she could come to a complete stop, Jacques flew out of the passenger seat to be surrounded by the small horde hugging, kissing and laughing.

They all spoke at once. "Philippe, you're so handsome with that moustache… His name is Jacques, remember… Caroline you have a new baby… His name is Paul like his *Papa*… We call him *p'tit* Paul… Ginette is that your little boy… Jacques you've put on weight… it's all muscle Phil unlike that little paunch I see there… Paul you look well… Not as well as you… *Monsieur* Roland it's a pleasure to see you again… likewise… What a big girl you are Geneviève… Youpee, youpee, youpee…"

When the excitement subsided and Jacques felt the last of the slaps on his back, they turned to Frank and Jodie who were standing by the truck smiling broadly, caught up in the exuberance.

"This is Frank and his formidable daughter Jodie." Jacques held his arm out to the pair. "And this is *Monsieur* Roland, his son Paul and his lovely wife Caroline with little Geneviève and *p'tit* Paul, also; Paul's cousin Phil, his wife Ginette and their son…" Jacques paused looking at the tiny boy.

"Yves, his name is Yves." Ginette blushed.

"*Entrez, entrez,* we were about to sit down to eat. There's plenty for everyone. We always cook copious amounts on Sunday."

They did much catching up at the dinner table. After dinner, the conversation turned to the reconstruction of Belgium. The politics revolved around the Flemish and their collaboration with the Germans, the latter having promised them independence after the war. Frank was taking notes having heard the other side of the argument a week earlier.

They regaled Frank and Jodie with stories of the resistance. "We were paranoid about being caught by the Huns. We were so secret that all the time I had known Caroline as a friend of the family; I never knew she was Paul's handler, up to her neck in dangerous missions. I mean, look at her, little innocent mother of two; who would believe," laughed Jacques.

Jodie was listening attentively. She was observing Jacques among his own people. *But he was with them for only three years yet he behaves as though they had been his family all his life.*

Quietly she conveyed this thought to Paul who was sitting beside her. Paul spoke slowly that Jodie might understand his French better. "I cannot imagine what it would be like to lose my memory but it must be devastating because in the process you lose everything, family, friends and country. Without a memory you are nobody. Philli... er... Jacques was adrift. For his own sanity, he built himself a new family and adopted a new country. We were all he had and he became a part of us. The love goes both ways."

And so Jodie hung on to every word that was being said, learning what she could of Jacques' life.

The party finished late. The couch in the main house was offered to Jodie and the one in the cabin was relegated to Frank while Jacques chose to sleep on the porch on this most pleasant summer night.

Jodie was having trouble falling asleep. *They really are like family to Jack. There's no lack of love there... on both sides. He's lived through an awful lot for his 26 years. He fought in the war, he lived through a plane crash, he recovered from his injuries and was saved by this family, he was a member of the resistance, and he lost a wife and child. He also lost his memory... completely... I can't imagine what that was like... like being in a vacuum.*

He must think I'm nothing but a spoilt brat. I don't think he realises just how handsome he is. Does he even know he has the most endearing dimple in his left cheek when he smiles… and he smiled plenty this evening. I really like him but I'm not his kind… we would be bad for each other. I would drive him crazy… it wouldn't last. It would be so good though… for a while.

Out on the porch Jacques was sitting on the steps staring at an almost full moon. He too was unable to sleep. Memories of his life on this farm were swirling in his mind. Mostly, he thought of Angeline. Her features were dimming and he was chastising himself for not bringing her photo. Nevertheless he could easily make out the smile that never failed to warm his heart. She was so tall. A flash of her long legs wrapped around his body made him shiver.

Generally Jacques preferred petite women. *Adèle is petite and so is Jodie… but you can't compare the two. Adèle's a real beauty, so feminine. Not that Jodie can't be feminine… but it's not the same… boldly sexual… more womanly than her nineteen years… and then she switches to looking like an untidy youth. I just can't figure her out. One minute she's really nice to talk to and the next she's insufferable.*

The front door creaked open startling Jacques. "Sorry Jack, I was tip-toeing so as not to wake you but I see that you can't sleep either."

"Too much moonlight, I guess." Jacques shrugged.

"Maybe too much excitement for one night." Jodie judged correctly.

"Maybe… it was just great to see everyone again. Will you just look at this moon!" Jacques marvelled. "Come, sit with me."

Jodie sat beside him. "It's magnificent but I prefer the dark nights when in the countryside; you can see the stars and the planets at their best. Two weeks ago they were amazing. Daddy and I watched for hours picking out our favourite constellations. Mars was there as orange as it could be and as for Betelgeuse, it looked like a veritable ruby. I made a wish on a shooting star."

"And where was I during this star-gazing episode?"

Jodie giggled. "You were in the Land of Nod."

"Do you often stargaze with your Dad at night?"

"Not so much in the city. They just don't shine the same way with all the competing city lights… but we often do when we're out in nature. It was something we did with my Mom. She was an amateur astronomer and carried her star charts everywhere. She showed us where to find all the constellations and the planets. She took me to the observatory to see Jupiter with its moons and its big red spot. The most beautiful was Saturn with its glorious rings circling it."

Jacques was staring at her.

"Why are you staring at me like that?" Dressed in a plain sleeveless cotton nightie, Jodie shivered as a breeze brushed her naked shoulders.

Jacques put his arm around her shoulders to keep her warm. "You never cease to amaze me Jodie Gresham. Why can't you always be like this?"

"Like what?" Jodie was feeling more heat than was necessary from Jacques' friendly embrace.

"Like the nice interesting young lady you can be when you want to, that's what." Jacques smiled, the dimple making Jodie melt.

Jodie removed his arm from around her. "That's it... enough nice... I'm going to sleep."

Jodie was up and through the door in a flash. Jacques groaned. *What a weird person she is!*

The next day they were shown around the farm noting the many improvements, Jacques making sure that all was caught on film. Frank interviewed Paul and Caroline in depth and Jodie played with the children as though she was their age. Later they drove into Couvin so Jacques could show off the picturesque town he had so loved.

Copious amounts of red wine ensured that dinner was as boisterous as it had been the previous evening. Everyone posed for group pictures and promised to stay in touch. Much needed sleep came easy that night, hoping to be well rested for their journey to Rheims departing at first light the next morning.

————◆●◆————

There were three days left in Paris before setting sail from Le Havre homeward bound for New York. The Marquis' were delighted to play host once again looking forward to the discussions detailing the expedition.

Returning to the lap of luxury was a heavenly experience; a hot bath, scented soaps, a proper bed and clean linens. Tired from their travels and with so much to be discussed, the first evening was spent '*en famille*'.

Frank and Jacques spent the better part of the next day planning the National Geographic article while Jodie went shopping for the latest trends with 'auntie' Isabelle. At dinner that evening, to Olivier's delight, Jacques begged off on a proposed night on the town.

First light was breaking when Jacques was awakened by the sound of Jodie's bedroom door closing. At breakfast Frank chided his daughter. "I can't imagine how you young people do it. It was three in the morning when I heard you come in and here you are planning an entire day of sightseeing with Jack. You'll wear yourself out."

Three in the morning? Jacques was doing some calculations. *She didn't get to her room until five... hmmm... where could she have been?*

Jodie kept her word about taking Jacques to the Bois de Boulogne. It promised to be a hot summer day. They left by tram with a large picnic basket in hand. "I don't see why it's going to take a whole day to see a park," commented Jacques.

Jodie laughed, "Well then, you're in for a surprise. The surface area of the Bois de Boulogne is probably much bigger than the little town you come from. It holds a zoo, a horse racing track, restaurants, lakes and... well... lots more."

"Can we go to the zoo then?" Jacques suddenly sounded like an excited little boy.

"We'll make it our first stop." Jodie was amused by Jacques' reaction to the Zoo. Having misjudged the size of the Bois de Boulogne, he practically exhausted his supply of film at the zoo.

By one in the afternoon they were happy to sit in a shady spot by the lake for their picnic lunch. "How can you manage to walk for so long in those pointy shoes with those funny heels?"

"Actually, my feet are killing me. Let's get comfortable." Jodie sat on the blanket, took off her shoes, undid the top buttons of her blouse and rolled up her sleeves.

As she busied herself taking the food from the basket, Jacques followed her example and removed his jacket, undid his top buttons and rolled up his sleeves. "*Oooh*, that's so much better. It's hot and that basket was getting very heavy."

"Imagine for a moment Jack, in this same spot by the lake, Van Gogh or Renoir, paintbrush in hand. They did some of their best work here you know."

"What about you? Wouldn't you like to paint here?"

"Oh, I did, when I was here two summers ago." Jodie tore a piece from the fresh baguette and spread a generous helping of *foie gras* on the soft bread.

"Will you be famous someday?" Jacques was struggling with the cork in the red wine bottle... POP.

Jodie held out her glass and laughed. "Nooooo... never! Well I'm not bad... in fact some say I'm quite good... good enough to hang on a parlour wall but not in a gallery or museum. I've accepted that but it doesn't stop me from enjoying my painting. I'm happiest when I'm painting."

In the heat the melted Brie spread like butter on Jacques' bread. "Well, I know very little about art and my tastes are conservative. I must admit that some of your work confuses me but I find most of your landscapes beautiful even though I prefer paintings that look more like photos."

Jodie leaned her back against the tree trunk. "Be that as it may, my paintings will never be anywhere near as valuable as your photographs. You are the genuine article."

Jacques blushed. The praise made him uncomfortable, especially coming from Jodie. "Thank you. I'm also happiest when I'm lost in the darkroom getting the best out of negatives."

The heat, the food and the escapades of the previous night had their effect and Jodie dozed off. Jacques went for a short stroll along the lake.

Upon his return, he found Jodie stretching and yawning. He sat beside her and without any preamble, he asked, "Are you sleeping with Olivier?"

Jodie sat bolt upright and yelped, "What? How dare you... this is none of your business." She was visibly flustered.

"No denial? What would your father say if he knew?"

"You leave my Dad out of this... and you... Jack Armand... are certainly not my father. You have no right..."

"Whoa, you can get off your high horses. I'm only asking because you're so young and I'm worried about your reputation."

"My reputation... my reputation... you must be some kind of dinosaur living in prehistoric times. What about you? Did you have sex before you were married?" Jodie had recovered and was ready for a debate.

"That's not the same thing."

"Really... and why not, may I ask?"

"It's just not the same for men." Jacques could find no better argument.

"Now there's something I would love you to explain. Are we not doing the same thing... does it not take two to be intimate? It's exactly the same thing."

"Jodie you know that society doesn't see it that way."

"Oh, I know very well... for doing the exact same thing the man is congratulated for proving his manhood while the woman is judged a harlot. I can see no sense in that."

"But Jodie, you could get pregnant... Olivier can't get pregnant."

"I would never have irresponsible sex and what if I did get pregnant? Would it not be Olivier's baby too? Would he not be just as responsible?"

"I can never win with you. Everything you say is true but the fact remains that people don't see it that way and you could get hurt. Could we please change the subject?" Jacques was so sorry he had broached this subject. *Why in heavens name did I ever bring this up? She's right... it really isn't any of my business.*

"I'd be happy to change the subject. I can only surmise that you're jealous." Jodie had a smile that trumpeted 'victory'.

"Jealous! You must be joking!"

"I thought we were changing the subject. Let's pack up; we're off to the horse races."

—◆◆◆—

In contrast to the turbulent interaction between Jacques and Jodie, the ocean crossing was smooth. Frank and Jacques spent most of their time in each other's company putting together their ideas for the article. Frank came to appreciate his determination and commitment to detail.

Watching Jacques fussing over some schematics, he thought; *he's a solid young man... genuine. I wish Jodie would see his worth instead of those empty heads she goes out with. She obviously likes him, otherwise she wouldn't bother annoying him with her taunts... but she's also afraid of him... afraid to get close. My fear is that she'll drive him away.*

At dinner on their last evening aboard ship the conversation revolved around the ballet, *'La Belle au Bois Dormant'*. The Marquis' had invited everyone to the *Palais Garnier* on their last night in Paris to see the performance of 'Sleeping Beauty'.

"It was the most beautiful building I'd ever been in and no photograph can do it justice. No matter which way I turned, it took my breath away." The thought alone of the Opera House could still overwhelm Jacques.

"You said it was your first ballet, what did you think of it?" enquired Frank.

"Our lumberjack probably thought ballet was for sissies," said Jodie unkindly.

"How perceptive of you," Jacques replied sarcastically. "As a matter of fact I did. Lumberjacks wouldn't be caught dead prancing around in tights." He turned to Frank. "I've really grown to like jazz thanks to Jodie but this was something altogether different. It was powerful. The orchestra with those acoustics, the dancing, the emotions... it won't be my last."

"Well, our country mouse is evolving, fancy that." Jodie snickered.

"Kindly excuse me, I need some fresh air. I'm all packed, let me know when we are to depart." Jacques left for a promenade on the deck.

"Jodie, why are you so relentlessly nasty to Jack. You've always been a tease, but this... this is something else... it's not how we raised you. You've gone too far."

"I don't know why... he just annoys me." Jodie looked petulant.

"He annoys you because you don't control him like the usual assortment of bubbleheads you frequent. Jack is a good man, undeserving of this treatment. I know you like him. What are you so afraid of that you push him away in this fashion?" Frank knew he had hit a nerve when he saw his daughter blanch.

"Daddy... please I'd rather not talk about this. I promise to think before I speak from now on. Tomorrow's a long day so I think I'll head for my stateroom. I love you Daddy." Jodie gave her Dad a kiss on his forehead.

The arrival and subsequent train ride to Washington were uneventful. Jacques noticed that Jodie spent her time quietly with her nose in a book.

The following two weeks saw Jacques ensconced in the dark room, emerging only for meetings with the editors for the article. Most nights when he reached Q street, Jodie was either out with her various beaus or hidden in her studio.

They usually came in contact at the breakfast table. Jodie would enquire politely about his work, listen attentively and then turn to her Dad for further conversation. One would think that Jacques would have been relieved at this turn of events but Jodie's civil behaviour puzzled him. He was somewhat miffed. *I must be crazy... imagine being offended because Jodie's stopped offending me! I should be pleased. The truth is that she's ignoring me. I must have done something to displease her. I'm leaving in two days and I really don't want to leave with things this way. I'll try to find some time to have a talk with her.*

The next day Jacques completed his work for the article and made the rounds to say goodbye to the friends he made during his stay. He left National Geographic on excellent terms with the promise of further collaboration.

He arrived early in the afternoon at the Q Street Gresham home with plenty of time to tend to his packing before dinner. Jacques was due to catch an early train bound for New York the next morning and he found himself longing for home. He missed his family and friends and looked forward to recounting his experiences and catching up with all that was new at home.

Dinner was a quiet affair with Frank. "Is Jodie out?" asked Jacques.

"She had some sandwiches sent up to her studio. Apparently she's in a moment of creativity that can't be interrupted."

For all of Frank's many travels, he had never been to Canada. "I sometimes think that Americans believe that there's nothing but a frozen wasteland north of the United States.," Jacques complained.

"That's a shame and I would like to do something about it," replied Frank. "You have represented your country well Jack, and it's given me a desire to visit. I already have an article in mind for your lovely Province of Québec and there could be no better photographer for the job than yourself. I intend to remain in touch with you."

"I would like nothing better. If you'll excuse me, I would like to skip dessert and interrupt your daughter's creative process." As Jacques stood to leave the table, Frank looked at him with raised eyebrows.

Jacques tapped at the studio door and waited. Just as he was about to knock once more, the door opened. There stood the Jodie he first met in dirty coveralls, smudges of paint on her cheek and forehead, a surprised look on her face.

"I'm busy."

Entering the room, Jacques brushed past her. He headed for her easel. As surreal as it was, it was unmistakably the portrait of a lumberjack!

"You have no right, this is private work." Jodie looked cornered... afraid.

Jacques went straight into it. "Why have you been ignoring me these past two weeks? Have I offended you in some way?"

"I can't win can I? Either I'm insulting you or I'm ignoring you. What do you want from me?" Jodie's voice was small.

"I thought we were friends. We've shared many good moments together these past few months. The trip would not have been anywhere near as enjoyable without you. I don't understand why you do it, but I can take the bantering... I'm not made of paper..."

His rant was suddenly cut short when Jodie grabbed his head and brought him down to her pressing her lips on his. Jacques lifted her up; her legs encircled his waist as he returned her kiss. Passions mounted as their tongues explored each other's mouths. With Jodie still in his arms, Jacques walked the two steps to the tall stool by her easel and sat her down, lips still locked in the kiss. It was an inordinately long kiss. Each explored the others body with groping hands. Jacques feeling Jodie's small rounded breasts and she with her hands under his shirt feeling the well-muscled torso.

They were on the point of no return when Jodie broke off the embrace just as suddenly as she had started it. Breathing hard they stared at one another, a puzzled look in Jacques eyes.

"I'm not ready to take the plunge... I hope to be someday... I hope that you won't have forgotten me. You must leave now... right now... go... I promise to be in touch... J a c q u e s." She pronounced his name with a perfect French accent as she pushed him out the room.

Stunned, confused, euphoric, Jacques slowly made his way to his room caressing his lips with his fingertips.

1923-1927
Agathe

Against the backdrop of a universe aeons old, the years slipped by as they are wont to do in the fleeting life span of man.

Adèle's third pregnancy was an easy one except for the first three months of nausea which she always forgot once the good months set in. To Joseph's endless delight, his first son Roger saw the light of day on May 25th, 1923.

It had always been Adèle's plan to space her children some three years apart. It would seem that the fates and her irregular menstruations conspired against this plan. This time the calendar watch seemed to be working as the months rolled by... until an enjoyable night of liquid cheer on Christmas Eve of 1924 was responsible for the couple's irresponsibility and put Adèle in the family way once again.

Young Joseph (Joey) greeted this world on September 15th, 1925. Adèle felt that she now possessed the perfect family; two boys, two girls. Time to stop... but how did one stop?

Four children all under the age of five is more than a handful. Child rearing, cooking and cleaning took up all of Adèle's time. She missed helping Joseph downstairs and meeting people in the store. She longed for the free time she would have once the children were all at school. Five years and then, at the drop of a hat, she could go into Ottawa to the library, the museum, shopping, a luncheon with Mary Labelle. She could do five years… provided she stopped having children.

In late November, Adele had the go ahead from her doctor to resume marital relations. Baby Joey, belly full, was fast asleep at his mother's breast after a late night feed in his parents' bed. Joseph took his son from her arms. Lovingly he caressed and kissed the infant and laid him gently in his bassinette.

Joseph gave his wife a questioning look. So full of hope were his eyes that it made Adèle laugh out loud. "Shh… don't wake Joey. Well?"

Adèle mustered up a serious look. "I'm so sorry Joseph, but the doctor says that there are complications and we should wait another six weeks." No sooner were the words out than she could no longer contain herself and her frown turned to a lascivious smile.

"*Grande taquine*[*], how can you tease a starving man in this fashion?"

"You're starving… well I'm famished. The time is right and the time is safe so what are you going to do about it Joseph Lafleur?"

Joseph loved that his wife was bold in bed. He took her gently knowing that there would still be some soreness after the birth. Adèle loved that her husband delighted in foreplay. It was the difference between making love and having sex.

Afterwards, feeling warm and cuddly Adèle broached the subject she had been mulling over. Any woman worth her salt knew full well that the afterglow was the best time to get what she wanted from her man. "Joseph, I've been thinking."

"Oh, oh, what do you want?" Any man worth his salt understood what was going down.

"I would like to stop having children."

"What! Is this your way of telling me this was our last night sleeping together?" Joseph looked horrified.

Adèle giggled. "*Dieu non*… but… I've never wanted a big family. I was always up front with you on this subject. I have as many as I can handle and although I love our family life… I also want a life for us outside of the children."

Joseph was silent, processing this unexpected discussion.

Adèle continued, "When you add up the four pregnancies, I've spent a whole year throwing up and four months with swollen feet that I can't fit into shoes. I've had enough Joseph."

"I understand and I agree with you, but you have many more childbearing years left. What do you propose we do about it?"

"We could use condoms."

More silence.

"Say something, Joseph."

"Birth control is a mortal sin Adèle."

"But we have no problem abstaining on risky days even though the priests say it's a sin." Adèle was not about to give up.

"You and I have always used our common sense when it comes to what the priests have to say Adèle, you know that. No priest will ever make me believe that God created sex for the sole purpose of creating children. God made man and woman to be one, to love one another. Choosing when to make love and when not to make love kills nothing and harms no one. Condoms, however, kill sperm and that is wrong."

Adèle let out a mournful sigh. "I know."

Joseph continued. "If we did that then we would have to confess. We couldn't even say that it was an accident and that we didn't mean it because condoms are so very premeditated."

"*Tu as raison...* I can't imagine myself going to *Père* Tremblay and confessing the same wilful sin week after week."

Joseph smiled. "Week after week, huh, I like the sound of that."

Adèle smiled back. "Insatiable pervert... could we at least be very careful."

"Have I ever pushed you Adèle? Have you ever made love to me when you didn't want to?"

"Never... I love you more than words can say... now go to sleep."

Careful seemed to be working and a year after Joey's birth Marie-Anne began school. Four more years and her perfect little family would all be at school. Perhaps Adèle could realise her dream of further education. She would have time to do some university courses. Why not?

Joseph and Adèle had carefully researched Marie-Anne's educational options. "I want her to have every advantage in case she should one day decide on a university education. Would you mind if I decided to pursue some of my own goals once the children are all at school?" The longing expression on Adèle's face saddened Joseph.

"Do you sometimes wish you had gone to university instead of marrying me?"

Adèle brightened, "And give up all this... just look at Marie-Anne. She's the most adorable little thing in her uniform holding her lunch pail like it was a trophy."

It was Joseph who drove his daughter to the *Annexe d'Youville* of the *Couvent St. Joseph* on *rue Notre Dame de l'Île*. Adèle had declined to go. "I'm just going to cry and I don't want to upset Marie-Anne. At the moment she's being very brave about the whole thing and I want her to enjoy her first day. In any case I'd have to get Madame Gauthier to babysit so it's better if I stay home. I'll cry anyway as soon as you drive off."

So true; as soon as Joseph drove off with their first-born in their 'new' second-hand Oldsmobile sedan, Adèle had a quiet cry. *It seems like she was born only yesterday and now my baby is starting school. I'll miss her. I couldn't have asked for a more perfect little girl. She's so caring and sweet... already thinking of others at this young age... always ready to help.*

Loud wails from Monique brought Adèle out of her reverie. "What's wrong Baby?"

"*J'pas un bébé*. I want to go to school too. I want to go to school too!" Monique cried louder.

Adèle took her in her arms. "You can go to school soon, it won't be long now. Marie-Anne will be home this afternoon and she'll tell you all about it." Comforted, Monique ran off to play with Roger.

I wonder if my girls will like school and want more after the convent. Things have changed in the last few years and this convent is dedicated to turning out teachers so when Marie-Anne is finished her primary at the Annexe, she won't be relegated to learning nothing but sewing and cooking.

Joseph and Adèle cherished their evenings together after the children were abed for the night. In bed that night they discussed their hopes for their growing children. "Our girls will do well at the convent. I'm impressed with *Soeur* Marie-Thérèse. She seems very modern in her outlook." Joseph had had long discussions with the principal before deciding to enrol his Marie-Anne.

Adèle added her views. "I've done some research on *Soeur* Élizabeth Bruyère, the Grey Nun who founded this convent. We never think of nuns when we speak of the avant garde women who furthered our cause for emancipation. But here was a remarkable woman way ahead of her time. Between the years of 1845 and 1876 she founded many convents on both sides of the Ottawa River, not to mention an orphanage and hospital. She was a true pioneer in the development of the Outaouais Region."

"Perhaps you should have been a nun." Joseph laughed.

"Well, I would have ended up a sapphist... or better still, I would have bedded the chaplain if he was young enough." Adèle had the most wicked look on her face. "Let's play, I'll be the nun and you be the chaplain."

"Come into my confessional, *Soeur* Adèle." Joseph opened his arms.

———◆●◆———

The confession of *Soeur* Adèle and the resulting penance meted out by *Père* Joseph resulted in the birth of Caroline nine months later in June of 1927.

The bedrooms of the large apartment above the store were filling up in a way Adèle had not envisaged. Although the pregnancy had been relatively easy, Adèle was unable to shake the post-delivery 'baby blues' and she found herself unable to cope. Lorraine Turcotte sent her own baby, now fourteen years old to help her big sister. As the baby of her family, Babette had not had the experience of caring for younger siblings. She did help Adèle with the housework but most of the time she was more of a hindrance than a help.

Joseph was close to despair when *tante* Hélène showed up one morning at the store. "Joseph, we need to have a little talk. Let the Help look after the store." They proceeded up the backstairs to the kitchen.

Adèle had just put the baby down to sleep. Businesslike, Hélène took over. "Babette, go look after the children, we need some adult time. Joseph, Adèle, let's sit on the porch."

"What is it, *ma tante* Hélène?" Adèle looked worried.

"Don't look so worried. I have a proposition for you which should help. You know that I work with the orphans when time permits…"

Adèle cut her short. "You're not going to suggest that we adopt a child!"

"*Du calme,* Adèle; let's hear what your aunt has to say." Joseph put his arm around his wife.

"You probably haven't given much thought to women giving birth out of wedlock… well, you wouldn't have reason to… but I would like you to hear me out."

"Go ahead."

"As you well know these women are branded the worst of sinners by the church. They're judged as deviants. Meanwhile our society treats them as social outcasts for what we deem to have been pervert behaviour. Even when the poor thing has suffered rape, it would seem that the fault is with her."

Forgetting her own troubles, Adèle perked up. "It's true, I've never really thought about it but you're right *ma tante,* yet another great injustice that women have to bear."

"Where are you going with this?" asked Joseph.

"Well, from time to time I've helped such women. In particular I'm thinking of Agathe Laroque."

"Laroque… Laroque… hmmm… there's a Laroque farm to the north of the Armand farm… large family… more than a dozen children I believe; any relation?" Joseph was trying to place the name.

"That's the family." Hélène nodded her head. "Isodore Laroque is a horrid man. He's drunk most of the time, beats his wife and children regularly and has them living in a state of abject poverty. *Père* Jacob has reprimanded him on numerous occasions but beyond that no one does anything about it. He has a shotgun and anyone approaching his farm is discouraged from going any further."

"I'd heard that he was a tyrant but I didn't realise how bad it was." Adèle looked horrified. "But what about Agathe?"

"What I'm about to tell you must be held in the strictest of confidence. You must promise."

In unison Joseph and Adèle nodded. "Of course… we promise"

"Agathe arrived on my doorstep some seven months ago, in an appalling state. She was dirty, and when she removed her ragged coat I could see that her clothes were torn and blood was showing through the shirt on her back. She had been beaten badly and it was obvious that she was with child."

"*Oh, Mon Dieu!*" Adèle made the sign of the cross. Joseph tightened his grip around Adèle's shoulders.

"Her drunken father had thrown her out of the house and she hid inside the barn. When Isodore passed out, her mother found her half frozen. She gave her a coat and told her to run to the Armand farm."

"*C'est incroyable,* how can such a beast be allowed to live?" Joseph was incensed.

"Gérard Armand brought her to me. He vowed that he would keep her whereabouts a secret. He used more than a few swear words to assure me that his own gun would keep Isodore off his farm."

"Gérard Armand is a good man," Adèle affirmed.

"Anyway, I fed Agathe and tended to her wounds. After a long scented bath, she had recovered somewhat. For two days the girl refused to speak. Eventually she opened up to me. The child she carried was her father's child."

The couple gasped.

"Agathe was afraid to return home feeling that her father might very well kill her. Ever since she had started showing, he had been beating her and calling her a whore. The poor thing was desperate and didn't know what she would do with herself."

"So what happened in the end?" Joseph had taken his arm away from Adèle and they were now sitting on the edge of their seats.

"I did what I've done with others in the past. I paid her passage to Montréal and arranged for her to be received by the nuns at the *Hospice de la Miséricorde.*"

"*Hospice de la Miséricorde?*" queried Joseph.

"*Pour les filles mères…* women know that's where unwed mothers go to have their babies." Adèle spoke knowingly.

"Sacrifice… I now remember something. Adèle you were unwell that Sunday and didn't come to church. I'd taken the three oldest to *St François de Sales* so they could see their grandparents after church. On our way out, this drunken man completely out of his mind was shouting and ranting that his daughter had been kidnapped by someone in the congregation. He wanted his daughter back. The children were terrified and then some men took him away. That was Isodore Laroque. We didn't have a clue what he was talking about and we dismissed it as the ravings of a demented drunk."

"I remember that Sunday well," said Hélène. "To this day he's clueless as to the whereabouts of his daughter."

"*Ma tante*, what has all of this to do with us?" Adèle looked her aunt in the eye.

"I'm coming to it, be patient. You know I was in Montréal last week... well I took the opportunity to visit Agathe. She gave birth to a healthy baby boy a month ago. Unfortunately she had been under the mistaken impression that she would be keeping her baby. Naturally, both the church and society don't accept that unwed mothers can bring up their children. The child was sent to the *crèche** for adoption and Agathe believes that God has forsaken her. She loves children and she's good with them. At the moment she's working in the laundry at the Hospice."

"How old is Agathe?" Adèle asked what neither had thought of asking before.

"She's just turned sixteen and nothing has gone right in this young girl's life so far. She deserves a chance at happiness. You know as well as I do that she'll be branded when she comes back. Through no fault of her own she'll be seen as a scarlet woman."

"You obviously have come to ask for our help in some way." Joseph was now thinking in practical terms.

"I've come to ask you to help her and help yourselves at the same time."

"What did you have in mind?" Joseph had not yet caught on.

"Adèle you need help, real help. Babette is well-meaning... but... well... you know. Would you take Agathe into your home as sort of maid and nanny? The nun's at the *hospice* tell me that she's hard-working but deeply unhappy."

The couple stared silently at Hélène.

Joseph spoke first. "Could we think about it for a while?"

Adele had already made up her mind but she didn't want to make the decision without Joseph's go-ahead. "*Merci ma tante*, it's a great suggestion and we'll get back to you very soon. Now, how about a cup of tea? You must be thirsty after all that talking."

That night in bed the couple discussed their options. "You want this, I can see it in your eyes," said Joseph.

"I have much to be thankful for Joseph... beautiful healthy children and a loving husband... but... my life is about housework and children seven days a week. I would like to have some time to be downstairs in the store with you, and to be just by myself for a little while to read or maybe go into town. Céline would say that I'm being selfish."

"Come here." Joseph took her into his arm and kissed her forehead. "All I want is for you to be happy. Lately you remind me of myself when I was in the trenches. For months I was like an automaton, going about my duties without thinking or feeling."

"Well I'd hardly compare my duties to the trenches of the war." Adèle smiled.

"Nothing compares to that, I know... but what I meant is that you have been depressed and sad and it hurts me to see you that way."

"Can we afford it?" Adèle looked hopeful.

"You do the books, so you know as well as I do that it would be no problem. Look at you... I haven't seen you really smile for weeks. Let's do it. Agathe can have the small room. The other two large rooms are big enough to hold a bunch more children.... oops.... I didn't mean that... sorry." Adèle hit him over the head with her pillow.

"Joseph what about Agathe's sisters?"

"We can't take them all in, Adèle."

"It's not what I meant silly. It's horrifying to think about what's going on in that home. These are vulnerable children. There must be something that can be done to stop that man."

"The only thing I can see happening is people having a talk with the man. It's his home and he will run it as he sees fit. Let's discuss it with Maurice and Mary Labelle. It's high time our representatives got this issue out in the open."

———•••———

Agathe arrived one week later, a small suitcase in hand. The poor little thing looked more like a young girl of fourteen at most. She was frail… skin and bones might be a better description. Her listless brown hair fell to her shoulders. She was plain looking with sallow skin, thin lips and a long thin nose… but it was the brown eyes a little too close to her nose that broke Adèle's heart. There was no other way to describe them except to say that they were lifeless… dead eyes.

"My three eldest are playing in the back yard. Joey and Caroline are having their afternoon nap so we can take this quiet time to show you where everything is. I'll take you to your room now and you can freshen up. You must be a little tired after your trip from Montréal." Adèle was talking fast, a little nervous because she was unsure what tone was appropriate to address a maid, her first maid.

Agathe kept her eyes down. "*Merci madame.*"

To Adèle's surprise, the frail little thing had boundless energy when it came to housework. She took all of the household chores including the washing and ironing (Adèle hated ironing) away from Adèle leaving her with only the cooking.

The two women shared the childcare… dressing, grooming, bathing, feeding and playing. To Joseph and Adèle's astonishment, Agathe's plain face with the dead eyes came to life when she was with the children. She behaved like a big sister and the children took no time in falling in love with their 'Gagatte', an appellation that would be hers for the rest of her life.

———•••———

Except for her time with the children, it was evident that Agathe was nervous and fearful. She never went further afoot than the park nearby where the children loved to run around. Little by little she opened up to Adèle. From these few confidences Adèle learned that the girl thought herself an unworthy person, she seemed to trust no one and lived in fear that her father would discover her whereabouts.

As such, Agathe refused to cross the Lady Aberdeen Bridge into Pointe-à-Gatineau when the family attended church on Sundays, visiting alternatively with the Lafleur's and then the Turcotte's after Mass. A day in town at the Lafleur's was bad enough but just the thought of an outing to the Turcotte farm sent Agathe crying to her room.

On the first Sunday after Agathe had begun her duties with Joseph and Adèle, it was the Turcotte's turn to host their growing family. Martin who would inherit the farm lived there with his wife and their two children. Yvette, her husband Gilles and their three children had just moved into a newly built cabin on his parents farm while Annette was to be wed the following year to Gaston. Gaston, a former lumberjack, was now employed by the new pulp and paper mill. Luc and Laurent spent the majority of their time in the lumber fields while Babette had her hands full helping her mother run the household.

While the women discussed children and household matters, the men were debating the pros and cons of the gargantuan Canadian International Paper mill newly constructed in Gatineau on the banks of the Ottawa River.

"*C'est trop vite.* The town is growing faster than we can cope with. The houses built by the mill are filling up with too many men tired of the lumber fields. In my opinion there will be brawling, drunkenness and trouble." Louis Turcotte lit his pipe; he had never been comfortable with change.

"*Vous m'insultez, Monsieur* Turcotte." Gaston looked properly offended.

Louis Turcotte realised his faux pas. "Oh, I didn't mean you Gaston. You're a proper young man; hardworking and honest."

Adèle who had been listening in, edged her way to the side of her husband. This was more interesting than diaper rash.

"But that's exactly how I view my fellow workers at the mill." Gaston argued. "Most have worked the lumber fields long enough and are now looking to marry and settle with a family."

"Pointe-à-Gatineau is booming." Joseph, forever the business man gave his opinion. "My father and Robert can't cope with the increased volume of customers. They've hired more help and they'll be opening a new store near the mill within a month or two. Pointe-à-Gatineau has always been Hull's poor neighbour. I predict that it will surpass Hull before long."

"More food is needed and the farmers are also benefitting. We planted our abandoned field by the creek to meet the demand." Gilles agreed with the younger men.

"You can't stop progress but I must admit that I miss the beauty of the Chelsea falls up the Gatineau River." Adèle had a melancholy look.

"But the dam was necessary if the mill was to have enough electricity to operate. Think of all the benefits for the people of the town who like creature comforts, *mon amour.*" Joseph put his arm around Adèle.

Amid these deliberations, Adèle noticed her mother heading for the kitchen to start the dishes. Annette rose to follow her as did Adèle.

The two younger women took their posts to the side of Lorraine, towels in hand. "You seem very quiet, *Maman,* is something wrong?" Annette had always been solicitous of her mother.

Lorraine seemed to be making up her mind whether to speak or not. She took a deep breath and began. "Your *tante* Hélène was here Friday and she told us what you and Joseph have done, Adèle."

"Done? What have we done?" Adèle looked confused.

"Taking in that depraved young girl to look after your children... what was Hélène thinking of... what were you thinking of? What if your children found out what she did when they grew up... what if..."

"*Maman arrête!*" Adèle cut her mother off. "Stop this right now." Annette and her mother jumped at Adèle's sudden outburst.

"You're supposed to be a good Christian woman. Did *Jésus* not forgive *la Magdalene*? Would you have been throwing stones at Our Blessed Virgin Mother when she found herself with child and no husband? Like Mother Mary, Agathe did no wrong. The poor girl was assaulted by her own father. Why are you criticizing her and not her good-for-nothing father? How could you, *Maman*..." Adèle had tears in her eyes.

"Adèle is right, *Maman*." Annette put her arms around her mother. "A woman is raped; the man is admonished; and the woman is branded for life. *C'est pas juste.* As women we can't make it worse, we must support one another."

Tears rolled down Lorraine's cheeks. "*Vous avez raison.* I'm proud of you two. Starting tonight, this poor unfortunate girl will be in my prayers."

———◆●◆———

One night while discussing Agathe's situation Adèle remarked to Joseph, "This poor child is greatly damaged. She believes herself to be nothing but a sinner and she's terrified that her father will return."

Joseph agreed. "Did you notice that she came within two feet of me for the first time yesterday? I always step back when I see that I'm too close to her. It's better to let her decide when it's time to trust me. She's definitely afraid of men... sad."

"She's been such a great help to me and she's fantastic with the children but it's going to take time, patience and kindness before she can come close to being normal again."

Joseph hugged his wife. "It's beginning to work... I can tell that she's warming up to you. The problem is that her father is bound to discover where she is. Our community is too small, too nosy and too gossipy for it not to happen."

Joseph had put his mouth on it. The very next morning, Isodore Laroque showed up at the store somewhat inebriated but too early to be passed out drunk. Shouting, he demanded to see his daughter. He used every swear word known in the French Canadian vernacular. Customers began to walk out and Joseph called the police.

Isodore was still going strong when the police arrived. He greatly resisted his arrest for disturbing the peace making matters worse for himself. As he was dragged out he threatened Joseph. "*Maudit salaud*, I'll be back tomorrow morning and I'm bringing my gun. She better be here waiting for me when I come."

The policeman in charge asked the constable to wait outside with Isodore. He questioned Joseph. "Do you have his daughter?"

"His daughter lives with us. She's our maid," answered Joseph.

"If she's underage, you'll have to let her go with her father," cautioned the policeman.

"You have to understand that there are circumstances, officer. Isodore Laroque beats his wife and children senseless. He practices incest with his children and impregnated his daughter when she was fifteen."

The policeman winced. "We'll let him cool off in the cells this afternoon and we'll have a talk with the coward but the law is the law. Maybe he'll let it go when he sobers up."

Fortuitously, the children had been at the park with their precious Gagatte at the time of the incident. Adèle who had heard the shouting threw herself in Joseph's arms when he reached the top of the stairs in the kitchen. "I'm so scared, what are we going to do?"

Joseph related his conversation with the policeman. "They must be crazy. We can't let her go with that madman."

"Let me think," said Joseph. "If he comes back tomorrow, we can't call the police. If we do, they very well might hand over Agathe to her father. Give me some time, I think I have a plan... not a word of this to Agathe. She might just run away in the middle of the night."

That night Joseph went down to the store to call François. He wanted to be out of Adèle's earshot.

"François, am I right in assuming that you don't work on Saturdays?"

"Yes I'm off tomorrow."

François listened to Joseph's lengthy account of the happenings. They formulated a plan. "I'm calling Jacques Armand as well. We'll both be there tomorrow morning. You can count on us."

Joseph returned upstairs. "What is going on, Joseph Lafleur?"

"Adèle I'm going to have to ask you to trust me. I want you and Agathe to take the children to the playground tomorrow. I want you all out of the house by nine. All will be fine, I promise. Stay there until lunchtime."

Adèle had never seen Joseph this serious before. The softness in his chestnut eyes was gone. She judged correctly that this was not the time to question him. She would trust him but it didn't stop her from being afraid.

Jacques and François arrived shortly after the women and children's departure for the park. François on the lookout, they waited close to an hour before the signal came that Isodore was coming up the street, gun in hand.

Joseph asked his confused clients to kindly vacate the premises as an emergency was forcing him to close for the next couple of hours. At the door he turned the *"OUVERT"* sign over to the side that said *"FERMÉ"*

Isodore Laroque came barreling in, waving his shotgun, without as much as a glance toward Jacques and François. *"Christie'*, do you think a little "CLOSED" sign is going to stop me coming in? Where's my daughter?"

Before he knew what hit him, François had grabbed and twisted the dirty little man's left arm behind his back while Jacques had wrested the shotgun out of his other hand. "Whaaa..." Cutting short any retort, Jacques' clenched fist pummeled his nose... crack... blood spurted out.

His eyes bulging in fear, the smelly alcoholic was lifted off his feet squeezed between the two men, one tall and strong, the other short and strong. They took him in the storeroom away from any possibility of prying eyes, Joseph following with a long kitchen knife in hand.

This is so wrong. On so many levels this is so wrong, thought Joseph. *But God help me, this feels so good.*

A rag was stuffed in Isodore's mouth to stop the infernal screaming. In complete silence, the men went about their work efficiently. Jacques was tying the pervert's hands so tightly behind his back that the rope cut into his wrists. François tied his legs at the knees and ankles just as tightly while Joseph was pulling down his foul-smelling pants and underpants.

François broke the silence. "Who gets the honour to cut off this degenerate's balls?"

"I think it should be me," said Joseph checking the sharpness of the knife's blade with his thumb. "After all, it is my store."

Isodore's eyes looked as though they were about to pop out, muffled screams tearing at this throat.

"I beg to differ," argued François. "I'm the eldest here and as such I should have the privilege to have a go at this deviant."

"Be that as it may, I have the most experience." Jacques was not to be outdone. "It is I who butchered the animals on our farm. It will be expertly done so that this *débauché* would hardly feel a thing."

"But surely that isn't what we want," countered Joseph. "The idea is to make this incestuous pervert suffer. I believe that slow tearing cuts would have the desired effect."

"I have a better idea," said François. "Why don't we cut off his prick? Doesn't it say that somewhere in the Bible? Something about if your eye offends you, pluck it out and if your arm offends you, cut it off. It seems to me that the offending member here is the prick."

Involuntarily Isodore peed and fainted. They pulled him up and slapped his face till he came to.

"Now look at the mess you've made. You're no better than a baby. You should think about wearing diapers." Jacques turned to his accomplices. "I think that cutting off both his prick and his balls would be the best solution. One would make sure that the coward never screws another child and the other would make sure that he can't impregnate any child ever again. Joseph, you're quite right, the store is yours and he did threaten you so the honour is yours."

"It's most kind of you and I pride myself in being a fair-minded man. I get the prick, you get one ball and you take the other François. I go first." Joseph took his knife to the poor devil's penis.

This time his bowels loosened before he fainted.

When Isodore came to, his hands and feet were free. He immediately looked down at his crotch to find that all was still intact.

François barked at the shaking man. "Take this rag and clean up your mess. NOW!"

Isodore started to cry like a baby and did as he was told.

Of the three, François had the most intimidating voice and he now addressed Isodore while the other two breathing down his neck held him down.

"We've decided that you aren't worth the trouble. You keep fainting like an ailing woman and we need you awake while we do the cutting. We're going to let you off with a warning this time... but... mark my words... if you ever come back here again... if you ever come near Agathe... if we ever hear of any more of your cowardly, incestuous, perverse behaviour... we won't care whether you're awake or aware... we <u>will</u> cut off your balls!"

"Get out of my store, pervert, before we change our minds." It was Joseph's turn to speak with authority. "Don't look for your gun. We're taking it to the police. When we told them what you've done they agreed to let us handle the matter so you won't be getting any help from them. Now, GET OUT!"

Pulling at his pants Isodore scrambled out as best he could.

At noon Adele entered her parlour with Caroline in her arms; the brood following with Agathe. Sitting comfortably were three slightly inebriated men, a half empty bottle on the coffee table. "Why is the store closed? Jacques, François, how nice to see you, but what's happening here, will someone tell me?"

The three men looked at one another grinning from ear to ear.

"Well... stop smirking and say something. Did Isodore Laroque turn up?"

Joseph spoke up to the sounds of muffled laughter coming from Jacques and François. "Let's just say that the problem has been dealt with. We shall not be mentioning his name in this house again."

1922-1923
American Visitors

Jacques returned to his beloved Ottawa Valley in time for the vibrant display of autumn leaves. It was good to be among family and friends again and especially good to be speaking French. Though his accented English was fluent, the French came easier, the love talk more expressive, the swear words more satisfying.

His career as a photographer had taken off. Jacques became a free-lancer and as such he worked for Mr. Jamis on contract basis. It was impossible to commit to full time employment as newspapers vied for his photographs. He submitted work to 'Le Devoir' and 'La Presse' in Montréal as well as the 'Ottawa Citizen' and the 'Globe' in Toronto. The proposed book for his war pictures finally went to press. It was received with moderate success.

Jacques was busy and contented with his lot. He was able to afford himself an apartment on St Patrick Street near the ByWard Market and paid for indoor plumbing at the family farm as a Christmas present for his mother. He avoided some of the *soirées* at the Labelles when he could, preferring the company of family and close friends such as François and Shirley. He resumed his ice-hockey and attended the cinema frequently.

He did keep in touch with Frank and Jodie on a regular basis. She had written first and he had agonized over his reply due to his lack in writing skills. In the end he roped in Shirley for help. "The letter must be entirely yours," she had told him. "You tell me what you want to say and I'll write it down correctly but then you must do your own copy in your own handwriting."

Jacques never showed the letters he received from Jodie, so Shirley was getting a one-sided conversation. It was enough for her to comment to François, "I think that there's something going on there with this Jodie girl."

"What does he say that makes you say that?"

"Well Jacques doesn't actually say anything compromising but I get the impression from his answers that she does." Shirley looked perplexed.

"That's not much to go on, is it? In any case Jacques has never spoken to me about Jodie in that way. I get the impression that she's a spoilt brat and can be quite annoying." François was dismissive.

"Hmm… I don't know but something tells me that there's more to it than that."

In the late summer of 1923 Jacques received welcome news from Frank.

Hello Jack,

I've got the go-ahead for an article about your neck of the woods. In a nutshell, we want to take in the wilds of northern Quebec, the logging industry and the French Canadian culture. NG agrees that you would be the best person for a guide come photographer.

Jodie and I would do a stint in autumn, one in the dead of winter and finally in spring for the log drive down the river. This is only a heads up. You should be hearing from me with the final details before long. In the meantime I would welcome your ideas on a preliminary itinerary.

All is well here in Washington. I shall wait to see you in person to relate our trip to Yosemite Park. You will want to hear all about Ansel Adams' photographs.

Jodie sends her regards,

Sincerely,
Frank Gresham.

Jacques had been expecting such a letter and had already given much thought to a proposed itinerary. He felt that it would be best to arrive by late September in time for the autumn leaves. They would camp in the Gatineau Hills and make their way up the Gatineau River by train stopping at Wakefield for a short stay and on to Maniwaki to witness the preparatory activities for the winter logging season.

In contrast to the wilds of Gatineau, a proper visit of Ottawa would showcase Canada as a civilized nation contrary to the American vision of a frozen wilderness. For the second trip, the felling of the trees in winter would be interesting as would the log drive down the river in Spring for the final stint. He would arrange an invitation to the wedding of Joseph's younger sister Lucille in April which would provide the perfect setting for Frank to study the French Canadian culture and cuisine.

With the ever-present help of Shirley, Jacques transmitted this information to Frank along with his recommendation that they stay at the Château Laurier for their stay in Ottawa. "It will be your only opportunity for luxury as we'll be roughing it for most of your stay in Canada," Jacques had written.

The reply from Frank had given Jacques barely ten days to prepare for their arrival date on Friday, the 21st of September.

For reasons Jacques did not want to fathom, he worried about the reaction of his family and friends to Jodie. He decided that it was best to prepare them. The next evening at François and Shirley's dinner table he broached the subject.

"I'm looking forward for you to meet my American friends," he began. "They've traveled the ends of the earth and have interesting stories to tell. You'll find that Frank is a regular salt of the earth type of man."

"And what about Jodie?" Shirley did not waste time in giving Jacques the opening he was looking for.

"Well, you may find that Jodie takes a little bit of getting used to."

"In what way?" Shirley was finally going to get some information about this mysterious girl who had been writing to Jacques.

"Well, she's an artist." Jacques was searching for a way to describe Jodie.

"So?" It would seem that Shirley would have to pull teeth.

"Artists can sometimes be a little... different."

"Does she have horns and a pointed tail?" Shirley was getting impatient.

"Shirley... really... leave the poor man alone. We'll meet this Jodie soon enough." François chastised his wife.

"Well, he started it and now I'm curious."

Jacques decided to have another go at it. "It's just that Jodie can be a little irreverent at times... brash... bold... even brazen. She dresses like a messy boy one day and a shameless woman the next. She can be out dancing until the wee hours of the morning. The truth is that Jodie is completely spoilt and at times without any manners. She says whatever she thinks and can be most insulting."

Jacques had never meant to say all of these things but once he got started, it just spilled out and he couldn't stop himself. Now he sat silent with his head down, wondering what had possessed him.

Shocked by the unexpected outburst, it took a few moments for Shirley to recover. "Jesus, Mary and Joseph, why ever would you want anything to do with such a woman?"

Chagrined at his disloyalty to Jodie, Jacques started to recant. "I'm sorry, Shirley, I think that I've been unfair to Jodie. It's true that she can be all of the things I said but she also has a very good side. I really shouldn't have said anything and you'll have to judge for yourselves. Could we please leave it at that and change the subject."

Shirley gave François a knowing smile that said she had been right to think that there was something going on there.

———◆◆◆———

Jacques knew that he had to warn his religiously ultra conservative parents about the Greshams but he wasn't about to make the same mistakes he made with François and Shirley.

He had lunch at the farm the Sunday before the arrival of Frank and his daughter. "*Maman,* my friends arrive on Friday. They were very kind to me in Washington and I was hoping that you could invite them here for lunch next Sunday for some of your wonderful cooking."

"*Les Américains, mon Dieu,* I wouldn't know what to serve these people." Jeanne Armand had a panicked look in her eyes.

"*Tabernacle*, Jeanne, they're just people like anyone else. You're a good cook and if it's good enough for us, it's good enough for them." Gérard Armand was not one to fawn over anyone.

"*Papa's* right and they just want to sample what we eat in Québec so your *tourtière* and some *boudin'* would be exactly the kind of dishes they probably have never tasted."

"I don't think that we'll meet at church because they're Protestant so I'll drive them up myself. And… please… try not to look shocked at the way the young modern people dress nowadays in the United States. They're nice people and they speak enough French to get along but I think that our accent will be difficult for them to understand us."

"*C'est assez*, stop it Jacques." His *Papa* spoke gruffly. "What do you think we are, cave men? We know how to behave in front of company. I've never seen you so nervous."

Jacques stared at his *Papa* for a moment and then began to laugh. "*Mais oui, excusez-moi!* It's just that they took me in and treated me like family and I want to be able to do the same with them."

At bedtime Jeanne confided in her husband. "What kind of people do you think he's mixed up with?"

"Well they go on National Geographic missions so they're probably scientific types who don't believe in God. The girl probably wears dresses that leave her half naked. Whatever they're like, we won't forget our manners and the sooner they leave the better."

"Do you think that our Jacques will become like them? I don't think he goes to church at Notre Dame as often as he says he does." Jeanne looked worried.

"We brought him up well, don't worry. Just go to sleep."

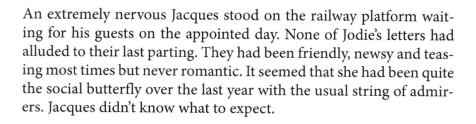

An extremely nervous Jacques stood on the railway platform waiting for his guests on the appointed day. None of Jodie's letters had alluded to their last parting. They had been friendly, newsy and teasing most times but never romantic. It seemed that she had been quite the social butterfly over the last year with the usual string of admirers. Jacques didn't know what to expect.

The train lumbered in, the engine shrouded in misty steam, hissing and screeching to a slow halt. In a flash, crowds of people filled the platform. A head above most, Jacques craned his neck trying to single out his party when he heard the familiar voice coming from behind.

"Yoo hoo, Jack, over here!" Jodie was waving energetically, a happy smile lighting her face. She ran to him, propelled her small frame into his arms for a hug, kissed him on both cheeks and stepped back. "Well, you big galoot, still as ugly as ever, I see."

Jacques laughed. "And I can see that you've lost none of your usual charm and graces. Where's Frank?"

"Come this way. He's looking after the luggage. I swear we've brought the whole of Washington in our trunks. We're all set for camping, partying and every eventuality. We'll have to arrange transport for all this stuff; how far is this famous hotel of yours?"

"Just across the street; so you see I've arranged nothing but the best for my American friends." As they reached Frank, the two men hugged slapping each other heartily on the back.

Having arranged for delivery of the luggage to the Château Laurier, the Americans took in their surroundings as the three friends walked through the massive train station. "Wow, maybe you guys don't live in igloos after all," Jodie marvelled.

Jacques' heart swelled with pride as they exited the palatial Union Station looking across the street with the parliament buildings to their left and the magnificent Château Laurier directly before them. Father and daughter were silent until they entered into the hotel's lobby. "Oh my, this is so very grand. You did it Jack, we're flummoxed." Jodie adopted an awed tone.

Frank laughed. "Forgive us Jack. It isn't as though we haven't been anywhere grand before. You of all people know that very well. It's just that we're not accustomed to thinking of Canada in this way. In fact we're not accustomed to thinking about Canada in any way. We're going to change that with this article. Keep bringing it on Jack."

Once they were checked in, they agreed to meet for dinner later at the hotel for a briefing of the proposed visit.

At the dinner table Jacques was just as curious as his guests having never gone beyond the lobby of the hotel before. He seemed somewhat uncomfortable. "Stop fidgeting Jack. I know you hate being in a tuxedo but you're in your own backyard now." Jodie felt his discomfort.

"How well you know me. This dining room is too rich for my taste. I am after all just a lumberjack." Jack tried to make light of it but essentially he was speaking the truth.

"For tomorrow, I've arranged a private tour of the parliament buildings with one of our Ministers who's a friend of mine and we shall be dining at his home afterwards in Hull across the river in Québec."

"Well... lah... dee... daah... we are connected. All this time you've been hiding this sophisticated side of yourself and I thought you came from some backward little town."

Frank admonished his daughter. "Jodie, I thought we had agreed you would leave this childish behaviour of yours behind."

"Sorry, Jack."

"No, Jodie's quite right. I am from a backward little town which you'll see on Sunday when we have lunch at the farm where I grew up. The border between Ontario and Québec runs down the river. Tomorrow as we explore Parliament Hill, you'll see the town of Hull to the north across the river. A bit further to the north east is the Gatineau River flowing into the Ottawa River."

"Pointe-à-Gatineau, the town near the farm where I'm from, is on the point where the Gatineau and Ottawa Rivers meet. It's not far and I guarantee that it is indeed very conservative. Most people there have never travelled, at least no further than Montréal. Everyone obeys the parish priest and the parish is mostly made up of lumber-jacks, farmers and mill workers."

"Daddy's right. You know I love villages and the countryside. I never meant to call it backwards and meeting your family will be the highlight of this trip." Jodie's tone was sincerely apologetic. "Will we attend church with everyone in the village?"

"Wellll... I didn't think you'd want to attend Mass, but we can if you want to."

"I think that an article depicting French Canadian culture would be severely lacking in something if we didn't bring in the Church." Frank interjected.

The explorers had just finalised plans for the expedition up the Gatineau to Maniwaki as the brandy arrived. Jacques reached inside his jacket. "I've brought you a map of our region. You can study it before our tour begins tomorrow."

"Do you live far from here?" Frank enquired.

"It's only a short walk from here. I've put off buying a motor vehicle because I'm in the centre of town, a stone's throw from everything and the trams run regularly." Jacques chuckled. "My friend François says I'm an old fuddy-duddy and believes that I'll never attract the girls until I get myself a sporty automobile."

Jodie smiled. "Is that the famous François who found you in Ypres and gave you back your memory? Will we meet him?"

"Of course you will. I've arranged for you to meet everyone but you have to promise to be on your best behaviour." His laugh made a joke of it but the pleading look in his eyes belied it.

Father and daughter were visibly tired after their long journey yet they insisted on accompanying Jacques to the lobby for the 'goodbyes', hugs and 'see you tomorrows'.

To Jacques' pleasant surprise, the Honorable Maurice Labelle himself turned up for the tour of the parliament buildings. The tour was lively as well as informative and Frank's pertinent questions were answered intelligently. The tour included a walk along Parliament Hill with the history of the locks of the Rideau Canal running between the parliament buildings and the Château Laurier.

After a light lunch in the ByWard Market, Jacques left the pair to do a bit of shopping before what Jodie termed; 'her preparation for an evening of hobnobbing with Ottawa's high society'. "François and Shirley will be passing by for you at half past six. I'm afraid that it'll be a tight squeeze for the three of us in the back."

"Oh joy, I get to cuddle in the back seat with the handsome lumberjack." Jodie's words dripped with sarcasm.

"Not a chance, the two of you are more likely to scratch out each other's eyes. I shall make sure that I'm sitting between you two children." Frank's smile was heard in his voice.

At the appointed hour, the three Canadians sat in the motorcar at the entrance of the Château Laurier awaiting the Americans. "I can't wait to meet this creature," Shirley exclaimed. She had barely finished the sentence when Jacques heard the intake of her gasp.

Whatever expectations had held Shirley's imagination, she was not disappointed. The petite woman was garbed in a most revealing shimmering silk dress tiered in glistening frills. Waistless and loose the material flounced about at her every move. Jodie's shoulders were bare and the V went deep between her small breasts, her long pearl necklace swaying as she walked.

Approaching the motorcar, Jodie pulled an intricate feathered shawl across her shoulders that matched the feathery contraption serving as ornamentation in her short, glossy blonde curls. Closer up Shirley admired the depth of the blue in her eyes and marvelled at Jodie's ability to apply such elaborate makeup. Then of course there was the incongruity of the heavily bearded man who accompanied her, looking as though he had just stepped off an archaeological dig despite his splendid evening suit.

The three friends got out of the car and Jacques made the presentations.

"My dear you look like you just stepped off the cover of Vogue Magazine. I don't think that I could ever be bold enough to paint my lips so red." The down to earth Shirley had spoken in a good natured way.

Before François could be introduced he gave Jacques 'the look', while Jacques gave back the most innocent of looks.

The soirée at Maurice and Mary's home was a lively affair with some twenty in attendance. Judging by the elaborate dress of the women who came close to competing with Jodie, this was indeed a 'high society' do. Jacques was relieved to see Joseph and Adèle enter the large drawing room.

Jacques could not deny his attraction to Jodie's alluring style but Adèle was the picture of feminine loveliness. Her appearance contrasted sharply with the heavily made up, bare-shouldered women. Her dress was satiny with beautiful bouffant sleeves. She wore just enough makeup to enhance her natural beauty. She had never cut her hair and it was now tied in the habitual loose bun at her nape.

The bun was laced with sparkles while curly wisps of the raven hair framed her face, her black eyes sparkling with intelligence.

Jacques was proud to introduce Jodie to Adèle because it was time people saw him with a woman by his side. He was also proud of Adèle and was glad to introduce her to Frank and Jodie. The two perceptive women noticed something in Jacques' voice when the introductions were made not knowing that Jacques had suddenly pictured himself untying the bun, loosening the hair and seeing it spill over crisp white pillows.

Banishing the thought he quickly turned to Joseph to introduce his American friends.

Everyone enjoyed reading the National Geographic and everyone had suggestions for the Canadian article. Frank and Jodie were well received and mingled beautifully.

During a quiet moment Jacques sat beside Adèle. "Roger must be a few months old by now. Is it very different having a little boy?" The two former lovers spoke of mundane matters enjoying each other's presence. Not far away, Jodie was espying Jacques' behaviour as he conversed with Adèle. *Hmmm... there's something there... I just can't put my finger on it...*

"What about you Jacques? Jodie's a beautiful woman, are you two an item?" Did Adèle's voice hold a hint of jealousy? *She's way too worldly for Jacques, he'll get hurt again...*

"*Mon dieu, jamais!* She's the most annoying brat you could every want to know." Jacques was sorry at his vehement tone.

"Ah... I see...," said Adèle, a knowing smile on her face.

"What do you see... there's nothing to see." Jacques was getting flustered and Adèle burst out laughing.

"What was it Shakespeare said? Ah yes... me thinks you doth protest too much."

The next day Jacques borrowed François' automobile for the trip to Point-à-Gatineau. He arrived at the hotel with some trepidation, wondering at Jodie's chosen outfit for Mass and the subsequent lunch at the farm.

He was greatly relieved to see Jodie in a tan skirt of appropriate length and a lacy long-sleeved blouse. Feeling the autumn nip in the air she donned the matching jacket which she had been carrying on her arm. The only allowance to frivolity was her big wide-brimmed hat worn low down to her eyes with a silk flower arrangement atop. She looked terribly young when she was devoid of makeup; almost vulnerable if such a thing were possible with Jodie.

As Jacques held the back door open he was staring. "You surprise me at times, Jodie Gresham."

Jodie sat herself down, pulling on a pair of tan gloves. "I can't possibly imagine what you might be alluding to Jack Armand."

Across the Alexandra Bridge Jacques parked the car in just the right spot across the Ottawa River for a view of Parliament Hill and its surroundings. Blue skies and well established autumn colours were reflected in the river. Each took turns taking a photo of the other two with the picturesque backdrop.

Their late entrance into the St François de Sales Church caused a small fuss as all eyes turned to the latecomers. "*Les Américains!*" One loud whisper was heard. "Shh...," hissed another. Although Jacques was seldom seen at this church since his return from war, everyone recognized him and everyone knew his business.

They settled a few pews behind his family who were craning their necks with surprised looks on their faces. There had been no time to warn them of their attendance at Mass, the Armands having no telephone.

Jacques was pleased when *Père* Tremblay climbed to the pulpit. The Greshams listened attentively to the homily outlining the depths of God's love towards man. Although the accent was unfamiliar to them and the priest spoke somewhat faster than they would have liked, the pair understood the gist of the sermon.

Afterwards during the usual social mingling outdoors, Jacques presented his friends to his family; his parents, Gérard and Jeanne Armand; his brother Albert and his wife Lise, a toddler pulling at her skirt, a baby in her arms and another one visibly on the way; his brother Charles and his fiancée Albertine; his brother David who looked sickly; and finally the two younger ones, Guy and Martine.

"Pleased to meet you... how do you do..." and "*enchanté*" was heard all around.

Jodie tried out her best French. "*Quelle belle famille!* And you Martine tell me what it's like to have five older brothers. Do they tease you all the time or do they spoil you?"

Martine looked shy. "They do both *Mam'selle.* How many brothers do you have?"

"I have no brothers and no sisters. I'm an only child."

Both Guy and Martine spoke together. "Wow!"

"No one... not even one..." Guy was incredulous.

"It must be lonely." Martine looked sad.

Jodie laughed to show that she was far from sad. "I have lots of friends and a wonderful *Papa.*"

Gérard began to usher his family to the newly acquired truck Jacques had helped finance. "*Allons... allons...,* Maman wants to make sure that things are ready at the farm."

As they departed, Jeanne whispered to her husband. "Just exactly what was Jacques trying to tell us about this Jodie girl? She seems normal enough."

Jacques escorted his party to another knot of people. Frank and Jodie immediately recognized Joseph and Adèle. As they approached, a small girl hid behind Adèle's skirt. Joseph was holding a smaller girl in his arms while Adèle held a baby. A number of adults were clustered around them.

"*Salut mon ami!*" Jacques took Joseph's hand and kissed Adèle on both cheeks.

The Greshams added their greetings and Joseph undertook the long introductions to his family.

"Lucille is the one getting married in April and we understand that you would like to cover a good French Canadian wedding. You are most cordially welcome and we look forward to receiving you." Rose Lafleur spoke in her best English and Frank thanked her profusely.

Meanwhile, Jodie had cajoled Marie-Anne from behind her mother's skirt and had her giggling in no time. When she turned her attention to the girl in Joseph's arms, she exclaimed, "What a beauty! Just look at those eyes Daddy!"

Frank admired the little girl. "She's a beauty indeed! Jack, I think that this little one rivals you in the green eye department and

I predict many beaus in her future. You'll need to keep a keen eye on her, Joseph, my friend."

Jodie noticed that Adèle was blushing deeply as was Jacques. She also noticed a number of young ladies looking intently at Jacques and some of these looks could even go so far as to be described as 'ravenous'. Jacques for his part seemed oblivious to it all.

Adèle was feeling uneasy. *She's so pretty and stylish. She's traveled the world and experienced things way beyond her age... way beyond anything I'll ever experience. I must look so dowdy compared to her. No wonder Jacques seems smitten even though he denies it.*

Having stretched out the socialising, Jacques now drove slowly to the farm wanting to give his mother ample time to prepare.

"I found the priest's sermon to be inspiring," commented Frank.

"Not to mention just how handsome he was. He had all the women spellbound." Jodie let out a wistful sigh.

"You were lucky to have *Père* Tremblay; our parish priest is an older man by the name of *Père* Jacob. He would have preached hell, fire and brimstone or else a sermon on the evils of sex. It would have been a better representation of the usual fare in our Catholic churches throughout Québec... and not as pleasant a sight for your salacious eyes Jodie."

"So... you grew up here. Everyone seems to know everyone. Did you always know Joseph and Adèle?" Jodie spoke nonchalantly.

"Yes we were all friends. François has always been my best friend and he's Adèle's older brother. Our farms are adjacent so we all played together as children. Later François and I worked in the lumber fields together and then... well... you know the story of our wartime together. Joseph worked at his father's general store close to the church so we weren't as close to him but he's a good chap, a bit weird at times but when he married Adèle, he became family."

"In what way is Joseph weird?" Jodie's curiosity was piqued.

"Well... actually you would probably enjoy chatting with him at length. He reads anything and everything and he has strong notions about women's rights, science and politics. Adèle's the same way so they're well suited I guess. I must admit that I'm usually lost when they all get going with Maurice and Mary Labelle."

"How is it that you speak English so well, Jack, and none of your family do? Isn't most of Québec French speaking?" Frank leaned in from the back seat to ask his question.

"Most of the Province is French speaking but in Montréal many speak English if they want to do business and here in Hull and Point-à-Gatineau, being so close to our capital, most of the townspeople can speak English more or less, but it's not so common among the farmers. I was in the lumber fields from the time I was thirteen and that's where I learned my English." Jacques recognised that Frank was in his fact-finding mode.

Lunch at the farm was a crowded noisy affair. Jeanne Armand had outdone herself. There was a nourishing *soupe aux gourganes*; the pastry on the *tourtière* was flaky; the *boudin* was well spiced; the *cretons* were garlicky; and the sugar pie was scrumptious.

Frank and Jodie ate it all up, even when it was explained that *boudin* was blood pudding wrapped up in pig's intestines. They had eaten weirder things in their travels.

The Armands wanted to know about Washington and once their initial shyness disappeared, the questions were flying. Jodie was taken in with the three grandchildren and Martine was taken with Jodie.

"*Mama* thinks that Jacques should get married and give her some more grandchildren. He was supposed to marry Adèle but then she married Joseph when we thought that Jacques was dead. *C'est bien*, Joseph is a nice man. Are you going to marry Jacques then?" Martine had not yet acquired the niceties of conversations with strangers.

"Martine!... " Lise stopped the girl before she could go any further. "We don't ask such questions and I'm sure *Mam'selle* Jodie isn't interested in any of our past history."

"Oh, but I'm very interested Martine. Jack is a good friend but I don't want to marry anybody."

Both Lise and Martine looked incredulous but it was Martine who spoke. "*Jamais*... you never want to get married? But you won't have any children... and doesn't God say you have to get married and have children?"

"Well you see I'm going to be traveling with my *Papa* all over the world so I won't have time for a family."

Jacques came to Jodie's rescue. "I believe that Frank has learned everything he wants to know about the hardships of farming in the north. My father is passionate about what he calls 'his piece of God's earth'. I can see that Martine is giving you the third degree but it's time to get this motorcar back to François."

Saying goodbye was a lengthy affair, so many hands to shake, cheeks to kiss not forgetting the many hugs and parting words for one and all.

—◆◆◆—

Monday was devoted to sightseeing. The day began with a visit at Mr. Jamis' studio. "It was I who sent the war pictures to National Geographic that landed Jacques his assignment with you last year," boasted Mr. Jamis.

The touring began in earnest when Jacques took the Americans further south along the Rideau Canal; showing them the Museum of Natural History without actually visiting it; going back north along the other side of the canal they visited the University of Ottawa; then a little further to the east they travelled north along the actual Rideau River to its eventual falls tumbling into the Ottawa River below.

The view from that vantage point explained the popularity of the area for a settlement. Jacques explained that you could canoe northwest along the Ottawa River leading to waterways that led to the Great Lakes while canoeing southward led to the mighty St. Lawrence River and on to the Atlantic. Across via the Gatineau River one could reach the northern wilds of Québec while the Rideau River on this side meandered south-westward.

On the east side of the Rideau River they took a tour through Rockliffe Park, culminating with a visit of the magnificent grounds at Rideau Hall, the Governor General's residence.

With the help of Joseph and Adèle, Jacques had prepared well for this tour and was able to answer knowledgeably the Americans' many questions. Frank was surprised to learn that despite the Indians' millenia of travel and habitation along this network of waterways, the Europeans did not settle here until the early 1800's even though they had explored and hunted the area and beyond for furs since the early 1600's.

Shirley was cooking for eight that evening as it was their turn to receive Jacques' friends. She had extended a long overdue invitation to *tante* Hélène and Adèle had surprisingly begged for an invitation as she was taken with Jodie and wanted to get to know her better.

Jacques had informed Frank and Jodie that the evening would be a very informal affair as they were visiting family and friends in a modest setting. They took the public transport to Eastview, François having promised them a ride back that night.

Once again Jodie had dressed appropriately looking so young giving the mistaken impression of modesty. She was in good spirits and delighted to be riding the street car. Across the Rideau into the Eastview district, Frank noted the modesty of the homes, many of them wooden structures. Jacques had told him that although most people spoke English in the Capital, this area housed the largest French speaking population, most of them working class folk.

Aromatic smells of lamb cooking in rosemary greeted them as soon as the door opened. "*Mmm... mmm...* what a lovely smell, I'm hungry already." Jodie kissed François on both cheeks. "Where's Shirley?"

"It's the boys bath time. They'll be out shortly. They love company. Kisses and goodnights to all the aunties and uncles allow them to delay their bedtime."

"*Salut François,* thanks for inviting us." Jacques shook his friend's hand and Frank followed suit.

"*Entrez, entrez,* you already know Joseph and Adèle but I want you to meet our very favourite aunt, *ma tante* Hélène." François proceeded to make the introductions.

Before he could finish two little boys smelling of soap came bounding in, straight onto *tante* Hélène's lap. Shirley was right behind them. Breathless and laughing she addressed Fank and Jodie. "I'm afraid that you're in for a good old Irish stew, none of that fancy stuff you've been eating at the Château." Shirley sounded humble but she was confident that her stew would make the grade.

Shirley made the rounds to greet her guests. François addressed the boys in French. "David, Patrick, kiss *ma tante* Hélène goodnight now and come meet our new friends. This is Jodie and this is Frank. David looked awed as Jodie bent down to kiss him. *"Tu es une belle mam'selle!"*

Jodie smiled broadly. *"Oh merci.* You will go far in life with that line young man."

When the boys had done the rounds... twice in some cases... François took them in for their bedtime. Adèle motioned to Jodie to come sit by her side. Frank found an empty chair next to Hélène.

Everyone had a glass in hand except for the new arrivals. Shirley offered them gin or a sherry; all three opting for gin. When François re-entered the parlour, Joseph stood with a loud "Ahem..."

All eyes were on Joseph. "We have something to celebrate tonight and I would ask you all to raise your glasses for a toast to our new pilot, François Turcotte who passed his solo flight this very morning... *félicitations!"*

"Saint Esprit! What a scoundrel! We knew you were taking lessons but you've kept this under wraps. Congratulations!" Jacques was visibly happy for his friend.

The group settled into lively conversations making the atmosphere most convivial. Adèle and Jodie were in a deep *tête-à-tête.* Adèle was a little more than envious of Jodie but she was also intrigued with her upbringing and travels while Jodie was unreasonably jealous of Adèle's past with Jacques yet she was also interested in the one room schoolhouse on the outskirts of town that serviced the farmers' children.

As such the conversation was somewhat frosty at first but surprisingly the two disparate youmg women found themselves warming to each other.

Then in her usual forthright fashion, Jodie brought up the subject that had absorbed her thoughts since the visit at Jacques' farm. "I understand that you were engaged to be married to Jack at some time."

Adèle was taken off-guard and blushed deeply. "Did Jacques tell you that?"

Jodie laughed. "Good grief, no... getting Jack to say anything about himself is like pulling teeth. It was his little sister Martine."

"We were never engaged as such. We were kind of childhood sweethearts and everyone expected that we would be married when he returned from the war. We kept in touch until he disappeared." The last was said with a slight tremor in her voice.

"Anyway, it all turned out for the best in the end. Joseph and I are made for each other." Not to be outdone Adèle could give as good as she got. "What about you and Jacques? Are the two of you sweethearts?"

It was Jodie's turn to blush deeply. She paused and mustered up a shocked look. "God forbid! We would be at each other's throats and someone might commit murder."

"My, my... what passion!" Adèle winked at Jodie.

Jodie laughed. "I'll admit to exaggerating but we do tend to get on each other's nerves and to be truthful we are more than collegues as I would consider Jack to be a good friend. The three of us make a good team."

With that out of the way, the pair returned to safer ground. "I envy your travels. It was my dream to attend university, settle into a career and do some traveling." Adèle's voice seemed a bit plaintive.

"Well why didn't you?"

"I had to make a choice. University would have taken me to Montréal and on an altogether different path. I would have lost Joseph. To be truthful, I've had qualms from time to time but in the great scheme of things, I have no regrets especially when I think of my three angels." Adèle reddened. "My goodness, I don't know what possessed me to get so personal. We hardly know one another."

Jodie reached out and put her hand on Adèle's arm. "Don't worry about it. I feel like we're kindred spirits you and I... and... I do know what you mean about making such a decision. I myself have decided against marriage and a family. Though I look forward to an exciting life of discovery, I'm well aware that there will be times when I may come to regret not having a family of my own."

The newly found friends talked throughout dinner almost to the exclusion of the others.

Meanwhile another friendship was blossoming between Hélène and Frank. Frank loved her French accent and could have listened to her for hours on end. Her questions about his travels were intelligent and she in turn spoke knowledgeably about life in a small French Canadian town. She managed to sound erudite with enough coquettishness to be alluring.

What a lovely lady, thought Frank. *We need to see more of her.*

I like this man, thought Hélène. *He looks like he just walked off the National Geographic page. Very professorial.*

After dinner the ladies went into the kitchen to help Shirley with the dishes while the men lit up their pipes and cigarettes.

In deference to Shirley and Jodie, English only was spoken.

"You have the most delightful little boys. The redhead is just like you and little Patrick is the image of his Daddy." With Jodie's usual nosiness and lack of good manners, she was able to learn that something had gone terribly wrong when Patrick was born and Shirley could have no more children.

"I'm so sorry!" The sadness with which Shirley told her tale made Jodie wish that she hadn't gone there.

Adèle was very quiet, lost in her thoughts. *I wouldn't give up any of the three I now have but I don't think I would be sad to discover that I was unable to bear more children.*

In the parlour the men discussed the upcoming trip into the Gatineau hills for the autumn colours and the subsequent visit to Wakefield and Maniwaki.

1923
Autumn Expedition

Frank and Jodie awaited their transportation outside the grand entrance of the Château early the next morning. Though chilly, the skies seemed to promise a clear day. Having checked their trunks wth the concierge for safekeeping until their return, father and daughter were dressed in camping outfits with pup tent and knapsack on their backs.

A week earlier Jacques had appealed to *tante* Hélène, (he had claimed this Turcotte aunt as his own from boyhood), to drive his party to the Gatineau hills. Free from the constrainsts of work and family duties, Hélène was happy to be of service.

As the two got out of the motorcar to greet their guests, Jodie pointed to the contraption tied atop the car that consisted of two six foot long poles with some sort of thatching in between looking a bit like a stretcher used for carrying the wounded. "What is that thing? I thought we were allowed nothing but what our backs could carry."

Jacques laughed. "It's used by Indians and meant to be pulled behind to carry supplies, in this case, my photographic equipment, my fishing rod and my hunting gun. I can also use it to carry you should a bear decide to eat you… they're particularly fond of young ladies… mind you… any bear would probably mistake you for a mere lad in this getup, not ripe enough for their liking."

"You can't scare me, Jack. I've come face to face with lions and survived. Is there extra space on your contraption?"

"I guess so." Jacques was puzzled.

"Just give me a moment, I'll be right back." Jodie ran back into the hotel.

"Now what's she up to?" Frank had the tone of an exasperated father.

"In the meantime let's pack up our things in the boot of the motorcar." Jacques was determined to waste no time.

"*S'il te plait* Jacques, could you do the driving. We ladies can sit in the back to relax and chat." Hélène did not relish the mostly unmarked dirt roads they would encounter in the hills.

Jodie came out shortly, package in hand. "My art supplies, please say yes."

Jacques groaned and rolled his eyes faking irritation. "If you must, but you owe me. Let's be on our way then."

Hélène installed herself in the back and before anyone else could make a move, Frank quickly eased in beside her. "If you don't mind *madame,* I would much prefer your charming company. We can leave the children to their bickering in the front."

And they were off on a new adventure with a certain amount of excitement in the air.

Hélène opened the conversation. "I understand that your daughter is quite the artist."

"I think she is but Jodie's extremely critical of her own work. At home she's often covered in splashes of paint with emotions running high. She's either deliriously happy or throwing a fit... never in between. I'm afraid that I failed at discipline after her mother's death and now she has the better of me. The only saving grace is that she loves her Daddy to bits." Frank sighed heavily.

"In Canada we have a group of seven artists who have banded together to start a new style. Their work consists mainly of Canadian landscapes, bold and quite wild some of them. They had a showing a couple of years ago in Toronto. I've seen pictures of their work and I'm looking forward to seeing the real thing this winter in Montréal. It would be wonderful if somehow Jodie could see their work." Hélène's face was animated and she was gesticulation with her hands.

Frank was mesmerised.

Jodie was eavesdropping.

She had never considered her Dad sharing his life with someone else before. Though she knew that Frank loved the company of ladies, this somehow seemed different and she couldn't help the small foreboding nagging at her.

"Oh say I can go, Daddy, please." Jodie interrupted the conversation behind her.

———●●●———

Frank learned that the Gatineau Hills lay at Hull's doorstep, widening and stretching toward the northwest some hundred miles. Heavily forested and endowed with pristine lakes, it was part of the Canadian Shield and seen as foothills to the greater Laurentian Mountains to the northeast. "That is as scientific as I'm going to get. Joseph has promised to fill you in on the geology and topography when we get back." Jacques had exhausted his knowledge of facts regarding an area he knew well physically.

They began the gentle climb into the hills and made their first stop at Pink Lake. From atop, standing on the rim of a bowl they peered below at the small lake nestled within.

"Why on earth would they name this 'Pink Lake'? It's a sort of funny greenish colour." Jodie sounded puzzled.

"I've seen this before." Frank seemed to know what he was talking about. "It has something to do with the tiniest of algae growing near the surface."

"So Joseph tells me, but apparently it's also special because it's very still and it's waters don't mix so the bottom has lost all it's oxygen and the fish can't live there. We also had mines down there that are now closed." Jacques was regurgitating knowledge acquired from Joseph.

"Oh, what were they mining," Frank enquired.

Jacques looked sheepish. "I really don't know... but we must get going as we part company with *tante* Hélène shortly at Kingsmere Lake where we must set up camp and catch our lunch. Tomorrow will be a long climb to the western edge of the escarpment."

At Kingsmere Lake they ran out of road and said their goodbyes and thank-you's to Hélène. She was sincere when she said that she wished she could go with them.

"*Tante* Hélène, I just can't imagine you in hiking gear getting all dusty, dirty and smelly. You always look so proper." Jacques was smiling at the thought and Frank was wishing it could be so.

"You have no idea what I'm capable of my young man. Be careful out there." Hélène drove off leaving a trail of dust behind.

Frank and Jodie went about setting up camp in an efficient manner while Jacques went fishing. They were adding the last of the twigs on the campfire when their fisherman arrived with plenty to appease their hunger.

Famished they ate in silence. Once their bellies were full, they were in a better frame of mind to appreciate the show Mother Nature had put on for them. The breeze had completely died down leaving the lake smooth as a mirror reflecting an exact copy of the colourful display hugging its shore. Quaint summer cottages dotted the scenery on the opposite side.

Jacques pointed toward the cottages. "Do you see the second cottage over there? It belongs to our Prime Minister."

"It's very modest for such a high office," Jodie noted.

"Well... we're not a rich nation like the United States but then again, just having a cottage in this area is not for the lowly. Look further... count four more cottages... the blue one... that belongs to the Labelles."

"We could break in and sleep in comfort tonight." Jodie smiled mischievously.

Frank cajoled Jodie. "What... and miss a beautiful night under the stars with a full moon shining on us. Where have you misplaced your sense of adventure, daughter of mine."

"She's afraid we'll discover her true nature when she gets on all fours and starts howling at the moon," Jacques said mockingly.

Jodie elbowed him in his side. "This dangerous wolf is about to start a masterpiece. Just look at these colours... and the sky... have you ever seen anything bluer?"

Her eyes immediately came to Jacques' mind.

Jodie pointed to a spot about 75 yards further on. "I think I'll set up my easel over there."

"Good idea. The conditions are perfect for photography as well. I'll get my equipment."

Jacques lingered on, watching Jodie as she sat at her easel, oblivious to all but the scenery she intended to capture on canvas.

Most birds had flown to warmer climes and the quiet was broken with a few trills and tweets added to the occasional shrill sound of an insect. Jacques' mind wandered. *Five days... not once has she mentioned our goodbye in Washington... to be fair we haven't had a chance to be alone... but she behaves as though nothing happened.* He relived the kiss and shuddered. *It's all I can do to stop myself from grabbing her in my arms and kissing her again. How could I've let her get under my skin that way... I knew she wasn't the kind to settle down.*

Looking up from his notes, Frank became aware of the intensity with which Jacques was staring at Jodie unaware of the turmoil churning in the poor man's mind.

"You're in love with my daughter." Frank's voice was soft.

Showing no surprise, Jacques turned to Frank. "It's more of a love-hate type of thing."

"I can well understand that. Would it surprise you to know that Jodie is also struggling with her feelings for you?"

"Has she told you that?" Jacques was hopeful.

"No. I don't think that it's something she would even admit to herself... but I know my daughter. Her Daddy is the only one she trusts with her heart. Jodie's terrified of becoming attached to someone else. Her relationship with her mother was unusually close and when she died it was more than she could bear. She's erected some pretty high walls around her heart. I've seen the way she discards men... they've never been more than mere playthings. With you it's different."

"Doesn't seem all that different to me... she certainly makes me feel like she's just playing a game with me." There was bitterness in Jacques' voice.

"Well... for one thing she's shown you her serious side which she's never done with any other man. You've seen her compassion in war torn Europe... her love of children. She even behaved herself with your loved ones… she would never have done that for any man, let alone want to meet the important people in his life. Ah yes… I almost forgot… she's never invited a man in her studio other than you. I rest my case." Frank looked triumphant.

"I wish I knew how to get through those walls." Jacques looked miserable.

"She's still so young Jack… give her time. She'll sort it out. There's a whole heap of love bottled up in that big heart of hers. She adores children and would be a good mother provided she found a man strong enough to cope with her temperament… well… you know what a handful she can be."

This was all a bit too emotional and personal so Jacques cleared his throat and got up. "Thanks Frank, but right now I'm in danger of losing this good light. We've got to have photographs to match the clever words you're writing for this article."

———◆●◆———

The next morning's northwesterly trek along well worn paths was all uphill. Though the climb was far from arduous, it was nevertheless constant and heavily forested. The adventurers took a small break to refresh themselves at a tiny lake which was named Black Lake according to Jacques.

"Ah I was hoping we would see one of these. A visit to Canada would be incomplete without coming across a beaver. The beaver dam is just over there to my left… see… shh… we'll approach quietly and remain very still." Jacques pulled out the small Kodak.

"*Oooh…* this is exciting!" Jodie crossed her lips to indicate that she would be quiet.

Crouched close by like stone statues, they were rewarded five minutes later when two beavers arrived with twigs and set about putting finishing touches on their abode. A click of the camera sent them scurrying into the depths entering the safety of their castle from underneath.

"Wow! Did you get that shot?" Frank was smiling broadly.

"I sure did. Let's fill up our canteens and be on our way." Jacques gave his marching orders.

"Wait… just wait. Look over there by the big tree. Chanterelles… lots of them. What's for dinner?" Jodie was already busy picking the mushrooms.

"Whatever comes into gun sight. I'm hoping for a nice big hare or some grouse. Are you sure those are safe to eat?"

"Jodie's mother was the expert and she taught her well. Should be a nice addition to our meal. I'm hungry thinking about it." Frank smacked his lips.

A few hours later, Jacques led them to a small clearing and without warning they were on the edge of the escarpment with the entire Ottawa Valley stretching below them as far as the eye could see.
"Oh my!" It was all Jodie could say.
"Just let us look and then you can explain it." Frank was equally spellbound.

"I'm near starving. You two set up camp and I'll get us something to eat. There'll be plenty of time to explain your surroundings." Jacques picked up his gun and disappeared into the woods.

Frank was building the camp fire and Jodie was picking some wild bergamont when the faint sound of two gunshots signaled that dining was imminent.

Grouse stuffed with minty bergamont and chanterelles made for a sumptuous meal. The leftovers would serve as an evening snack and breakfast.

"Better than any fancy restaurant," proclaimed Frank. "Now what's all this loveliness lying before us.?"

Jacques went into his guide mode. "We're approximately 1,000 feet up on the western edge of the Gatineau Hills. The hills far to the north are part of the Canadian Shield. Before you is the Ottawa Valley…"

Jodie shut out his droning and looked across with her artist eyes. The faraway mountains were blue-black… too far to be forbidding. The patchwork of farms alternated between straw coloured for the harvested fields and green for those awaiting the sickle. The Ottawa River snaked its way down from the northwest, its indigo colour contrasting sharply with the myriad shades of orange, red and yellow of the trees running along both banks of the river.

She picked an area on the closest horizon where a forested area glistened with colour against a deep blue sky sporting just enough cloud to give it character. Installed at her easel she went to work shutting out the world.

Jacques set up his tripod.

Frank was writing.

The perfect lazy afternoon was coming to an end as the sun began to sink peeking here and there behind small bands of broken clouds.

Frank was dozing and Jacques was standing quietly by Jodie watching the scene come to life on canvas. Jodie took no notice of his presence.

And suddenly, in a flash, there was magic. As the sun made its final plunge it robbed the trees of all their glory leaving behind mere dark shadows, whilst splashing the stolen colours across the western sky.

Without looking away, without a word, the two held hands.

The sudden chill of the sunset woke Frank. He approached the couple quietly so as not to break the spell. The three watched until the last of the sky's embers had expired.

Frank spoke first. "That was an awe inspiring sunset. You just can't capture that on film."

"But you can paint it, can't you Jodie?" Jacques wanted her to say yes.

"I intend to," Jodie replied.

"We could include it in the article." Jacques turned to Frank for approbation.

"That's not a bad idea. Let Jodie paint it and then we'll see."

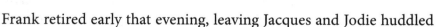

Frank retired early that evening, leaving Jacques and Jodie huddled by the fire staring at the hypnotising flames.

At last we're alone and I can finally have it out with her once and for all. I've no intention of playing her games. Why isn't she saying anything... she always has something to say... she doesn't shut up sometimes. What should I say... this is so awkward.

Jacques put his arm around Jodie's shoulders. "Are you cold?"

Jodie sidled closer. "A bit, thank you."

More silence.

Finally Jacques took the bull by the horns. "Why did you kiss me in Washington last year?"

"It was just a kiss... does there have to be a reason." Jodie was almost whispering.

"No, it wasn't just a kiss." *She can't get away with this,* thought Jacques.

"You're right... it wasn't just a kiss...," still whispering.

Jacques withdrew his arm. "Well... why then? I'm not just one of your many conquests to be discarded when you've had your fun." There was irritation in his voice.

Jodie spoke up louder. "You might be surprised to know, Jack Armand, that of the two of us, your conquests would far outnumber mine."

"That certainly isn't the impression you've given everyone."

"I know... but, in reality I'm nothing but a big tease. Not that it's any of your business but my one and only conquest was Olivier last year in Paris... and I only did it to make you jealous."

Jacques didn't know what to say to that.

"Well, don't you believe me?" Jodie stared at the fire.

His arm encircled her shoulders once more. He spoke in a soft voice. "Jodie, you're playing games with me. I didn't mistake the passion in your kiss and you know full well that it was returned... then... nothing... not a word in your letters. You arrive here as though nothing had happened. What am I to understand by this behaviour?"

"I'm really sorry Jack. You've been in love at least twice that I know of. It's obvious that you and Adèle were very much in love and may still be for that matter. Then you married Angeline and almost had a family. You know your way around real relationships and anyone can see that you're ready for marriage and a family. You stick out like a sore thumb with all your married friends and family. I'm just not ready for all that." Jodie started to cry softly.

Jacques tightened his grip. "I'm in love with you Jodie." His voice cracked. "Tell, me you have no feelings for me and we'll end it here."

"Oh, I have feelings for you, lots of feelings but I'm not ready to be a wife and mother and I may never be for that matter... but... I don't want it to end."

Jacques looked into her eyes and took the plunge. He cupped her chin in his hand and drew her closer. The kiss was soft and gentle. As the flames of the camp fire died, the flames of passion ignited in the two lovers. The kiss intensified. Grabbing at one another they rolled on the ground.

Gasping for breath, Jodie broke the hold. "Stop... stop. I'm not ready... I don't want it like this."

Jacques sat up breathing heavily. "I understand. I can wait. I'm not asking you to marry me. I'm not asking you to have my children... but... would you be my girl? Can we openly love one another... no more beaus."

Jodie beamed. "I can do that. I promise I won't make you wait forever."

During the final trek eastward across the hills, Frank did not fail to notice that his early bedtime at the escarpment had borne fruit. Jacques and Jodie's bickering had turned to friendly banter. Touching often, the pair also laughed often.

The clement weather held, the sun sharing the skies with interesting cloud formations; excellent fodder for the camera, the canvas, as well as the pen. After a stay at Meech Lake, it was time to make their way further east to Chelsea where they would catch the train northward along the Gatineau River all the way to Maniwaki.

In Chelsea, Jacques took his American friends to see the Chelsea Falls. "Now's the time to take photographs and immortalize these falls because they plan to dam the river at this point within the next year or so. Maurice Labelle warns us that the demand for electricity is escalating to the point that the day will soon come when both rivers will be dammed from one end to the other." Jacques sighed heavily.

"It's the price of progress, it would seem." Frank was being pragmatic.

"Imagine the views we saw with the farms spread before us, the small villages dotted along the river and then the cottages at Kingsmere. Now imagine all of that gone... to be replaced by forest...

everything wild. Not much more than 100 years ago, that would have been the case."

"My goodness, that isn't so long ago. Was there no one here then?" Jodie was curious.

"Well the Indians were here of course but remember I told you that the white man didn't establish himself here until the turn of the 1800's. For centuries... actually Joseph Lafleur says it's thousands of years... the Algonquins travelled these rivers in their canoes; breaking camp when the season changed; living in harmony with nature. I have Indian friends from the lumber camps and I believe we're destroying their way of life as well."

"That's a terrible shame. They were such proud people with a noble way of life and we've ruined it believing ourselves to be better. Surely we'll have our comeuppance someday." Jodie spoke harshly.

"I guess we can be quite destructive. You've no idea just how often we've seen examples of this throughout our travels... atrocities all in the name of the almighty dollar." Frank spoke equally harshly.

Jacques took out his watch. "*Oops...* time to go or we'll miss that iron horse the Indians still marvel at."

It was a short train ride to Wakefield, a quaint village hugging the Gatineau River. After checking in at the *auberge*, Jacques said he had a view to show them well worth the short uphill trek.

"I'm not going anywhere until I've had a bath and a real meal. We may have gotten used to it, but didn't you notice the man at the reception wriggling his nose with a look of great disdain.?" Jodie did a good imitation of the hotelier's grimaces.

"What do you mean... 'a real meal'... what was wrong with my hunting skills... fresh fish, hare and grouse... not to mention every variety of mushroom and herb you could lay your hands on... oh... and what about those delicious berries... it was gourmet at its best!" Jacques did his best to look offended.

Frank laughed. "Tsk-tsk-tsk," Frank wagged his finger at his daughter. "Lesson number one, my daughter, never belittle a man's ability to provide for his loved ones."

Frank turned to Jacques rubbing his stomach. "While we dined like kings under your care, Jack, what I need now is a great big steak, potatoes, vegetables and my berries in a pie."

Bathed and fed, the three friends set off on an uphill trail by the side of a small river rushing down helter-skelter over rocks. Less than a mile up, the river was dammed in order to drive a lovely old flour mill built of log and stone.

The mill, the old house and the dam with its consequent falls were all photographed. Frank dallied with the intricate iron machinery at the top of the dam.

"We're on MacLaren property. We'll go to the right behind their lovely old home and up to their family cemetery where the trail goes behind and up the escarpment you see there." Jacques was pointing up to the right.

When they reached the cemetery Jodie exclaimed. "Oh my, I've never been to a cemetery before that made me feel happy... almost joyous I'd say. Would you just look at this view... so peaceful. This is where I must be buried. I see other family names on the headstones so I guess I'll have to marry into one of these families or perhaps a MacLaren if I want to end up here? Do you have any connections, Jack... can you introduce me to a strapping young Scot by the name of MacLaren?" Jodie winked at Jacques.

"I doubt you could get any Scot interested in marrying a spendthrift like you." Jacques winked back.

They picked up the trail leading up to the escarpment. The grade was steep but the view at the top was indeed lovely. Unlike the grand vista of the Ottawa Valley, this was a more intimate view. The Gatineau meandered below much closer, its surrounding hills in their autumn colours rose nearby all around the small valley.

———◆●◆———

The scenery was varied on the last leg of the journey to Maniwaki. The train steamed its way northward sometimes along the river; other times entering a forest that would eventually give way to neat farms; and at one point along the dazzling waters of Blue Sea Lake. They passed a series of tiny villages with mainly English names such as Farrellton and Gracefield, a few sounded French and one village in particular delighted Jodie.

"Kazabazua! I don't believe it! Kazabazua... I love it. It must mean something to somebody... don't you just love it Daddy?" Without waiting for a reply she chattered on. "I could move here and build a home just so I could put Kazabazua on my return address. It would amuse all of my friends... Kazabazua."

While the two Americans enjoyed the unfamiliar scenery, Jacques dozed, lulled by the swaying of the train.

Maniwaki was abuzz with the preparations for that winter's logging. Jacques organised a ride for the three on a horse-drawn wagon heading for a new camp with supplies. The ride on the newly laid out road into the forest was long and arduous.

"It's times like these that I wish I could have a nice big layer of fat on my poor rattled bones." The tremble in Jodie's voice matched the unevenness of the ruts in the dirt road.

The foreman, Alister McTavish, had been briefed about the strangers' arrival. Visibly annoyed at this intrusion, his mood improved when he was made aware of Jacques' logging experience. He was one of them. For Jacques' sake and because he now understood that he and his gang would be featured in the National Geographic, he gracefully accepted to be their guide for the next few hours.

The camp was abuzz with the noise of hammering, sawing and swearing. The foreman began his lecture. "We choose the areas we want to harvest well in advance and then we build a road to reach the spot where the camp is going to be. We put up tents and start working. It takes only two weeks to get a camp like this ready for action. We're almost finished here."

"That's really fast." Frank looked impressed and the foreman looked pleased.

He began to relish his role of guide and spoke in a more officious tone. "The camp is divided into four main areas. We build the cabins with sticks, plaster and mortar in between the logs, and over there... that large cabin... it's where the men sleep in bunk beds. I, have my own cabin. The other large cabin on the other side there is for the kitchen and the eating area. The one beside it is the office and the store, so the men can buy their cigarettes and anything they want. Back there is the barn for the horses and the blacksmith shop and that's real important because the horses are just as important as the men."

"How many men live in the sleeping quarters?" Jodie felt uncomfortable when the foreman stared at her before answering. *It's a sensible question,* she thought. *Why is he looking at me that way?*

The foreman fnally realised that the scruffy looking youth was a woman. This was a men's camp. If the woman had to be here then the least she could do is remain quiet.

Ignoring Jodie, the foreman turned to Frank. "We can house 50 to 100 men in a cabin. We're expecting 70 or so here this season. When the camp is bigger and there are more than 100 then we build another sleeping cabin."

Jacques looked at the red-faced Jodie. He shrugged, held her hand and whispered in her ear. "Women are sort of unwelcome at a logging camp. It isn't personal."

When Jacques saw her ready to deliver an angry retort, he quickly put his finger to his lips. "Shhh… not now, we'll talk about it later."

Offended by the foreman, Jodie was not about to keep quiet. She pinched her nose. "Pee-yew… can you just imagine 100 sweaty men sleeping in one cabin after a meal of pea soup and beans… ugh."

Frank and Jacques couldn't help themselves. They burst out laughing.

She'd won over the foreman who joined in the laughter. "You're quite right, little lady. Don't forget the dirty socks and the language. Between the French Canadians with their holy swear words and the Irish, it can be pretty shocking. A pretty young thing like you would surely faint."

Jodie rolled her eyes.

They were invited to eat with the workmen that evening. Plates, bowls and cups were made of tin and the meal was hearty. Jodie kept her head down avoiding the stares. Not much effort was made to curb their language.

The next morning Frank did his interviews and gathered his information while Jacques busied himself with tripod and camera, Jodie sticking right by his side. A few hours later they climbed into an almost empty wagon to make their way back to Maniwaki in time for the afternoon train.

———◆◆◆———

As previously arranged, Hélène was at the train station in Hull to take the bedraggled party back to the lap of luxury at the Château Laurier.

Hélène had been looking forward to seeing Frank again with great anticipation. When he disembarked, she could feel her heartbeat racing. *Quelle idiote... what's the matter with me. I'm behaving like a young girl... but I do like this man. Watch yourself now... he leaves the day after tomorrow and you'll never see him again. There's no future to any of these feelings.*

Frank and Hélène did nothing to hide their delight at being together. They took the back seat without any preamble and began chatting as though no one else existed. Left standing by the automobile, Jacques looked at Jodie with a meaningful smile but Jodie was not smiling.

Jacques sat behind the wheel and Jodie flounced into her seat next to him with a scowl on her face.

"What's the matter Jodie?" Jacques looked concerned.

"Nothing."

"But I can see something's bothering you."

"I said... nothing... now leave me alone." Jodie crossed her arms and looked away.

"Alright then, if that's the way you want it."

The two in front drove to Ottawa in silence, each mulling his own thoughts.

The two in back chatted away merrily.

Jacques thoughts were confused. *What's the matter with her? One minute she's happy and the next she's angry. I didn't do anything... did I?* He examined his recent actions. *No I don't think it was anything I said.*

The happy chatter in the back broke into his thoughts. *That's it! She doesn't like what's happening between those two. By golly... she's jealous of tante Hélène... ho ho.*

Jacques started giggling to himself.

"What's so funny?" Jodie was not in the mood for laughter.

"You are."

Jodie elbowed him in the side and Jacques laughed louder.

At the drop-off in front of the hotel, Hélène reminded Frank of her invitation for a farewell dinner at her home the next night.

"Looking forward to it." Frank waved goodbye smiling broadly while Jodie stomped into the Château without so much as a look back, a goodbye or a thank you.

Hélène sat herself beside Jacques for the short ride to his apartment. "What's the matter with Jodie?"

"*Oh rien, rien...* nothing really, she's an extremely moody person and shouldn't be taken seriously when she gets like that. I did warn everyone that she could be that way." Jacques shrugged.

"You sound like you have some experience with her moods *mon cher garçon.*"

"That I do. Enough about me. What about you and Frank, *tante* Hélène? You two seem awfully close." Jacques gave her a wicked look."

"*Regarde* we're almost there. François and Shirley won't be coming tomorrow night. David and Patrick have the measles but François will lend you the car and I expect you by five. I've invited Joseph and Adèle..."

Jacques interrupted. "*Non, non, non...* you can't just change the subject like that."

But she did get away with it because they had arrived. Hélène hurried out of the car before any more uncomfortable questions came her way. Jacques got his gear out of the boot and Hélène kissed him on both cheeks. "*Bonjour, à demain,* remember 5 p.m." Hélène sat behind the wheel and waved goodbye.

———◆●◆———

Their last day in Ottawa was a quiet one. Jodie must have spent an hour immersed in a hot scented tub. Packing took up the rest of the morning and after a sumptuous lunch, father and daughter took a walk by the river.

It had rained the day before but the sun was now competing with the clouds for its share of the skies.

"I really like this town Daddy. It's a small civilization surrounded by wilderness. But it's this river I love the most. I could see myself building a home here... somewhere on the outskirts... high up with a view of the Ottawa River."

"Could it be the tall, handsome lumberjack you also love?" Frank's voice was very soft.

"Please Daddy, don't push." Jodie's eyes were pleading.

Dinner was an intimate affair that evening. While the women helped Hélène with the finishing touches to her meal, the men discussed the National Geographic article. Frank was getting precious information from Joseph who seemed to know everything about everything.

"We're still waiting for the Government to designate the Gatineau Hills as a federal park. We've been promised since before the war and we're still waiting." Joseph was interrupted by the call to the dinner table.

Hélène had gone all out... french onion soup... *coq au vin... pommes de terre au gratin...* buttered beans with roasted almonds and pumpkin pie. She had wanted to show off her cooking skills to impress Frank.

Frank was duly impressed and would probably have been impressed had she opened a tin of beans.

The Greshams were becoming well acquainted with Jacques' friends. The dinner conversation was friendly and lively. Adèle was able to take Jodie's mind off the blossoming romance between her father and Hélène.

"Who is looking after your children?" Jodie wondered.

"We're fortunate to have a kindly widow, *Madame* Gauthier who lives a few houses up, to look after them whenever we wish to have a night out." Adèle proceeded to explain the beginnings of their business and the relationship of *Monsieur* Laflamme with Joseph. Jodie regaled her with her impersonations of the misogynist foreman at the lumber camp.

Meanwhile, Frank and Hélène managed to have some intimacy without ignoring the rest of the guests.

"You must teach me to skate when we come back in January."

"You're coming back?" Wide-eyed, Hélène spread her hand on her chest.

"Why yes, didn't you know? We're doing this in three parts; the autumn colours with the logging camp preparations; the actual felling of the trees in winter; and the drive down the river in spring."

"*Mais non,* I didn't know... how delightful! *Certainement,* I will take you and Jodie skating on the Rideau Canal by the university."

"I was hoping that you could join us in Washington in the spring when the cherry blossoms are out. You could be our guest. There's plenty of room for both you and Jack." Frank was looking at her hopefully.

All this was sudden and unexpected and moving too fast to digest. Hélène was a bit confused. "Jacques will be there too?"

"Well yes, Jack travels with us tomorrow for ten days in the photo labs of National Georgraphic. He will be doing the same after the winter photo shoot and the one in spring. That's when I thought you could come down with all of us... that is... if you're interested. I'm sorry if I'm being so presumptuous." Frank looked down... a little afraid of her answer. Had he been reading too much in her manner towards him... maybe she was just being friendly.

Hélène beamed. *Steady... steady,* she told herself. *I musn't seem to be too easy.* She couldn't help it, chicanery was not her style. "*Mon Dieu, oui, oui...* I would love that." She recovered herself and spoke in a more neutral tone. "That is, I love to travel and I've never been to Washington."

Everyone noticed Hélène's jubilance and looked their way.

"What are we missing, *ma tante* Hélène?" Adèle enquired politely.

"I've been invited to Washington... in spring... to see the cherry blossoms... *n'est-ce pas merveilleux!*"

CHAPTER 2 5

1923-1924
Winter Expedition

It was good to be back on Q street to be pampered by Bessie and Coco. Jacques was also happy to reunite with the photographers at National Geographic and found it satisfying to be working in the state-of-the-art photo lab once more.

Jodie returned to her usual city self. Though she went out less often, she was just as gaudily dressed; just as teasing and flirtatious with her men frends in the speak-easies; the difference being that she was obviously in Jacques' company. She hung on to his arm and danced every dance with her tall, handsome escort.

Daytime would find her in her studio, covered in paint, assidu-ously recreating the sunset on the escarpment. Having seen Hélène's pictures of the Goup of Seven paintings, she chose Frederick Varley as her inspiration. Unlike most of his Canadian landscapes, she added two small figures in the foreground, standing hand in hand, admiring the magical sunset. No one was allowed into the studio until the work was finished which didn't seem to be anytime soon.

Jodie was happy and good-humored. Her taunts toward Jacques were done in fun and apparent affection. It was plain to everyone that they were witnessing a budding romance. Frank was delighted, the servants tittered softly in the kitchen, happy for Miss Jodie.

It was the first time Jodie had committed to anyone and she gave much thought to her newfound relationship. She was falling in love and doing nothing to resist. She did, however, need to resist her strong desires for Jacques. Her tryst with Olivier had been a drunken affair lasting but a few frenzied minutes leaving her wondering what the hoopla was all about.

In her thoughts she conjured up a nude Jacques. She envisioned long legs with well-muscled thighs; a trim waist and firm abs; the broad chest and arms not overly muscled but well-defined. His torso was hairless but curly brown hair surrounded his manhood and she imagined it to be stirring, growing, hardening... much bigger than Olivier's. She had no doubt that the reality would be much better than with Olivier. With no religious conscience to contend with, Jodie readily abandoned herself to this fantasy.

Jacques for his part knew what Jodie looked like in the nude. The photograph on her dresser had left nothing to the imagination. Lying in his bed at night, he found Jodie's proximity on the floor below extremely difficult to bear. It was all he could do to stop himself from tiptoeing down to her room and possessing her.

Heavy-hearted, the time came to say goodbye. Just as his last departure from Washington, the kiss was repeated. This time Jacques was not left in a quandary, knowing full well the meaning of this kiss and knowing that they would meet again soon.

In the Ottawa Valley, the snows were not long in coming and the three months went by quickly. Jodie's letters were entertaining and more intimate without being romantic. It wasn't her style. Frank wrote Jacques with his arrival dates in mid-January informing him that they intended to stay on a couple of extra days for recreation.

Jacques prepared for his guests' arrival; made the necessary arrangements with the lumbercamp foreman, Mr. McTavish; made the reservations at the Château Laurier; arranged for a day of skating on the Rideau Canal with *tante* Hélène and perused the coming attractions at the cinema.

Jacques was not Frank's only Canadian correspondant. He had written to Hélène shortly after his arrival in Washington in October. She had been only too happy to respond and the letters to and fro were frequent. Her letters were addressed to Frank Gresham in care of the National Geographic in accordance with the return address on his envelopes.

In this manner, Jodie was ignorant of these missives. Frank felt a bit guilty of this duplicity but he was not ready for what he knew would be a confrontation with his daughter.

He was by and large an organised man, well-settled in his ways. Preferring the company of women to that of men, these encounters never resulted in anything more than friendship. With Hélène he was in unfamiliar territory. He had no idea where he was going with this relationship; it was out of his control. Though he found this somewhat disturbing, he wasn't fighting it. For the last few years his life could have been described as a contented one, until now. Hélène made him happy.

Organised, well-settled and contented was also an apt description of Hélène's life. Adolphe had died before they could celebrate nine years of marriage. Several eligible bachelors and widowers of a certain age had tried to court her at first but none of them interested Hélène. Soon she would celebrate her 38th birthday putting her beyond the normal age for courtship.

Her comfortable life was now in turmoil. She was experiencing feelings that were more akin to those she had for her young man lost to the priesthood rather than those she had known with her husband, Adolphe. She too was not in control and willing to throw caution to the wind.

——————◆●◆——————

It was 10°F when father and daughter arrived in Ottawa. Jacques had warned that Canada could indeed look like the frozen wasteland imagined by most Americans. Consequently they came prepared and were dressed for the occasion; Jodie looking lost in an oversized fox fur coat with hat to match, the earflaps hidden inside to be used in dire cold. Frank looked comfortable in a lambswool overcoat just as substantial as Jodie's.

As had been the case in September, the first night was spent dining quietly with Jacques at the Château discussing their plans for the visit. The next day was to be a festive one.

It being Sunday, Hélène was able to organise a large skating party on the canal. The guest list included Maurice, Mary and the two boys; Joseph, Adèle and the two eldest; François, Shirley and their two boys; Céline and Gérard who brought Xavier and the twins; the Americans; herself and Jacques. Having asked Frank for shoe sizes, she had purchased the required skates for the guests of honour.

Jacques and his friends walked the modest distance from the hotel to the appointed spot on the canal. Jodie had purchased hardy ski wear for winter activities and trekking in the timberlands of the North. Both hers and her father's coat-jackets were of heavy wool, belted tightly at the waist, flaring out fashionably above the knee over worsted wool pants tucked into warm winter boots. Jodie's coat was trimmed with a fox fur collar, wearing the same fur hat she had arrived with; earflaps down over her ears this time. Frank's coat was trimmed with lambswool, wearing a matching hat with ear flaps. Jacques was looking handsome in his red plaid mackinaw coat trimmed with raccoon fur; a raccoon hat complete with tail giving him a 'Davy Crockett' look.

All along the canal families were out in their numbers; most skating gracefully; some on their bums more than on their feet. Children in multicoloured tuques squealed, parents shouted warnings, boys slapped pucks with their hockey sticks and the steady scrape of blades cutting through ice served as background noise. It was a happy, noisy, colourful sight.

The scene put a spring in our walkers' step. Before long, Jacques spotted Adèle gracefully executing figure skating moves. Most everyone had arrived. With *tuques* down to their eyes and scarves across their mouths, it took a while for Jodie and Frank to figure out who was who.

One such figure hurtling toward Frank came to an abrupt stop, blades braking sideways, ice chips scattering. Hélène pulled down her scarf, gave Frank the warmest of smiles and all was right with the world.

Céline had been dying to meet the Americans. "Adèle, *regarde…* she looks so fashionable in her outfit. The two of you make me look like a whale." She laughed loudly. "The more of me to love, *hein*? Come on, introduce me."

The two ladies skated up to the three who were putting on their skates. Adèle made the introductions. "Frank, Jodie... this is my very best friend, Céline. We've been friends since we were at school."

Despite this nice itroduction, the usually brash Céline turned shy and reddened. She waved for her husband Gérard to come over. With the 'hello's and 'enchanté's' out of the way, Gérard pointed out his son and twin daughters to Jodie who wanted to know all about the children.

Hélène undertook the skating lessons for Frank. It was a good excuse to hang on tightly to each other. Falling frequently, they laughed exuberantly as they picked themselves up in each other's arms.

Hanging on to Jacques trying her best to balance, refusing to fall, Jodie was too busy to notice her father's shenanigans with Hélène. Adèle soon took over the lessons. "The men want to play hockey, Jacques. I'll have Jodie skating like a pro in no time."

"You seem to be floating on air, Adèle. You make me envious." Jodie complimented her.

"They have us on skates as soon as we can walk. Just look at the speed of the men and look at the tiny ones. Monique is not yet two, but there she is trying to skate and so determined. It's more like they're walking on their skates instead of gliding but that will come later. *Oops...* down she goes." Adèle laughed.

Under Adèle's patient tutelage, Jodie eventually got the hang of it. She wasn't the steadiest but she was skating and she was ecstatic. She made her way to the children. They found her unsteady gait funny. Jodie initiated a game of tag and the fun began. When Jodie fell, she joined in the children's hilarious laughter.

Jacques looked behind him to see what the commotion was all about. The more the children tried to get Jodie up, the more she ended back on her bum. He waited a while before going to her rescue, enjoying her fun. *What a wonderful mother she would make. Children everywhere love her.*

Frank and Jodie stayed on the ice till they were exhausted. Sitting on the sidelines they gratefully sipped hot chocolate purchased from a vendor in a covered cart who was enjoying a brisk business. They marveled at the colourful spectacle before them; the men deftly passing the puck to each other; one of the twins crying for her mother; Céline's bulky frame moving with speed and grace to her fallen child; Hélène and Adèle dancing together on the ice.

"I do love it here Daddy!" Jodie warmed her hands around the hot cup of chocolate.

"So you've said before. They're a nice bunch of people… no pretentions… just nice." Frank was admiring the pair dancing on ice.

Jodie followed his gaze. "What's going on between you and Hélène? Aren't the two of you too old for that sort of thing?"

"Jodie Gresham! I never realised that you see me as an 'old' man and anyway… this isn't any of your business." Frank was visibly offended.

"But it is my business. I thought you and I were happy together. We don't need anyone replacing Mom. We're fine just the two of us." Jodie sounded like a petulant child.

Frank softened. "No one can ever replace your mother, Jodie… but it's been a while now and can you not understand that a man needs the companionship of a woman other than that of his daughter?"

"You've been fine up until now and I've seen how some women look at you. You've never been interested before. What's so special about this one." Jodie waved the back of her hand dismissively toward the dancing duo.

"Alright, maybe it is your business. I like Hélène very much, Jodie. She makes me happy… but I must confess that this is all new to me and I have no idea where it's going."

"I don't like her." Jodie was back to being petulant.

"You liked her enough before you noticed that I was interested. She's a lovely person, much like her niece Adèle with whom you're so chummy. If you truly loved your Daddy as you say you do, you'd be happy for me. You would be doing me a great service if you put aside this unwarranted jealousy. It is most unbecoming." Seldom had Frank used such a severe tone to admonish his daughter.

Jodie was shocked and hurt by her father's tone. She remained silent with head bowed.

Seeing his daughter's discomfiture, Frank adopted a conciliatory tone. "Look around you Jodie. Families… nice big families… loving families. Maybe two of us aren't enough, anymore. Already we've added Jack to our circle. Wouldn't you miss him terribly if we were never to see him again... I know I would."

He thought he detected a lone tear streaking down Jodie's cheek. She remained silent and he continued. "Being a grandfather would be the greatest gift you could ever give me. Having a husband and a family would add a wonderful dimension to your life without taking anything away from our relationship. A wife would complete my life, yet she could never replace my love for you... she'd be adding to our life, both yours and mine if you could only get to know her."

"I thought you didn't know where this was going?" Jodie looked her father in the eye.

Frank's eyes rounded with genuine surprise. "No I didn't. I'm just as surprised as you are at the words I've just spoken. Well... well... we've a lot of thinking to do, you and I. Brighten up girl, here comes your beau."

"Why so glum Jodie?"

Jodie shrugged.

"Never mind her... just another one of her moods."

Jodie glared at her father.

"Well off with your skates. We're all exhausted and the party is moving to warm up at your hotel where Maurice has reserved a small party room for all of us. We're all chipping in. There'll be warm soup, beef stew and warm bread pudding for the children."

People were cold and famished. Seated around two long tables, red in their cheeks, the party was loud and lively. Jacques had learned from experience to leave Jodie alone when she went into one of her moods. Adèle, however, did her best to cheer up the girl but in the end it was the children who got the better of Jodie and brought a smile to her face.

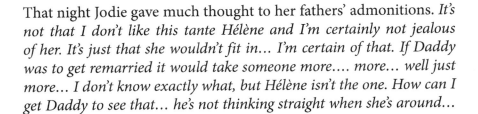

That night Jodie gave much thought to her fathers' admonitions. *It's not that I don't like this tante Hélène and I'm certainly not jealous of her. It's just that she wouldn't fit in... I'm certain of that. If Daddy was to get remarried it would take someone more.... more... well just more... I don't know exactly what, but Hélène isn't the one. How can I get Daddy to see that... he's not thinking straight when she's around...*

hmmm. He wants me to get to know her well... I'll do just that and maybe she also needs to get to know us better.

Jodie was quiet at the breakfast table the next day. "A penny for your thoughts." Frank knew she was mulling something over.

"I was thinking Daddy..." Jodie paused.

"Yes?"

"Well, I truly want to see the exhibition of that Canadian group of artists in Montréal. Hélène has invited me and you did say that I should get to know her better... so... would it bother you if I were to skip the lumber camp tomorrow and go to Montréal with Hélène instead?" Jodie did not meet her father's eyes.

"What a great idea. I do believe that Jack and I can handle that foreman you liked so much on our own. Wait... you do plan to behave yourself with Hélène?" Frank cupped Jodie's chin in his hand and forced her to look him in the eyes.

Jodie feigned surprise. "Daddy! Really! To be truthful, it's the paintings that beckon me... and... I also thought that I could get to know this aunt that Jack likes so much."

"It's a deal then, let's call Hélène after breakfast.

Frank was shocked at the change in the landscape since their last train ride to Maniwaki. "Wow, what a difference a couple of months can make. The forests are naked. The farms and the river all meld into one... nothing but fields of white. I don't recognize anything. It's actually quite hypnotising."

"All that white along with the rocking of the train just puts me to sleep." Jacques eyelids were drooping. "I don't think Jodie's missing much."

"I know that she was impressed with what little she saw of these Canadian artists but still... it was a sudden decision. I do hope she's not up to something mischievous. She did say that she wants to get to know your aunt better." Frank sounded a little dubious.

"She really isn't my aunt."

"So you've said before... but then we all have an auntie or two in our lives who are not related and, nevertheless, we feel just as affectionate towards them. You're nodding off... I'll trouble you no further." Frank picked up the newspaper.

Once again they rode into the timberland in the supply wagon only this time it was a winter supply sleigh... a glorified wagon on runners easier for the horses to pull on snow. The ride was smoother than before.

Smoke was curling from the chimneys of the log cabins as they arrived into the camp yard. The lumberjacks were away, working their stint and all was quiet. At the sound of the horses, Mr. McTavish came out of the office to greet his guests.

"The lads are working some three miles to the northeast of here. Where's the wee lassie?"

"Gone to an art show in Montréal," replied Frank.

"Ah... I see... much more appropriate for a young lady." Despite his earlier disapproval, Alister McTavish sounded disappointed. "Well, we best be going."

They could hear the sawing, the whacking of the axes and the cussing of the men well before reaching them. "Stay with me at all times." The foreman cautioned them as they neared.

The lumberjacks wearing mackinaws of reds, yellows, oranges and some blues made quite a contrast against the dark tree trunks and the white of the snow.

Frank let out a whistle. "Wow... they're all dressed like you Jack. I've got to get myself one of those jackets."

"Why, Frank, is that whistle for me. I do cut a fine figure in my makinaw, don't I? Seriously, it could be a matter of life and death if you aren't clearly seen out here," Jacques explained.

The foreman pointed out that the lumberjacks were working in teams of three. "The guy with the axe makes some cuts, a kind of niche, on the side that the tree will fall and the other two use the bucksaw in tandem on the other side of the tree until... there it goes..."

There was a resounding cracking noise followed by a piercing yell. 'TIMMMBERRRR."

It was like watching slow motion as the towering tree fell to its demise... and then the final muffled boom as the tree shook the ground it fell on.

Frank felt it through his body. "Man, oh, man... that was exciting. Although I can't help feeling sorry for that majestic tree. We're cutting them down faster that they can grow back. A day might come when we lose our forests."

"You sound just like Joseph."

The chopper wasted no time wielding his axe to cut off the branches while others squared the logs for easier transportaion. There were specialized teams for road building, sliding the logs, and working with the indispensable horses.

On the way back to the camp Frank asked Jacques if he missed being a lumberjack.

"It's back breaking work and it can get lonely up here, even among all these men, you do miss your family. This is the first year I've been back since I was eighteen and I have to confess that I feel a little nostalgic."

The only noise heard at the dinner tables was the slurping and the chewing. These men took their eating seriously. Frank was amazed at the amount of food they could put down.

"Between keeping warm in these frigid temperatures and doing hard physical labour, our labourers need the energy. Believe me, no one gains any weight while working here. You do put on some good muscle though." Jacques flexed his biceps.

As quiet as dinner was, things became downright riotous and rowdy afterwards. One guy fiddled, two worked the harmonica, another guy played the spoons while someone was able to get some harmony out of grating some doodad against an old metal washboard.

Singing did not require the men to be on key. To Frank's great amusement the men started dancing with each other. Those playing the woman's role made exaggerated female moves right down to batting their eyelashes.

Jacques was laughing heartily. "There you go Frank, that guy is making eyes at you. You've got it made."

Some men were arm wrestling and a small number were gambling. "The gambling can be a problem for some. There are always an unfortunate few who go home penninless after a season's hard work."

Frank spent the rest of the evening in conversation with Alister with whom he was now on a first name basis. His many questions were answered knowledgeably. Jacques for his part relived old times as the men invited him into the singing and dancing.

It was early to bed for the exhausted men for whom it would also be early to rise for the next day's stint.

Hélène met Jodie in the lobby of the Château early Tuesday morning. Jodie stood to greet her. "*Bonjour tante* Hélène. You don't mind if I call you *tante* I hope. I just thought that since everyone else of my generation is calling you *tante*... well... it might be more polite for me to address someone your age as '*tante* Hélène' instead of plain 'Hélène'." Jodie gave her the most innocent smile.

Now that makes me feel old, thought Hélène. "*Mais certainement,* Jodie, *tante* is much friendlier... er... have the men left yet?" She looked around wistfully.

"They left half an hour ago. I'm looking forward to this adventure. I've never been to Montréal and I'm hoping we'll get to know one another better." Jodie was smiling brightly.

Hmmm... I didn't get the impression that this girl liked me very much. I'm sure it's all about the art and she's trying to be polite. "Me too. We certainly can get in a good chat. It's almost three hours to Montréal."

When the two ladies had settled in and the train whistle signaled their departure, Hélène opened the conversation. "Frank tells me that you're experimenting with a number of modern styles with your paintings. I'm truly looking forward to seeing your work in the Spring."

"Well... I'm not good enough to show my paintings to anyone and so far I've only let family into my studio... and Jack of course."

"How fortunate for me that you're now calling me your aunt. I do believe that makes me family and entitled to entering your studio. How marvelous!" Hélène was just as adept as Jodie in the innocent smile department.

Jodie reddened. "But of course, any aunt of Jack is an aunt of mine... but... be warned... my work is amateurish at best."

"I'm curious... have you always painted... I mean, as a child, did you like to draw." Hélène was honestly interested.

Ah... good... we're going to talk about my childhood, thought Jodie. "As a matter of fact, yes, from early childhood. I travelled with my parents everywhere, mostly in remote uncivilized areas. It could be quite lonely at times. Drawing was a good pastime for me."

"What an exciting life!. I also love traveling but I've been nowhere compared to you." Hélène looked dreamy.

"Oh but we're not talking about the same kind of traveling you would like to do. Many of our expeditions are months long, living under harsh conditions... sleeping on dirt floors... no running water... no sanitation of any kind... weeks without bathing. In some areas we have to watch out for dangerous animals. At four years old I faced a family of lions. It's one of my first memories. I wasn't frightened but apparently my parents were terrified. Other times we had to beware of bandits..."

"*Mon dieu, Seigneur...* it was no life for a child," Hélène interrupted.

"Oh but I was happy. My mother home-schooled me and what I learned in our travels is priceless. I was usually the only child around and everyone spoiled me. The three of us were extremely close and I felt nothing but love."

Jodie had her companion spellbound and she continued. "My mother never complained and made everything seem wonderful no matter how rough our conditions were. My Dad says that Mom was one of a kind and he says no other woman could put up with such a difficult and dangerous lifestyle."

Then Jodie became genuinely sad. "I miss her terribly, no one could ever replace her."

Fait accompli.

Hélène found her voice. "I guess not every expedition is as easy as the one in Québec. I mean... surely you don't see us as an uncivilized and dangerous mission."

Jodie laughed. "I love Ottawa and its surrounding areas. What a beautiful setting! The autumn was breathtaking and I love this winter wonderland. I'm looking forward to spring and I must come back in the summer just to go canoeing and explore the rivers and lakes."

It was pleasing for Hélène to hear her homeland being praised. "Do you go on all your father's expeditions?"

"Yes I do, we're a team. Daddy says no one else can get the children to talk like I do and you'd be surprised how much one can learn from children."

Hélène agreed. "Oh I'm well aware of that. Most of my work is with children."

Jodie gave her a curious look. "I didn't know that you worked?"

"Well I don't get paid, so it isn't a real job, but it is work. I volunteer to help with the abused, the impoverished and widows who are left with a brood of children and no real means of support."

"Jack tells me that you lost your husband some time ago. I'm sorry for your loss."

"Thank you, but it's been a long time now. Adolphe was a wonderful companion and I did miss him terribly at first but I have my books, my volunteer work and my nieces and nephews who are constantly in my life."

"Did you never want to remarry, you must have been still young at the time" *Oops, why am I going there...* "What I mean is how can you survive with no paid work and no husband... oh my... this is really none of my business... do forgive me."

"*Oh c'est rien...* I don't mind at all. I much prefer it when people say what's on their minds. For one thing I never found anyone else to hold my interest before. Also, Adolphe, bless his soul, left me provided for. So you could say that I'm a bit of an heiress."

"Well, we have that in common. I'm an heiress too." Jodie looked triumphant. This was now going the way she wanted.

"Oh?"

"My mother was related to the Rockefeller family by her father's marriage. She fell out of favour with them when she married my Dad. They'd picked out a solid banker from New York for her intended husband but she literally eloped with Daddy."

"How romantic! But what was wrong with her marrying your father? He's well educated, earns a good living, and such a lovely person." Hélène was offended at the thought that anyone should pass over the man she admired so much.

"Maybe so, but my Mom was expected to marry real money, produce heirs and take her rightful place in high society. Instead she studied archaeology and ran off to the ends of the earth with an anthropologist. It was all very noncomformist."

"How did you come to be an heiress if she was disowned? *Mon Dieu...* now I'm the inquisitive one, asking impertinent questions."

Hélène touched Jodie on the arm and gave her a look that begged forgiveness.

Jodie laughed. "I too much prefer people to be up front. I never said that she was disowned. No... but... we were shunned and never invited to the family affairs. After she died, my grandmother wanted to get to know me. I'm now on the invitee list."

"So have you been to any of these grand affairs?"

"Lucky for me, we were away for most of them... but yes... I've been to a wedding and a debutante ball. Talk about ostentation, glitz and glamour... whew. I was a curiosity... black sheep you might say. I could feel the whispers behind my back. Grandmother tried to be nice but she's so stiff and stuffy."

"Not your cup of tea, I gather."

"Oh don't get me wrong. I'm quite accustomed to high society. In Washington, Dad and I attend high society do's all the time and I can play the game just as well as any other socialite... just ask Jack. He hates it. I've never seen anyone more uncomfortable in a tux." Jodie laughed at the thought.

"No, I can't imagine Jacques enjoying himself among high society." Hélène was pensive.

"I wouldn't imagine that you would enjoy it either. It's all so hypocritical and you have to know how to carry yourself or they'll eat you alive. With her upbringing, my mom was amazing at any prestigious affair. She was always the belle of the ball. One minute she could behave like a princess and the next she's digging in the mud for artifacts. She was exceptional."

But Hélène had gone very quiet. Jodie continued. "Anyway, you'll see for yourself when you're in Washington. We're bound to have to attend something so make sure you bring the appropriate clothes."

Hélène looked downcast. Feeling guilty, Jodie moved to a more harmless topic. They discussed the seven Canadian painters.

Hélène recovered and the remainder of the voyage was very pleasant. Try as she might, it was difficult for Jodie to dislike *tante* Hélène. She was well read, witty, kind, without a mean bone in her body.

Jodie had persuaded Hélène to spend the two days at the Windsor Hotel with her rather than going to her sister's as was her custom. The location was perfect. They would have the train station, the downtown area and the art show at hand.

The Château Laurier had nothing on the opulent Windsor Hotel and once more Jodie was astonished as they entered the magnificent rotunda to register.

Hélène commented on Jodie's amazement. *"Et bien...* what did you expect. After all, Montréal is our biggest city. We do have a certan amount of culture here in the great northern wilderness."

"Oh, I'm finding that out."

After a day at the art show and a day of sightseeing, Jodie was becoming very friendly with her newly acquired aunt.

That night at the dinner table Jodie made an announcement. "I've been to the concierge and obtained the name and address of the best jazz club in Montréal. Eat up, we've got to change into our party clothes."

Hélène looked wickedly at Jodie. *"Oooh...* how naughty, I'm game."

"You're very much like Adèle... or I guess I should say that Adèle is very much like you.," Jodie observed.

"She's my very favourite niece. She and I are very close, more like sisters. We're each other's confidante."

Suddenly Jodie had a hankering to be part of that. *This isn't turning out as I'd expected. I was supposed to scare off tante Hélène. Nothing I've said about the difficulties of our life seems to have affected her. Instead I'm finding that I really like her.*

Jodie could not have been more wrong. Her depiction of life with the Greshams greatly affected Hélène. *What was I thinking? I can just imagine myself in some tent, living in the mud for weeks on end. How could I possibly fit in with Frank's upper class friends? How could I ever measure up to a woman like his Miriam? I must have mistaken his friendliness toward me. Obviously he likes me, so it must be friendship he's after. I won't be making a fool of myself... friendship it is then.*

———◀●▶———

When the two parties returned to Ottawa, it was agreed to meet for dinner in order to compare notes on their respective trips. It was left to Hélène to make the reservations for the foursome. She chose a small French restaurant, a short distance from the hotel.

It was snowing, great big fat flakes that fall gently and linger on the eyelashes. "Oh please let's walk," begged Jodie. She stuck out her tongue to catch some flakes.

Frank was visibly happy to see Hélène and he offered her his arm. "Lead the way *madame*. We are at your bidding."

Jodie took Jacques' arm and the party drowned out the crunching noise of their boots in the packed snow with their lively chatter.

Rosy cheeked and invigorated by the winter walk, the cheerful friends handed their coats to the *maître d'* before being shown to their table.

Jodie looked wide-eyed at her father as he aptly described the feelings he experienced when a tree was felled. He then regaled them with his version of the evening's festivities exaggerating the role of the would-be female dancers. The two women were in stitches.

The women were just as expressive when it came to describing the art of the Canadian group. In their haste to tell all, they often finished each other's sentences and by all accounts it was obvious that the two had had a grand time.

"When it comes to landscapes there's nothing as beautiful and romantic as a Turner or a Constable, Daddy, but their style could never have captured the wilds of Canada. Although each of these Canadian artists in the group has a distinctive style, they all possess the boldness necessary to depict North American nature."

"I totally agree with Jodie… I for one found them very refreshing." Hélène winked at Jodie.

Both men were watching the women intently. Both men had the same thought. *Well, well, quite the budding friendship here.*

Frank was delighted that Jodie came around to liking his lady friend.

Jacques was delighted that Jodie came around to liking this favourite *tante* of his.

1924
The Proposal

Jacques had planned a day of snowshoeing up the Ottawa River just above Aylmer. Jodie was excited at the prospect of trying something new. Frank wanted to be alone with Hélène so he begged off.

"You children go and enjoy yourselves without me. I've got much more sedentary plans in mind for myself." No sooner had they gone than he telephoned Hélène to invite her to lunch.

Once again through the good graces of François, Jacques and Jodie traveled by car across the Chaudière Bridge into Hull. From there they headed northwest to the quaint town of Aylmer close by. They passed several gates with curved driveways leading to lavish homes.

Jodie turned sideways to get a good look. "Goodness, is this millionaire row? How come we haven't been invited to any of these homes?"

"Ah... these are the folks that made their fortune in timber. We call them the lumber barons... you could say that they were my former bosses... but... never got an invite."

"Will they be included in the presentation? Shouldn't you be taking pictures?"

Jacques chuckled. "While you ladies will be chatting over tea at Adèle's tomorrow, we men, are going ice-fishing via the sawmills. Joseph will have all the facts, figures and history of the timber trade.

You can bet that the lumber barons will feature in the discussion. As for me, rest assured that I'll have my camera with me."

"Oh you must take a picture of Daddy ice-fishing. It's part of the custom around here, is it not?"

"I promise. By the way… did you buy long johns in Montréal like I told you to, and are you wearing them. Although it's mild today, it will be cold out on the river, the wind can cut right through you."

"Yes mummy." Jodie spoke in a child's voice. "I also bought a beautiful Irish wool sweater and I'm wearing it all. Daddy will be properly dressed for his ice-fishing. I've seen to that so there's nothing for you to worry about."

They left the car shortly after Aylmer and made their way down to the river with their gear. "Brrr… you call 20°F mild? How cold can it get?"

"Well below zero I'm afraid. You've been lucky so far." Jacques laced Jodie into her snowshoes. "I want you to know that these are the genuine article made by the Indians. Trying to walk in deep snow would be heavy going but with these your weight is dispersed and you don't sink all the way down."

Jacques grunted as he bent down to lace himself in. "The Indians have used these for hundreds of years… well thousands actually, if you believe Joseph."

Jacques looked over at Jodie. "You're very quiet. What's the matter?"

Jodie looked very stiff, standing on her snowshoes, legs apart. Her hat was pulled down, the earflaps secured by a strap under her chin. A scarf hid the bottom of her face and large sunglasses took care of the upper part. The newly acquired sweater under her coat made her look fat. It was a comical sight. "How in heaven's name am I supposed to walk in these?"

"Hold that pose!" Jacques pointed the Brownie camera hanging around his neck at Jodie. "Smile!"

"What do you mean… 'hold that pose'… I can't move." She pulled down the scarf and stuck her tongue out at the camera.

Click.

"That was one for the grandchildren." Jacques laughed.

"Don't worry, you learned how to skate and this is easier. People actually run in these things. Just watch me and follow." Jacques held out his hand.

Jodie's gait was awkward at first but she was determined. Once she had mastered it, she began to take in her surroundings. It was a beautiful sunny day. She now understood Jacques insistence that she wear sunglasses as the myriad sparkles in the snow were sure to blind.

The couple had trekked for an hour in comfortable silence. Jodie was deep in thought. *'One for the grandchildren', he said. If I had a child, I could have grandchildren. I'd like that.*

Jodie suddenly stopped and shouted out. "I recognize this place! We're heading north aren't we?"

"Yes, we are. What do you recognize?"

Jodie pointed. "There on our right... inland a bit... there's a higher shelf that runs parallel to the river and beyond that are the Gatineau Hills. That's where we were camping atop the escarpment in autumn looking down on this valley and the river... right where we are now."

"I'm impressed." Jacques looked proudly at Jodie.

"This is all so lovely. Can you imagine the nice view from above on that shelf. That is exactly where I want to build a house. A nice big house. One of those modern homes... all geometric shapes... walls made of windows... and a circular wing that sticks out in the front like a rounded prow of a ship." Jodie was enthusiastically gesticulating, making shapes.

She was happy and her enthusiasm was very appealing. Jacques wanted her so badly. "Jodie, open your coat, I want to see that lovely sweater you bought."

Jacques eyes were burning and Jodie did as she was told. He approached her as he unbuttoned his mackinaw. He stood astride her snowshoes, pulled down her scarf, put his arms around her under her coat, he drew her close to his chest and embraced her tightly.

He whispered, "I love your new sweater." He bent down to kiss her.

They held nothing back, body and soul went into that kiss. When they came up for air, they took off their sunglasses and looked deep into one another's eyes. They held the gaze for a very long time, speaking their love without words and eventually started kissing once more… small kisses… soft kisses… and then long, lingering, passionate kisses.

When Jodie went weak at the knees, Jacques held her up. They stopped. They were both breathing heavily, holding on to one another, slowly coming back to their senses.

Jacques loosened his grip slightly and spoke in a husky voice. "I want to be with you all the time, Jodie Gresham. What are we waiting for, say you'll marry me."

"I want you with me all the time too. I can't bear the thought that you'll be coming back here without me after your week at National Geographic."

"Well, then let's do it." Jacques was pleading.

Jodie pushed him away gently and buttoned her coat. "It's not as simple as that. Before I could take such an enormous step in my life, there are many things we need to discuss."

"Well, yes, I can see that. For one thing I can't afford the kind of kooky house you were just describing. Not too long from now I should be able to build you a lovely little house on that same spot if you wish and I promise that you'll not want for anything."

"You really don't know, do you?"

"Know what?" Jacques looked wary.

"Let's head back, Jack. I'm famished already and we're a good hour away. We can talk on the way."

Jacques made the about turn. "It'll be lunchtime by the time we reach Aylmer and I know a nice little tea house that serves a delicious soup."

As they veered back Jodie spoke first. "Jack, I know now that I want to get married and have a family and I can't imagine wanting to do that with anyone else but you. But… I could never be happy being the docile little housewife, living my life in one spot for the rest of my life. And if I was miserable then I would make you miserable."

"I'm listening. Tell me what it is that would make you happy."

"Well, you would make me happy so it would have to be you but I don't want the rest of my life to change. I'll always want to go on expeditions. I'd want to bring up a child the same way I was brought up. The only thing I would change is that I'd want that child to have a sibling... but no more. We would be a very close-knit family. You have no idea how happy we were; Mom, Dad and I."

Jacques was quiet.

"Well?"

"I'm thinking, I'm thinking."

After a long silence Jacques put his thoughts into words. "I too want to go on expeditions. I can see it being a big part of my photography career. Expeditions can be long and I wouldn't want to be away from my wife and family for any great length of time. I think that what you propose would be something I would also want... although..." Jacques paused.

"Yes?"

"Although I wouldn't know where to begin bringing up a family under such conditions and how can you be so sure we would only have two children unless you plan to abstain?"

"Remember that I have first hand experience as a child brought up while traveling the world. As for the rest of it, I know how to take care of myself. I might as well not get married if I'm to abstain." Jodie gave Jacques a lascivious look.

"What do you mean, 'you can take care of yourself'?"

"I know that you're not one much for reading but you do read copiously when it comes to photography. I'm going to lend you a book by Margaret Sanger. If you're going to be a husband you should know the female part of my anatomy and you should be *au fait* with birth control. Oh dear, I'm sorry... I forgot... your religion doesn't permit birth control."

"First of all, I intend to get to know your female anatomy intimately and secondly, I have no religion... this is so strange... I'm not accustomed to having this kind of talk with a woman." Jacques looked a little uncomfortable.

"But I'm not just any woman, I'm your woman and I expect that we'll be able to say anything that's on our minds. When have you ever known me to be proper, Jack Armand."

Jack was grinning. "I love you, Jodie Gresham and I see no objection to the kind of life you have in mind for us. What was the other thing you said I didn't know earlier?"

"I'm starving. I'm done with this serious talk until I'm sitting in front of a bowl of hot soup."

It was to be a thick pea soup to the great satisfaction of their stomachs.

They finished slurping and were awaiting their slice of *tourtière* when Jacques remembered. "You were to explain something I was unaware of."

"I had assumed that you knew about my financial situation…"

Jacques interrupted. "Anyone can see that your father's well-off but he won't be looking after our family, I will."

"No Jack, it's not my father, it's me. My mother was related to the Rockefellers and I've inherited from her. We're not talking about well-off here… we're talking about filthy rich. Why do you think we're so welcome in Washington's high society and why do you think so many young men are throwing themselves at me?" Jodie looked down.

Jacques was silent, mouth agape.

The *tourtière* arrived. Sensing the awkwardness at the table, the waiter served them speedily and left.

"Say something Jack."

"I don't know what to say."

"So I'm rich. I'm still the same person you fell in love with. I'm the same person you proposed to. I'm the same person you're contemplating having children with. I'm the same person you were so passionate about just an hour ago Nothing's changed."

"I won't be a kept man." Jacques fists were balled up.

"I can certainly understand that, Jack, and I promise it wouldn't be like that. But I do have this money and it allows me to do things that are very important to me."

"What things?"

"I'm involved in a great number of charitable projects… all anonymously. I couldn't give that up. I own the house we live in but Daddy looks after everything else. It could be like that for you and me too. I have no desire whatsoever of living the opulent lifestyle of my maternal relatives; our life would be simple."

"Nothing is ever simple with you Jodie."

Fat tears spilled from Jodie's eyes. "I never asked to be rich. I could give it all away but that makes no sense. Can't you love me this way?"

Jacques softened, his fists loosened and took her hand in his. "Jodie I love you any way you are. This is a shock and you're naïve if you think that this won't change my perception of the life I had envisioned with you. You've made all kinds of demands of what you want in a marriage. Let me give this some thought and I'll let you know exactly what it is I would like."

"When will I know?"

"Soon, very soon, and if all goes well, we can announce our engagement."

Jodie was smiling again. "If you married me right now, you wouldn't be marrying a rich girl. Right now Dad holds the purse strings. He's the trustee for my fortune until I turn 21 in a few weeks. I love you Jack."

"And I love you."

———●●●———

Frank and Hélène had lunch at the Château. He was waiting for his guest in the lobby far from the entrance that he might admire her approach.

She walked with a lively step. Hélène was petite like her sister Lorraine and her niece Adèle. Unlike them, however, Frank knew that under the rabbit fur coat her bones were well covered, yet her waist was small and she was busty enough to give her a curvaceous hourglass shape. Hat in hand, her glossy jet-black hair curved into a short bob over her ears. As she neared and smiled, he was once again disarmed by the dimple in her right cheek that gave her a saucy look. She took his arm and they proceeded from there to the dining room where the *maître d'* showed them to the table Frank had specifically reserved beforehand.

The couple sat and Frank ordered champagne. "My, my, to what do I owe this lavishness?"

"Having lunch with my favourite Québec girl is cause enough for celebration."

"Ah, so I'm your girl now... and how many other Québec girls do you have?" Hélène teased.

They heard the 'pop' in the background and the sommelier arrived with the chilled bottle. He poured, he left, and they toasted one another.

"To my Québec girl."

"And to my… er… what do I call you Frank?" Hélène looked embarassed.

"Am I not your favourite Washington beau?"

Hélène blushed. "*Et bien Monsieur* Gresham, it sounds to me like we might be courting."

Now they were both blushing realising that they were acting silly and way ahead of themselves.

Frank recovered first and cleared his throat. "Ahem… well it would seem to me that courtship is all about getting to know one another better, wouldn't you say? I count you as a friend that I do want to know better."

Hélène was relieved that the awkward moment had passed. She raised her glass. "To friendship then, *et bonne santé!*"

Their glasses clinked and their smiles broadened. *There's that charming dimple again,* thought Frank.

They spoke of books, cinema, art and politics. Frank spoke of his travels and Hélène spoke of the constraints imposed on Québec women by the government, the church and society.

During dessert Frank proposed a walk down by the river. "Jodie and I had a lovely walk there before we left in autumn and I want to experience the same walk in winter."

"*Absolument,* we must take advantage of this mild sunny day." Hélène was very agreeable to a walk by the river.

"So you consider 20°F mild?" Frank hugged himself tightly as though he were cold.

Down by the river Frank marveled at the difference in the scenery. "It's just so different… just as beautiful… but different."

"I believe that Jacques showed you the Rideau Falls when you were here last… is that not right?"

"Yes, he did."

"Come then, let's get the car. If you want to see different, this you have to see." Hélène had made an about turn and was heading back up at a pace.

"Whoa... wait for the old man." Amused, Frank followed.

He was not disappointed. Sparkling columns of frozen water replaced the autumn falls he had viewed before. Here and there a stream of water not yet frozen spilled down.

"Thanks for bringing me. It is indeed lovely."

Frank put his arm around Hélène and she leaned in against him. They stood in silence, quite content. Their nearness began to have an impact. Hélène looked up at Frank. He cupped her chin and kissed her softly on the lips. With great restraint he went no further... not wanting to scare her away... not knowing that she would have welcomed more.

They rubbed noses and Hélène giggled. "Your beard tickles."

"I'm looking forward to your visit in spring," said Frank.

Hélène suddenly looked uncomfortable. "I wasn't sure if you were serious about that... I mean... it was mentioned last autumn but you haven't brought it up since... and... well..."

"Well of course you're coming. I've seen the capital of your country so it's only fair that you see mine. What's the matter... something is troubling you." Frank looked concerned at her discomfiture.

"It's just that... Jodie was saying... well I don't think I would fit in very well... and I don't have the right clothes... *mon dieu*... I'm babbling... sorry."

"Just what did Jodie say?"

"She was only describing her life in Washington and it would seem to me that you move in a high society circle where I would be most uncomfortable." Hélène let out a big sigh.

Frank burst out laughing. "That little devil. I knew she was up to something." He laughed some more.

"*Mais c'pas drôle*, I really fail to see what's so funny." Hélène looked offended.

"My dear, I'm not laughing at you. I believe Jodie had a plan when she went with you to Montréal and I suspect that it might have backfired." Frank still looked amused.

"*J'comprends pas...* I'm still at a loss here."

"I'm afraid you were not Jodie's favourite person, simply because she was afraid that she was losing her Daddy to another woman." Frank chuckled. "Even though she's my own daughter, I have to admit that she's spoiled and can be childish at times. It's obvious that her objective was to frighten you off."

"*Mais non...* we got on very well in Montréal."

"Exactly my point. She hadn't planned on you being the lovely person that you are and you won her over." Frank laughed some more.

Hélène blushed at the compliment. "But... was she telling the truth."

"Jodie wouldn't lie... she's really a good girl and her heart is in the right place but she sure can exaggerate."

"Well her upbringing has been far from normal and she can be quite complicated at times but I find her refreshing and likeable." Hélène was being honest.

"What you need to understand is that I enjoy your company tremendously. I can't tell you exactly where our friendship is heading, but I do want to explore the possibilities... and as for the clothes, I'm sure that Jodie will be overjoyed at the prospect of a shopping spree with you in Washington. So... are we still on for Washington?"

"To be honest, I really did want to go to Washington and now I look forward to it." Hélène smiled at him, dimple and all.

"Ice-fishing. You Canadians must be crazy." Frank commented to Joseph when he picked him and Jacques up early the next morning.

"And when we're done, it's off with your clothes and we jump in the water." Jacques was dead serious.

Frank blanched. "Please tell me that you're joking."

Joseph couldn't keep a straight face. "You should have seen your face... scared you, huh?"

"A man could get heart failure at the mere thought of it." Frank sighed relief.

"Oh we were only partly pulling your leg. A number of guys do take that plunge. It's actually supposed to be healthy." He could tell that Jacques wasn't jesting this time.

"What are the chances it could happen while we're there? Jack, just think of the photo opportunity."

"He's always on the job." Jacques explained to the others.

On the way to the Gatineau River, the men visited the sawmill in Hull and Jacques took the appropriate pictues.

"There are a number of sawmills within easy driving distance from here and we hear rumours of a big pulp and paper factory setting up in Point-à-Gatineau in the next couple of years. If that were to happen the town would boom overnight." Joseph was always a fountain of knowledge.

"I appreciate you taking the day off, Joseph. I know you'll be a big help for my article."

"I left the grocery in good hands. *Monsieur* Laflamme enjoys helping me out from time to time. Some days he just comes in to talk to his old customers. I think he's lonely."

When they arrived at their destination there were others on the river sitting on wooden boxes waiting patiently by a hole in the ice. Here and there stood tiny wooden structures to protect the serious fishermen from the wind. One hole had a pup tent erected over it.

With the help of a small pickaxe and saw Jacques cut a hole in the ice almost two feet in diameter. They set up their boxes and sank their lines in the frigid waters. Jacques stood back a little and took pictures of the two men intently looking down the hole. Before settling down to the business of fishing he photographed other groups and some of the tiny shanties.

"What are we likely to catch here." Frank enquired.

"Pike, speckled trout and maybe a..." Jacques turned to Joseph. "How do you say *doré jaune.*"

"Walleye."

The idea was to keep quiet and be patient just like summer fishing.

Frank would have been bored out of his mind had he not scored twice while Jacques and Joseph caught one fish each. "*Woo hoo...* nothing like showing your teachers how it's done," boasted Frank on his second strike.

As they were packing up to leave, Jacques made his way across to one of the shanties. After a little while he came back accompanied by a strapping young fellow.

"Fellows, I want you to meet Jean-Luc Fortier. Just five dollars Frank and he takes the plunge. What do you say?

"Hell yes, get your camera ready Jack." Frank started pulling from his pocket.

Another man came running from the shanty with a blanket while the brave Jean-Luc stripped and before giving it a second thought, he jumped in.

Frank was whooping and clapping.

Jacques took the shot as he was half immersed on his way out.

The men finished their day at one of the popular taverns in Hull. They gulped the first beer down and while they sipped the second Joseph answered all of Frank's questions about the history of the most successful lumber baron families; names such as Wright, Symmes, Conroy and Egan.

Hélène felt lonely after Jacques and his guests left for Washington. She looked forward to Sunday mass where she would see her family.

In preparation for mass and communion, she was in the habit of going to confession on Saturdays, not that there was ever much to confess. Without being a fanatic, she was nevertheless devout. Her relationship with her Lord was solid and as such she belived in having a spotless soul before the sacred communion.

The line at the confessional was long. As usual Hélène was making an inventory of her sins.

Realising that this confession might be problematic, in her mind she reviewed her knowledge of sin taught to her by the nuns and committed to memory. 'Any thought, word or deed against the law of God is deemed to be sinful.' *Hmmm…this does leave a great deal of room for sinning.*

'Furthermore sin is divided into three categories; the first being original sin which everyone commits by the act of being born. None can escape and the only thing that can erase this sin is Baptism.' *I've often thought how cruel it was to leave the babies who die before being baptised in limbo.*

'The second is mortal sin which is a deliberate transgression against the moral law of God and is extremely serious. Immediate confession is highly recommended lest a person should die before receiving pardon and doing the required penance, because the consequence of mortal sin, even a single one, is eternal damnation.' *I don't think I've done anything as bad as all that.*

'The third kind is venial sin. It also requires confession and penance but it is much less grievous because a person dying before receiving absolution would find themselves in purgatory for a time with heaven being the eventual destination.' *That seems fair.*

But I wonder how the priests decide which category a sin falls into. Of course things like murder are obvious but it seems to me that there's an awful lot of grey areas. What if I really believed that my sin was venial while another puts it in the category of mortal? After all there's no tribunal where a person could appeal.

Hélène had been quilty of only one mortal sin in her entire life. *Père* Jacob had decreed that her reading of *Madame Bovary* was mortal and as such had extinguished her soul. Unfortunately, this had taught her very little as she found herself confessing to reading an equally salacious book to *Père* Tramblay who seemed to think very little of this sin. The moral of this story is that one tried to confess one's sins when *Père* Tremblay was in the confessional.

However, today *Père* Jacob had taken *Père* Tremblay's place for whatever reason and Hélène found herself thoroughly examining her list of sins.

It was her turn. She entered the confessional.

"Bless me Father for I have sinned. It has been one week since my last confession...."

Hélène started with the small stuff... a sin of omission... an unkind word... a moment of laziness.

Père Jacob yawned.

When she finished with those, she took a deep breath and confessed to her impure thoughts concerning Frank.

Père Jacob was suddenly alert. It was a very small town and he knew who he was dealing with. "*Ma fille*, are you involved with this Protestant friend of Jacques Armand?"

"*Oui mon Père.*" Hélène was shaking.

"What exactly have you done with this heathen."

"Nothing really, just a small kiss."

"My child, you must stop seeing this man at once. It is clear that you are more than friends and the relationship has no future.

The Church would never marry you unless this man converted to Catholicism. I need not tell you that any other action will lead to your immediate excommunication."

There was a sharp intake of breath on the other side of the screen. He could as well have said 'executed' instead of 'excommunicated' and the reaction would have been the same.

"Now, I want you to recite ten rosaries for your penance and think carefully on what I have told you."

The persons next in line did not fail to notice the length of time Hélène spent in the cubicle nor her ashen face as she exited. Tongues would wag… a sin in itself to be sure, but then so easy to confess.

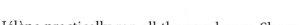

Hélène practically ran all the way home. She was in a mess. Pacing the floor she decided that her first step was to execute the prescribed penance. Ten rosaries! The most she had ever gotten was one rosary; with a few 'Hail Marys and a few 'Our Fathers' being the norm.

Ten rosaries take a long time. Perhaps they would have a calming effect on her. It was not to be. The recitations did nothing to appease her state of mind.

It was lunchtime. Hélène forced a piece of bread wth cheese down her throat and phoned Adèle.

She waited three rings. "*Oui, allô.*"

"Adèle, *c'est tante* Hélène." The tremor in her voice alerted her niece.

"Is something wrong, *ma tante*?"

"Well I would like to talk something over with you, if you have some free time this afternoon."

"Of course, Roger is down for his nap in another hour and the girls will be tobogganing with the neighbours at the park. Do come over, I'll have a hot cup of tea waiting."

Hélène met the warmly bundled up girls on their way out with their neighbour and her three little ones. "*Ma tante* Hélène," they shrieked in unison.

Big hugs were in order. Hélène stopped a moment to give the neighbour a few words of greeting and appreciation for her good care of the children.

The women settled into the two large armchairs in the parlour, tea cups in hand. Adèle looked comfortable sitting sideways with her feet tucked under her bottom while Hélène, sitting straight backed, looked stiff.

"*Et bien ma tante*, you seem worried, what's the matter."

"I don't know where to begin. Actually I feel a little silly now." Hélène looked embarrassed.

Adèle waited patiently.

Hélène took a deep breath and looked up at her niece. "It's about Frank Gresham."

Adèle smiled. "Everyone can see how well the two of you get along. Joseph and I were hoping that something good would come of this for you."

"Well that's just it. I think I'm falling in love. I know you may think that it's silly at my age but if I'm reading things correctly, I think that Frank might be feeling the same way too."

Adèle's smile broadened. "*C'est merveilleux*, I couldn't be happier for you and I can't imagine anyone considering you too old for love."

Tears ran down Hélène's cheeks.

"*Sainte Marie*, what's wrong… please tell me." Adèle put her cup down and went over to her aunt. She knelt by her, took away her cup and held her hands. "*Là, là, ma tante…* everything's going to be alright."

Adèle was not sure what to do as this was a reversal of roles. How many times had her aunt comforted her. She wanted to do the right thing.

Hélène held on tightly and blurted it all out. "It's not so simple. Frank lives in hovels across the world half the time… the rest of the time he lives in high society… I don't even have the right clothes… Jodie doesn't really like me… and *Père* Jocob is going to have me excommunicated."

Adèle was dumbfounded.

Hélène was now audibly crying.

Adèle pulled her aunt out of the chair and held her tight until the crying stopped. She handed her a hankerchief. "Now, come and sit here on the sofa next to me and we'll go over this slowly."

Calmer now, Hélène was able to explain things clearly to Adèle. "*Maudit Père* Jacob! Damn that priest." Adèle was livid.

Her aunt was shocked. "Adèle! You can't damn a priest."

"He's not just a priest, *ma tante,* he's also a man and a dishonest one at that. He broke the confessional seal after one of Joseph's confession and used that to call me out in front of the whole congregation. He's mean and all of his sermons are full of venom. Neither Joseph nor I would ever confess with him again."

"Well, I don't know what to say about that."

"Look at what he's trying to do to you. There's no sin in love *ma tante*. Jesus preached nothing but love and God is supposed to be all love. This is a brand new relationship and you don't know where it will lead. If he wants to marry you, and he would be a fool not to, then he may very well want to convert. You can cross that bridge when you come to it. *Père* Jacob thrives in making people miserable."

"You're right, I've done nothing to be excommunicated… at least not yet anyway." Hélène was feeling a little better.

"And what's this about Jodie not liking you? I saw how she behaved toward you when we had tea here the day the men went ice-fishing. She adores you. We had such a good time. Marie Labelle phoned me to tell me we have to do this more often and that it would be at her place next time."

"I know, I know. Whatever Jodie had against me, has been resolved." Hélène told Adèle the story of their Montréal trip.

Adèle laughed. "She never achieved her objective and you turned the tables on her and made a friend of her… that's funny."

"Actually she didn't fail altogether in her mission. She really did make me see that Frank and I are from two very different worlds."

"See, there you go again, getting ahead of yourself. Live in the present *ma tante*, enjoy his company. Things have a way of resolving themselves. In fact, if I remember correctly, a very wise aunt of mine gave me the same counsel some years back."

By the time the two had exhausted the subject entirely, the children had come back and Joseph had finished work for the day. In much better humour than when she had arrived, Hélène was easily persuaded to stay for dinner.

CHAPTER 27

1924
Spring Expedition

Jacques had spent much of his week in Washington either working in the photo labs of the National Geographic or deep in meetings. Jodie spent the better part of her days in her studio emulating some of the Group of Seven artists.

Their evenings were spent together. They thoroughly enjoyed seeing 'Safety First' at the cinema one night. On another occasion Jodie took Jacques to an out-of-the-way jazz club where Jodie knew no one for a change. It was a hole in the ground but the music was haunting and worthwhile. The night before Jacques left, they ate in a cozy French restaurant and walked for hours afterwards talking about everything and nothing. Otherwise, their time on Q Street was spent with Frank, playing cards or in companionable discussions.

They kissed frequently; their bodies yearning for more; knowing, feeling, and believing that the time to become one was not far off.

In the following weeks the two Canadians did much soul searching as did the two Americans. Meanwhile the letters between the Ottawa Valley and Washington were frequent.

Jacques often asked himself why he was so enamored with this complicated young woman. *Just exactly what is it I see in her?* He recalled their first meeting two years previously and he laughed to himself. *She looked like some dirty boy and right from then she got under my skin and it wasn't in a good way. She knew how to provoke me and it was truly annoying. I must say though that I gave back as good as I got.*

Frank has made me understand a lot. I know now that she was scared... scared to let anyone get close... scared to get hurt. It's taken me a long time to peel back the protective layers but it was worth it. She's funny, witty, interesting and so sensual. It's all quite intimate now... she tells me just about anything because she trusts me... but.... she's frail and vulnerable and I don't want to hurt her or she'll go back in that shell forever.

It's that damn money! Whew... I sure didn't see that one coming. I can't just ask her to give it all away... ground rules... that's it... we've got to set some ground rules... rules that we can both live with. We've got to work that out because when she comes back in spring, we're going to make it official with a wedding just around the corner because I just can't wait any longer.

——●●●——

Hélène was in a disturbed state most of the time. Though Frank's kiss had been quite chaste, it had nevertheless awakened feelings that she hadn't experienced in years. She had accepted long ago that the sensual part of her life was over. After years of suppression, one could say that the feelings were back with a vengeance.

Her weekly confessions to *Père* Tremblay were repetitive. With great sympathy, or perhaps it was empathy, he absolved her of her sins and gave her counsel to cope with the situation. Most of this advice required meditation and prayer.

Pray as she might, her mind wandered to visions of sleeping with Frank. These nocturnal thoughts fluctuated between reveling in Frank's arms, and worrying about her body image at what she called 'middle age'.

In the daytime she worried about the differences that could separate them. She was both excited and frightened by the prospect of visiting Washington and experiencing Frank's way of life. On the plus side, she felt that Jodie would not be a problem. On the contrary, she enjoyed her vivacity and felt that Jodie also had good feelings toward her. On the minus side, she worried about fitting into high society and knew that Frank's religious beliefs, or rather his lack of beliefs might pose an insurmountable problem.

Some days she would chastise herself for needlessly worrying over something that had been, after all, only a kiss. Yet, in the depths of her heart she knew... she knew that Frank was seriously interested in her... she knew that she was too. For the first time, a completely unknown future stretched before her which was both exhilarating and daunting. She would not be taking *Père* Jacob's advice on ending the relationship... she just could not. *C'est simple,* I've fallen in love.

Jodie had come out of her protective cocoon. It had been so safe in there, just her and her Daddy. But now the obnoxious little caterpillar was out spreading her adult wings. What seemed frightening a year ago was now liberating. The butterfly could soar and before her lay a life of endless possibilities. Her world could now evolve.

She began to dream of things that would never have entered her mind before. *Jacques could be with me all the time... and children... a mother... I would be a mother... my own child. Daddy would make such a wonderful granddaddy and Hélène would be a lovely addition to our family... she makes Daddy so happy... I swear he looks younger. Just the other day he was asking me if he should cut his beard.* Jodie laughed out loud at the thought.

Then she frowned. *But it's the money. Jacques is such a masculine type of guy always in control of the situation. He could never be a kept man even if he just thought he was, it would destroy who he is slowly but surely. Anyway, I've some ideas about how we can get around it and hopefully Jacques will agree because I just can't wait anymore.*

Much like Hélène, Frank was also in a troubled state. He was well aware that there were gaping differences between them. One quiet Sunday morning, father and daughter sat at the breakfast table reading the papers over a strong cup of coffee.

Frank put down his paper. "Jodie, I need to know what you think of Hélène... and I don't need a flippant remark at this time."

Jodie lowered the section she was reading. "I would never think of doing that Daddy. I can tell how serious you are about *tante* Hélène. The answer is that I enjoy her company, she's very much like her niece Adèle. She's kind, knowledgeable, funny and lively… an all around lovely person, I'd say." She went back to reading the paper.

Frank took a deep breath and exhaled audibly. "My word… I didn't expect so much praise coming from you. It's just that you frightened both of us when you outlined our differences on your Montréal trip."

Jodie put the paper down and looked her father in the eye. "That was a mistake Daddy. It was foolish and it was mean. I was afraid that our life would tear apart. I'm sorry." The contrition in her voice was genuine.

"Oh I know full well why you did it, Jodie. However, you weren't altogether wrong. Her life in Pointe-à-Gatineau has not prepared her for our expeditions nor some of our high society events."

"Poppycock! Love will conquer all." Jodie smiled and winked at her Dad. "All that matters is that she's comfortable with us and that way she'll be comfortable with us anywhere."

"Jacques is comfortable with us but still hates wearing a tux and mixing with these characters you frequent," Frank pointd out.

"Well, I'm done frequenting these phonies with dollar signs in their eyes everytime they see me. We do have a few nice friends who frequent these parties and we can introduce Hélène to these people who know how to put a stranger at ease."

"That's true."

"*Tante* Hélène would love to come on many of our tamer expeditions and when she feels that a particular mission would not be her cup of tea, she could visit her family in Québec. We <u>are</u> talking about a possible marriage here, are we not?"

"When did you get so smart. Yes… I think so. I intend to see how things develop when she visits us in spring. If all goes well and if we can overcome these hurdles, I will ask her to be my wife and hope she accepts."

"I'm afraid that these so-called hurdles of yours are the least of your problems." Jodie put her hand on her Dad's arm.

"I'm not following." Frank looked perplexed.

"Jacques and I had a long conversation about you two before he left." Frank was preparing to object. "Hold on, hold on." Jodie put up her hand in a stop sign. "You might not have been aware of just how religious Hélène is. She could never leave her church. Jacques informs me that the Catholic church would never marry her to a Protestant."

"But I have no religion really."

"Ah... well, apparently that's even worse. I'm told that a Protestant is akin to being a heathen but an atheist is akin to being the devil incarnate in Québec."

Frank looked worried. "I hadn't given this any thought and I should have. What an idiot I am. This could indeed be a stumbling block."

"With our two heads plus Jacques... he's also giving it some thought... we should come up with a way out of this.

"Well what about you and Jacques. He's also Catholic... and we <u>are</u> talking about marriage here, are we not?" It was Frank's turn to wink at his daughter.

Jodie rolled her eyes. "It's not as much of a problem because you know he's not a practising Catholic... but... he wouldn't want to hurt his parents... so... we're discussing it."

Frank took his daughter's hand in both of his. "Lots happening here, daughter of mine. It's all so marvelous and all so frightening. Whatever the outcome, we'll always have each other.

The April spring melt in the Ottawa Valley brought the four lovers together once again. On this occasion the lumber camp foreman had to put up with two females as Hélène accompanied the usual trio.

The more the workers displayed their pleasure at seeing the women, the more Mr. McTavish indicated his displeasure. "Perhaps the ladies would have been more comfortable viewing the latest spring fashions in Montréal and doing a wee bit of shopping."

Hélène nudged Jodie and whispered in her ear. "I see what you meant about this foreman of yours. Not the most evolved."

They were guided to the banks of a tributary of the Gatineau River where the logs had been skidded and hauled during the winter. They stood well back and watched with fascination as the logs were floated into the water, jamming together. Where the log-jams impeded progress the *draveurs* jumped from log to log with long poles to unblock the way.

The women held their breaths as the men deftly danced on the logs. "*Mon Dieu, mon Dieu...*" Hélène looked away as one of the men lost his balance and regained it a hair's breath away from falling where he would surely have been crushed between logs and drowned.

"Damn that was close." With nerves on edge Frank had watched it all.

"This is probably the most dangerous part of the logging industry," Jacques informed them. "It was my speciality."

Two bearded men made their way toward the visitors.

Grinning from ear to ear with right hand outstretched the first one cried, "*calvert!*", while the second exclaimed, "*sacrament!*"

"*Ti-Jean, Reynald... salut.*" Jacques shook both men's hands. "I can't believe you men are still doing this."

"Now that you're gone, Reynald here has broken your record and is still the man to beat." Ti-Jean was lauding the prowess of his comrade.

Ti-Jean pointed to Jacques feet. "You've got the right boots on... how about giving it a go for old times sake... or maybe you're a bit soft in your old age."

Jacques took his backpack off. "Get me a pole."

Jodie hung on to his arm. "Are you out of your mind, Jack. You haven't done this for years. It's too dangerous."

"Are you sure this is wise?" Frank looked just as worried as Jodie.

"*Jésus, Marie, Joseph...* he's going to kill himself." Hélène crossed herself.

"And I was led to believe that you loved a bit of excitement." Jacques called out to Jodie as he made his way to the river with the two *draveurs*.

Hearts in their mouths, the three watched as Jacques began jumping and rolling on the logs that were behaving themselves gently. As he lost and regained his balance a few times before getting back his *draveur's* legs Jodie cried out and hid her face in her father's jacket. Hélène was peeking through the fingers of her hands placed across her eyes.

As Jacques grew more confident he went further out where the situation was fraught with danger. "*Gie it laddie!...*the man's still got it," exclaimed the foreman.

Each time Jacques slipped or seemed to lose his balance Frank involuntarily tightened his arms around his daughter sending chills down her back.

Unharmed Jacques returned to his group. Breathing heavily, his face red, excitement danced in his eyes.

"Well... what did you think of that, Jodie."

"I couldn't look."

Jacques' face fell. "But Jodie...."

Frank stepped in smartly. "You were fantastic Jack. Hélène and I were greatly impressed."

Hélène elbowed Frank. "Speak for yourself Frank Gresham, it was a foolhardy thing to do Jacques. You terrified us and poor Jodie was frightened half to death that something bad would happen to you... *mais... oui...* you were quite exciting to watch." The last was said grudgingly.

When the logs reached open water in the larger river, they were tied into large rafts, the *draveurs* guiding the rafts with their long poles. The party of four made the trip to the Gatineau River in the horse-drawn wagon on runners. Though the temperatures were milder, snow was still on the ground.

Having bid their goodbyes to Alistair McTavish, the visitors now reported to Mike O'Flaherty who was the person in charge.

Unlike the Scot, this Irishman was quite comfortable in the presence of the ladies. With a twinkle in his eye he kept smoothing the tips of his handlebar mustache smiling deliberately at the women.

After watching the hardworking men swearing and sweating for the better part of an hour, Mr. O'Flaherty offered the goup a ride on a newly completed raft.

"Oh my, yes, could we please." Jodie was excited.

"*Non, non, non...* it can be quite dangerous." Jacques was forbidding it.

"Oh, so it's quite fine for you to try breaking your neck and have me suffering, but when it's my turn to have a little fun, then it's no... no... no." Jodie turned to Mr. Flaherty. "I would be delighted to try it out."

"I think I'd like that very much also. What do you say, Hélène... shall we give it a go." Frank seemed just as gung-ho as Jodie.

Miséricorde! I'm probably going to have more of this sort of thing if I'm contemplating a life with these two. "I'm scared Frank, are you sure it's safe." Hélène said timidly.

"I'll hold you tight, I promise."

Jacques sighed. "It would seem that I'm outnumbered." He turned to the Irishman. "The ladies will have to be carried onto the raft. It wouldn't do for their feet to get wet."

"And so it shall be." The Irishman was delighted as were the men put in charge of carrying the ladies safely onto the raft.

They rafted down the river smoothly at first, the *draveurs* showing off their poling skills and sneaking looks at the ladies; Jacques and Frank, each with his arm around his beloved. When the raft reached some mild rapids, bumping and shifting from left to right, the women started shrieking, much as though they were on a roller coaster, both frightened and thrilled at the same time. The *draveurs* laughed good-naturedly, purposefully poling the raft toward wild waters.

Exhilarated, the women were eventually carried off the raft with the help of their beaus at an appointed spot where the wagon-come-sled awaited them.

———◆●◆———

It was a whirlwind of activities for the Americans during their week in the *Outaouais* region. Shortly after the excitement of the log run the foursome went on a sugar party. Frank had been to one in northern Vermont in his youth but it was a first for Jodie and she was looking forward to tapping the sap from the maple trees.

Five wagonloads of people made their way to the maple shack. Joseph and Adèle brought their children as did François and Shirley. Jacques' parents were there with much of their extended family, most of whom Frank and Jodie had met before. Louis and Lorraine

Turcotte were surrounded by their extended family, most of whom were new acquaintances for the American pair.

It was a mild cloudy day, so mild, that large patches of yellow grasses were exposed. The farmers had come earlier to tap the trees and had hung the tin buckets filling with sap drop by drop. The buckets were now full and ready for the boiler in the shack. The fire was stoked, the sap boiled until it reached the consistency of syrup. Some was boiled longer to make taffy.

Many hands were needed to carry the buckets to the shack for boiling and back to the trees for more sap. Jodie listened to the drip, drip of the sap rattling the empty tin bucket. She was as excited as the children.

Some helped with the boiler fire; others were busy skimming the scum off the boiling syrup; women warmed lard beans in iron pots over an open fire; and the children made primitive-looking snowmen in the wet snow.

When the taffy was ready, Louis Turcotte made the call to one and all. The children abandoned their play and made a beeline for it. The taffy was spread in strips on the cold snow to cool and rolled on sticks to savour; the more creative ones made elaborate shapes in the snow with the hot taffy.

When tummies were satisfied with the delicious beans, the home baked bread and the yummy maple taffy, an accordion appeared seemingly out of nowhere and the music began. Some sat by the fire while some danced and everyone sang the familiar lyrics of the old French-Canadian folk songs: *Vive la Canadienne et ses jolies yeux doux... Ah les fraises et les framboises, du bon vin j'en ai bu... C'est l'aviron qui nous mène...*

Frank could not have asked for more insight into the French Canadian culture. He sat apart from the crowd making notes in his black book and admiring Hélène bellowing out the songs with great gusto. She had thoughtfully written out the words to the songs and handed the sheet to Jodie who was singing along with Jacques at her side. *If only time could stand still...* Frank thought.

Back at the farm it took a full twenty minutes to kiss, hug and shake hands before all the goodbyes were done. Frank made arrangements with Hélène for the following day and then climbed into the back of Jacques' new car for the ride back to the Château. "Not a bad little car for a secondhand. You did well," Frank commended his friend.

"Well, it was about time. Poor François was almost without transportation everytime we came here." Jodie yawned, tired out after the day's festivities.

"I think it'll be an early night for us." Frank had caught Jodie's infectious yawn. "Two more busy days before we depart for Washington to put this article to bed. Hélène is not on the guest list at tomorrow's wedding so I thought I would take her out to dinner after we're done. I'm certain you two won't mind having some time to yourselves." Frank was grinning.

"I'm afraid you might be disappointed with Lucille's wedding. Joseph's family are considered affluent in Point-à-Gatineau. Denis Lafleur's General Store does very well. He's bought land next to the soon to be Pulp and Paper factory. If that comes into being, the surrounding area will mushroom and he'll be right in the thick of things," Jacques informed them.

"I don't see how that affects the wedding?" Frank was curious.

Joseph looked down and smiled at a deceptively innocent-looking Jodie who had nodded off. He spoke in a low voice. "Other than the Lafleur family, the guest list will be the who's who of Hull and Aylmer. Rose Lafleur tends to be a little snobbish so she won't want her wedding to look like what she sees as a low-class family farm affair especially when the groom is a young doctor."

"So none of the fiddles, accordions, harmonicas and spoons then? I wanted to see the French Canadian version of square dancing." Frank sounded disappointed.

"Well, we'll have to wait and see but I think I know Rose Lafleur." Jacques seemed confident.

———◆◆◆———

At ten sharp the next morning, Frank, Jodie and Jacques were seated on the bride's side in a middle row of the St. François de Sales Church. People were dressed in their finest, some expensively so. All awaited the bride.

The organ belted out the traditional wedding march and the heavily veiled bride all fluff and lace entered on her father's arm; a maid of honor, two bridesmaids and a darling little flower girl brought up the rear, all smiles and giggles with basket in hand. She forgot to scatter the petals around.

When the wedding party had settled, the bride and groom knelt before *Père* Jacob who made a series of signs of the cross and said some latin words before he began his preaching to the couple.

His stentorious voice echoed through the church. He spoke at great length in a monotone about the sanctity of marriage and the seriousness of this sacrament.

Bored, Jodie's mind wandered. *It must hurt to be kneeling for so long. It's a good thing the bride's dress has ample material to cushion her knees.*

Suddenly, *Père* Jacob raised his voice considerably and adopted an admonishing tone. The guests awoke.

"Woman is by nature evil and a temptress. It was through Eve that mankind lost paradise." The priest looked down pointedly at Lucille, his voice positively strident. "As a consequence God decreed that you would bear young with great pain. He instituted the Sacrament of Marriage for the purpose of bringing life into this world. It will be your conjugal duty to service your husband that you may have as many children as God desires for you. You must not fail in this duty toward your husband for the flesh is weak and you must not allow temptation from outside the sacred bonds of marriage to befall him."

The priest turned to the groom. "It will be your duty to protect, and provide for your wife and children. You are the head of the family and as such you must be a good disciplinarian of sober mind."

Back to the bride... "You must obey your husband in all things..." almost as an afterthought he added, "provided of course it is in accordance to God's law."

"Finally, I remind you both that it is your sacred duty to bring up your children in the fear of the Lord and to be holy in your dealings with one another. We will now procede to the vows."

Frank and Jodie had almost dozed during the first part of the preaching but the admonishments to the young couple were delivered slowly and deliberately so that both the Americans understood perfectly.

Father and daughter looked at one another meaningfully. They shared a common thought. *In no uncertain terms was this priest to have anything to do with marrying them.*

Jodie turned to Jacques and whispered. "What was that all about? No one seems perturbed, least of all the bride and groom. I would be devastated if that were me getting married."

Jacques whispered back. "We're all used to it by now. It's his usual wedding sermon. I guess we don't pay attention to it anymore."

"Why wouldn't she use that other gorgeous young priest? He certainly would have brought in the word 'love' at a wedding."

"*Père* Jacob is head of this parish and I think that *Madame* Lafleur wouldn't want a young assistant presiding over the ceremony."

"Well they deserve what they got then."

Jacques had been correct. The wedding reception was generic; a well decorated hall; classic piano music; dancing to a waltz; champagne; *coq au vin* accompanied by *pomme de terre au persil.* Hardly a fun-filled, lively affair like the Katie O'Malley wedding.

Jodie was delighted that Joseph and Adèle were seated at their table. She was curious to hear Adèle's thoughts on *Père* Jacob's preaching.

At first Adèle laughed it off and then she took on a more serious look. "Actually, it's really no laughing matter because that priest meant every word of it. Any problems brought to him by a married couple will invariably be blamed on the woman. If a man were to confess to an infidelity, *Père* Jacob will call on the wife to find out if she has been fulfilling her conjugal duties. As soon as two years go by without a pregnancy, he will investigate the same conjugal duty obligations or worse still, the possibility of birth control."

"And these woman take him on?" Jodie was shocked.

"He terrifies them."

"I don't understand. He can't send them to prison or anything. He holds no real power over them."

"Oh but he does. He can refuse absolution in the confessional and there's always excommunication which is death to the soul and eternal damnation." Adèle was quite dramatic.

"That's odious... why would anyone ever want to be Catholic... *oops*... I'm sorry if I'm offending you... but... honestly, I'm afraid it's the way I feel about it." Jodie looked sad.

"Oh dear, I never meant to put you off Catholicism but I must admit that *Père* Jacob does not sell us well. His only saving grace is that he will not abide drunkenness. The good father will stand by a wife should her husband beat her while intoxicated... otherwise a husband has every right to discipline his wife."

Joseph broke in. "Hey, you two, this is a wedding, a happy occasion and you both look like doom and gloom."

Jacques used Frank's dinner appointment as an excuse for an early getaway. Adèle was sorry to see them go because she was not sure when she would see them again now that the research for the National Geographic article was completed.

"Oh you can count on seeing us again. We love it here and feel that we've made some real friends. It's only an *au revoir*." Frank was very sincere.

———————◆●●————————

Desirous of privacy the two couples separated for dinner. Frank and Hélène ate at the hotel while Jacques and Jodie chose an intimate eating place near the ByWard Market.

Frank related the day's events at the Lafleur wedding. "Jodie and I were quite taken aback by the priest's lack of warmth during the marriage ceremony. He said awful things about the state of marriage."

"Ah, that would be *Père* Jacob. They're not all like that you know... although... I must admit that his position on marriage seems to represent the teachings of the church in Québec." Hélène hated saying this but if the relationship was to go anywhere, Frank would have to know what she was involved in.

Frank changed the subject. "Well, enough of that. It was a most boring day without you my dear. I look forward to tomorrow's lunch at the Armand's although I believe we'll skip mass this time. It was kind of them to include you in the invitation."

"The Armand's and the Turcotte's are good friends. We were neighbouring farms for at least three generations that I know of. At times it was difficult to tell who belonged to which family." The smile was back on Hélène's face.

"Yes, Jack has explained as much. I'm afraid that Washington's spring was weeks ago and you will have missed our cherry blossoms. Are you all packed? We'll be leaving early Monday morning."

"Almost; I'm pinching myself in case it's all a dream. I can't believe two whole weeks in Washington. There's so much I want to see." Hélène did a quiet clap of the hands.

Jacques and Jodie had finished their nervous small talk when their soup bowls were removed. Both of them wanted to broach the subject of their relationship but didn't know where to begin.

It was Jodie who eventually took the bull by the horns. "Jack, we need to talk."

"I know."

"Well?"

"You go first, I'm listening."

"I've had some ideas about our money problem."

Jacques perked up. "Go ahead."

"I'm twenty-one now and can do as I please with this small fortune. What if I was to put the majority of it in a charitable trust in both our names…"

Jack interrupted. "But I told you that I don't want your money."

Jodie put her hand on his arm. "Please Jack listen to my proposition." When she felt the tension ease in his arm, she continued. "The money would not be yours or mine. I don't need all that money either. The trust would be managed by the two of us for charity. Anytime either of us saw a worthwhile need, we could discuss it and be of some real help. Just think, Jack… helping a poor budding photographer or an artist… building a school where illiterate peple want to learn… or a hospital where there is none… anything that would make a difference. We could do that together."

Jacques was silent. Jodie could almost hear him thinking and she let him.

When he looked up his eyes were bright. "Right now I can't seem to find anything wrong with that idea... in fact... it's a great idea. I'd like very much to be a part of that; Jodie, you're a genius."

Jodie beamed. "But I did say the majority of the money and not all. I would have two requests."

Spoke too fast, thought Jacques, *what is she going to come up with now.* "I'm all ears."

"I was very serious about that house on the ridge overlooking the Ottawa River... very serious. I want it more than anything. I've never had real friends before, let alone women friends, and it's here that I would like us to have our family home where we could spend the majority of the year. There's plenty of room on Q Street when we're in Washington for work. I'm happy here Jack and the artist in me has a house all figured out. It won't be anywhere near as grand as I was saying. Please allow me to build it."

"You said two requests... that was one."

"Yes, well... if you said no to this one it would be alright... I guess... I'd like to keep a small allowance just for myself." She saw Jacques' frown and hurried on before he could put in a word. "Say I wanted to buy Daddy a little something for his birthday that really came from me... or say I wanted to buy a special dress... or maybe buy you a small present that would be a total surprise. Nothing to do with our day to day living. Our family would rely on you totally. What we couldn't afford we would do without. You know very well how little I really need, you've seen me sleep on the ground and all I really need is you to make me happy."

Once more she let him mull it over.

The main course arrived.

Finally Jacques spoke. "It seems to me that you're really trying to work something out here and you're actually willing to give up what I would imagine is a substantial amount of money for the good of others. I guess it's only right for me to meet you half way."

Jodie started to clap. "Yes... yes... yes!"

"Hold on a minute, I'm not finished. I know the house will probably be weird, but then, I suppose it will undoubtedly represent you well... but... it shouldn't be a huge house, I wouldn't feel right living there and if you must have an allowance it should only be for frivolities. I'm sure I can provide well enough for my family with enough for me to be able to buy you a surprise present from time to time."

They held hands across the table. "Wow, is that it? Are we going ahead? Is it really going to happen?" Jodie had tears in her eyes.

Jacques got up, knelt on one knee, searched his pocket and held out a small diamond in a plain silver setting. "Jodie Gresham, will you do me the honour of being my wife?"

Everyone in the restaurant stopped eating and held their breath until Jodie cried out her 'yes' through her tears. Words of congratualtions came from the surrounding tables.

"We should eat... I'm suddenly famished and this food is getting cold." Jacques was back to practicalities.

"I think I'm too happy to eat." Jodie was drying her tears.

"I'll talk to your Dad in the morning and then I'd like to announce our engagement to the family tomorrow. How does that sound?"

"I'd love that. When are we planning to actually marry. I really don't want to wait long, what about you?" Jodie looked hopeful.

"I've been thinking about that. There's no way I'd ask you to convert to Catholicism.... I don't even practice myself. My parents wouldn't consider us married unless we married in a Catholic church... and I really don't want to hurt them so I really don't know how to get around that... unless we eloped and told them we got married in a Catholic church even if we didn't."

"I've been thinking about it too. I don't want to hurt your parents either. I'd want them to be at our wedding so no eloping... but... I don't want to be a Catholic... definitely wouldn't want that horrible priest to have anything to do with marrying me... on the other hand I don't want you lying to your parents."

It was all business now as they talked between bites.

"Oh..." Jacques suddenly had a thought. "I beg of you, no big high society wedding."

"Jodie laughed. "Not a chance, I can promise you that. Could we aim for three months, maybe four at the most? As for the church, I've been hatching a plan and I don't want to say anything until I know it can work and I'll know very soon."

"That sounds very mysterious. For now, all I need to know is that before long we won't have to be apart anymore."

————◆●●————

It was difficult for Jacques to get his family's attention amidst the hubbub around the table. The clinking on the rim of his glass didn't do the trick so he let out a shrill whistle. That worked.

All eyes were on Jacques as he stood. "*J'ai une petite annonce...* I have asked Jodie to be my wife and happily she has consented."

Everyone turned to Gérard and Jeanne Armand, some with mouths agape. The silence was very uncomfortable... awkward even. Gérard held his wife's hand tightly and broke the silence.

He raised his glass and smiled. "*Nos félicitations!*"

The noise level rose to a new level as everyone raised their glasses. The men got up in turn to clap Jacques on the back and the ladies went to kiss Jodie on the cheek.

Jeanne remained seated, somewhat in shock, a small forced smile frozen on her face.

This did not go unnoticed by Jodie but she understood. *I'm certainly not what she would have wanted for a daughter-in-law. Obviously she would have preferred a good Catholic French Canadian girl for her son. This must be difficult for her. I hope my plan works.*

Frank had a permanent smile on his face since his breakfast with Jacques that morning. He had finished their conversation by raising his orange juice glass, laughing and saying, "Well, she's your problem now son."

Smile pasted on his face, he looked around the noisy table and thought...*life can take such unexpected turns... I would never have believed this. My Jodie... my baby... a woman at last, making the right decision for once in her life.*

CHAPTER 28

1924
Jodie Fixes
Everything

Jodie took her new *tante* to the art galleries, the shops and a bit of sightseeing during the first days of Hélène's stay in Washington while the two men worked. The nights were spent out on the town. Jacques and Jodie took the older couple to a speakeasy jazz club one night.

"My, my, this is all so cloak and dagger. It's quite exciting... are you sure we won't be arrested." Hélène's voice had a little tremor in it.

Frank laughed. "Now, wouldn't that be exciting! If we hear the sirens, we'll sneak out the back door and make a run for it.

"*Sainte Mère...* he's joking, right?" Hélène looked doubtful.

"Oh but he's dead serious. He had to come and bail me out one night when our getaway was blocked." Jodie recounted.

"You went to jail!" Jacques sounded incredulous.

"Well, not quite. Most of our parents got there before we were processed.

It took half the night before Hélène could stop imagining herself in jail. The music eventually got the better of her and she abandoned herself to the enjoyment of the evening.

In turn Frank and Hélène took the younger couple to a classic concert. Though the genre was different from jazz, the selections were just as energetic.

After a few days, Hélène had been run ragged. Jodie offered her a quiet day at home on Q Street. "I have business to attend to just outside Washington tomorrow. I thought I would drop the men off at work and drive myself to Alexandria. I know Daddy's planning to take a few days off next week to really show you around so you might appreciate a day to yourself."

"*Merci,* it's exactly the kind of day I would love. You go and do whatever it is you have to do and I'll be just fine. I can't wait to get my hands on some of your father's books."

The three bid her goodbye the next morning after breakfast. "If you want anything, just ask Bessie." Frank kissed her on the cheek.

Frank let Jodie take the wheel and sat behind the couple. Having noticed his daughter's unusually modest attire, he enquired, "Jodie, just exactly what is this mysterious business of yours in Alexandria?"

"All in good time, Daddy."

Frank shrugged. Jacques looked at Jodie with question marks in his eyes. All to no avail.

Jodie drove the ten miles south to Alexandria going over what she would say when she reached her destination. Quaint Alexandria was a nice change of pace to the hustle and bustle of the big city. She arrived on time for her ten o'clock appointment with Father Keegan at The Saint Simon's Catholic Church.

An Irish lady by the name of Bernadette Cassidy who had also married into the Rockefeller family many years back had been a friend of Jodie's mother due to the fact that they were both snubbed by the family; one because of her elopement with a poor anthropologist and the other for being a devout Catholic. Jodie knew that aunt Bernadette had married in this Church and was one of its benefactors. She had shamelessly dropped her name in making the appointment.

Father Keegan greeted his guest with undisguised curiosity. "How may I help the niece of our beloved Bernadette?"

"It's most kind of you to make time for me," began Jodie. "I'm wondering if I may begin by seeing your delightful chapel."

The priest nodded his head and stretched his arm to the right. "By all means, if you will follow me please to St. Mary's chapel."

It was indeed a lovely little chapel but a little on the run down side. "Yes, this would do very nicely. My fiancé and I are contemplating our wedding in this very chapel. Is there somewhere we could talk?"

Comfortably settled in two armchairs at the rectory, the priest opened the conversation. "My congratulations on your upcoming nuptuals. Pehaps you could give me more information so we may plan ahead."

"We were hoping for an August wedding. A very small affair of course as the chapel is small. I did notice however, that the chapel is in need of a new roof. Am I correct in this?" Jodie had done her homework.

"You are very perceptive my child. It's at the end of its life and does tend to leak when the rains are heavy."

"If you were to permit me, I would be happy to have it repaired or even replaced if it could be done before the end of August." Jodie removed her gloves.

"That would be most generous and how could we be of service to you in return." The experienced priest knew that nothing was ever free.

Jodie's heart was beating fast. "We are probably looking at a double wedding. My widowed father has met a lovely companion with whom he would like to spend the rest of his life. We are a close family and it would be grand if we could be married at the same time."

The priest smiled in relief. This could easily be arranged. "How delightful, father and daughter marrying at the same time."

Jodie continued. "We could have a small problem but I'm confident that we can come to some arrangement."

Now the priest looked wary. "And what might that be?"

"My fiancé and my father's fiancée are devout Catholics who would not consider marrying anywhere but in a Chatholic church. My father and I, however, are of the Anglican faith."

Father Keegan made a steeple with his fingers under his chin. "I see… well… that does pose a problem. We normally ask that you convert to Catholicism."

"Well, I believe that we are interested in taking lessons but not ready for a commitment that cannot be taken lightly. Our fiancés come from Québec in Canada and for reasons of work, transportation and other tiresome logistics we would want to be married by the end of August." Jodie adopted a nonchalant pose trying not to seem overly eager.

"I could certainly meet with the other persons in question. You should be made aware that as non-Catholics, you and your father would have to make certain promises as well as follow catechism lessons with a view to conversion."

"Our fiancés are in Washington until the end of next week. Would it be possible to arrange a meeting with the four of us before then?"

"It would be my pleasure to discuss the promises you're willing to undertake in order for us to come to some understanding... Er... have you noticed how the stained glass in the chapel is in need of a restorative cleaning? We could have them shining before the end of August should the funds be available."

Jodie smiled... *got him!* "We certainly would want the chapel to be at its best for the wedding. My fiancé and I would be only too happy to see to it."

Jodie was beaming when she picked up her two men. "I just can't wait to get home. Daddy I'll want to speak to you first, in private, and then Jack... oh I can't wait... I just can't wait."

Her excitement was infectious. "Well, step on it then, I can't wait either." Curiosity was eating up Jacques.

Upon arrival Frank asked after Hélène and was informed by Bessie that she was out on the back patio reading. "Don't disturb her just yet." He turned to his daughter. "Let's go then. You're going to burst." They went into the library that also served as Frank's office.

Jodie had barely sat down before she blurted out. "Daddy you are going to ask Hélène to marry you this week, aren't you?"

"Now just a minute. This is very personal."

"Oh, Daddy, please, it's me, Jodie, we tell each other everything and this is important."

"I'm very much in love, if you must know and I believe Hélène feels the same way... but."

"But what, Daddy?"

"It's my impression that she won't marry out of her church and I could never bring myself to converting to her faith. It would be the height of hypocrisy."

"Is that the only thing stopping you?" Jodie had a mischievous look on her face.

"Isn't that enough?"

Jodie spilled the beans. In her excitement she talked too fast and ran her sentences together.

Frank was dumbfounded. "You did what? How could you presume to make arrangements for me.?"

Jodie was surprised at her father's reaction. "Well I was really doing it for Jack and I. I added you two into the bargain just in case. If you decided that this wasn't for you then Jack and I would go alone and say that you were making other plans."

Frank was silent and Jodie waited patiently.

"What kind of promises?"

Once again Jodie had done her homework. "Oh things like 'no birth control' and your children being brought up in the Catholic faith. He'd want you to commit to a few catechism lessons with a view to conversion. Surely you could do that for your Hélène!"

"I've got to think about this Jodie. You've obviously been planning this for a good while and I'm hearing it for the first time. Give me some time and go find Jack. I'm sure he'll be delighted. We could bring down his parents and some of his friends to attend with no fear of their reaction. Go… go!" He waved her off.

Alone, Frank lit a cigarette. *That child will never stop amazing me. She's too bold for her own good… but then again… how very resourceful. I shall never have to worry about her… she can handle anything.*

I can't fault her logic. We were both faced with a serious problem and she found a solution. When Hélène was telling me about her first marriage she let me know that she's barren so promising 'no birth control' and a Catholic upbringing for the children is not a problem. A few catechism lessons could be interesting research and help me understand Hélène better.

Good old Bernadette, we'll certainly have to add her to the guest list.

After an hour's quiet solitude and deliberations, Frank emerged from the library and winked at Jodie as he took his place at the dinner table. Hélène could tell that something was afoot. Her three dining companions could hardly sit still smiling like Cheshire cats.

"Who is going to tell me what's happening? I'm feeling a little left out here."

Father and daughter replied at the same time. "All in good time."

Saturday was the night of the annual Charity Ball. The two petite women looked dazzling in their ball gowns. Their shopping sprees had paid off. It would be Jodie's first social affair with a fiancé on her arm and she was looking forward to it. It was Hélène's first real ball and she was apprehensive. Jacques was twitching in his tuxedo and Frank seemed to have lost his usual calm.

It took no time at all for Hélène to put aside her fears as she realised that she looked just as good as anyone there and all the people Frank introduced her to were interested and intrigued with this French lady from Canada.

As Frank twirled her on the dance floor, she felt like Cinderella, the Belle of the ball. The evening wore on and between the drinks and the dancing, Hélène needed a bit of fresh air. Frank accompanied her to the gardens.

In a secluded corner of the gardens Frank pulled his love into his arms. Hélène stood on tiptoe to receive his kiss. This could in no way be described as a chaste kiss. *Père* Jacob be damned, she gave herself to the kiss wholeheartedly. She felt Frank's manhood against her and she melted further into his embrace. She wanted this man, she wanted to feel like a woman again, the wicked Eve of *Père* Jacob's sermons.

Frank pushed her gently away trying to regain his voice. "Ahem... come sit with me here on the bench. I have something to ask you."

He guided her to the bench and they sat, both of her hands in his. "My sweet Hélène, I've fallen hopelessly in love with you. I can no longer bear to live here while you are so far away. Please say you'll be my wife." Frank's voice was quavering.

Hélène burst out crying.

Frank was not prepared for that. He didn't know what to say so he held her against him until she calmed herself.

She sat up straight and he gave her his handkerchief. "I love you too Frank and I miss you terribly when we're apart but… my priest says I can't marry you. You may not be able to comprehend this but it means everything to me."

Like his daughter earlier, he asked, "Is that the only problem?"

She looked up at him. Tears welling up again, she nodded.

He took the handkerchief from her and set about dabbing at her tears himself. "There, there. I have a story to tell you."

It didn't take Hélène an hour's deliberation to reach a decision. She couldn't believe that it was possible to be so happy.

The couples were married on the last Saturday in August. St. Mary's Chapel was gleaming. Although Jodie had promised Jacques that her Dad would not go overboard with an expensive wedding, she had splurged on flowers, hundreds of flowers of every colour, making the chapel a cheerful, sweet-smelling place.

The grooms waited impatiently at the altar. Jacques stood fidgeting with his best man François by his side. Frank kept looking to the back of the church in anticipation; his good friend and colleague, Johathan Finney from National Geographic standing at his side.

As promised, it was a small affair with no particular seating arrangement. In the pews were Jeanne Armand, Shirley Turcotte, Joseph Lafleur, aunt Bernadette, and a handful of Gresham friends.

Five minutes later three petite women entered to a violin's rendition of the bridal march. Gérard Armand proudly escorted the brides, one on each arm, neither of whom wore veils over their faces. They were followed by Adèle, maid of honour to each of the brides. All three were dressed in cream-coloured satin. The simple dresses falling elegantly to the ankles for the brides and below the knee for the maid of honour.

The priest had been instructed by aunt Bernadette to keep it loving and warm. Father Keegan would do anything for 'their beloved Bernadette.'

The party of sixteen repaired to a reserved dining hall in one of the historical inns of Alexandria, the main fare being rack of lamb.

Rather than seating the guests at four separate tables, all were seated at an extra long table allowing for a merrier atmosphere.

The brides were radiant with happiness. Jeanne Armand looked at her son. *Mon beau Jacques... he seems so happy. Jodie chose a lovely chapel for the wedding... and the flowers... I've never seen so many lovely flowers. If only I spoke English, I could have understood the priest. I can't believe I'm here... sometimes I think I'm dreaming.*

The entire Canadian party had arrived a week previously so that the newcomers could be shown around Washington by their host before the wedding. The honeymoon night was to be in the old inn and Jonathan Finney would now be in charge of the Canadian guests, ensuring that they would be delivered safely to their hotel in Washington and on to the train station the next day.

———◄●●———

No explanation is necessary to understand why Jodie had made certain that the newlyweds' rooms were far apart.

The *avant-garde* Jodie was the furtherest thing from being a prude, yet she had chosen not to bed her handsome Jack until the wedding night. Regretting her drunken escapade with Olivier in Paris, she'd wanted this to be special. Waiting until the wedding night added meaning to the occasion for her.

She had bought the most *risqué* nightgown and had planned a sensually suggestive approach from the bathroom to the bed. She had imagined Jacques removing it slowly... however... the months of waiting had proven to be too much and the sexy nightgown had been an unnecessary expense. Without further ado the couple had torn the wedding attire off each other upon closing the door behind them.

Jodie discovered the difference between a naughty escapade and the act of lovemaking. Their first coupling was intense, almost violent, in an attempt to relieve the ache in their loins from months of unquenched longings. Inebriated by the experience they laughed, they caught their breath, and then proceded to explore one another's body inch by inch, kiss by kiss.

The second encounter was slow and tender, drinking each other in, feasting on one another, Jodie crying tears of joy, murmuring her lover's name in perfect French... J a c q u e s. Afterwards they talked, happy lover's talk. Their third time around was simple greed, just because the energy of youth was on their side.

Down the corridor, the mature couple entered the room apprehensively. Hélène took an inordinately long time in the bathroom while Frank waited nervously in his pyjamas sitting on the side of the bed.

Unknown to anyone, Frank had had a liaison not long after Miriam's death. It had been an attempt to erase the pain of separation from his beloved wife. Unsatisfied, he had left feeling as though he had cheated on his dead wife. Now, as he waited for Hélène, he was no longer sure.

Hélène eventually came out of the bathroom, looking the picture of femininity in her lacy nightgown. She gave Frank a small tentative smile and when the dimple appeared, Frank melted. He patted the bed by his side, motioning for her to sit.

Sensing his bride's nervousness, Frank took his time and approached her gently. He kissed her softly and felt her apprehension ease. He slowly began to unbutton her nightgown. Although the low ambient lighting was favourable for masking flaws, Hélène wished that the light could be turned off.

Frank pushed the nightgown off her shoulders and it fell to her waist. Having had no pregnancy or nursing to contend with, Hélène's full breasts were still firm. Frank ogled them appreciatively. "My God… but you're so beautiful," he gasped.

All misgivings disappeared when Hélène saw the earnest look of appreciation in Frank's eyes. A jolt went through her body when he cupped her breast and suckled it gently. She became ravenous and wanted none of this gentleness. She undressed her man in a flash and pushed him down on the bed straddling him. Totally taken by surprise at this turn of events, Frank was turned on.

His chest was covered in soft curly hair. She nuzzled it and giggled. With Hélène still on top, he entered her, the warmth and softness surrounding his manhood sending thrills throughout his body. He lasted a long time giving the lovers an opportunity to experiment with a variety of positions.

Hélène had enjoyed her lovemaking with Alphonse but had never experienced real passion before. Here she was, enthralled and all within the sanctity of holy wedlock. She could wantonly let herself go. She could love this man to her heart's content without ever thinking of reporting to a priest.

Exhausted, the satisfied couple fell naturally into a spooning position and were in dreamland before they could finish saying, "I love you."

It was room service and breakfast in bed for the newlyweds at either end of the corridor.

1928-1929
A Tirade

In early February of 1928 Jacques and Jodie were hosting a dinner party at their Eardley home a few miles past Aylmer. They were preparing to leave for an extended expedition to Polynesia and wished to see their friends before their departure.

Joseph and Adèle had brought their four eldest, leaving the eight month old Caroline with Agathe. François and Shirley's two boys were also present, always happy to be with their cousins. Jodie's twin boys were delighted to be with their playmate Joey, who at two and a half was only a few months their senior.

The adults had settled into the large living room leaving the children in the twins' playroom. "Everytime I step into this room, the view takes my breath away." Adèle was standing by the large windows overlooking the winter wonderland of the Ottawa Valley.

"It's the most beautiful home I've ever been in." Marie Labelle had let herself in with Maurice close behind."

"Come on in"... "*salut*"... "*ça va?*"... "hello"... "*bonjour*"... "glad you made it"... Greetings were coming from all sides.

Shirley whispered to her husband. "She says that everytime she comes here, but I think it's the craziest home I've ever been in."

"Shh... tastes are personal and Jacques seems to love it so that's all that counts." François hoped she hadn't been overheard.

"I made a good strong punch, *très bon,* anyone interested?" When everyone assented Jacques went to pour the punch into the awaiting glasses.

Jacques was proud of their home. He had put in his own labour throughout the entire year of its construction, working harder than any other labourer on the job. He had explained to Jodie that it was the only way he would feel that it was 'their' home and not 'her' home.

They had collaborated on the furnishings and hung both her art and his photo-art on the walls. The painting of the Ottawa sunset with the couple holding hands was prominent on their bedroom wall. It was an ultra modern home in the Bahaus style, all curves and angles with banks of large windows.

Jacques had been through some tough times; the plane crash; the loss of his wife and child; the loss of Adèle; and the frustratingly difficult relationship with Jodie. But he was a happy man now. To be sure, Jodie would always be challenging but her loving side overshadowed any difficulties.

The twins, Frankie and Gerry, were his whole world. He had lived the most horrifying moments of his life during the difficult delivery. At times it seemed as though history would repeat itself and he would lose his family once more. He had vowed never again to put Jodie or himself through such an odeal.

"*Besoin d'aide?* Here, let me take this tray in for you and you can bring the rest." François was always ready to lend a helping hand.

The lively chatter was as bilingual as it could get with some sentences beginning in French, English in the middle with some more French at the end and *vice versa.*

"I can't imagine travelling all the way to Polynesia and be away for five months with a two year old, let alone two of them." Adèle rested her hand on Jodie's forearm.

"We were in the wilds of Patagonia in Argentinia for two months last year, one on my back and one on Jack's back. It was just fine especially with *tante* Hélène there to help out. We'll miss her terribly on this trip. I really don't know how Daddy will manage."

"I know *ma tante* will miss him too but we'll be here to make sure she's kept busy. I imagine Patagonia to be a very lonely, barren sort of place…"

"Oh no." Jodie barged in. "Think of it as another planet alto-gether, different from anything on earth with its own beauty. Haven't you seen Jack's photos especially the coloured ones?"

"I'm afraid not."

Jodie got up. "Just a minute, I'll get them… be right back."

Meanwhile Mary and Maurice were deep in conversation with Frank about the proposed Polynesian expedition while the other three men were discussing hockey.

Hélène turned to Adèle. "You look a little pale… ça va?"

"*Mais oui ma tante,* I think that the punch didn't sit well with me. I've switched to a Coca-Cola. *J'suis bien…* don't worry."

And so the day progressed in good fellowship with the occa-sional interruption from a crying child in the playroom. The mother recognising the cry of the child in question would sort it out and be back in no time.

"It was Monique again I'm afraid. She swears everyone's unfair to her. Not a week goes by at the convent without receiving a call from the nuns regarding some mishap or other involving Monique. I've threatened to lock her up in the guest room if I hear one more cry." Adèle seemed worn out.

At the dinner table François was curious about the method of transport to Polynesia. "We're looking at a good three weeks' travel. We sail out of San Francisco to Japan and then we'll sail south on a liner bound for Australia, but, we get off at Papua New Guinea where we board a smaller expedition boat to our destination."

François looked ill at the thought of so much time at sea. "*Tabernacle,* that would be the death of me, I'm sure. Now that Lindbergh's shown it can be done, it's only a matter of time before planes will be built to transport passengers to every corner of the world. Weeks and even months of travel will be cut down to mere days and in some cases, hours. Mark my word, we'll live to take advantage of it."

"I heard somewhere that Lindbergh was in Ottawa, am I right?" Frank was addressing François.

"He was here for Ottawa's 60th anniversary last year… with his aeroplane of course. I got to sit in the pilot's seat of the Spirit of St.

Louis and actually got to speak with the man. You can imagine how great that was for me."

"It was all he could talk about for weeks." Jacques added. "With all his talk about the future, he had us flying to the moon before the century was out."

"What a preposterous thought!" Maurice laughed.

"But no... what imagination, my love." Mary corrected.

"She's right," said Joseph. "Man had to imagine flying or else we would never have invented the plane. We're living in an age of wonders, trains, cars, steamboats, the aeroplane, the telegraph, the telephone, moving films, the radio and the list goes on. None of this would be if man had not dared to imagine first."

"No one knows where our imagination will lead in the next hundred years," Mary continued. "For all you know we very well might end up on the moon."

Everyone laughed at the thought.

At the end of a most pleasant visit, the well-fed guests said their thank yous and goodbyes, wishing their hosts *un bon voyage.*

Halfway home Adèle begged Joseph to stop the car. She got out and promptly threw up the whole of her meal with the worried children looking out. "*Maman est malade... poor Maman.*"

Joseph joined her to see how he could help. When she was finished he held her up. "Oh no, not again... maybe it's just indigestion."

The dejected Adèle got back in the car. "Not a chance."

————◆●◆————

The first trimester of Adèle's pregnancy was the same as all the others. When she came out of the three month ordeal, she looked forward to a good four months of well-being, good eating, involved family time, and, lovemaking without fear of pregnancy. The last month or so always brought on the back aches, the swollen feet and the great longing for it to be over.

One morning in late September, Adèle awoke with a scream that made Joseph's blood curdle. "*Mon Dieu... Adèle mon amour...* what's the matter?"

Adèle held her bulging abdomen and let out another scream. Marie-Anne came running in, a frightened look on her face. Monique followed shortly.

"Agathe!… Agathe!" Joseph yelled.

Agathe was there in a flash as Adèle let out yet another scream. "*Sainte Mère*… what's happening?"

Caroline could be heard crying in the background.

"*Maman, Maman…,*" cried the girls.

"Don't worry, *Maman*'s not well but I'm going to look after her. Agathe, please keep the children away."

"*Oui, Monsieur Lafleur.*"

They left with their frightened Gagatte, the young girls looking backwards until out of view.

"Adèle, speak to me. What's wrong." Joseph was beside himself.

Another scream. "*Mon Dieu* Joseph, I've never felt anything so painful. I'm only seven and a half months gone but something is awfully wrong. I know it in my bones."

Joseph went to get Adèle's overcoat. "Put this on, we're going to the hospital."

Adèle didn't object and let Joseph take over.

In a few short minutes, Joseph had instructed Agathe and had Adèle sitting in the car bound for the *Hôpital du Sacré Coeur de Hull.*

Joseph paced the waiting room. The doctor came out of the examination room in a relatively short time. His face spoke of doom.

"*Monsieur* Lafleur, we believe that your wife's matrix may have become detached or maybe even ruptured."

"Her matrix?"

"Yes, her uterus. We must act quickly if we are to save the baby. We will be performing a Caesarian and you may want to speak to your wife now because I'm very sorry to say that we can only save one or the other." The doctor looked very sad.

"Well, there's no question, you will save my wife."

"The teachings of the Church and this Catholic hospital are very clear on this. The child comes first. We will do everything we can for your wife certainly, but…."

"WHAT!" The same adrenalin that had once propelled Joseph on the battlefield took over. The small man grabbed the doctor by the lapels and lifted him off the floor, crashing him against the wall.

He spoke in a menacingly low voice. "*Maudit fou,* if you save the child at the cost of my wife's life, I will persue you and this hospital to the highest court of the land and you can be sure that the Supreme Court of Canada couldn't care less about this archaic Catholic teaching of yours."

He took a deep breath and let the doctor go. "Get in there and save my wife."

The shaken doctor straightened his lab coat and left without a word.

The commotion had brought a small crowd to the waiting room. Ignoring them, Joseph sat down, put his head down in his hands and began praying.

After what seemed to be an interminable time, the doctor came into the waiting room. Keeping his distance, he addressed Joseph. "*Monsieur Lafleur...*"

Joseph looked up. His face was tear-stained, his voice tentative. "*Oui?*"

"Your wife has pulled through the operation. She's asleep now and if we can keep infection at bay over the next few days, she should recover fully."

Joseph jumped up and picked the doctor off the floor once again, this time in an ironclad hug. "*Merci, merci.*"

The doctor disengaged himself, disliking the hug almost as much as the violence. "*Du calme Monsieur,* I'm afraid that your son is unlikely to survive. The nuns have performed an emergency baptism. I shall take you to him now."

Joseph sobered up. He now faced the fact that he had a tiny son... a son who in all probability would not survive the day.

On the way to the nursery, the doctor spoke in a more positive voice and with seeming pride. "We do have some excellent news... we were able to save your wife's uterus. If all goes well, she should be able to bear more children."

Joseph groaned.

In the nursery, he was handed a very small bundle. The sister spoke to him gently. "We baptized him Jude after St. Jude to whom we pray for hopeless causes."

"*Merci, ma soeur*... I shall pray to him too. If he lives we'll call him Bernard Jude."

He cradled the tiny creature and looked down at the ashy, wrinkled face. He kissed his little forehead and rocked him gently, whispering. "*Là, là, mon p'tit Bernard...* you must fight hard now. I'll stay and hold you until your *Maman* wakes...then we'll both go to her... you must fight my little man, your *Maman* wants to see you..."

Joseph held him close, rocking him and talking to him in this fashion until he was told that Adèle had awaken.

He started to follow the nurse when the sister held out her arms. "I'll take him now."

"No, Adèle will want to see him." Joseph held on to his son.

"Is that wise, *Monsieur*? The pulse is so weak the breathing is shallow and his colour is gray. In my experience the poor little thing has a few hours at most. Would you not want to spare your wife?" The sister held out her arms once more.

"I know my wife, she would never forgive me." Joseph followed the nurse with his son close to his chest.

Although the paleness and obvious weakness of his wife shocked him, he wore his brightest smile. "*Tu es belle, mon amour...* what did I ever do to deserve such a beautiful wife."

Adèle forced a little smile. "Is that Bernard? You don't have to spare me, the doctor told me everything. I didn't think I would see him." She held out her arms.

Joseph handed over the precious little package.

Adèle bared her breast and stroked Bernard's cheek to wake and entice him but he would not suckle. Tenderly she continued caressing him and talking soft words of encouragement. Eventually a tiny mewl was heard bringing a smile to both parents.

The nurse came in. "*Monsieur* Lafleur, you must let your wife get her rest now. We'll take good care of her. *Madame*, I'll take the little one to the sister."

"*Non!*" It was a desicive no. "Bernard will remain here close to my chest where he will be warm. Bring me an eyedropper and some sugar water. Thank you, but I want my son with me as long as the Lord permits it."

The nurse was about to protest when she noticed the fierce look in Adèle's black eyes. "Very well, I'll check in on you regularly."

Joseph kissed Adèle on her moist forehead and took a long last look at his son. "I'll be back tomorrow morning. Pray to St. Jude, Adèle, and get the hospital to telephone me if you need me for anything. *Je t'aime ma chérie.*"

Joseph went straight to the *Notre Dame de Grâce* Church in Hull to pay for a mass dedicated to his wife and son. The priest was very sympathetic and knelt with Joseph and prayed to St. Jude on his behalf.

After a restless night Joseph returned to the hospital expecting the worse for his son. To his surprise the infant was still alive. Tired looking with brown circles under the eyes, Adèle was still holding him close to her breast. Joseph lifted the blanket to see. It was the same wrinkled grayish face, the body motionless. It seemed no more hopeful than the previous day.

"He's still alive Joseph and he swallows the sugar water."

The husband put on an encouraging smile for his wife. "That's wonderful news *ma belle.*"

He bent down to kiss her. "*Monsieur* Laflamme is in charge of the store and he sends his best wishes. The priest celebrated a mass first thing this morning for little Bernard and I've notified everyone. They all send their love, their good wishes and their prayers."

The next day brought no change, but the day after that Bernard began to suckle at his mother's breast.

The change in Adèle was remarkable. Though the circles remained under her eyes, her face was alive with hope. It was all Joseph could do to keep from crying when he saw his wife. *Please, God, it would be too cruel to take this child now that there's hope. I think it would be more than Adèle could bear. I implore you Lord, let this child live.*

"He cried this morning Joseph... Bernard actually cried."

Over the next few days, the nurses and sisters used every little excuse to enter the room to peek at their 'miracle' baby. As soon as the fear of infection was gone, Adèle and tiny Bernard were released.

It was a long hard recovery for both mother and child. It was a full three months before Adèle felt like herself again. It was a full three months before Bernard could look like a healthy infant no more than three weeks old. Nevertheless, by Christmas the danger had passed and life returned to normal.

The word 'normal' pertained to the day to day routine. For three months Adèle had devoted her entire time to her own recovery and that of her infant son. She had barely left the house and even Christmas had been celebrated at their home.

'Normal' meant that Adèle now possessed the strength to resume her share of the household duties and caring for her other five children. She drove the three eldest to school, shopped for their clothing, prepared the meals, resumed her bookkeeping for the store, and so on.

Her state of mind, however, was far from normal. Where she had once read the daily newspapers voraciously, she now skimmed through them with little interest and had not resumed her trips to the library. Conversations at the dinner table were unusually mundane.

The worst thing, however, was her lack of sexual appetite. The couple had not had marital relations since early September and Adèle was fully aware that her ever patient Joseph was suffering. She stayed up late many a night waiting to hear his soft snoring before going to bed.

Joseph was worried. This was not his Adèle. They had always been able to talk through their difficulties. Though Adèle listened politely, she had little to say. The previous night he had taken her out for a romantic dinner. Even though Adèle seemed to be making some effort, the evening ended with a weak goodnight and a kiss on the cheek. He was now at a loss as to what could be done.

The next morning Joseph telephoned *tante* Hélène from down-stairs in the store.

With the pleasantries out of the way, Joseph came to the point. "Adèle has been working hard and I find her a little tired. I thought it would be a good idea for her to have a day off and visit with her favourite aunt."

"*Bonne idée,* I could actually pick her up and we could drive up to Jodie's. Would you believe that the men are going ice-fishing today! The three of us could have some good girl time."

Hélène waited for his response but there was silence at the other end.

"Is there something wrong Joseph?" Hélène asked the question perceptively.

"It's just that I thought she might want to spend some time alone with you seeing as you and Frank are leaving for Washington at the end of the week. Jodie plans to be here until the spring so she could see her friend some other time."

Joseph knew this sounded lame but he didn't want to be discussing his marital problems with anyone but his own wife yet he knew that if anything was bothering Adèle, Hélène was the person she would most likely open up to.

Hélène caught on quickly. "It would be my pleasure to spend some quiet time with Adèle. We haven't had a good *tête à tête* in a long time. She did look tired when I saw her at Christmas, a day off would do her wonders."

Joseph was grateful for this understanding woman. "One last thing… could you call her and invite her… er… I don't want her to think it was my idea."

"*Toute suite,* I'll dial her the moment you disconnect. Goodbye Joseph."

When Hélène saw how difficult it was to persuade her niece to have lunch with her the next day, she knew something was wrong. "But Adèle, I really don't know when we'll be back and I so wanted to see you before we left for Washington."

"I really don't want to leave Bernard… but… very well then, I'll speak to Joseph tonight and see what can be done."

———◆●●◆———

"*Vite, vite,* come in and shut the door, it's freezing out there…brrr…" Hélène pretended to ignore the listlessness of Adèle's hug.

"Come, sit down. How's Bernard?"

Adèle perked up a bit. "He's always hungry now. I think he's going through a growing spurt. I extracted a large amount of milk for him before I left and Agathe will be fine with him I'm sure. She has been quite the Godsend. It was lucky for us that you went to check on Agathe in Montréal when you got back from Patagonia last year. I don't know what we would do without her. When do you leave?"

"The day after tomorrow. There isn't that much to pack. We leave behind all the heavy winter clothes. After our two week Christmas holiday, Frank's eager to get back to work."

"It was a wise thing for you to keep this house. You've used it quite a bit since your marriage."

"Is Bernard still sleeping in your room?" Hélène was fishing.

"Yes, he's still so tiny. He's more like a one month old rather than a three month old. Agathe will take him as soon as he's sleeping his nights."

Hélène launched her bomb. "Luckily your bedrooms are large. The three girls could easily accommodate another and the boys can certainly accommodate more if it becomes necessary."

Adèle blanched, and stiffened. There was fire in her eyes and her aunt expected to see smoke come out of her ears.

"*Mon Dieu,* Adèle, is something wrong"

"IS SOMETHING WRONG… IS SOMETHING WRONG… I'll tell you what's wrong!" Adèle was hyperventilating.

That's it, thought Hélène, *let it all out. I'll wait till you finish.*

"I'm not just a baby machine… that's what's wrong. I nearly died last time. Did you know that? If Joseph hadn't practically beat up the doctor he would have let me die on the table just to save the baby."

Hélène nodded.

"It's the church, *ma tante* Hélène… the church. Can you imagine… save the child and let the mother die! Just tell me if you can see what sense there is in that, it leaves the infant motherless along with all his brothers and sisters… no one to look after them… no sense. Who are they to decide that this is God's will? What gives them the right… can you tell me that?"

Hélène nodded.

Adèle paused to take a breath and she was off again. "Since I was ten years old, all I've done is look after children. First at home to help *Maman* and then at school and now at home. One baby after the next... I can't even catch my breath." She caught her breath. She stood and started pacing to the window and back.

Hélène nodded.

"I don't even know who I am. Oh yes... I'm Babette's big sister... I was the schoolchildren's teacher... I'm Joseph's wife... I'm Marie-Anne's mother and... but... just who am I, me Adèle?" She pounded her fist on her chest.

Hélène nodded.

"According to the church my body isn't even my own. The doctor and the husband decide if I'm to live or die. No one asked me... no one. According to the Government I'm not even a person. Since Canada became a country of its own, none of us women are persons under the law. Poor Emily Murphy and her band of brave women fought this all the way to the Supreme Court to be told last April that WE ARE NOT PERSONS... I'm somebody's something... but... I am not a person..." Her pacing quickened as her ardour intensified.

Hélène nodded.

"I'm just a baby machine *tante* Hélène. That's all I am and I've more children than I want. Six times three months... that's a year and a half. Do you realise that I've spent a year and a half throwing up. You should see me naked... I'm skinny all over except for an ugly pouch of fat hanging from my stomach... and my breasts have the shape of two fried eggs. If that wasn't enough I now have a bright red scar the all the way down my abdomen."

Hélène nodded.

"If I hadn't married... if I hadn't had any children, I could have been somebody. I could have been a scientist making discoveries... I could have been a doctor... maybe I could have been a writer... I could have traveled the world... I could have been... somebody."

Adèle burst into racking sobs and threw herself on the sofa. The tirade was over.

Hélène got up to sit beside her niece. She put her arm around her shoulder and let her cry it out.

When Adèle eventually calmed down, the aunt spoke.

"I don't doubt that you could have been anything you set your mind to *ma chérie*. You probably should never have married Joseph. He's a man after all and perfectly satisfied with his work spending all of his time engrossed with the store and his plans to build another one in Aylmer while everything else is left to you. You must be very lonely."

Adèle sniffled and thought for a bit. "Well… that's not quite fair *ma tante*. Joseph includes me in everything. He's a wonderful father and spends a lot of time with the children. He got Agathe to help me so I could have time to myself."

"Perhaps, but then marriage must have stifled your desire to learn. Nothing but children and household chores has to be boring."

"Well… it hasn't been quite like that. Joseph's interesting and he's a fountain of knowledge. We do an enormous amount of reading, discussing and arguing over our findings. He's made sure we have interesting friends like the Labelles… and Frank and Jodie have added a whole new dimension to my life… no… it would be unfair to say it was boring." Adèle was beathing easier now.

Hélène adopted a matter-of-fact tone. "Yes, but all those children. It would have been so much better if you could have stopped at Marie-Anne. I remember how much you wanted her. You really could have done without Monique, she's been a constant source of trouble."

"Oh no, not Monique, I couldn't do without Monique. She's a real beauty that one and so intelligent, it frightens me… no not Monique.

Hélène offered another possibility. "Well, perhaps two children would have been enough then. The boys are too much work, always getting dirty, up to no good tricks."

"Not Roger, *ma tante,* he's a good boy… the image of his father. Always looking after his *Maman*. He's kind and considerate… surely you've noticed what a perfect little gentleman he is. It's Joey… sometimes I think he's the devil incarnate. But he makes me laugh… no one can make me laugh like him. He's so full of joy." Adèle became a little dreamy thinking of her Joey.

"Who then? Four children is already a handful, maybe Caroline was one too many and as sad as it is to hear, it might have been better if Bernard hadn't survivied."

"*Ma tante!* How could you say such horrible things. I fought with all my strength that Bernard might survive... all my children are precious... I couldn't do without any one of them. This isn't like you." Adèle noticed the small wicked smile forming on her aunt's lips. "Oh, I see, you're playing with my head."

"You needed to put some things in perspective for yourself. Wallowing in self-pity tends to cloud the issues. But you do have real concerns, legitimate concerns and maybe now we can talk seriously." Hélène patted Adèle's hand.

"Let's eat first, I've got *un p'tit ragoût* simmering on the stove and there's nothing like a bit of chicken stew to make everything better."

Adèle suddenly felt so much lighter and she was ravenous. "*Mmm...* it smells so good."

They ate silently, dipping chunks of bread in the gravy in an unladylike fashion.

Over a cup of tea the satisfied Adèle was ready to resume her conversation with her aunt. "I may have exaggerated *ma tante* but there was truth in what I said."

"It isn't easy for women in a man's world and it is a man's world. Our Prime Minister, McKenzie King, is going to be helping Emily Murphy with her appeal and I believe that it's only a matter of time before this atrocity towards women is rectified. But enough of that, I want to talk about you, Adèle. Talk to me *ma p'tite.*"

"Ever since the hospital, little by little, it's been like walls were closing in on me. I've felt so suffocated that I haven't even been there for my family and Joseph... I mean... I function but in spirit I'm not there. Poor Joseph, I know he's been trying so hard to reach me... but I just couldn't do it. I couldn't come out of it." Adèle took a deep breath.

"*Et maintenant,* how do you feel now?"

"*Beaucoup mieux,* I feel lighter and all I want to do is go home to Joseph and talk to him. I miss him so much and the poor man has been there all along."

Adèle paused a while and Hélène could see that she wanted to say something else so she waited.

"My biggest problem right now is that I'm afraid to get pregnant. It's ruining my private life with Joseph. It's not just that I don't want another child... although truthfully I really don't... but I'm afraid of dying."

"My poor girl, I can't begin to understand what you're going through. Here I am wishing I could have had a child and envying those who can... yet I wouldn't have wanted more than two or three myself... and nothing has ever brought me face to face with death."

Adèle sighed. "I just don't know what to do."

"I know how personal this is... but... have you considered birth control?"

"Oh, we've talked about it from time to time and I do watch my calendar. Even though it would horrify *Père* Jacob our conscience is completely clear on that. The problem is that my monthlies are quite irregular and it works for a few months but then it only has to go wrong one month. It's so frustrating."

"I wouldn't want to put you up to something that would go against your conscience but I believe you should speak with Jodie and read her book by Margaret Sanger."

"You surprise me *ma tante.*" Adèle's eyes had rounded.

"You know that my faith means a lot to me... but I've questioned a few things since I married Frank and I've read my Bible in great depth, something we Catholics don't do. It seems to me that our Church has come up with a number of things designed to keep women in their place that are in none of Christ's teachings."

They drifted into other topics, speaking of Frank's adventures and of her reuniting with Frank in August. Hélène complained of the heat during the Washington summers and her joy at spending the Holidays in Pointe-à-Gatineau "Unless we're traveling, Frank promises that all our Christmases will be here. He loves a white Christmas and the family atmosphere."

Time flew by. "Oh dear, it's getting late and I'm picking up the children at school." Adèle rose from the sofa.

"Are they back in from the Holidays? When did they start?"

"Two days ago to Monique's great dismay. *Merci ma tante,* you've been so good to me today. It's time I went home to my family and my Joseph. We've a lot of talking to do."

The women hugged affectionately and Adèle left to pick up her children.

———•••———

As the family sat down to dinner that evening, Adèle's bright mood was obvious to everyone and it was infectious. Each child had something to say to their *Maman.*

"*J'ai fait un gros bonhomme de neige.* Did you see it *Maman?*"

"*Mais oui, chouchou,* It's the most beautiful snowman I've ever seen."

Monique complained that the sisters were unfair to her at school. Marie-Anne got a star for her homework. Roger triumphantly announced that he had scared away the class bully at recess. Agathe reminded him not to talk with his mouth full and Caroline, still in the high-chair, started giggling for no good reason.

Joseph looked upon the happy scene coming close to tears.

Adèle's heart melted when she saw the look on his face. "Did you know, Joseph, that Emily Murphy is going to appeal the Supreme Court decision?"

"*Oui, ma chèrie...* it's been in all the newspapers... you may have missed it," Joseph said kindly.

"I've missed far too much lately, tell me what they're saying about it."

Life was indeed back to normal in every sense of the word. *Merci tante Hélène,* thought Joseph.

Adèle made it early to bed that night freshly bathed in her best nightie. "I'm so sorry Joseph. I'm afraid that I've neglected you terribly for the longest time."

"Sush, sush... you've not been well and I understand."

"No, you don't understand. I've been quite well in body for a good while now but I've not been myself and I need to explain things to you."

Much of what Adèle had said to Hélène was now revealed to Joseph... this time in a calm state of mind.

They talked to one another, each expressing their fears. Joseph related his state of mind when he thought Adèle would die on the delivery table and his feelings of despair at not being able to reach Adèle over the past months.

They were still talking when Joseph suddenly kissed Adèle. She froze momentarily and Joseph withdrew, a pained look on his face.

Adèle recovered quickly. She put her hand at his nape and drew his head toward hers. "I want this Joseph, I really want this."

They kissed, softly at first, then deeply until they became voracious. They came up for air, long enough to tear off their night clothes.

When Adèle saw his readiness she assured him that all was safe. "Don't worry Joseph, this is the safest time of the month."

Joseph reached for his bedside table and came up with a package of condoms. "We're not taking any more chances."

"When and where did you get those?"

"Last week... in Ottawa." Joseph proceeded to open the package.

By the time he was ready to put one on, his erection was almost gone. "It sort of breaks the mood, doesn't it."

Adèle laughed and with a wicked smile she took the condom from Joseph. "Let's play a game."

She began to manipulate him. "Come now 'little Joe', you must stand up for me... you need to get dressed... that's it... nice and tall... we put the cap on your head... and now we roll it down... there... all done."

Before Joseph could wipe the incredulous look off his face, Adèle had straddled him and put 'little Joe' in his favourite place.

It was a night of pure joy for the familiar lovers. During the afterglow, Adèle lay in the crook of her husband's arm. "Little Joe, huh...I didn't know you saw it as 'little'... and where did you learn how to put on a condom?"

Adèle laughed heartily. "You men, all you think about is size! 'Little Joe' is all that I want him to be and putting on a condom is common sense... much easier than dressing the children in their snowsuits and nobody teaches you how to do that."

Joseph laughed, he was so happy.

Bernard awoke crying for his feed. Joseph watched his wife nursing his son. "I could swear that he's grown visibly this last week."

Adèle took on a more serious tone. "Are you ok with this Joseph... I mean the condoms?"

Joseph replied just as seriously. "I'm not sure yet... but the one thing I'm sure of is that I never want to come close to losing you again."

"I'm going to be borrowing a book on the subject from Jodie. *Ma tante* Hélène says that I must read it. When I'm done and I have all the facts, we can discuss this again, right now I'm too content and sleepy to think straight."

—————◆●●————

A visit with Jodie was long overdue. The day after Frank and Hélène's departure, Adèle left the baby with Agathe, dropped off the older children at school and made her way to Eardley with Joey and Caroline.

As soon as the car was heard entering the driveway, the twins called out excitedly to their mom. "Mommy...mommeee...they're here!"

Jodie emerged from her studio in her paint-spattered work clothes in time to greet her guests arriving at the door. Adèle looked Jodie up and down. "That's a fine way to be dressed when receiving important guests." She winked.

Making no apology, Jodie laughed. "I lose all track of time when I'm painting. Come on in, let's get these kids out of their boots and coats." Frankie and Gerry were jumping up and down impatiently.

When the children were settled in the playroom, Jodie invited Adèle to sit at the kitchen table. "I'll make us a nice cup of tea."

Jodie started to fill the kettle and then stopped. "Wait... I don't really want tea... my painting's finally going the way I envisioned and I feel like celebrating. How about a sherry... lets live a little."

"A sherry in the morning? Why not... it's a great idea, I'd love a sherry."

Jodie got the bottle and poured. "Have you left Bernard with Agathe then?"

"Yes, and I've left plenty of milk so we should be good until end of the school day."

Jodie handed a glass to Adèle and sat opposite her. "Remember the time the men got together to scare the living daylights out of

Agathe's father? I laughed so hard when Jacques told me the story, I nearly wet my pants!"

Adèle chuckled. "You got the story the same night, it was weeks before Joseph would tell me what they had done to that incestuous man and I really don't believe that he ever told me the whole story. The important thing is that we never heard from Isodore Laroque again and it's taken almost two years, but Agathe's finally beginning to breathe easier."

Jodie changed the subject. "You look well Adèle, I was worried about you when I saw you just after Christmas."

Adèle gave her friend a small synopsis of her reasons for her depressed feelings without the drama she put her aunt through.

"I know how much you love your children but I just couldn't cope with anymore than my two terrors. I've always looked at you with great admiration and all the other people in Jacques' family and the other French Canadian households who seem to cope with such a large number of children. I don't know how you do it."

"On the contrary I've coped very badly. My friend Céline Hébert is going to have her eighth next month and she expects more. She's never been anywhere outside Ottawa and her excursions into town are rare. She takes it all in good stride. Her life is entirely devoted to her children, her husband, and a clean house... although... sometimes I believe that the clean house comes first."

"*Oops...* look around you... I'm afraid that a clean house is last on my list of priorities. I work myself ragged before *Madame Armand* visits here and still I can see the look of disapproval on her face when she inspects the place... and believe you me, it is an inspection." Jodie rolled her eyes.

She put her hand on Adèle's arm. "All jesting aside, you are not Céline. From what I've heard she never has a day of morning sickness and pops them out like it was nothing. You very nearly died Adèle, and as much as you love your children, you have much wider horizons than family life."

"I know... but why is it that we must choose between a life of our own or family life? Why can't we have both?"

"I'm not trying to boast but I believe that in a way, I've achieved that. Jacques and I plan to continue traveling with the twins and do a mixture of homeschooling and formal education. I can continue my painting and do the things I love. It all comes down to having no more children."

"At times I envy you atheists but I can't deny what I know to be true in my heart. We've started to use preventative methods but it isn't without a good deal of guilt."

"Why does everyone always assume that we're atheists? Daddy is definitely agnostic and says that he's open to any possibility. You might be surprised to know that I do believe in a higher power and I'm quite spiritual. There's too much beauty in this world not to believe. Everytime I commune with nature, I connect with God. Whenever, I feel powerless I try to tap into His immense power. I just don't believe in religion."

Adèle was wide eyed. "Really! We've never had this conversation and you surprise me. I'm afraid that I do believe in my Church, however... but... lately I'm beginning to wonder if some of the priests aren't misogynists. The Church is run by men and the worst of the priests don't see us as much more than procreating animals it would seem."

"It doesn't seem like the Jesus I've read about," said Jodie.

"You've read the Bible!"

"Why yes, and the Koran as well as other religious teachings. Haven't you? I know you love books."

"I suppose *Père* Jacob would damn me forever, if I read any teachings other than our own. It's a part of my education that is sadly lacking and now I'm intrigued." Adèle's eyes were full of curiosity.

"*Ma tante* Hélène told me that I must ask you to lend me the book by Margaret Sanger."

"Ah... it's a must read for all women. I must warn you, however, that your Father Jacob would not approve." Jodie laughed.

After more chatter and a second glass of sherry, Jodie started to get lunch together. She called out to the children. "Frankie, Gerry, go knock on your Daddy's darkroom and tell him it's lunchtime."

"*Papa...Papa...*" The twins screeched on their way downstairs to Jacques' studio and darkroom.

"It's just like in Shirley's home, I find it amazing how they'll only talk to you in English and only in French to Jacques. Don't they ever get it wrong?"

"Never, it's the best age to learn languages. I was nine years old when we followed Mom to Machu Picchu for the archaeological dig and even at that age I learned to speak Spanish in mere weeks just playing with the village children."

After a simple family luncheon, Jacques returned to his work and the children resumed their play. In a much better mood than that of their previous meeting, Adèle was now ready to enquire about Polynesia.

She was pouring over pictures while Jodie regaled her with their adventurous tales. "These pictures are wonderful, they bring to life, all that you're telling me. Jacques is really quite the photographer." Adèle became pensive.

"What is it?" asked Jodie.

"I was just remembering him with his old brownie when we were in our youth. He photographed everything; the cows, the pigs, the horses pulling the plow, and all of us with mud on our faces. My mother still has a boxful of these old photos… I must ask her for them and I'll bring them next time."

The afternoon flew by and the time came to head for the school. The tired out children fell asleep in the car and Adèle drove with the Margaret Sanger book by her side, determined to make the best of her life with the genuinely wonderful man she had married, the best friend a woman could want.

1929-1935
The Crash

The 'roaring twenties' were coming to a close. It had been a decade of change in the way of prosperity, innovation and culture.

Economically, the decade started slowly for Canadians but by the mid-twenties the demands for the country's exports grew; notably its copper, asbestos, hydroelectricity, timber, pulp and paper to name but a few. With the building of the Canadian International Paper mill in 1926 and its opening in 1927, the population of the Gatineau area boomed.

The Hébert's handcrafted furniture business had more than doubled while the second Lafleur general store near the pulp and paper plant was doing even better than the one in town. Meanwhile Joseph continued with his plans to open a second grocery store in the small town of Aylmer.

As the decade progressed cars almost became a necessity, electric fridges began to appear in the more affluent homes along with the Hoover vacuum cleaner, radios grew in popularity and everyone went to the movies. Consumerism was alive and well.

The most significant changes were probably cultural and mainly affected the young woman. During the 20's her skirt rose from the ankle to the knee, her arms were bared, the neckline plunged and pants became the rage. The modern woman painted her face, smoked, drank, danced and behaved in an unladylike manner. Young people danced the charleston, the cake walk, the shimmy and the black bottom. They listened to jazz and utilised phrases incomprehensible to their parents.

It is important to understand, however, that these activities and behaviour could be ascribed mainly to the young people of the big cities and did not represent the majority. Furthermore, all aspects of this 'vulgar' lifestyle was deemed scandalous and strictly forbidden by the Catholic Church.

By and large the folk in Hull and Pointe-à-Gatineau experienced very little change in their mores. Nevertheless, they did prosper in the late 20's and in the early spring of 1929 Joseph was ready to open his new store in Aylmer.

As was their custom, Joseph and Adèle were discussing their finances after the children's bedtime. "I've done it... I've sold my shares in Montreal Power and Imperial Oil and I can tell you that the investments have paid off handsomely. Maurice tells me that I shouldn't have sold yet as they're bound to rise some more. But that piece of land we were looking at on Norway Bay has come up for sale. We have to buy now if we're to have a cottage on it by summertime and the money from the sale of the shares will cover the price of all that and allow me to open the store in Aylmer as well."

"Didn't you tell me that you were getting a loan for the store?"

"*Mais oui*, I've secured a small mortgage which only covers half of the costs because I didn't want us to be tied down to a heavy loan. Cashing in these stocks will pay for the balance I need."

"When do we open?" Excitement danced in Adèle's eyes.

"Two weeks... I signed the Deed of Sale this morning and the goods have been ordered. I've got two candidates in mind to manage the store. I was wondering if you'd help me with the final interviews tomorrow."

"Won't the candidates find it strange to see me there?"

"Adèle, I don't know anyone more discerning than you when it comes to character and anyway, I'm the boss, and they're the ones looking for a job so why should they object?" Joseph winked at his wife.

"Épicerie Lafleur...it really sounds like it's all ours," Adèle said proudly.

"Well, since *Monsieur* Laflamme died two months ago and Laflamme's is all paid for, this store is ours even more. Just because I promised Henri Laflamme to carry on the name doesn't make it any less ours." Joseph sounded just as proud.

"I know... I know... but... well I just like the sound of it... Lafleur's Grocery." She enunciated the name slowly and distinctly.

Summers in the small town of Aylmer was a popular destination for the Ottawa population. Some had cottages near the part of the Ottawa River that widened into *Lac Deschênes* while many came by train to spend the day by the waterside to picnic and swim. The town was growing and prospering as did the new store.

Earlier that summer on a bright Saturday a large delegation of Turcottes, Lafleurs and friends gathered on the newly acquired land at Norway Bay. Eight able-bodied men made up the construction crew for the new pine cottage; Adèle's brothers, François and Martin as well as her dad, Louis, and her brothers-in-law Gaston and Gilles; Joseph and his dad, Denis, as well as everyone's good friend, Jacques.

The women built a fire, cooked the food and assisted the men. The work progressed swiftly to the tune of the children's laughter playing by the waterside. With all hands on board it took four weekends to complete. On the last Sunday, the men put in the large stone patio while the women and children painted the cottage. It was a small cottage consisting of a spacious living space with a food preparation area tucked in one corner and a large loft that would sleep a dozen. Though plans were drawn up for an indoor bathroom, an outhouse would have to suffice for the first summer.

Some 35 miles further along the same road where Jacques and Jodie lived, the Ottawa River bulged into Norway Bay. This attractive, peaceful bay was perfect for swimming and boating and the cottage was made available to all who had helped with its construction. This way the cottage was sure to have been a great investment for the many to enjoy from the last of the snows in spring to the first of the snows in late autumn.

The Lafleur family was in the best of spirits by the end of that summer. Business was good, the children were well, birth control seemed to be working and Adèle was ebullient.

On October 4th Joseph received a call from his friend Maurice Labelle. The stock market had hit a low and he was being advised to buy now. "I've secured a mortgage on our home and I'm buying whatever I can. I believe that we're going to make a killing." Maurice proceeded to advise Joseph on the best stocks to invest in.

The next evening Joseph and Adèle were enjoying an intimate dinner at the Labelles. "What did I tell you! The prices are rising already, the market has rallied well. Did you take my advice?" Maurice was enquiring of his friend.

"Yes I did. At least I put in what little I had short of mortgaging anything we own. I've only just begun to clear a profit from my investment in the Aylmer store and I already have a small mortgage on it." Joseph had been more conservative than his friend.

"You'll regret not having invested more."

The two men had not married submissive women and as such Adèle put in her two cents worth. "Joseph and I discussed it at length and we came to the conclusion that we couldn't risk our stores. We did well with the stock market these last few years, especially this year but we just didn't want to take the risk. Everything is good right now and it would be foolish for us to tempt the fates."

"Tempt the fates! Not strong on economics with that term. You surprise me Adèle. Let me explain how the system works…"

Mary stopped her husband in mid sentence. "Maurice, please, Adèle is an informed individual. She and I have discussed the topic before and I can assure you that she fully understands the system."

With Mary's support Adèle continued. "It seems to me that when a company sells its shares at the outset for one dollar, that's all well and good. In this way the company raises money and can get down to business. If a business does well and experiences real growth then I can understand that the value of the shares must go up. Am I correct so far?"

"Yes but…"

Adèle did not let him finish. "However, when the shareholders begin to sell these same shares on the market at an elevated price just because another person wants them… and… if that person bought these shares for the sole purpose of reselling them in turn at a higher price to another and so on then this smells like gambling to me." Adèle was sitting on the edge of her chair.

"But you must take into account…"

It was Mary's turn to interrupt. "Let us finish, please. All year, the shares have been rising in price because buyers are willing to pay more and bet that the shares will continue to rise. People who can't afford it are borrowing in order to buy on the market and none of this has anything to do with the real worth of the companies themselves." It was clear that Mary was not in agreement with her husband on this topic.

Mary motioned Adèle to continue. "The way I see it, investors are buying nothing but the hot air on which the prices are soaring. I may not be an economist but this smacks of greed to me and it's bound to blow up in our faces at some point. So… yes… I see it as tempting the fates." Adèle sat back, there was nothing more to say.

Joseph was looking at his wife, beaming with pride. He turned to Maurice. "For the first time, the market has been very unstable these past few weeks. I have to admit that it's making me a little nervous. On the other hand the Financial Post says that all is well and mining stocks should become blue chip within the year. I hope they're right."

Maurice squirmed in his seat. "Ahem… I do apologise if I seemed a little condescending earlier. You ladies have done your homework and I should have known better with you two… but it's a bit more complicated than that."

"It's as complicated as it's going to get tonight, my love. I never got the chance to tell you that we've received a letter from our Charles today. He's all settled in at the University of Toronto and…" Mary had succeeded in changing the subject.

Despite the Financial Post's initial predictions the market continued to destabilise over the next few weeks. Tensions mounted and nervousness crept in until Thursday of October 24th when a frenzy of selling sent the market spiralling downward; a day that earned its appellation of 'Black Thursday'.

Adèle and Agathe were joyfully assisting Bernard with his first steps when the radio announcer's voice became louder. Adèle paid attention to the news broadcast for a few minutes and then went running downstairs.

"Joseph, Joseph… *c'est une catastrophe!*" Joseph and clients alike circled around Adèle to get the news.

"Something is very wrong with the stock markets. Big crowds are gathering at the markets everywhere; Montréal, Toronto, New York... and... well... everywhere. They've had to call the police in some places." Adèle was out of breath.

"*Du calme* Adèle, it can't be as bad as all that. It will recover."

As it turned out, things got even worse as the market continued to slide until its complete crash a few days later on October 29th.

Not many years before, the stock market had been viewed as the domaine of millionaires and big businessmen. The 1920's saw the common man in all walks of life joining in to play the market. Both wealthy and not-so-wealthy alike were tempted by rising prices to invest heavily, often doing so on credit.

Furor and frenzy followed the October 29th crash. One man jumped to his death from a New York high rise and with the prevailing hysteria false rumours had men all over New York and Chicago jumping to their deaths.

It was a very pale Joseph who informed his wife of their situation following the crash. He spoke in a lifeless voice. "We have no money whatsoever. I lost every cent in that damn stock market."

His voice suddenly rose to an angry pitch. "*Sacrement,* I never listened to that little voice in my mind that told me to hold off when Maurice was urging me on. *Maudit fou,* what have I done." Dejected, Joseph put his head down in his hands.

When Adèle heard the desperation in Joseph's voice, she rightly judged that it wasn't the time for an 'I told you so'. "With all our money tied up in the market, it was just as silly of me to spend my university nest egg on furnishing the cottage and buying canoes."

This last reminder was intended to shoulder some of the blame herself. However, it was no help as Joseph groaned louder, got up and went downstairs to sit in his storeroom with the door shut.

A few hours later Adèle went down to entice him out. "Joseph, *mon amour,* it's time for dinner. Please come out, the children are asking for you."

"Leave me alone, *tabernacle!*"

Never had Joseph spoken to his wife in such a manner. Adèle thought that she had detected a slur in those few words. She remembered the rumours of suicides in the wake of the crash and went running back upstairs.

In the bathroom she grabbed Joseph's razor then did the same with the dangerous kitchen knives. She wrapped them up in a towel and hid the bundle.

Joseph did not come out of his storeroom until the next morning. It was the first time the couple had slept apart in their home since their wedding night. The children looked up with surprise from their breakfast as their bleary-eyed father entered the kitchen. Sensing the awkwardness between their parents they quickly looked back down into their bowls of oatmeal.

"You must be hungry." Adèle said quietly.

"Yes..."

Unafraid to make her feelings known, Monique looked at her *Papa* and pinched her nose. "Pee-yew, *Papa*... you smell bad."

Everyone held their breaths.

Joseph burst out laughing. "*Oui ma belle...*your *Papa* smells bad." He ruffled his daughter's hair. "Adèle, I'd love a cup of coffee but I'm going to clean up first."

A few minutes later Joseph yelled from the bathroom. "Adèle, where's my razor?"

Adèle went to the bathroom. "I really don't know. I'll look for it when I have time. You look just fine... it'll do for today."

When the older children were off to school and the household settled into its routine, Joseph asked Agathe to take over while he talked to his wife. "Let's go in our room Adèle, we need to talk."

Sitting on the bed, Joseph took his wife's hands in his and looked earnestly into her eyes. "I can't believe that I've put the welfare of my family at risk the way I did. But what's done is done and I can't take it back no matter how much I would like to."

"Joseph, we still have both our stores and we're all healthy, it isn't the end of the world."

"No, it isn't but I've done a lot of thinking and I see hard times ahead. I've got creditors for all the store supplies who'll be wanting to be paid... and..."

"But we have clients." Adèle interrupted. "People have to eat and they'll have to buy food. Sales might come down a bit but we can tighten our belts. We'll be just fine." She gave her husband an encouraging pat on the shoulder.

"Don't worry I'll make sure of that because if I have to, I'm ready to shovel horse shit to feed my family." Joseph looked determined.

Adèle got up and went into the closet under her box of pictures on the top shelf. She brought down the bundle, opened it and handed the razor to her husband. "Well then, you'll need to shave if you're going to make love to your wife tonight."

Even though the number of those venturing into the stock market had risen to new heigths during the decade, investors only made up a small percentage of the general population. Despite this, the effects of the crash seemed to snowball. The bankruptcies among the wealthy investors put people out of work. The unemployed had no money to spend. Consumerism went down the chute putting more businesses, large and small, in peril thus increasing the ranks of the unemployed. The downward spiral seemed to have no bottom. Depression set in.

Perhaps the economy could have righted itself in time had the governments not panicked. Protectionist measures in other countries seriously affected Canada's all-important export trade. As the ranks of the unemployed grew, so did demonstrations and strikes demanding that the government do something. Making grand promises to right the economy, Richard Bennett soundly defeated MacKenzie-King in the 1930 election.

Bennett had been big on promises… but once in power, it turned out that his great plan was to do nothing, confident that Capitalism would survive on its own.

Things got worse.

As bleak as it seemed in the eastern provinces, the prairies seemed to be suffering the biblical plagues of Egypt. Years of severe drought set in, followed by enormous dust storms and then the locusts. Gone were the fields of golden wheat gracefully swaying in the wind. Gone was the bread basket of the country.

Joseph had struggled hard to keep his grocery stores open. After a short year he had to let his store manager in Aylmer go. He took on the running of that store while Adèle ran Laflamme's in Hull. Although the economy was dead, bartering was alive and well. Joseph was quite willing to take in some chickens, eggs or even a good pie in payment for goods but his creditors were not.

One evening in early 1932 Joseph came home from Aylmer after another disappointing day at the store looking as though he had aged a good ten years.

Concerned, Adèle asked him if something was wrong. With a tired look he answered his wife. "Please don't ask any questions right now, I have to go back out and I have to act fast."

Joseph went straight to the phone and dialed his father's number. "*Papa, c'est* Joseph. It's time. Meet me there with your truck." He then made a similar phone call to François, and to Louis Turcotte. He then went into the kitchen and buttered a piece of bread to take with him along with a piece of cheese. Without further ado, he went downstairs and got into his old truck.

The children had just gone to bed when he returned. "Adèle please bring Agathe and come down. I need your help."

Parked in the back by the storeroom, the old truck was ladened with dry goods. "*Sainte Marie*, what's all this," exclaimed Adèle.

Joseph spoke in a low voice out of Agathe's earshot. "I need your help to unload this so I can go for a second one. Your father and Martin have loaded up their truck and are on their way to the farm. *Pa* has done the same and François has loaded his car. I've got time for another run but I'll need your help. Maybe you can drive the car to Aylmer and that will give us an extra small load." Joseph never stopped unloading as he was speaking.

"Why are we doing this?" Both Adele and Agathe were in the swing of things.

Joseph nodded towards Agathe's back. "We'll discuss this when we're alone."

When all was stacked in the storeroom, Joseph spoke to Agathe. "*Merci beaucoup. Madame* Lafleur and I have to pick up some more goods we bought today so the house is in your hands until we return."

It would never have occurred to Agathe to question why her employers were picking up goods in the middle of the night. She lived and breathed for the Lafleur household and knew little outside that sphere. "*Oui Monsieur* Lafleur, I'll take good care of everything."

Before getting into the car, Adèle pulled Joseph by the arm. "Whoa, I'm not going anywhere until I know what's happening here."

Joseph held her by the shoulders and looked her in the eye. "A little bird... a very informed little bird... told me that they will be foreclosing on the store first thing tomorrow morning."

"Oh no we're losing the Aylmer store, *j'suis désolée*, Joseph. You've been working so hard managing all by yourself over there, I'm so sorry."

"I could see it coming, Adèle. My clients can't pay me and I can't pay the mortgage. In fact the store lasted longer than I thought it would. If they're coming tomorrow then I want this food in the hands of friends and family rather than the bank's. Maurice may have given me bad advice when it came to the stock market but he was right when he advised me to make Lafleur's a limited company. Yes, we'll lose that store but they can't come after me for anything else."

They parked in the back of the store in Aylmer and worked with very little light so as not to draw attention to their nefarious undertaking. In the wee hours of the morning when all was safely stowed in the bulging Laflamme's storeroom, the aching couple dropped to sleep in their bed fully clothed.

——— ◆●● ———

By 1933 the depression had deepened. The demonstrations were more frequent, bigger, and even violent at times. Signs of malnutrition and its ensuing diseases began to appear. The government could not manage with welfare. Furthermore, government employees accepted cuts in wages; a far better outcome than being jobless.

Joseph and Adèle had severely curtailed their lifestyles in order to keep the older children in private education. Fortunately the nuns were willing to do a certain amount of bartering. Between the store supplies and the produce coming from the Turcotte farm, the family would not starve. The trick was to satisfy the creditors enough to keep the store open and Joseph was faced with some difficult decisions. He could no longer justify keeping his assistant at the store nor could he continue to pay Agathe her wages.

Sometimes it seemed to Adèle that the only topic of conversation between herself and her husband had to do with finances. On this particular occasion Joseph was complaining to his wife. "There's not enough coming in to continue paying Jean-Marie and I just can't seem to work up the strength to face him tomorrow when I let him go."

"Jean-Marie has been with you since *Monsieur* Laflamme retired. He just got married last year and they're expecting their first child. Joseph, what will he do? There's no work anywhere" Adèle was pleading.

"Adèle you keep the books... you know I can't pay him anymore." Joseph was truly anguished. "We can't even pay Agathe anymore. I'm afraid that I'll have to manage the store by myself and you'll have to do the same with the household."

"*Non... non...* Joseph Lafleur, not Agathe. She's part of the family and has nowhere to go. You just wait here a minute." Adèle opened the bedroom door calling out for Agathe.

Agathe arrived at their door in her nightgown. "*Madame* Lafleur, is something wrong?"

"Come, let's sit in the parlour, I have something to ask you." Adèle motioned to her husband to stay put.

She returned to the bedroom a few minutes later. "That's settled."

Joseph had no idea what his wife was up to. "What did you tell her?"

"This is Agathe's only home, Joseph. She loves our children as though they were her very own. She's quite willing to stay here and work for room and board. I've promised that her wages would resume as soon as we can and if possible we would try to make up the lost wages."

Joseph was relieved. "I wasn't thinking straight. The children would have been devasted and we would have been throwing her to the wolves. I should have thought of this solution myself."

"As for Jean-Marie, you would be able to pay him reduced wages if you stopped giving credit to Samuel Frenette. You'll never get a cent out of him and I could name a few others."

"Adele, think for a moment, please. Have you seen how skinny Samuel's children are. As it is I sell him only the bare necessities and if I stopped starvation is sure to set in."

The businesses that survived the depression would be faced with these hard decisions in the years to come. Joseph and Adèle eked out a living from their store helping those less fortunate whenever possible. Meanwhile Jean-Marie continued in Joseph's employ on a part time basis, receiving irregular wages and food supplies when there was no money.

Of all their friends the hardest hit in the year of 1933 were the Labelles. Maurice had lost his elections in 1930 and although lawyers were always in need when bankruptcies, evictions and repossessions were plentiful, it was next to useless if clients didn't pay.

Unable to manage their expensive lifestyle; the fees for Adam's education at Ashbury College; the fees for Charles' education at the University of Toronto; and the large mortgage payments; something had to give.

Fortunately Charles had graduated the year before but unable to find work he returned home to live. The relief from having to pay the university fees was not sufficient. By the end of 1933 the Labelles lost their lovely home on *rue* Alexandre Taché.

The family did not adjust well to the two bedroom apartment rental. Mary blamed her husband for his foolish venture in the stock market and Maurice blamed his wife for hanging on far too long to her expensive lifestyle. It broke Joseph's and Adèle's hearts to witness the marital tension between their two friends. They vowed never to let this happen to them.

———●●●———

Despite the constant struggle, Joseph and Adèle were happy. In September of 1934, tiny Bernard's first day of school was a bitter-sweet event for Adèle. She had looked forward to this day. At long last she would become an independent woman during the school year. Yet, the idea of letting her baby go was causing unexpected emotions to tug at her heart.

She had insisted on walking the three youngest to the nearby public school.

Eleven-year-old Joey had protested. "Don't come *Maman*, I'm old enough to take care of Caroline and Bernard. I'm a big boy now and next year I'll be going to the big school with Roger."

"I know you are Joey and I'm expecting you to look out for your brother this year. He's so small, I worry that he'll get hurt."

Joey flexed his biceps. "*Regarde Maman...* I'm very strong. No one will hurt Bernard, I promise."

Adèle gave her son her most endearing smile. "I'm so proud of you Joey and I trust you to look after your brother and sister... but I really want to come along just this one day."

Joey nodded.

"Are you proud of me too, *Maman?*" Caroline looked up hopefully at her mother.

"I'm very proud of you Caroline, you're such a good girl."

Caroline beamed.

Adèle held it together waving from the pavement as Bernard went through the schoolhouse door.

On her way back she let the tears flow. Her baby was grown up and it was Joey's last year at public school. *I really don't know where we'll get the money to send him with Roger. Joey's so bright, he's bound to want to go to university someday and he needs to have the best chance. Roger says he wants to start work at the store as soon as he can but he may change his mind and want to go on with his education. Then again Monique's the brightest of them all and she'll be the first one ready for university. Where would we get the funds? Surely this depression has to end at some point.*

Her thoughts were interrupted when she entered the apartment to the sound of crying coming from Agathe's room.

She rushed to the room and put her arm around the sobbing Agathe. "*Là là...* shh... shh... I understand... I cried too, all the way home. He's so tiny and you're going to miss him around here during the day."

Agathe calmed down and spoke haltingly. "*Mais non... mais oui...* er... I mean... I will miss him but I wasn't crying because of that. It's because you really don't need me anymore. There's nothing for me to do here. What will I do? Where will I go?" The crying resumed.

"What are you talking about? *Sainte Marie,* we still have six children, they're only gone during the school hours. There's still the housework, the clothes to wash..."

Adèle softened her voice and held her tighter. "*Ma pauvre fille...* what would the children do without their Gagatte. You're family Agathe, for goodness sake you don't even get paid right now so you must be family!"

She handed the girl her hankie. "Come on dry those tears. It's Jean-Marie's day off and I have to help downstairs and I need you up here. There's lots to do around here so get off your lazy bones... go, go, go." These last words were said mockingly with a broad smile on her face.

"*Merci Madame* Lafleur... *merci...* I'm very happy here and now that I have more time, your house will be so clean, you'll see... *propre... très propre.*"

Adèle's heart went out to the poor girl. "I know it will, you always do such a good job, but remember, it's your house too."

———●●●———

At the worst many lived through catastrophic events and at the very least most everyone suffered hardship. Yet, throughout it all life did go on. People got married, had children and found ways to enjoy life when they could.

Joseph would have gladly sold the Norway Bay cottage; furniture and canoes included, to bring relief to their financial problems but the offers were too few and far between not to mention ludicrously low. Although the cottage deteriorated due to a lack of maintenance funds it didn't prevent the Lafleurs, Turcottes and Armands from enjoying the property.

On a bright Sunday in the summer of 1935 the Lafleur's were entertaining Jacques, Jodie, and the twins at the cottage. After a refreshing swim they settled to a picnic consisting of simple but plentiful fare.

Politics and the economy were the main topics of discussion. The two couples were thankful for the fact that their homes had been mortgage-free at the time of the market crash.

"I'm certain that we would have suffered the same fate as the Labelles had we been mortaged. When the market crashed and all those banks failed in the States, we immediately lost our charity trust... so much money. I was in a state of shock for days on end." Jodie was reliving painful memories.

"At least you weren't hit personally." Adèle was trying to find a silver lining.

"Oh, I took it very personally. So many people depended on us. A much needed school went unfinished and all the projects we had on the drawing board evaporated into thin air. Our promises for a better life were broken for many... I was devastated." Jodie looked sad.

"I didn't know what to do to get her out of her misery." Jacques remembered and he turned to his wife. "I don't think you ever really got over that loss even though I keep reminding you how fortunate we are."

Joseph thought that the conversation should turn on to a happier path. "I guess the newspapers still need photographs and the National Geographic is still publishing."

"That's right," agreed Jacques. "Nevertheless the pay is less and the portrait business dried up as did the demand for wedding and special events photographs. In times like these, folks figure that their Brownie will do the job."

"But I've found a market for some of my paintings in New York." Jodie piped in.

Adèle clapped her hands. "That's wonderful news, Jodie... but who has the money to buy artworks nowadays?"

"Oh there's plenty of money out there. The very wealthy are still wealthy. It's quite disgusting actually. Seeing the Astors, the Rockefellers and the Vanderbilts pictured living high off the hog in the society pages of New York is a slap in the face of the starving masses." Jodie was being quite dramatic.

"It's all very depraved as far as I'm concerned. The rich are getting richer, gobbling up desperate people's properties for next to nothing. They're living in the lap of luxury oblivious to the suffering around them." Jodie's face had disgust written all over it.

"You exaggerate Jodie, many of these high society women are working in soup kitchens to help out and... " Jacques was trying to be fair.

"Oh sure... and how do you know that? I'll tell you how you know that... it's because you saw their pictures in the papers. It's probably just a photo opportunity, a chance to feature in the society pages as being a generous soul… nothing but a publicity stunt." Jodie was getting overexcited.

"I give up. When you've made up your mind on a subject there's no middle road for you, Jodie Gresham." Jacques was laughing.

Adèle laughed in turn. "You men seem to be all alike. Whenever I'm doing something Joseph agrees with I'm 'Adèle Lafleur'… but… if it's something not to his liking then I'm 'Adèle Turcotte'."

Joseph deemed it a good time to change the subject. "It seems a sure thing that Bennett will lose the election this autumn."

"It's his own fault for letting things get out of hand this badly. He says he's going to put all kinds of measures in place to alleviate the situation but it's too little too late." Jacques had always been a Liberal die-hard.

Adèle had been devouring the papers as was her custom. "I agree that the man had no vision and has done little to nothing but in all fairness I don't think any government could have done much better these past five years. The priests preach that we're paying for the sins of the depraved 20's and some economists say that it's natural for economies to go up and down. I've no idea who's right here but this depression seems to me like a monster with a life of its own."

Joseph and Jacques' predictions came true. The disillusioned Canadians changed the government once more in the hopes that MacKenzie-King would be their saviour. To the delight of his friends, Maurice Labelle was elected to the House of Commons once again, restoring some of his pride and alleviating the tensions in his marriage.

1935-1936
Depression

It had been an enjoyable year for Adèle. Her newfound freedom gave her the opportunity to work closely with Joseph and enjoy interacting with the customers. She also had more time for helping the needy, reading, and having tea with Jodie and *tante* Hélène whenever they were in the Ottawa region.

Mary Labelle never invited anyone to their small apartment so the Lafleur's invited the Labelles to their home or for a day at the cottage. Although Adèle understood Mary's discomfiture at their lowly circumstances, she thought that Mary ought to get on with life and realise that they weren't alone in their affliction.

One day Adèle dropped in unannounced at the Labelles' apartment. Mary answered the door; a surprised look on her face.

"Well, aren't you going to invite a tired woman in?"

Mary had no choice really. "Of course, do come in Adèle."

On the right of a small entryway was the parlour and through the door on the left Adèle perceived the master bedroom. Down the passageway she could see three other doorways which she figured would lead to the kitchen, the bathroom and the other bedroom.

Adèle sat herself down heavily on the sofa. "*Ouf...* I'm so glad to get off my feet. We're saving on gas so I find myself walking everywhere now."

Mary sat herself opposite Adèle. "Where've you been?"

"Caroline forgot her lunchpail. Imagine that, only the second day back at school and already I find myself rushing over there. You're the halfway point back home so I thought I would take a rest and catch up on your news. It's been a long time."

"I know... way too long. I've been meaning to call you but Maurice and I have been so busy with the campaign. You're lucky you found me at home." Mary looked uncomfortable.

Adèle gave the room a look all around. "I must say, you've done wonders here. The place looks so warm and homey."

Mary brightened a bit. "I've tried my best under the circumstances."

"Well it shows." Adèle changed the subject. "You must tell me everything about the campaign. I'm dying to know so don't leave anything out."

"My goodness, where are my manners. How about a cup of tea?"

"I'd love one," said Adèle enthusiastically.

When Mary got up to go the kitchen, she hadn't expected Adèle to follow her. "Oh, you can stay seated and rest, I'll bring the tea out."

"Don't be silly, I'll give a helping hand." Adèle resolutely followed her to the kitchen. "My, what a lovely airy kitchen. It holds this big table with plenty of space to spare."

"It's been a big adjustment to eat all our meals in the kitchen. I really miss my dining room. I miss entertaining." There was sadness in Mary's voice.

"I grew up eating in the kitchen. It's so much more intimate and family-like. I've always thought that the kitchen is the happiest room in a house." Adèle was trying to put a positive light on everything.

"Maybe so... but when you're running a campaign you're severely handicapped if you can't entertain."

"Entertainment or not, Maurice is bound to get elected next month. Every client I've served says that he has their vote."

The talk turned to the particulars of the campaign and then to their children. Mary enjoyed her friend's visit and although she was not in a position to hold dinner parties, this was to be the first of many teas in her kitchen with Adèle.

The mid-thirties saw things at their worst with no apparent light at the end of the tunnel. The labour force counted one in three out of work. In Pointe-à-Gatineau the pulp and paper mill had done its share of layoffs and pay cuts.

Denis Lafleur had battled longer than most with his second general store but it had finally succumbed in early 1935. Like Joseph, it was a constant struggle to keep the town store going. Unlike Mary Labelle, Rose Lafleur gave up any pretenses and severely curtailed her lifestyle at the first sign of trouble. When the chips were down, the practical Rose gave all she had to keep things together.

It was the Héberts who were a cause for great consternation. Their custom-made furniture business had all but dried up. The week after her visit with Mary Labelle, Adèle discovered that her friend Céline was once more with child. It was to be her eleventh. They had met after mass at the St. François de Sales Church.

Adèle was shocked everytime she saw Céline. Over the last two years the heavy woman had dwindled in size until her stretched skin was visibly hanging from her bones. She looked easly ten years older than her age. The usually jolly Céline had unenthusiastically invited Adèle to come by for a visit someday.

Adèle was strangely silent on the drive back after mass; Bernard on her lap, Caroline in the middle, and the four eldest squeezed in the back.

Joseph sneaked a look at his wife. "Why so glum?"

Joseph and Adèle kept worrying conversations away from the children so she hesitated to answer. She paused and then spoke. "Are the Héberts going to be alright?"

"Alexandre Hébert has a crush on me." Monique had been listening.

"He does not," Roger countered.

"Yes he does."

"That's enough of that. Monique, you're too young to be talking of such things." Joseph was talking in his best disciplinarian's voice.

"But I'm a woman now, I've got my monthlies." Monique declared proudly.

"MONIQUE!" Adèle shouted.

"What's a monthly?" Joey was curious.

Marie-Ann turned red. "*Vraiment* Monique, have you no decency."

"We'll discuss that when you're older, I promise." Adèle was giving Joseph a dirty look in the hopes that he would wipe the smirk off his face.

"Oh, so it's one of those woman things, we can't talk about then." Joey was resigned.

"Who wants an ice cream?" Joseph shouted.

"Me"… "me"… "me"… "*moi aussi….*"

"We can buy three so you each get half but you must promise to share equally… did you hear me Monique.?"

"*Oui Papa, merci Papa.*"

"Nicely done, *mon amour,* but you will need to have that talk with the boys soon. Think of it as a science project." It was Adèle's turn to smirk.

When the couple found time to be alone later that day, Adèle revisited the Hébert topic. "Did you get any more news about the Hébert business at church today?"

"Yes… and I'm afraid that none of it's good. *Pa* was telling me today that their business is hanging by a thread. There are three large families depending on that business and I understand that old *Monsieur* Hébert is very ill."

Adèle was on the verge of tears. "Have you seen how poorly Céline looks? She told me she was pregnant again. That will be eleven children, Joseph, eleven! Everyone in the family is skin and bones. I haven't seen Céline this skinny since school."

"Anyway, she sort of invited me to come by her place and I intend on going this week but I don't want to arrive empty handed. Can we afford to give away some groceries?"

"We can't afford it but we'll find a way, their need is much greater than ours."

Two days later Adèle phoned Céline only to discover that their phone was disconnected. *Fine, if I could drop in on Mary unannounced, I can do the same thing with Céline. She never leaves home so she's bound to be there.*

Céline opened the door to her friend with the same surprised look Mary Labelle had given Adèle. "Adèle, *quelle belle surprise…* come in, come in."

"Wait, is Xavier here, I need his help with something in the car."

"*Non,* he's out looking for work… everyday he goes out looking but so is everyone else." Céline looked back into the house and called out for Alexandre to come help his 'auntie' Adèle.

Alexandre kissed Adèle on both cheeks. "*Allô ma tante,* you need my help?"

"*Oui mon beau* Alexandre. Can you bring in the boxes from my car into the house, please?"

Adèle turned to Céline. "I knew that Xavier had quit school but what is Alexandre doing home.?"

"Don't just stand there, come on in. I tried to talk some sense into his head but he hates school and Gérard agreed that he could be of more help at the workshop but today he's helping with some repairs at the back of the house."

Alexandre started bringing in the boxes. Céline looked perplexed. "What's all this? We don't need this. I know that it's hard for you to find clients, Adèle, but we can't afford all this right now."

"It's a gift, Céline."

Céline sat down and went silent.

Alexandre brought in the last box. "*M'man…* you stay and talk with *ma tante* Adèle and I'll upack these groceries for you."

"*Non* Alexandre. Take them back to the car, we can't accept this."

Adèle held the boy back by the arm. "Alexandre do me a great favour. Take the two little ones with you, I need a moment with your mother." She looked around. "Where's Mimi?"

"She's having her nap. Don't worry *ma tante* I'll take care of the little ones. Try to talk some sense into *m'man.*"

Adèle sat beside her friend on the sofa and put her arm around her. "Céline, *ma chère amie,* there's no shame in this…"

Céline stopped her. "I know we're seeing hard times right now but so is everyone else and we haven't been reduced to begging… not yet… and Gérard would never accept charity."

"None of us can survive this *maudite dépression* without help, Céline. If it wasn't for help from the farm, I don't know what we would have done when our creditors stopped selling us fresh produce… and all of us have had help from Frank and *ma tante* Hélène in one way or another."

Céline remained silent.

"Your children are hungry and… look at you… you're disappearing in front of my very eyes. The baby you're carrying won't survive unless you start eating more. Are you going to let your stupid pride stand in the way of feeding your children… come on Céline, wake up and do it for them." Adèle was getting angry.

Céline remained silent.

"Have it your own way then. You can give the groceries away if you must but I'll not be taking them back with me."

Adèle got up to leave. "I never thought I'd see the day when two best friends couldn't count on one another."

When she reached the door, she heard Céline's voice all choked up. "Wait."

Adèle turned back to see her friend in tears. She went to her and held her till she stopped crying.

"I'm so tired, Adèle. You have no idea how tired I am. Sometimes I feel as though I would like to drop down dead. For the first time ever, I'm pregnant and I don't want the baby. *Père* Jacob tells me it's a sin to think that way… but I just can't cope anymore, God forgive me."

Adèle was alarmed by her friend's despondency. "You need to eat and you need a good iron tonic. You'll find a good tonic in one of the boxes. I promise it will help you to regain your strength."

When Céline saw the alarmed look in her friend's eyes, she sought to reassure her. "*Merci* Adèle, for all these groceries. I promise to eat and you needn't worry so much because it's not all bad, we do have some good news."

"Oh?"

"Your brother François got some work for Gérard. It's only a cleaning job in maintenance at the aeroport but right now there's nothing for him to do at the workshop. There would have been quite a line up for that job but François made sure that Gérard got it, bless his soul."

"Well that's good news. Has he started yet?"

"Yes but it takes him forever to get there. We had to sell the car… but he's managing. You shouldn't worry about me either because Lou Lou and Gi Gi are quitting school at the end of this week to help me."

"Oh no, they're bright girls. Isn't there anything else that can be done.?"

"No, Adèle, there's nothing else and I just can't do it alone anymore. It's only for this year until the baby's born and I'm on my feet again. As you said they're bright girls and they'll go back in next year."

When Mimi awoke, Adèle took her leave. The two friends embraced and Céline repeated her thanks. Adèle took a last look around as she reached the door and her friend was heading for the bedroom. What she saw was a dilapidated house and her friend's stooped back.

Adèle couldn't seem to shake her discouragement at her friend's situation. For a week she seemed listless and lost her appetite. When she began to vomit, she knew that her loss of appetite had nothing to do with her friend's woes.

⬤ ⬤ ⬤

Adèle's morning sickness was over in time for Christmas. No one would allow her to feel low or sorry for herself; not Joseph; not Jodie; not her mother; and most of all, not *tante* Hélène. The advice from each of them was basically the same... bite the bullet and count your blessings.

Frank and Hélène had arrived for the Christmas season in early December. When Hélène arrived for a visit at the Lafleur apartment she naturally enquired about Adèle's health. As Adèle prepared herself to answer, Hélène could sense a complaint about to escape her niece's lips.

"Uh, uh, uh... wipe that look of gloom off you face and put on your happy face before you answer me." Hélène gave her niece a big hug and kissed her on the cheeks.

Adèle took a deep breath, put on a smile and tried the positive approach. "No more throwing up so I feel great. The children are excited about this, even Bernard who says that no one will be able to treat him like a baby anymore. There hasn't been an infant in the house for seven years and Marie-Anne's maternal instincts show up strong everytime she mentions helping with the new baby."

"Good, that's the spirit. I can see that this little one will not lack attention. Your colour is great, I've a good feeling about this Adèle," said Hélène encouragingly.

Every night Adèle prayed to the Virgin Mary for the strength she would need to keep a positive outlook on this unwanted turn of events.

Joseph had promised that positive feelings would keep her healthy and see her through. Privately, he was terrified to lose his wife and he had to make double efforts to keep the positive attitude and hide his own fears from his wife. *Seven years and just once the condom had a small tear... tabernacle... it wasn't even supposed to be a dangerous day. She must be the most fertile woman that ever lived.*

Christmas was a happy affair at the Turcotte farm. Everyone brought a dish and though the food was simple, it was plentiful and tasty. The Christmas presents were mostly homemade and everyone felt proud of their achievements.

Père Jacob had been ill, leaving *Père* Tremblay in charge of the high mass. The choir sang the carols beautifully and the sermon made the folks of Pointe-à-Gatineau forget that they were living in dire circumstances.

On the last day of 1935, news travelled fast of the death of *Père* Jacob at the ripe old age of 81. While the congregation mourned his passing, Adèle could not muster up the required grief.

———◆◆◆———

1936 did not come in with a bang. It was more like a squeak with very little hoopla. The economy showed little sign of improvement after the first quarter.

Despite this, the Lafleurs were a happy lot. Counting their blessings and finding inexpensive ways to enjoy life kept the family close-knit. After Christmas the boys went around the neighbourhood collecting all the discarded fir trees. Following a heavy snowfall, the family built a large snowcastle in the backyard and planted the fir trees in the snow at the other end.

The fir trees represented Sherwood Forest where Robin Hood and his men hid. The snow structure was Nottingham Castle where the evil sheriff lived. Mountains of snowballs were fashioned as ammunition. This provided weeks of winter fun for family and friends. Half would take turns being Robin and his men in the forest while the other half defended the castle. A snowball fight would ensue and when the castle was successfully breached, the players changed roles except for Monique who insisted in keeping the role of beautiful Maid Mary at all times.

The weeks flew by quickly. In early March Joseph received a phone call at the store.

"Allô, Épricerie Laflamme..." Joseph smiled when he heard his father at the othe end.

As he listened to his father's message, he went deathly pale. "Oh no... *c'pas possible*... when?... I see... I'll break it to her gently... *merci pa*." Joseph disconnected.

"Jean-Marie, I have to go out and I don't know when I'll be back. You're in charge." Joseph took off his apron and headed for the stairs.

He found Adèle in the kitchen. Come into the parlour Adèle, I've something to tell you. He led her by the hand.

"*Mon Dieu*, something's wrong.... I can tell... the children... are the children alright?" Adèle was panicking.

"The children are fine, *mon amour*, just sit down and listen, please."

They sat on the sofa and Adèle was preparing for the worst. Joseph spoke quietly. "It's Céline."

Adèle's hand flew to her mouth as she gasped. "*Mon Dieu, non, c'pas possible.*"

"She's early and the midwife came but something went very wrong and she sent for Dr. Fortin. But as soon as he saw her he got her in his car and took her to emergency at the hospital here in Hull."

"What are we waiting for, let's go." Adèle was already reaching for her coat and calling for Agathe.

They found Gérard and François in the waiting room. François was pulling gently on his friend's arm. "We have to go now Gérard, I'll take you home. There's nothing more to do here, the baby won't be released for a few days. Come with me *mon ami*."

Gérard just sat there in shock mumbling the same thing over and over again. "We had to save the baby... we had to save the baby..."

"*Sainte Marie*, François, what's happened?" Adèle knew in her heart.

Joseph held his wife.

"She's gone Adèle. Céline is gone. I'm so sorry." François was still holding on to Gérard's arm.

Joseph sat his wife down and went to his friend. He took Gérard's right hand into his own. "I'm so sorry, *mon ami,* so sorry."

Gérard looked at Joseph without seeing him. "We had to save the baby… we had to save the baby."

Realising that Gérard was not there, Joseph turned to François. "What happened here."

"I'm not really sure. *Sacrifice,* it all happened so fast. The doctor came out and said something about not endangering the baby's life any longer and in order to save it, Céline didn't stand much of a chance. Gérard went in and kissed his wife and came back here. We didn't have time to finish a rosary before the doctor came out to say that Céline was gone but the baby was safe."

"Was it *docteur* Gendron by any chance," asked Joseph.

"I think so."

"I'll find him." Joseph's jaw was tight.

Adele got up and put her hand on her husband's arm. "Joseph, *non.*"

"Oh, you won't find him here. He's gone home. Gérard's seen his little daughter and he's been sitting there for half an hour in total shock. I need to get him home and get back to work." François needed help.

Together the two men got him up and guided him outside. "Has anyone informed the family yet?" Adèle thought to ask.

"No, not yet."

Joseph looked at Adèle and she nodded. "You get yourself back to work, I know they'll understand Gérard's absence. We'll take care of this. We know the family better."

"Thanks my friend… you look well Adèle… take good care of her Joseph." François waved and headed for his car.

On the way to Pointe-à-Gatineau, Gérard stopped babbling and started crying softly. The children were waiting anxiously with *Madame* Hébert who had left her husband's sick bed to be with them.

They all rose when the three entered, worry written all over their faces. Before Adèle could say anything, the words and tears spilled from Gérard. *"Elle est morte...* my Céline is dead... your *m'man* is gone."* He fell to his knees.

After a momentary shock, the wailing began. From the eldest to the baby, everyone wailed.

Adèle rushed outside.

Joseph followed her. "What's wrong?"

"I can't do this, Joseph, take me home now."

"Get in the car, I'll give my condolences to *Madame* Hébert and I'll be right out."

The only good thing that could be said about Céline's funeral was that *Père* Jacob was not alive to officiate. Adèle would not have been able to bear his platitudes about God's will.

No amount of counting blessings and positive thinking worked over the next few weeks. Adèle was afraid... afraid to die.

Joseph had to act or else the worry would take over everything. After a number of inquiries he chose a doctor in Ottawa who came highly recommended and made an appointment. Having examined Adèle and heard her history, arrangements were made for her to deliver at the hospital in Ottawa. Doctor Williams gave strict instructions for a diet intended to make sure Adèle would be well and strong.

On the ride home, Adèle questioned her husband. "Just how are we going to pay for all this?"

"Enjoy the ride home, *mon amour,* it will be your last in this car. I've got a buyer."

"This large family needs a car, Joseph."

"What this family needs is a good mother. The old truck will have to do. We should be thankful we have the truck. We'll manage just fine."

It was no surprise that Adèle was seized with the same pain as last time a full month before she was due. Once in the examination room at the hospital, Doctor Williams came to a quick decision.

He approached Joseph in the waiting room. "As expected we will have to perform a caesarian. Your wife is strong and the baby's heartbeat is also strong. We don't anticipate any real problems except that we need your permission to perform a hysterectomy should it become necessary."

Joseph gave a nervous laugh. "I can just hear my wife wanting to know why you're asking me and not her. Yes, doctor, all that matters to me is that my wife will get through this."

The doctor nodded and left.

It seemed to take much longer than last time and just when Joseph thought he could wait no longer, he was greatly relieved to see the doctor enter the waiting room with a smile on his face.

Joseph rose to meet him.

Doctor Williams did not believe in letting anyone suffer a minute more than necessary. "Mother and daughter are fine Mr. Lafleur. Come let's sit."

The two men sat facing one another.

"I'm afraid that your wife's womb was badly damaged and to be quite frank, Mr. Lafleur, I deemed it inadvisable for your wife to bear another child. We did perform a hysterectomy but I left her ovaries intact and in this way Mrs. Lafleur will not suffer the effects of sudden menopause."

Joseph was beaming.

The good doctor continued. "I understand that you have a lovely family and this is something you two will be able to live with easily."

Joseph's smiled widened. "You have no idea, Doctor Williams, what a pleasure it is to find an enlightened man such as yourself."

The doctor blushed. "I too have a wife I love dearly, Mr.Lafleur. Speaking of which yours will be asleep for the next little while and I would imagine that you want to see your daughter."

As they walked to the nursery, the doctor explained the workings of an incubator. "Have you ever seen one, Mr. Lafleur?"

Joseph had been listening with great interest. "No but I've read all about them and it all sounds so incredible."

Arrived at the nursery, Doctor Williams introduced Joseph to the nurse and took his leave. "I'll check in on your wife, my congratulations Mr. Lafleur."

Joseph thanked him and asked the nurse to see his brand new daughter.

She looked so tiny in that glass box that served as a pseudo womb. Joseph was relieved to see her pink colour as opposed to the ashen skin tone at poor little Bernard's birth. Nothing pleased him more when she began to kick and cry.

As she scrunched up her face, he laughed out loud. "You're a feisty little one, *ma p'tite* Louise. Hurry up, get strong and join us in the real world where I can hold you in my arms."

Adèle was fully awake when Joseph reached the ward. He kissed her on the forehead and sat by her bedside. "She's beautiful... our little Louise is beautiful. She's very tiny but she looks strong."

"You look wonderful. You don't look like someone who's undergone a big operation."

Adèle looked happy. "I'm glad I'm alive, Joseph, I've done nothing but worry since Céline passed. The doctor has explained everything to me. He's such a nice man."

"I agree, he really impressed me."

"Imagine, Joseph, no more children. It's over. I feel as though I can take on anything right now and I've been thinking about something..."

"Tell me, Adèle."

"It's sort of a promise I've made to God if he could see me through this. And now that I know there'll be no more children, I feel like we have to do this."

"For goddness sake Adèle, I've no idea what your talking about."

"It's about the Héberts. Obviously Lou Lou and Gigi will never go back to school and even though they're willing to run the household and the family at such a tender age, it's too much for them. Since *Céline* lost her mother years ago there's no help from that quarter. Mimi's been farmed out to a relative and *Madame* Hébert is doing her best with the newborn but she can't cope with her household, her sick husband and the infant."

Joseph's voice was very tentative. "Sooo... just what are you proposing."

"Let's take in the infant, Joseph." Adèle was speaking quickly to avoid being interrupted. "Louise is so much younger than the others, she'll need a playmate. We'll raise Giselle as our own... I owe it to Céline, Joseph."

"This, coming from the woman who wanted three children, four at the most. Are you sure you can cope?"

"I feel I can do anything I want now… the children are at school most of the time… and I have Agathe… and Marie-Anne will help."

"Monique can help too, after all she does have her monthlies now." Joseph was laughing.

"I doubt that one has a maternal bone in her body. Her qualities must lie elsewhere." Monique had the power to exasperate her mother at times.

"I'll tell you what. The doctor believes that Louise should be ready to go home with you in a week and if you still feel the same way then, we'll make the offer to the Héberts and see what happens."

Ten days later, Giselle was accepted into the Lafleur household ensconced in Agathe's bedroom. As far as Gagatte was concerned this orphaned baby was her very own and she became the child's veritable mother. Adèle was confident that her childhood friend was smiling upon them from her well-deserved place in heaven.

1938-1939
The Accident

At last, a dim light at the end of the tunnel began to appear during the year of 1938. At least it was so for Laflamme's Grocery. Jean-Marie fortuitously found himself in the right place at the right time one day which procured him full time work elsewhere.

Everyone knew that there were enough Lafleurs to take his place and he would not be missed financially, yet he had been a loyal employee for many years and the parting was emotional on both sides.

Marie-Anne had graduated from the convent the year before. With one less in private school, Agathe's wages were restored. Giselle and Louise found themselves with three mothers at their beck and call. The two little girls were inseparable behaving as twins would.

And now at the dinner table in June of 1938 Joseph and Adèle received two announcements from their daughters.

Marie-Anne spoke first. "*Papa*, Pierre Poulain has asked me to marry him."

That went over like a lead balloon. Everyone went silent, stopped eating, and looked at their father expectantly.

A year older than Marie-Anne, Pierre lived up the street. He and his siblings had been playmates of the Lafleur children since the beginning. It was he who was the leader of the gang, it was he who planned the Sherwood Forest project behind the store. He had finished his secondary education the previous year and was currently working as a clerk in the government. The job was a reward from Maurice Labelle for the boy's tireless efforts during his campaign in 1935.

Joseph gathered his thoughts before speaking. "*Ma chère* Marie-Anne, Pierre is a fine upstanding young man but you are both much too young. Wait a few years and I'll be only too happy to give you my blessing."

"But *Papa*... he'll be asking you for my hand tomorrow and I was afraid you would think this way and I really don't want you to refuse him. Please hear me out." There was desperation in the young lady's voice.

Joseph had never refused to listen to his children. "Go ahead."

Heads turned to their sister. Marie-Anne took a deep breath, she had to make a good case. "We plan on being engaged for a year before we marry. I'll be eighteen then. We don't want a big wedding so it won't cost anything and his probation period is over, his job is now permanent. We can do this *Papa*...I love him *Papa*, I've loved him since I can remember."

Heads turned to their father. Joseph looked at his wife across the table and then spoke. "I won't say yes and I won't say no right now. Your mother and I will discuss it tonight and we'll let you know our answer tomorrow before the boy comes to see me." There was finality in his voice.

"*Oui Papa, merci Papa.*"

Always searching to be the centre of attention, Monique spoke up. "Well, I too have an announcement to make. After I graduate from the convent next week, I've decided not to take the university scholarship exam. I find school boring and I want to work in the store with *Papa* and be a business woman."

Adèle slammed her fork down rattling the plate. "*Ah non, jamais!* You're graduating with the highest honours, you're to be the valedictorian, and you're a shoe-in for that scholarship. *T'es folle...* you're either out of your mind or this is a very bad joke."

Monique's green eyes flashed with anger and she shouted at her mother. "It's what you want *Maman*, not what I want..."

Joseph stopped her in her tracks. "*C'est assez...* you'll not raise your voice to your mother like that. Apologise at once."

Monique looked properly chastened. "*Pardon Maman.*"

"This too is a matter to be discussed between your mother and I. Now... this dinner your mother lovingly prepared for us is getting cold. Roger, tell us where the Scout Camp will be this summer."

Sitting in their bed that night, the couple found that there was indeed much to be discussed.

Joseph was wondering if he paid enough attention to his children. "I always knew that the two were close but I always thought it was more brotherlike until last Saturday when Marie-Anne asked us permission to go to the movies with Pierre. How long has this been going on right under our noses?"

Adèle had also been surprised. "Marie-Anne never really talks about herself. I wonder when they found the time to talk of love... I mean... they're never alone... and we sent Monique along with them to the movies as a chaperone."

Joseph laughed. "Ha... Monique as a chaperone... she was probably bought off, if I know her. In any case, where there's love there's always a way I suppose."

"That's very true," Adèle suddenly looked sad. "It's just that in another two years, Marie-Anne will probably be a mother and religious as she is, I'm afraid she'll be having one after the other, the poor thing."

"Not everyone thinks like you on that subject, Adèle. Marie-Anne is very maternal and would probably be happy with a large family. Look at how happy Céline was... *oops*... I'm sorry *mon amour*, I wasn't thinking... all I meant to say was that some women like having a big family and have no ambition beyond being a wife and mother."

"We didn't bring them up thinking that a woman's only choice was as a wife and mother." Adèle still looked sad.

"You're right. They were brought up thinking that they could choose to do anything they wanted in life and even though this would not have been your choice, it's Marie-Anne's choice."

"I know… I know… maybe I'm just not ready to be a *grand-maman.*" Adèle smiled at her husband. "I guess we'll be having our first marriage next year then."

"I guess so, but it is sad in a way. The memory of when you first held her is as clear as though it were yesterday… you were glowing. I'd never seen you more beautiful. We're letting our baby go." Joseph was dewy-eyed.

"You're such a softie, Joseph Lafleur… go on… go tell her now. She's bound to be awake… let's put her out of her misery."

When Joseph returned to the room, Adèle looked up expectantly. "Well?"

"Well, she's crying. Why women cry when they're happy is beyond me. Anyway, she can sleep peacefully now."

"Oh she won't sleep tonight. She would have been kept awake by the anxiety of not knowing and now she'll be too excited to sleep."

"Women!" Joseph rolled his eyes.

"Are we avoiding discussing Monique's foolish plans?" It was obvious how Adèle felt.

"I too think she's making a big mistake… on the other hand we can't force her to go to university. She does love working in the store. If I'm to be truthful, I'd say she can run it better than I can. She's a boon to business, I've never had so many young men for customers."

"She always was your favourite."

"That's not fair, Adèle, I love all my children equally." Joseph's feathers were clearly ruffled.

"It wasn't meant as a criticism, *mon amour.* Through all my sicknesses it was you who looked after her. She was by your side in the store from the time she was a baby. It's only natural that the two of you would have developped a special bond."

Joseph was somewhat mollified. "As I said, we can't force her but it is a waste of a good brain and I'll have a quiet talk with her pointing out the benefits of further education. I can at least try to show her that it will be anything but boring. However, there seemed to be a lot of resolution in her voice tonight… I'll make sure she understands that she can decide to go to university at a later date if she changes her mind."

"Perhaps you could mention the fact that she would be surrounded by young men at the university." Adèle gave Joseph her best impish smile.

It was impossible to have a small wedding when so many large families were involved. One year later the Turcotte, Lafleur and Poirier clans were gathered at the farm along with the Armands, Greshams and Labelles.

With everyone's co-operation it was easily affordable to hold this happy occasion. Borrowed tables and tablecloths set with an eclectic collection of crockery along with old milk bottles filled with wild flowers decorated the tables in the large front yard. Ribbons flowed from the veranda railing.

Tante Hélène had brought the most beautiful satin and lace from Washington which Marie-Anne fashioned into her wedding dress. She had always struggled with the the three R's at the convent but had excelled at cooking and sewing. The dress turned out better than any she could have bought.

Frank who had been delighted at witnessing a truly French Canadian country wedding had given the lovers a weekend at the Château Laurier as a wedding present.

The economy was recovering, people were happy and the weather co-operated as though the heavens were showering rays of sunshine and blessings on this union.

Bursting with pride and overcome with emotion, when Joseph and Adèle finally made it to bed that night they made love joyfully and passionately. They cuddled afterwards whispering sweet nothings and reviewing the best parts of this momentous day.

On a mid-summer's night Jacques and Jodie sat at the Lafleur dining table discussing the probability of war in Europe. They were dawdling over their dessert when the phone rang.

Joseph got up to answer and returned shortly. "Monique's ready. It'll only take me a few minutes, she's just across the bridge. Will you ride with me Jacques."

Jacques took his last mouthful of the raspberry crumble. "Sure thing. No need to take out the truck we can take my car."

When the men had gone, Jodie asked where Monique had gone.

"She went to see a movie with her girlfriend Margarite who lives in Ottawa close by. Joseph didn't want her coming home alone after dark. She's his little *chou chou** you know."

Jodie laughed. "She's a beauty that one. Joseph will have to keep his eye on her. How's Marie-Anne settling into married life?"

"She's in heaven. They've moved into a small flat on Ethel Street in Eastview, just a short walking distance to her *oncle* François. The furniture's simple but she's turned the whole place into a domestic paradise with her sewing skills. You should see the curtains and cushions… oh… and the most beautiful quilt ever on her bed. She'd been working on that project with Agathe the whole of last year." Adèle couldn't keep the pride out of her voice.

"It's obvious that Marie-Anne was ready for marriage so you really have nothing to worry about."

"At least I prepared her for her wedding night much better than my mother did." Adèle gave her friend a wicked smile. "The twins must be happy to be home after a year of boarding school."

"They certainly are. But they do enjoy Ashbury College. It was Mary Labelle who recommended we send our boys there. My home schooling had them a year ahead of their age group and they seem to enjoy their studies. After traipsing all over the place with us they were happy to settle down and we've made it clear to them that they can stop and travel with us if boarding school isn't for them."

"Don't you miss them?"

"We both miss them very much. Luckily we've spent the better part of this past year here and we've had them with us most weekends."

"I wonder what's keeping the men?"

Half an hour later, the women were worried and Adèle placed a call to Margarite's parents who assured them that Monique's father had picked her up a good while ago.

Ten minutes after that the women were pacing the floor with negative thoughts going through their heads.

The phone rang.

Adèle answered in a weak trembly voice. "Allô?"

When Jodie saw her blanch she clutched at her heart.

"We'll be right there." Adèle put down.

Adèle was in total panic. "They've been in an accident. All three are being treated at the hospital in Ottawa but they won't say anything more. *Mon Dieu, mon Dieu... Jésus, Marie, Joseph,* help me." Adèle doubled over.

Jodie took her friend by the arm. "No time for that, let's go, get the keys for the truck. I'll drive."

When they reached the hospital Monique and Jacques were in the waiting room. With a bandage on his forehead and a sling on his left arm, Jacques got up to greet them.

Jodie burst into tears and threw herself into his chest.

Jacques encircled her small frame with his good arm. "There, there, I'm fine, just a scratch."

Adèle grabbed Monique. "Where's your father?"

Monique winced. "Ow... ow... ow!"

Adèle noticed that her daughter's right arm was bruised and her cheek was badly swollen. "I'm sorry Monique... but where's Joseph?"

Monique started to cry.

Jacques came over and spoke softly to Adèle. "*Calme toi,* Adèle. Joseph's in surgery right now. Out of nowhere, a drunken idiot crashed into the passenger side of the car, *maudit ivrogne*. Monique was sitting behind me and she's banged up a bit but she'll be fine."

"But what about Joseph?"

No sooner had she uttered the words than a nurse appeared at her side. "Are you Mrs. Lafleur?"

"Yes, yes... how is my husband?" Adèle's voice was frantic.

The nurse held Adèle's arms gently. "Listen carefully, Mrs. Lafleur. If you are to be of any help to your husband, you must calm yourself down. Your husband is seriously injured and there has been a great deal of blood loss."

Shaking, Adèle interrupted. "Oh please, give him my blood."

"Calm down… calm down. This is what we're going to discuss now. We have enough blood for the moment, don't worry yourself about that but he'll need more afterwards. His friend, Mr. Armand here has generously offered but he has a rare blood type AB and would not be a match. We have your type on record here and we need not test you as you're type O, a good match, but we would need another donor as well."

Monique had been following the conversation attentively. "Take mine, I'm his daughter, I'm sure to be the best match possible."

"How old are you my dear."

"I'm nineteen." Monique lied. The look she gave her mother defied any contradiction.

The nurse smiled. "There's no better match than flesh and blood. Would both of you follow me please so we can proceed."

As Adèle prepared to follow, a horrible thought struck her mind. *No better match than flesh and blood… mon Dieu… must my sin follow me here.*

She turned toward Jacques. Their eyes met and his tortured look told her that he had understood what she was thinking.

She followed the nurse meekly. "Are you going to test my daughter's blood for a match… I mean, what if she was AB or something bad for Joseph?"

The nurse smiled. "Oh no, my dear, that's quite impossible for the two of you to have an AB child. There really is no need to test as she's his daughter."

Adèle looked the nurse straight in the eye and spoke slowly and meticulously. "I insist, you must do the test."

The nurse looked puzzled for a moment and then came to a decision. "I see. You just sit yourself here and we'll begin with you while we test your daughter's blood."

Monique protested. "Why do you have to test my blood?"

The nurse had a ready reply. "It's a good precaution my dear. You never know what hidden disease could be lurking in that blood."

Meanwhile as the life-giving blood was flowing from Adèle's veins, inside her head was total chaos. For eighteen years Adèle had managed to push the thought of Monique's parentage somewhere in the back of beyond in her brain. On the rare occasion when it reared its ugly head, Adèle had firmly pushed it further back. And now... like anything pent up for too long, it broke its bonds and burst to the forefront invading her thoughts entirely.

The churning in her stomach matched the churning in her brain. *Mon Dieu... Sainte Marie... I thought you had forgiven me. How foolish of me to think that a confession and a few prayers for penance would pay the price for what I'd done. This can't be happening... what am I going to do? It will all come out now... but it just can't come out... what will it do to Joseph? If he had been told at the time he might have forgiven me but after eighteen years of deception I'll lose him for sure. Oh... I know... Joseph being who he is won't abandon his family but I'll lose his heart. I can't face life if he dies and I can't face life without his love.*

But it will come out now... and what will become of Joseph and Jacques' friendship... what of Jodie and I... and Monique... mon Dieu... Monique! It can't come out. Somehow I'll get the nurse to lie and my soul will be damned to hell but this sin is mine and it will do damage beyond repair.

Throughout these desperate rantings in her head, Adèle had closed her eyes. The nurse was priming Monique for her precious donation, disturbing Adèle's frenzied thoughts. Her eyes flew open and there before her was the most beautiful young lady all hooked up for her gift of life. She looked at her daughter as though she had never really seen her before and the tears welled up.

"What's the matter *Maman*? Surely you knew I wouldn't have some kind of disease in my blood."

Adèle was smiling through her tears. "Of course I knew... it was just a precaution, *ma belle fille*. It's a beautiful thing you're doing for your *Papa* and I love you so much."

Adèle sat back and let the relief sweep through her, washing away the malignant thoughts forever. She trembled with the euphoria.

When the two women re-entered the waiting room, Adèle's eyes sought out Jacques and she smiled at him. He nodded his understanding and smiled back.

Monique sat by Jodie explaining the whole process of giving blood with great animation. Jacques and Adèle stayed apart and spoke in low voices.

"All these years you've been thinking the same thing I have and you never told me."

"Adèle, it was you who insisted that we were to act as though it had never happened and were never to mention it."

"Are you happy Jacques... you seem to be happy with Jodie."

"I'm very happy. I have everything I've ever wanted, and more. When you came out and smiled at me, I knew immediately that Monique wasn't mine. The funny thing is that a small part of me had always wished she were mine and now that I know... well... all I feel is relief... great relief." Jacques let out a deep sigh.

"Me too." Adèle's sigh was just as deep.

"What are you two whispering about?" Jodie came over to them.

Adèle answered. "Would you believe me if I told you that your husband here was telling me how lucky he was to be married to you?"

Jodie took her husband by the arm and looked up at him. "Well it's about time he realised it."

At this point the doctor entered the room. All eyes were on him.

"Which one of you is Mrs. Lafleur."

Adèle stepped forward... Monique right behind her. All the anxiety had returned.

The doctor looked tired. "Your husband should pull through, Mrs. Lafleur. He's very weak and there was a great deal of blood loss but we've repaired the internal damage and stopped the bleeding. He suffered a number of contusions and his leg is broken but that will mend."

Adèle and Monique hugged, tears were flowing freely now. "Thank you so much doctor... when can I see him."

"He should wake soon and you may go sit by his side now. Undoubtedly he will be glad to see you when he wakes. However, I wouldn't allow any other guests at this time. He needs all the rest he can get."

Jodie put her arm around the disappointed Monique. "We'll take Monique home and make sure that everyone is informed."

Jacques walked over to Adèle, put his hands on her shoulders and kissed her on the forehead. "Go to your husband now. You couldn't have chosen a better husband, Adèle Turcotte."

As the Armands walked out hand in hand with Monique following, Jodie said, "What a sweet thing to say Jack. You do surprise me at times."

———●●●———

The first thing Joseph saw when he came to, was the face of his beloved.

"*Allô mon amour.*" Adèle kissed her husband softly.

His speech was very weak. "I must have died and gone to heaven. I see the most beautiful angel by my side."

"No chance of that, we're both going to grow old together and have a bunch of grandchildren and great-grandchildren."

Joseph was suddenly strickened as his circumstances dawned on him. "*Mon Dieu...* Monique... Jacques... what happened to them?" He tried to sit up.

Adèle gave him a reassuring smile and pushed him back down, patting gently on his chest. "They're fine... no more than a few scratches... you'll see them tomorrow. Look above there, that bag of blood flowing into your veins... it belongs to your daughter."

"She gave blood for her *Papa*?"

"Yes, we both did."

"Then how do you know this bag is hers and not yours?"

"I just know, Joseph, I just know."

They gazed silently in each other's eyes letting the love flow.

Then Joseph took his wife's hand. "Are you happy Adèle? You had such plans when I met you. You would go on and on about all the things you were going to do. You could have been anything you wanted but in the end you married me. Sometimes I think that you must regret it."

"Yes, I did have such grand plans, didn't I... lots of choices. Most of my girlfriends never knew there could be a choice other than marriage and motherhood. I know one girl who was forced down the aisle by her father and that was no choice at all... remember her, it was poor Jeanette Goudreau. But I did have choices Joseph, plenty of choices and I made mine consciously."

"I'm glad you chose me Adèle because I too have plans. Before you know our young ones will be at school and the older ones will be settled. With Monique and Roger to take over many of my duties at the store, I'm planning all sorts of interesting things for us to do together. It's never too late for some university courses, for either of us… oh and travel… yes we'll do that too. You won't regret your choice, I promise."

Adèle gazed at her Joseph, she felt her heart swell up; she thought it would burst. "Any other choice and I may not have had you or any of our wonderful children and that is something I could not bear."

Joseph had tears in his eyes… his lids were getting heavy.

"Go to sleep *mon amour*, I'll be right here by your side."

FIN

NOTES AND ACKNOWLEDGEMENTS

Many thanks to my sister Pauline, my daughter-in-law Annita and my friend Sylvie for their useful constructive criticism, and especially for their belief in my characters. They journeyed through this book as it was being written and it was their enthusiasm that kept me writing the next chapter. I'm also very grateful for my granddaughter Hannah's artistic book cover design. Thanks are also due to my husband Tony and my sons Eric and Gregory who were essential for giving me the male perspective. A special thanks to Flo Delorme who undertook to find so many of my million and one typos.

Although this story is a complete work of fiction set against the backdrop of historical events such as the Great War, the Spanish Flu and the Great Depression, I must credit my late grandmother for sharing many of her memories with me which have been woven into the tale. Much like the photographer in 'The Bridges of Madison County', all of my photographer Jacques' dealings with National Geographic are purely fictional except for the fact that Eliza Scidmore was indeed on the board of National Geographic. I shamelessly gave her a cameo appearance and hope that I was able to represent her well. Equally shamelessly I had the renowned photographer, Arnold Genthe do the nude photograph of Jodie.

BIO – HELEN GALLAGHER

Born in 1947 of Irish and French-Canadian parentage, Helen was raised in *la Ville de Québec*. The family moved to Barbados, in 1964 where Helen met her husband of 52 years and raised three sons in the tropical paradise. Retired, they now reside part time in Gatineau, QC, and winter in Barbados.

Helen obtained a History and French Literature degree at the University of the West Indies whilst working as a secondary-school teacher. In her retirement she writes and translates for Rotary.

Growing up she adored listening to her grandmother's stories about life in small-town Chicoutimi. Such stories became the inspiration for this first novel and its sequel now in progress.

GLOSSARY

Algonquin:	A predominant First Nations people in the Outaouais region.
baptème:	French-Canadian swear word; translates to baptism.
boudin:	Pork blood sausage.
Bytown	Original name for Ottawa named after Colonel By who was sent to oversee the building of the Rideau Canal. Known as Lower Town it was predominantly settled by labourers mainly Irish and French Catholic. This area located immediately east of the government is still called Bytown by the locals.
ByWard Market:	Open air Market located in Bytown named after Colonel John By, original surveyor and engineer.
Chou chou:	Term of endearment.
Christie :	French Canadian swear word; a diminutive of the word Christ.
Sacré Cœur :	French Canadian swear word; translates to Sacred Heart.
crêche :	Crib.
creton :	French Canadian pork spread.
désolé :	Sorry.

draveurs :	Lumberjacks who drive the cut logs down river after the spring thaw.
Drôle:	Funny.
Eastview:	Area of Ottawa east of the Rideau River with a large Francophone population. The area was renamed Vanier in 1969 after Governor General Georges Vanier.
Étaples :	Town in France away from front lines where Royal Canadian Medical Services had set up a general hospital.
faim :	Hunger; hungry.
folle :	Crazy; (*feminine*)
fou :	Crazy; (*masculine*).
gourgane :	Broad bean.
ivrogne :	Drunken man.
Jamais :	Never
La semaine prochaine	Next Week.
maudit :	Damn.
Oblates :	Order of priests active in education in the Ottawa region.
oncle :	Uncle.
Outaouais:	French phonetic representation of the name given by the indigenous peoples of the Ottawa region.
pauvre:	Poor.
Pond Farm :	Training camp at Salisbury Plains in First World War.
prochaine :	Next.

regarde :	Look.
réveillon :	Christmas Eve celebrations typically held after midnight Mass by French Canadians.
sacrifice :	French Canadian swear word; translates to sacrifice.
sapphists:	Lesbians.
St Jean sur Richelieu :	Town outside Montreal with a military training camp and military college.
tabernacle :	French Canadian swear word; pronounced *tabarnacle;* translates to tabernacle.
tante :	Aunt.
taquinne :	A tease; (*feminine*).
tard :	Late.
taverne :	Tavern.
tourtière :	Pronounced *tortière;* a pork pie.
tranquille :	Calm.
tuques :	Woolen stocking caps.
Voyageur :	French Canadians who transported supplies to and from distant stations and forts by canoe and through forests.
vraiment :	Really.

CPSIA information can be obtained
at www.ICGtesting.com
Printed in the USA
LVHW111947270219
608884LV00019B/34/P